Susanna Quinn has wo...
designer, hostess, club...
in Brighton with her p...
of seagulls.

Praise for GLASS GEISHAS

'A terrific read. A natural talent for plotting and an emotional punch.' Fay Weldon

'I enjoyed *Glass Geishas* very much. It's a gripping adventure story and a terrific fun read.' Joanne Harris

'Unputdownable. I was completely absorbed. Meticulously researched, *Glass Geishas* is a real page turner that celebrates the triumph of the human spirit, friendship and love over adversity.' Julia Crouch

'Susanna Quinn is a born storyteller.' Erin Kelly

'I stayed up late reading as I needed to know what happened next.' Natasha Solomons

'*Glass Geishas* is a gripping, thrilling insight into the very murky world of Japanese hostess bars. Susanna Quinn takes the reader deep into Tokyo's underbelly – I was shocked, fascinated, and sometimes terrified. A seriously skilful page turner where Quinn's research makes her world feel totally authentic, but never detracts from the terrific story at its heart. If you take it on a plane, you won't want to get off till you've finished. And don't read it on the beach unless you want sunburn.' Kate Harrison

'*Glass Geishas* manages to do for Tokyo's infamous Roppongi district what Alex Garland's "The Beach" did for the Khaosan Road and Thailand.' Simon Toyne

'A fascinating look at the seedy underworld of Tokyo – the writing is skilful and vivid and the tension doesn't let up. Su...

Visit www.bookclubbooks.com for book group discussion questions, information about me/how I wrote *Glass Geishas* and news about future novels.

GLASS GEISHAS

SUSANNA QUINN

HODDER

First published in Great Britain in 2012 by Hodder & Stoughton
An Hachette UK company

First published in paperback in 2012

1

Copyright © Su Quinn 2012

A CIP catalogue record for this title is available from the British Library.

ISBN 978 1 444 73357 0

Typeset in Plantin Light by
Palimpsest Book Production Limited, Falkirk, Stirlingshire

Printed and bound by CPI Group (UK) Ltd, Croydon, CR0 4YY

Hodder & Stoughton policy is to use papers that are natural, renewable and
recyclable products and made from wood grown in sustainable forests. The
logging and manufacturing processes are expected to conform to the
environmental regulations of the country of origin.

Hodder & Stoughton Ltd
338 Euston Road
London NW1 3BH

www.hodder.co.uk

To my sis, Cath, who is brilliant.

Prologue

Breathe in, breathe out.

Annabel hadn't noticed the clear liquid being dropped into her champagne glass. Nor had she tasted anything strange as she downed her drink and asked for another.

Breathe in, breathe out.

But she was certain, when she woke up with a pounding headache, queasy stomach and moth-eaten recollections of the night before, that her drink had been spiked.

One breath at a time, in, out.

She wasn't certain, though, where she was. Or why it was so dark. She could smell aftershave, stale beer and green tea.

Don't make any noise. Try to think. Try to remember. Check your underwear.

Pounding images of the night before flickered and flared. Annabel remembered sitting in her hostess club, pouring drinks, pretending to laugh at Takka's bad jokes, a usual night at work. But after that nothing. A big, black No Entry sign.

How much did I drink?

Two bottles of wine with Takka. But that wasn't enough to account for a memory blackout. Annabel was a serious drinker now, not the lightweight she'd been when she first arrived in Japan.

She became aware in the gloom of lying on some sort of slippery cushioning. Her French-manicured nails identified it as silky with swirly patterns sewn on to the fabric. Somewhere, a red light winked and the neon blue of a fire exit sign glowed.

Try to sit up.

She did, shivering, and rubbed damp, bare legs that felt like frozen pastry. Her taffeta evening dress rustled, a flock of birds taking off, deafening and frightening in the dark, and she vomited wine-flavoured bile into her mouth. She swallowed it quickly, her heart vibrating even faster.

It's only my dress.

The tears came then, warm and self-pitying. She reached under her skirt to check her underwear was still in place. It was.

Get up.

She swung her frozen feet to the ground and felt around . . . What was it, sand? No, carpet. Thick carpet. None of her clothing felt tampered with, but her dress rustled again and her hand knocked against something cold that wobbled noisily: a bottle.

A bar . . . Am I in a bar? A hotel bar?

Her eyes were adjusting to the darkness now, and she could see outlines, shadows. And then, just like that, the outlines became objects.

A glass table, cushioned chairs of the sort you'd see on a cruise ship, rows and rows of champagne and Suntory whisky bottles arranged behind a gleaming sheet of glass on the far side of the room.

I'm at the club. I'm at my *hostess club. What am I doing here?*

Calamity Janes was closed up for the night, so how had she ended up here, passed out without anyone noticing? Had the waiting staff just left her, thinking she'd wake up and find her own way out?

She knew the staff didn't like her. These days she was a far cry from the nice young woman with the pink plastic suitcase on wheels and no tolerance for more than two G&Ts. Everyone had called her Barbie back then, with her blue eyes and long, blonde hair. Now everyone called her 'the drunk one' or 'the girl asking for coke'.

More memories came. Drinking shot after shot with Takka; sneaking off to the toilets and snorting gritty powder to chase away the seeping tiredness that always overwhelmed her at one in the morning; tripping over in the toilets and vomiting into the sink; someone passing her a glass of *shotu* . . . She'd had a few sips of that before the world turned woozy, like she'd climbed inside the *shotu* bottle and was looking out. She vaguely recalled someone shaking her, but after that nothing.

A few feet away, a half-empty bottle of whisky stood on a glass table. She reached towards it for a quick drink to ease her into this unpleasant reality but, as she grasped the bottle, there was a breathing sound – heavy and rasping, like an angry cat.

She sat back quickly.

I should get out of here. Now.

Then there was another noise, a whirring sound, and Annabel's skinny body tensed. Through the glass door across the club she could see the outline of the elevator, the call light lit up.

No one should be using the building at this time. If Calamity Janes was closed, everything should be closed. Unless someone – someone who knew she'd been drugged – was coming up to get her.

The numbers above the elevator began to glow, one by one, and Annabel was wide awake.

Someone was using the lift.

With clumsy legs she ran straight into one of the glass tables, the angular surface hitting her knees with a painful clunk. She bit her lip. Again she heard breathing.

You're being paranoid, it's just the drugs.

Waiting here in the dark, her thoughts a frightened froth, every shadow felt alive. There was no way out, she realised, except past whoever was coming up. It could be a cleaner, or a maintenance man. But still, it wasn't clever to wait here, a shucked oyster, exposed and vulnerable. Better to hide until she knew who it was.

Annabel watched the numbers change above the elevator doors as the lift rose.

Two — three . . .

She thought about crouching behind the bar, but she could be easily seen if whoever was coming up here got a drink.

Four — five . . .

A panicked sob escaped her lips. She stumbled towards one

of the sofas. The dark recess beneath it looked far too small for her, and Annabel whimpered as she tried to pull her cold body under the frame.

The elevator doors slid slowly apart.

Someone stepped out of the lift and flicked on the lights, just as Annabel pulled herself into the tight space. Momentarily dazzled, she made out bulky shadows and long legs.

It was a man; no, two men, a tall one and a short one. She couldn't see their faces, but Annabel could see someone else now the club was bright.

A blonde girl, lying comatose a few metres away. Breathing heavily.

The girl was sprawled on one of the silk sofas, her slender body wrapped in a red evening dress and one arm dangling towards the floor. She was still, but her chest rose and fell. Her face was out of eyeshot, but her red dress and hair looked familiar.

The men's faces were hidden by the silk-covered beam above Annabel's head, but she daren't move to get a better look at them. It appeared, from their posture, That they were surveying the club. She gripped her bare knees.

'There's only one,' said a slurred voice.

'The other one . . . Maybe left?' The other voice was crisp and sober.

'Bad news. Bad idea. Better turn them off.'

There was a click as almost all the lights were cut, leaving only the bar glowing in the far corner of the room. The tall man walked towards it, and Annabel watched his suited torso and arms. He opened the wall-mounted glass champagne cabinet and ran his fingers along the Dom Pérignon bottles until he found a wooden box wedged between two of them.

From the box he took a thin cigar and a gold-coloured object about the size of a playing card. It looked like a small guillotine; Annabel saw it sparkle under the low lighting.

Carefully, the man placed the cigar into the hole, clicked down the top and let the snipped end fall away and roll around the pink shadows of the carpet.

He strode towards the smaller man, who stood by the glass door.

'Apology time,' he said, holding out the cigar cutter. 'Snip, snip. Any finger you like.'

Annabel's stomach turned to ice.

'Please,' the other man stuttered. 'Please.' His voice was soft and very familiar. 'A mistake, I know, but . . . My job . . . you know what it would look like.'

There was a long pause, and Annabel realised she was holding her breath. She could see the quick rise and fall of the shorter man's plump chest.

The blonde girl took a wheezy breath, but neither man turned to look at her.

Then the tall man lit his cigar. 'It had better not happen again.'

'*Hai.* Won't happen again.'

Annabel blinked as clouds of silver smoke floated towards her hiding place.

The tall man went to the unconscious girl, her black bra showing under a fallen dress strap, and began pushing red fabric up her legs.

The other man came to stand behind him. Everything was shadowy, but Annabel saw pale skin exposed under the dim, orange lights of the bar and then . . .

She closed her eyes, willing the images to go away, willing herself to be somewhere else, but she couldn't shut out the noises. The awful, frightening noises.

Eventually, the two men moved away from the girl, rearranging their clothing, breathing quickly.

'We need to put her back in the apartment,' said the tall man, picking up the blonde girl as though she were a bag of cement. Her blonde hair glowed see-through, a sheet of swaying, yellow tissue paper, as he carried her towards the glass door. He held the door open with his foot while the other man followed. Then he pressed the call button.

Annabel let out a low whimper.

They're going. It's okay. They're going.

She blinked and bit the insides of her cheeks, willing the images to stop flashing inside her head, and craning her stiff neck to watch the men step into the elevator. One of them pulled out a mobile phone and she heard: 'Take it . . . I have to . . .'

Breathe. Breathe.

Then there was a sound.

The room span as Annabel's gaze settled on a brown object a few feet away. Her Louis Vuitton handbag. It sat at the foot of the sofa, as obvious and out of place in the empty hostess club as a fast-food wrapper on a surgeon's instrument tray. And it was vibrating.

Breathe in, breathe, breathe in, breathe out.

The vibrating turned into ringing, low at first, like the tinkling breaking of glass. Then it grew to a loud, blaring electronic tune, deafening in the stillness of the closed-up club.

Oh my God, oh my God, please help me God.

It was Annabel's mobile phone.

Annabel chewed her cheeks harder, willing the noise to stop. Instead, the ring-tone grew louder and more frightening in the silence.

Acid-bright light flickered all over the club, merciless spotlights shining into every corner, chasing away any comfort offered by shadow.

Annabel saw the blonde girl lying half in, half out of the elevator, the gold-coloured elevator doors opening and closing against her unconscious body.

Both men walked back towards the club.

'. . . she's . . . told you . . . find her . . .'

There was a pause, then the tall man threw open the glass door.

'She could still be here.'

Another pause. Someone rummaged around the folds of the settee above her, and she screwed her eyes shut as the upholstery moved. When she opened them again she saw legs in grey trousers.

A mottled hand picked up the whisky bottle on the table in

front of her. Then the bottle was replaced with a clunk, and Annabel's stomach constricted as the grey trousers bent at the knees.

She screwed her eyes shut again. When she opened them a large face hovered inches from hers, the eyes bloodshot.

Annabel held her breath.

They'd found her.

I

Steph

'Smile is Best Makeup', said the sign at Roppongi subway station.

Steph, rucksack on one shoulder, dyed-red hair in long, salty tendrils around her unmade-up face, saw the message through a sea of lipsticked, blonde girls – and smiled.

With more blondes per square mile than anywhere else in Japan, Roppongi, she'd been warned, wasn't the least bit Japanese and definitely more yen than zen. Still, she thought, as the crowd carried her up and out into the noisy disco streets of Tokyo's notorious sex district, past fast-food restaurants, legal-drug shops and clubs called Climax, Red Lips and Private Eyes, Roppongi didn't smell half as bad as it sounded.

She fought to stand still by a traffic-jammed dual carriageway, under a vast green and white motorway overhang, while the crowd in its collective high heels tottered around her, young western women hurrying to meet Japanese men.

No one paid any attention to the blue-eyed British girl in frayed jeans standing outside Freshness Burger flicking through a Tokyo city guide. They'd seen it all before: western girl comes to Tokyo to make her fortune. But if they'd looked closer, they might have seen the scars on her arms, a hand that couldn't quite grip the guidebook, and realised that despite Steph's photogenic face with its symmetrical lines and strong jaw, she wasn't just another model looking for easy money.

Steph read neat, handwritten notes at the back of her guidebook.

Annabel@docomo.ne.jp – her friend Annabel's Tokyo email address.

Flin – Annabel's landlord and the person she was due to meet here.

Calamity Janes – the hostess club where her other friend, Julia, worked.

Finding Flin in this crowd of people wouldn't be easy, but as soon as she got her accommodation sorted and caught up with Annabel, she could find out where Julia's club was and ask for a job. If Julia's club didn't have work, she'd have to go door-knocking until she found something. Her savings wouldn't last the week in the world's most expensive city. She had to start working as a hostess, girlfriend-for-rent-but-honestly-there's-no-sex-involved, as soon as possible. Tonight, preferably.

'Hey girly.'

A man with black hair, white skin and red lips appeared at her shoulder, a tired-looking vampire holding a sheaf of *Club Orgasmic* flyers.

'I'm not a girly.'

He leaned towards her. 'Looking for work? Dancing work?'

Steph shook her head. 'Not at the moment. I'm looking for my new landlord.'

'So what are you doing here?'

'I just told you. Right now I'm trying to find my new landlord. Do you know the name of this road?'

'What am I, a tour guide?' The man rolled his bloodshot eyes. 'You looking for hostess work?'

'Maybe. Why, do you know someone who's hiring?'

'You won't find hostess work, not with those.' He nodded at the silver line running over her chin, and the scars on her shoulder and upper arm, twisted and bumpy like baked mud.

'Only dancing jobs.'

'Look, fuck off would you?' Steph turned around, swinging her rucksack so it clipped the man's shoulder. 'I don't need you to tell me . . . I'll find something.'

The man slunk back into the crowd, and proffered flyers to a group of shaven-headed Americans. 'Sir. Free topless. Free bottomless. Sir.'

Steph looked back at her book.

'Excuse me.'

'What?' Steph turned to see another man standing too close, this time an anaemic-looking Pakistani in a thin, white shirt. He had very flat features, so flat his face looked like it had been ironed, which was more than could be said for his shirt. She was about to tell him to get lost too, when he said: 'Stephanie?'

She stared in surprise. 'Yes?'

'I'm Flin. The apartment?'

'*You're* Flin?' She'd expected him to be Japanese. But, this was Roppongi – *gaijin*, or foreigner land. 'Well, great! I thought I'd never find you.' Steph stuck her hot hand into his sweaty one and shook it. 'The apartment. Perfect. Shall we go there now – it's near here, isn't it?'

'Very near. This way.' They walked back down the street, dodging a crowd of six-foot blonde girls shouting at each other in Russian. 'I wasn't sure you'd come,' Flin said. 'I thought maybe someone told you . . . Anyway, did you have a good flight? Not too tired? Jet lag?'

'I'm okay. I slept on the plane. How's Annabel doing?'

They stopped at a pedestrian crossing and Flin bounced from one foot to the other.

'I'll take key money,' he said, 'and then I'll show you the apartment. The key money is sixty thousand yen. Okay?'

'What?' Steph's smile slid away and the white scar on her jaw bunched into little creases. 'How much?'

'Sixty thousand yen.'

At Heathrow, Steph had changed all the sterling she had left in the world, and been handed the grand sum of 50,000 yen – about £250 – in a polythene envelope with a plastic seal. The money was supposed to last her the week until she found a job, but apparently it wouldn't even cover the apartment deposit.

'Show me the place first,' said Steph, stepping back as a scooter trundled past. 'Then we'll talk about it. Is Annabel there now? It'll be great to see her.'

'No, no. Key money first. Then we see the apartment.'

'No, show me the apartment first.'

There was a pause, during which the crossing light turned green and crowds surged towards them.

'Okay, okay,' Flin decided. 'It's not the usual way, but I'll show you the place.' They crossed the street, past Café Almond with its white and pink awning and array of colourful cakes in the window. 'You're really going to like it, I'm quite sure. It really is a great place if you want to live in Roppongi, a seriously great place actually. You want me to carry your bag?'

'I'm okay.'

Flin led her into a grubby, grey side street with stairwells stuck to the backs of the squashed-together buildings. 'You understand,' he said, as Steph followed him up one of the wrought-iron stair-cases, clang! clang! clang! 'that I need the key money as soon as you've seen the apartment. The key money is sixty thousand yen. There are plenty of banks on the crossroads, I'd be happy to show you to one. Citibank usually takes Visa, or the convenience stores . . . Family Mart, Lawsons . . .'

'Look, I'm going to be honest with you,' said Steph, watching him unlock a dented, metal door that looked like a sumo wrestler had run into it. 'Fifty thousand yen is literally all the money I have, and I mean in the world. Is there any chance I could give it to you in a week when I've got myself a job and—'

Flin unlocked the door. 'You don't have a job here?'

'No, not yet.'

He pushed the creaky metal. 'No key money, no place to sleep.' The door screeched as if bemoaning the squalor and the smells inside.

'As you can see,' said Flin, walking into the narrow hallway that smelt of cheese, toast and perfume, 'there's every modern convenience here. Microwave.' He patted a food-encrusted micro-wave that rested on a freestanding, pink plastic shelving unit in the 2-foot-wide entranceway. It wobbled. 'Bathroom.' He opened a door to what looked like a caravan toilet, a plastic-walled cocoon with a tiny shower hung directly over the lavatory. 'You'll be sharing with great girls, really great. In you room particularly, a Russian girl, very clean.'

'What?' said Steph, feeling her trainers stick to the floor. 'What are you talking about?'

Flin pulled open a chipboard door. 'This is your bedroom.' He moved into the room so Steph could see the metal bunk beds, low ceiling and metre of floor space. A chugging air-conditioning unit opposite the beds made grinding, spluttering sounds.

'I'm sharing with Annabel,' Steph insisted. 'My friend. I'm supposed to be sharing with my friend.'

'Annabel?' said Flin. 'No, no, she left. Disappeared without paying her rent. A-W-O-L.' He spelled the letters carefully. 'Absent without leave.'

2

'What do you mean she left?' Steph asked. 'In your emails you said . . . Only last week you said . . .' But as she thought about it, Flin had never mentioned Annabel in his email correspondence. Only what a great room she'd be sharing and how fantastic the apartment was. And Annabel hadn't replied to her emails for months – having too much fun, Steph had assumed.

'It was all arranged,' said Steph. 'Why would she leave without telling me?'

'I don't know. Girls leave all the time, boyfriends, new jobs. You'll have the top bunk, the other girl already asked for the bottom. Not a problem for you, right?' Flin didn't give Steph time to reply. 'Here one day, gone the next, these girls. Of course, I had to keep her key money. You're lucky with this room in particular. You're only sharing with one other girl, which again is very unusual. And for a very good price. In your email, you said you had another friend here. Perhaps you can borrow the key money from her?'

'Julia? I don't think so. She's not a big lender. Look, Annabel . . . She wouldn't just *leave* without telling me. Don't you know anything about where she went? Do you have a number for her? She hasn't replied to emails in ages.'

Flin drummed his fingers on the metal bed frame. 'No. Girls come and go all the time. She's probably found some man to take care of her and moved into his place. It's safe out here, no need to worry. Tokyo is one of the safest cities in the world.'

'That's not like Annabel,' said Steph. 'Anyway, she was looking forward to sharing with me. At least that's what she said back in . . .' Steph counted back the months on all ten fingers. 'January.'

'She worked as a hostess,' said Flin. 'Probably she met a customer and he rents her an apartment in some fancy part of the city.'

'No, she's teaching English,' said Steph. 'She's an English teacher.'

'She worked as a hostess,' said Flin with a sharp nod. 'I saw her coming back at all hours. Make-up every evening. Sounds like you don't know your friend so well.'

A wave of tiredness enveloped Steph. 'It's been a while since I've seen her,' she admitted. 'Ten years actually. We knew each other at school. Maybe she's changed . . .'

Flin shrugged. 'You want the bed or not?'

'Okay,' said Steph, running her hand along the dented bed-frame and feeling dust under her fingers. 'Fine. You've got me. I need somewhere to stay tonight. But, look, I can't give you all the money I have. How am I going to eat?'

'This apartment is excellent value,' said Flin, puffing out his chest. 'It's one of—'

Steph held up her hand. 'Spare me the sales pitch. I've got eyes. Look, I'm not saying I won't take it. But I didn't realise you'd need the key money straightaway, and fifty thousand is literally all the money I have. I mean that's it – everything.'

'No key money, no room. You won't find another apartment tonight – impossible. Where will you sleep, out on the street?'

'Maybe. You just said Tokyo was safe.'

'Maybe so, but girls still go missing in Roppongi.'

Steph thought of the news reports about dead girls found in concrete, serial rapists . . . She was sure the stories were exaggerated, but suddenly she felt worried for Annabel.

'Has anyone spoken to the police?' asked Steph.

Flin looked at her as if she was a lunatic. 'The *police?*'

'In case anything has happened to her.'

'Annabel?' said Flin. 'She's fine. Find your other friend. I'm sure she knows where she is.'

Steph nodded and chewed her lip. 'I suppose . . . Me and Annabel haven't seen each other since we were fourteen.

And it's not like we planned to come here together. Nothing was written in stone. Maybe she's just doing her own thing and forgot about me.'

'Yes. Probably she forgot. Too much drinking. They all do it, all the girls. Now about the deposit.'

Steph sighed. With the custom in Japan for references, key money and monthly apartment contracts, there was no way she could find another cheap place at short notice, and she didn't fancy a night on the street. She wondered, as she sat down on the bottom bunk, what possible reason there could be for Annabel leaving so suddenly. Probably there was a perfectly good explanation. The mattress sank a little too readily under her weight.

'No, no! You can't sit until you pay.'

'Don't be stupid. I'm just sitting down. So you think it'll be easy to get a job here? Julia told me it was easy, but I've been told that before.'

'I thought this was your first time in Roppongi.'

'It is. I meant back in London. Sometimes people have their own agenda when they tell you they have work. But I got the impression it would be easier here.'

'I think . . .' Flin glanced at her scars. 'Perhaps not easy, but I think you'll be okay.'

'Okay, fine.' She pulled a roll of yen from her jeans pocket, exactly 50,000 yen, and removed it from its plastic wallet. 'Would you settle for forty thousand?'

'You said you had fifty thousand.'

'Forty thousand and you can take it right now.'

'No. Sorry.' Flin folded his arms. 'No way. The price is sixty thousand.'

Steph began counting out the notes, and held 40,000 yen out to Flin. 'I'll give you the rest next week.'

'Absolutely not. No.' Flin backed away as if the notes had teeth.

Steph looked at the money. She sighed. 'Fine. Fifty thousand?'

Flin nodded. 'Okay, okay. But the other ten thousand yen by next Saturday, or you pack up and leave. Other girls want the beds here. Big waiting list.'

The smooth notes slipped all too easily from Steph's fingers. She'd been carrying the bankroll in her jeans since Heathrow, and it had cut into her thigh for the last 24 hours, but she was still reluctant to let it go. All the money she had in the world – gone, just like that. It felt like she might just have made a monumentally stupid decision.

'So you really think Annabel is okay?' Steph said.

'Yes, yes,' said Flin, flicking through the bills. 'Ten, twenty, thirty . . . She was a sensible girl. Drunk but sensible. You do have to be careful out here though. Forty . . . fifty. Get a nice, safe apartment.' He thumped the wall, as if to reassure her of the solidness of the building, and the thin plasterboard shuddered. 'You won't regret staying here, I promise you. It's safe, nice girls, nice landlord. Safety is very important. You're going to be working as a hostess, right?'

'Right. Do you think Annabel might come back?'

'I don't think she'll be coming back,' said Flin.

'It's a bit weird, isn't it? Just leaving like that. Maybe she found a better apartment . . .'

Flin shook his head tightly, as if such a thing couldn't be imagined. 'This is a very good apartment. Annabel was here a long time, always paid her rent. No complaints.'

'So why did she leave without paying you?' asked Steph. 'I thought girls earned lots out here.'

Flin stuffed the roll of yen into his pocket. 'They earn lots, yes. Girls get bonuses, clothes, trips to Tokyo Disney World, all sorts. Money, money, money. That's what girls come here for. That's what you're here for. Right?'

'Yes,' Steph conceded. 'My last chance, you could call it.' She ran the back of her hand along her upper arm. 'I'm looking to earn about fifteen thousand.'

'Yen?' Flin smiled at his own bad joke.

'Pounds. Fifteen thousand pounds. Then I can . . . Never mind. Anyway. Everyone says I can earn that out here no problem.'

'How much is that in yen?'

'I don't know in yen. Maybe twenty thousand dollars?'

'Twenty thousand dollars?' Flin absentmindedly pushed the yen deeper into his pocket. 'You'll have to be a top hostess to earn that. It depends . . . If you get the right customers, the right club, anything's possible. Here's the key. Call me on my cell phone if you have any problems.'

Only when Steph heard the metallic clang of Flin's feet on the stairwell outside did she realise he hadn't given her his phone number.

It was inside the air-conditioning unit that Steph found it: a simple, hardback notebook with a blue, woven cover.

Annabel's diary.

She'd been heading out of the apartment of find Julia's club, but the air-conditioning unit was making unhealthy gurgling noises, so she thumped it in the hope of shutting it up. It let out a high-pitched wheeze and sent its front panel clattering to the floor, revealing dark, dusty innards.

Looking closer she saw, amid the dead cockroaches and blossoms of blue dust, a hardback book, damp with condensation and slightly charred at one of the corners.

With some irritation, Steph reached in and grabbed it, wondering what sort of idiot would stuff such an obstruction into the air-conditioner. But then a dozen business cards fell from its white pages, fluttering and twirling towards the ground, the names of influential Japanese company directors and business owners coming to rest on the floor between cockroach and fly carcasses.

What is it – someone's address book or something?

It was well-used, the book – she realised that straightaway. The lined pages were puffy and wavy, and she noticed page after page of neat, bubbly, girly handwriting. 'Dear God,' she read over and over again. And 'Love Annabel' . . .

She got down on her knees to pick up the business cards, dusting insect wings and legs from their glossy, white surfaces, and was surprised to find, under a card for Ken Yokimoto, MD at Asahi, a dozen or so identical business cards for Sinatra's Hostess Club with Annabel Jones written on them in faded pencil.

The handwriting was so familiar. Suddenly Steph was back in English class, sitting next to her thirteen-year-old friend and watching Annabel write Take That over and over again on the foolscap cover of her exercise book.

Flin was right. Annabel is working as a hostess, Steph realised, staring at the little white rectangles in her hands. *Julia said hostesses have to give out their own business cards and collect other people's. Annabel must be working at this place – Sinatra's.*

Dropping the cards to the floor, she rushed outside and on to the stairwell.

'Flin! *Flin*!'

Flin was climbing into a little van that looked like a loaf of sliced bread.

'Don't worry about the shower,' he shouted up, 'I'll have it fixed by tomorrow.'

'No, I just wondered . . . Annabel. She's left . . . There's something she left behind. A diary. Why would she leave without her diary?'

'She left lots of things behind.' Flin stroked an earlobe. 'Girls do. Rush, rush rush. Drinking, drinking. Always leaving things. Some clothes . . . I threw them all away, just throw it away.'

'Oh. Okay.'

Steph went back into her airless room and slotted the panel back on to the air-conditioning unit. She took a seat on the saggy bottom bunk and felt the weight of the diary in her hands.

She left lots of things behind.

Who left clothes behind? And their diary? Something didn't feel right. Flin said girls went missing out here, but he seemed more concerned about his rent money than Annabel's sudden disappearance. Probably she was being paranoid and at the very least she should speak to Julia, but . . .

Steph opened the diary. Maybe there was a forwarding address inside or a telephone number. But there were no personal details on the first page, only row after row of neatly written text. The first words were: 'Dear God, I'm scared.'

Steph stared at the bubbly handwriting. A chilly feeling worked its way up her spine. Flin didn't know where Annabel had gone. Did anyone else know she'd left the apartment suddenly, leaving a load of things behind?

I'm probably worrying about nothing, thought Steph. *Big deal, she left a few clothes and a diary behind and didn't tell her landlord where she was going. And she forgot to tell me she was leaving. So what? We haven't seen each other in years. She didn't have any obligation to stay in some grotty apartment for my sake if she found somewhere better. Julia will know where she is.*

All the same, Steph couldn't shake the feeling that something wasn't right. She found her gaze drifting down towards the page, and she continued to read.

3

Mama

Kimiki 'Mama-san' Tanaka didn't like foreigners. She worked for foreigners, employed foreigners and, as the daughter of a Japanese pan-pan girl and a US soldier, was half foreign herself. But Mama preferred the Japanese ways. As age eroded her, quickly and inevitably, like a wave falling over a sandcastle, she clung to duty, honour, sacrifice – all things she was sure the fat British journalist standing on her doorstep couldn't possibly understand.

'Mama-san. It's good to see you again.' The journalist, whose name was George, extended a hefty hand covered in dark hair. She felt his surprise at her faded face and the little shoots of black springing from her nearly bald head.

The last time George had seen her she was the regal owner of a hostess club with heavy black hair cut in a fashionable bob, thickly pencilled eyebrows, full red lips, shoulder pads in her silk jacket and diamonds sparkling on every finger. Nothing like the shrivelled-up woman, who looked more than her fifty-five years, hiding behind the door in a tired old kimono and house slippers.

'So . . . ready to get started?'

Mama peeked around the door frame and extended her own hand cautiously

'George-san.' Her voice was croaky and weak. It had been many weeks since she'd spoken out loud. She noticed the Dictaphone in his grey shirt pocket and the spiral-bound notepad in his hand and felt tired. Recovering, yes, but she wasn't 100 per cent Mama Tanaka-san. Not yet. 'It's been a long time. Many months since the newspaper interview.'

'Almost a year,' said George. 'But the public haven't lost interest. If we get the timing right — '

'I know,' said Mama, sounding tired. 'Money, money, money.'

'We'll have to move quickly,' said George, putting on his serious news reporter face. 'The publisher is anxious to strike while the iron's hot.'

A laugh whistled from Mama's throat. 'George-san, so serious. Where is the young man I remember? The English guidebook writer who used to dance on the tables with my hostesses?'

'That was a long time ago,' said George with a cough. 'It was my job. I couldn't review your club without — '

'It certainly was,' Mama interrupted. 'You've come a long way since then. Journalist. And now book writer.'

'I wouldn't call myself a book writer just yet,' said George. 'You'll be my first.'

'Nervous?'

'A little.' George took a wheezy breath. 'I'll need much more from you this time. The deadline's extremely tight, and budget . . . I don't have much to pay for my interviewing time. I know you've been ill, but you look like you're recovering well, and — '

'*Well?*' Mama didn't do false flattery. 'I look like an old lady, *neh?*' She laughed a sick person's laugh, weak and half-hearted. Then her voice changed abruptly, the way it did when she switched from presenting customers with their bill to arguing over the total. 'I'm too tired, too tired. I'm not going to do the book. Sorry.'

George's grey face flushed red. 'You're not going to . . . You can't be serious. Mama, a publisher wants to buy a book about your life. Do you know how rarely opportunities like this come along?'

Mama smiled. 'People really do want to read about me, *neh*? After your newspaper article, I'm famous in Tokyo.'

'And not just Tokyo,' said George. 'In the UK, America . . . Wherever the article sold people want to know more.'

'Sorry, George-san.' Mama folded her arms. 'Too tired.'

'But the contracts are signed. Money's already changed hands . . .'

'Contracts yes, but not signed by me. By you.'

George scratched light hair, turned tea-coloured with grease. 'But everything's been arranged.'

'*Hai, hai,* but I'm tired.'

George looked like he'd been slapped around the face. After a moment he said lamely: 'This book really will be an excellent investment for you. When it starts earning royalties—'

Mama smiled. 'Maybe I'm just one mama among many. It could be a lot of work for nothing.'

'You? One among many? Sinatra's was legendary. Notorious. One of the most famous hostess clubs in Roppongi.'

'Sinatra's hasn't closed down, George-san.' Mama gave him a coy look under sparse eyelashes. 'Even though you haven't visited us in a while.'

'The prices are a little beyond my salary,' said George, flipping open his notepad. He began to read. 'Mama Tanaka-san – a celebrity of the Tokyo hostess circuit. From film stars to famous politicians, Mama has entertained them all.'

'Sorry, George-san.'

George looked flustered and flicked on. 'Some of the girls who worked for you – they're famous themselves now. Hollywood stars. There's so much more to give the public. Please. Please say you'll do it. It'll be a great book.'

With a sigh, Mama stepped back and opened the door a fraction wider. Japanese hospitality, even though she was only half Japanese. Her better half.

'Come in and we'll talk, but not for long. Shoes, George-san!' She held up her hand.

With a grunt, George pulled off his brown leather slip-ons and dropped them messily by the neat rows of sandals and boots at the door. They looked especially grubby and unpolished next to Mama's sparkling clean shoes.

'Will they be safe out here?'

'Of course! What a question. You should know by now. We're not in America.' Mama gave the slip-ons a disapproving glance, then turned and walked inside. 'Too tired. You understand. Maybe the newspaper article said enough, anyway. In here.'

She led George through an open, paper-screen door into a large living-room with a low table and leaf-patterned cushions on a bamboo-mat floor. There were no western-style seats, and George surveyed the furniture with apprehension.

'You've lived in Japan how many years now?' said Mama with a smile.

'Five.'

'You have an apartment in Tokyo, you wrote a guidebook about Tokyo, you work for a Tokyo newspaper—'

'An *English* newspaper *in* Tokyo,' George corrected.

'—and still you're afraid of Japanese furniture?'

George blushed. In his own apartment in the westernised area of Azabu Juban, nothing was Japanese. He'd purchased every sofa, table and chair from an American couple hosting a *sayonara* sale and there wasn't a *futon, kaisu* floor chair or low *katasu* table in the whole place.

'Would you like tea?' Mama asked. 'Miu has gone home, but I can make it.'

'What? Tea. Yes, great.'

A moment later, Mama brought through a tray, noticing George had swallowed up one of her floor cushions with his ample rear end. He was trying to cross his fat legs in their corduroy trousers, his back squashed against her dark orange, wood dresser with its beautiful wrought-iron handles. She was sure those handles would cut into him if he sat like that, but a little pain was no bad thing. In her experience, westerners didn't endure enough of it.

The tray contained a little iron teapot, delicate cups with no handles, and a tub of green tea powder. There was also a plate of plum-coloured Japanese gelatine sweets dusted with powdered sugar. Mama laid out everything precisely on the table.

'So I said we'd talk,' she said, in her near-perfect English. 'And what I'd like to say is there isn't the right time to write a book.' She set a cup in front of George, then sat daintily on her cushion, tucking bare feet underneath her, and spooned green-tea powder into the pot.

George nodded politely, anxiety stealing across his face. His preliminary part of the advance had been paid and spent. The second payment wouldn't come until the manuscript was delivered. With hefty repayments on his apartment and child support for a son back in England, he'd be bankrupt within a few months.

'You agreed before, Mama.'

'I know, but I'm tired. You understand? I've just finished treatment. I'm recovering, I have a long way to go. And I have to go back to work. I'm starting again tonight as a matter of fact . . .'

'We'll keep it as simple as possible. You won't have to do anything – just talk to me. Like you did for the "interesting people" article. Remember? Easy.'

'I didn't think anyone would really read that article,' said Mama. 'And you want more this time. Secrets. No, I'm too tired.'

George took a sip of tea, frowning at the taste. He was used to lattes with four teaspoons of brown sugar.

'Tell me about the chemotherapy.'

'Very hard, very hard.'

George nodded and cocked his neck attentively, ever the trained journalist.

'You take a tablet, you know?' said Mama. 'Just one tablet, every day. It looks like nothing. Harmless. At first, you don't think it can do anything. But then . . . Oh, everything hurts. I couldn't work, I couldn't do anything.'

'They told me you haven't been working for a few months.' George's lips puckered as he took another bitter sip of green tea.

'I'll go in tonight,' Mama said. 'Later. Maybe eleven, just to see how they're doing.'

'And your chemo's finished now?'

'For now.'

Mama sipped her tea, clearly not seeing the need to talk anymore. The room was warm; she hadn't risked letting the temperature drop since her illness.

'Mama, tell me,' George said, his left knee jiggling. 'You wanted to write this book for your daughter, didn't you? To give her an income. That's why you agreed to this.'

Mama bowed her head for a moment, and when she lifted it

up again wetness had worked its way into the wrinkles around her eyes.

'Yes. For Kaito.'

'I have a son. He's five.' George gave her his best attempt at a sympathetic smile, pale skin stretching around tired eyes. There was no need to mention that he hadn't seen his son in over two years and owed thousands in backdated child support. 'So, what's changed? Isn't Kaito important any more?'

'It's so much work. You want me to tell all and I don't think I can.'

'Too much work for your daughter?'

There was a pause.

'And Mama, when you're gone, don't you want your daughter to know about your life? How you earned enough to send her to college?'

'Maybe. Maybe I'd like her to know . . . I'd like her to understand. I'd like her to forgive me.'

'So why don't we try it, Mama? Just one interview today. See how it goes. If you want to stop, we'll stop.'

Another pause.

'If the book does well,' said George, shuffling on his cushion, 'Kaito will have an income. No more work for you.'

Mama sighed, a big sigh that let all the breath from her body. She looked at the photo of her daughter in a clear plastic frame on top of the dresser, and felt the smallness, the cheapness, of the apartment under her bare feet. The 1980s economic bubble had burst, the big spenders were gone.

The champagne had been drunk; the beautiful outfits worn and reworn until threads dragged along the floor and the colours had faded; the jewellery, almost all of it, sold and melded into this shabby one-bedroom apartment in Ikebukuro.

The apartment, and a drawer full of diamonds; that was all she had left to give her daughter. It wasn't a lot.

'George-san . . . We'll try. Just try, okay?'

4

Steph

Steph knelt on the thin mattress and, holding the blue book in her good hand, let her eyes sweep back and forth over Annabel's neat handwriting. She wasn't altogether comfortable reading Annabel's private thoughts, but needs must. The most important thing was to make sure Annabel was safe.

Dear God,

I'm scared. Please keep me safe in this mad place and help me make money and get more customers. Money, money, money, money, that's all I think about out here. Yen, yen yen. Every day the same, how much more can I make, how much have I missed out on. How can I get more customers, who has more customers than me.

Who *was* that guy last night? I'm not going mad, I swear he really was following me. Too big a coincidence. No men like that live round here, so what was he doing outside at four in the morning? *What was he doing?*

God, I know I can be crazy silly scared sometimes but things *do* happen if you don't keep your eyes open. The girls at Calamity Janes always have bad stories to tell . . .

Steph swallowed hard and tasted acid. *By the sounds of things, a man followed Annabel home.* And Calamity Janes . . . That was Julia's hostess club, wasn't it? She pulled her guidebook from the netted pocket of her rucksack and checked. Yes, it was. *Bad stories to tell.*

The business cards with Annabel's name on said Sinatra's Hostess Club. Presumably, that's where she worked now. Or *had* worked if she wasn't in Roppongi any more.

. . . how many times have those girls told me to watch my drink??? I can be so stupid sometimes. Just careless, but then, what are we supposed to do, take our drinks into the toilet with us? That's what I am now, careless. I used to be so scared of dating customers, now I go out with men all week and don't even tell the girls where I'm going.

The guy was so creepy, I feel like he was watching me all night, it makes my skin crawl. I was drunk, but not so drunk anything could have happened, but what about the nights when I drink and have blackouts and one of the girls gets me home? What if he follows me then?

La, la la la, de da. OK. Thinking of nicer things. It was great to sing last night, shame my voice went (why do I smoke now? I don't even like it). I could see them all thinking I was rubbish, they're all going to think I'm such a big head now, going 'la la la, I'm such a great singer'. I need to practise more, I didn't realise how out of practice I was, it's been what? 10 months?

I think creepy guy was following me when I left the club. But that might be someone totally different. I swear someone was watching me drinking at Hollywoods though, I got goose bumps.

It's hard to think clearly when you drink all the time.

I hate Hollywoods, they used to be nice but they're so mean, mean, mean, always one free drink, that's it. They look at me like I'm a total prostitute.

On the way home there was definitely someone, definitely. Japanese though, at least he wasn't Iranian.

Those Iranian guys, it's scary now they're in Hollywoods. They don't make sense to me, if they've got so much money why dress like that? They scare me so much after what happened to Estella.

I don't know how it works with them, if you keep clear they leave you alone?? All the bad stories are girls who get too close like the girl who had her cheek bitten off, she was a stripper. Stripping is so mad out here, why let someone touch you for 2000 yen when you can hostess for 3000 yen an hour?

I'm learning so fast out here, not so naïve any more. So embarrassing. I can't believe I asked Nishi about those Russian girls, sooo stupid! Did they come to Tokyo knowing they were going to stand out in the street with a '3000 yen for sex' sign or did they want to be models or something?

So many stories . . . all third or fourth hand, but they can't all be made up.

Help me God, please, because I'm scared to be alone today.

Love Annabel.

Steph closed the diary with a snap and leaned back against the wall. The diary felt sticky and she threw it on to a coverless pillow and put her head in her hands. She wanted to be sick.

It sounded like Roppongi wasn't safe after all, and now Annabel had vanished without a word, leaving a load of her things behind.

Talk to Julia, a little voice said. *If there was anything to worry about, she would have emailed you about it.* The space in her jeans pocket throbbed like a missing tooth. *Anyway, you need to earn rent money before you go running around looking for Annabel.*

Steph took a few deep breaths. She looked at the diary again. Then she snatched it up and headed out of the door.

The *koban* police box was empty when Steph slid open its squeaky glass door, and its interior smelt of mould and something else – perhaps some sort of tea. There was no real-life policeman to greet her inside, only a cartoon picture of a dog in a policeman's helmet stuck to the wall. Next to the police-dog picture was a bright yellow poster with a photo of an acne-ridden youth staring out into the little room – a Wanted poster.

Except for some white forms scattered around on pink counter tops and a couple of biros, everything was pinned or stuck to the walls. After turning a circle in the centre of the *koban*, Steph spotted a heavy, black telephone secured to one of the counter tops and picked up the receiver. She held it for a moment and then a thin Japanese voice crackled through the other end.

'Hello? I'd like police? Do you have the police?' *It sounds like I'm ordering a takeaway.*

More Japanese crackled through.

'Hello? Hello?' Steph shouted back, but the voice on the other end remained incomprehensible. She hung up and was about to leave when the black phone started ringing.

She picked it up. 'Hello?'

'Hell-lo. Er . . . You wanted the police?' It was a man's voice, young but formal.

'Yes, I need to speak to the police,' said Steph, grasping the diary and squeezing its furry cover between her fingers.

'Okay. Please wait. I'm coming.'

Steph checked her watch. 'How long will you be?' Outside the plastic windows of the *koban* box, the sky was getting dark. She was wasting time.

But the line had gone dead.

5

Twenty minutes later, a young policeman arrived outside the *koban* on a pedal cycle. He stared at Steph like a love-struck puppy for a few seconds, before climbing down and reaching out to give her hand a solid shake.

'You need help?' he asked.

'Not me – it's about my friend.'

'Ooooh.' The man nodded enthusiastically. 'We'll talk please at the police station. It's not far from here. Please.' He gestured for her to follow him, explaining, 'I'm one of the only policemen at the station who speaks English. But I'm not very good.'

'You're sure it's not far?' Steph asked, checking her watch again.

'Not far.'

At the police station, the policeman removed his shoes and took a pair of green police-logoed slippers from a wooden pigeon hole. He gestured for Steph to do the same, and she reached for a pair of rubbery green slippers from one of the many pairs stowed, and tried to put them on her feet. The slippers were too small, and her heels hung off the back.

'Do you . . .' The policeman lowered his head and muttered in Japanese, grasping for the correct English expression. '*Would* you like a drink?'

'I'm sort of in a hurry but . . .' Steph swallowed and realised her throat was dry. 'That would be great. Thanks. Just something quick.'

Steph followed the policeman through an admin room of fellow officers, who all stared at her. She stared back at one of them and he quickly turned back to his computer screen.

'Okay,' said the young policeman. 'I'll bring you a drink. My *boss* will interview you.'

Steph was led into a wood-panelled interview room, and the young policeman vanished. A moment later, a middle-aged policeman with a grey crew-cut like an army sergeant sauntered into the room and banged a stack of papers on the table. He looked Steph up and down and frowned.

'Please sit.'

'Okay.' Steph took a plastic chair. 'It's about the—'

'You're staying in Roppongi?' asked the army sergeant, taking the seat opposite and scratching rapid Japanese on to a pink form.

'Yes, but—'

'Why did you come to Japan?'

Steph's smile dropped. 'Holiday. I'm just on a holiday. But listen, it's about my friend Annabel—'

'You're working in Roppongi?' The army sergeant looked up from the pink form with alarming suddenness and Steph found herself leaning away from him.

'No, I'm not working in Roppongi,' she said, looking down at the table. 'I'm here on holiday. Look, I want to tell you about this diary.' She put the blue book on the table. 'It belongs to my friend. She was staying at my apartment but she's gone now. I'm worried something, you know, perhaps something bad has happened to her.'

'Apartment.' The policeman tapped the table with his pen. 'Where is the apartment you're staying, please?'

Even if Steph had known the address, she wouldn't have given it to him. But as it happened, she couldn't for the life of her remember the odd line of numbers and letters that made up the location of her apartment. So she gave him an honest answer.

'I don't know.' She returned his serious stare, fancying herself a wrongly accused heroine in a police drama. 'The addresses are hard here. Very different from back home.'

'You have nothing with you, no details for your landlord?' The army sergeant regarded Steph with deep suspicion.

'No.'

'Strange.' He tapped his pen even harder. 'What visa do you have?'

'A holiday visa,' Steph answered smoothly. 'But listen, I'm not here for me. My friend Annabel. She left her apartment without taking her diary and the landlord said she left some clothes too and—'

'*Holiday* visa.' The army sergeant seemed to give this answer a lot of thought. 'Do you have your passport, please?'

'No, *listen*.' Steph could feel her bad hand becoming tense. 'Why do you need my passport? Oh never mind. Anyway, no, I don't have it. But is there any way to check, at least to see, if Annabel is still in Japan? There must be records.'

'Your holiday visa, when did it start?'

Steph sighed. She felt as if she was trying to pull a bone away from a particularly stubborn Rottweiler. 'Yesterday.'

'And how long will you stay in Japan?' The man asked.

'I – maybe a month or two. I'm travelling. I don't know.'

'Ah. Okay. Fine.' There was a long pause. 'So. Your friend. English girl?'

'Finally. Yes – I'm here about an English girl. We were supposed to be sharing a room, but when I arrived she'd vanished. No forwarding address and she never emailed to let me know. I found this diary of hers in my room and my landlord said—'

'Strange to have a landlord, when you're here on holiday,' said the policeman, graciously accepting a hot coffee from the young policeman who had just re-entered the room. A cold carton of green tea was placed in front of Steph, and she pulled the straw from the side of the carton as the young man backed out of the room.

'Most tourists, they stay in hotels. Or other places. Strange.' The army sergeant sipped his coffee.

'Look,' said Steph, 'I need to make sure Annabel's okay. Her diary . . . It says she was being followed.'

'I think she's fine, this girl,' said the policeman. 'No girls have been reported missing this year, no family has telephoned to ask about their daughters. I think there's no problem. But you can make a statement, have a police investigation. It will mean we'll have to look into your apartment, your *working activities*, very closely.'

Steph flinched. She understood the implication. If she took things further, it was likely they'd keep an eye on her, check she wasn't working illegally. And of course, she fully intended to work illegally, if only someone would give her the opportunity.

She thought for a moment. Julia had never mentioned anything about Annabel going AWOL, and Steph knew the two girls had been in touch since Julia had moved to Tokyo. Surely if there was anything to worry about, Julia would have let her know. Until she spoke to Julia, there was no point making a big fuss over nothing.

'Fine.' Steph punched the straw into the green tea and drank the entire carton in one go. She put the empty box down on the table and slapped her hands either side of it. 'Thank you for your help. I've really got to get going.'

'Please take your book,' said the policeman, pushing Annabel's diary towards her.

Steph snatched up the diary and pulled open the door, slip-slapping through the admin room in her rubbery slippers.

On the gleaming steps of the police station, Steph watched traffic trundle along the busy main road and decided she'd better make contact with Julia as quickly as possible.

As she marched across the street, ignoring the red Don't walk light and the Japanese pedestrians waiting virtuously on the pavement, she hoped Julia's hostess club wouldn't be too difficult to find. The sky was a flat, slate colour, and Steph wondered what time it was. She'd been in the police station quite a while – maybe an hour or so. All those stupid questions.

Soon Steph reached the exhaust-fume-filled streets of Roppongi crossroads, where women shouted 'Massagie! Massagie!' at men with bowed heads and furtive expressions, and a 10-foot TV screen played pop videos interspersed with *Docomo* mobile phone commercials.

Calamity Janes. Where are you?

She ran across zebra crossings, ignoring the red Don't walk man and dodging between green taxis, lorries, scooters and businessmen in BMWs who watched the news on mini dashboard televisions. In the polluted air, she could already taste poverty.

Steph realised, as she was carried along by the crowd of tall blonde girls, short blonde girls, fat and thin blonde girls, that her biggest problem wasn't finding Annabel, but getting a job. It had sounded simple back in England. She swallowed air that felt like sand. If Julia's club wouldn't hire her, it might not be simple at all.

6

Chastity

From: C_C_Chastity
To: CanadianDaphne
Subject: re: re: re: last nite

Hey Daph,

Sounds like a total idiot. Get rid of him. Seriously.

Tammy's fine, doing well at school, loves it there so all good. She is a BRIGHT KID, knows more Japanese than I do. The school said if I kept taking her late she'd never pick anything up – shows what they know.

So, great trip, but back to Sinatra's and the dirty old world of hostessing. It sucks, I hate it. Well, sometimes I hate it. Today I really, really do but I'm sticking to the plan, working hard and trying to save cash.

When I think of all the money I wasted, OMG, all the stuff I bought when I first started, champagne, coke, all that crap I paid for myself. I even bought my own clothes. Idiot! So the plan is the plan, babes, I promise you. This time next year I'll be out of this place. Plus, no more modelling. I've called it quits, it's just a waste of time. Too much competition. Sunscreen and all that jazz, no thanks. Next to them I'm just another brown-skinned girl with green eyes, no big deal.

Thanks for saying I'm a good mum. I am, I know it, I just forget sometimes. People are always on at me for going out or doing coke or working where I do. It's like as soon as you're a parent you're not allowed to have a good time or you're neglecting your kids. I didn't even smoke when I was pregnant with Tammy, but people still give me a hard time.

I swear though, if I didn't go out I'd go mad. Having Tams is TOUGH. Hard work, 24/7. Seriously. Japanese kids are so well behaved, it's so bad how she talks to me, a right little madam – don't know where she gets it from. She still wants to live with her dad, I tell her all the time he's NOT a good person. I'm lucky if I can even pay for her school and child care out of what he gives me. But don't get me started on that, I could go on for hours. IRRESPONSIBLE. Say no more.

Visa raids, just like always, but so many this month. I think things here . . . I don't know, it's not good. It's not going to last for ever, that's basically it, and Tammy's growing up so fast. About hostessing and all of that, part of me doesn't care, that's life, but I don't want her school friends ragging her for what her mum does. Like history repeating.

Botox last week. You're right, it WORKS!!! I look five years younger. I'm still working on Daishi-san to pay for the next lot. He was one of Annabel's, but I snapped him up quick before Helena got her claws in, ha ha ha!

Things were so good for a while when Princess Barbie left, I was top girl for like three weeks in a row. But good things never last. Still, I've had Daishi for months now, and he is a GOOD customer, worth all the hassle, but things are still slipping.

Honest, Daph, despite the Botox I'm getting old now, thank god for cosmetics. All I see are lines, lines and more lines. And bags. And pores. Were they there before, or did I just never look for them? People say coke gives you lines, but whatever. I know it can't help but the booze can't either and it's not like I can stop drinking.

This customer called me an old maid the other day because of the lines around my eyes. 'Spoiled sponge cake' is what he said. Some Japanese thing, means you're past your sell-by date. This was *after* the Botox. SHIITTT!! BUT! Here's something funny. He told me he was president of this big Japanese company, then gave me his business card. I got Tammy to read it for me and guess what – Assistant Accountant! Ha, ha ha! I couldn't care less what he thinks now, he's probably already blown his month's salary on one night in the club.

But seriously Daphs. I know I don't have long. I'm not an idiot. Another year here, save up a load of money and then start whatever. No more sleazy customers. No more make-up everyday. They haven't caught that guy yet. The police don't even care, surprise surprise. I told Mama and you know what, she still fined me for being late that day, the old battleaxe. And stuck me on a table with the *sukabai*-ist guy, talk about no sympathy.

I forgot to tell you, Mama's been off sick for an age, but she came into work last night for the first time in months. The staff say she had cancer. She hates me right now. Helena keeps making a play for my customer, and Mama helps her.

Seriously though, Mama is being a real pain. Ever since Annabel, AKA Miss Perfect, left she's been in such a bad mood. I've gone from her favourite girl to the one she picks on. Chastity! Your hair smells. Chastity! I can see your tattoos. Chastity this Chastity that. She asked me to dye my hair blonde last night. I just laughed at her. Me with blonde hair? I'd look like one of those *yakuza* girls that hang out in McDonalds.

You wouldn't believe not so long ago Mama was talking about promoting me to Mama-san number two, but she doesn't say that any more, not since those new girls started.

I tell you what Daphs, no matter how hard it gets out here, no matter how bad my face starts looking and how Mama and the customers treat me, I'm not going to start sleeping with the customers like Nadia and Christina and those other girls do. There is a limit, you know? I've got a daughter to think of.

I've done bad things, stupid things, but that's where I draw the line. Those girls who do, don't get me wrong, it's up to them. No judgement. I mean, it's not like I don't get it. When you're new, you have no *dohan*, no bonuses and Mama on your back every day to make customers. I remember what it was like. But it's not like we don't make enough money – all you have to do is go bottle-backing after work, job done.

Talking of sex with customers – remember that boxer guy? Ha ha ha!

Love, love, love,

Chastity

7

Mama

George slid his Dictaphone from his pocket, and by the time it touched the table its recording light was already flashing.

'So, Mama. Where shall we start? This book should be . . . How can I put it? Saleable. That's what the publishers are after. So I suppose . . . Political scandal, intrigue – the big blockbuster topics.'

'Sex,' said Mama, nodding rapidly.

George looked bewildered. 'I don't know. I'd think people would want to read about the men in power. Your big customers. The politicians.'

'Yes, and their sexual habits. Sex is what sells. Trust me, I've sold it for long enough.' Mama thought for a moment. 'Shall I tell you about the first time I saw a man's penis?'

George dropped the cap of his pen, ignoring it as it rolled over the bumpy bamboo-mat floor.

'It was a western penis.' Mama's voice became light and fun again, the fire cracker party girl who lit up Roppongi. 'It has to do with my first job, so I suppose I should tell you all about that.'

George nodded uncertainly. 'Maybe you should tell me about Sinatra's first.'

Mama ignored him. 'Okay. Where do I start? Ah, of course. When I ran away to Tokyo.'

'You weren't born here? I thought your mother . . .' George pushed his pen against the notepad in an attempt to get the ink flowing.

'No. We lived in Kyoto when I was a teenager.'

'How old were you when you came to Tokyo?'

'Sixteen.'

Mama reached for the knife next to the plum-coloured *daifuku* sweets and began cutting them in half, tipping them open with the knife so their bright red middles were showing.

'My father lived here – I thought I could stay with him.

'I didn't want to get married. I was a young girl. Pretty. I had a *look*, people said. Half American, half Japanese. I was scared of wasting it all and just being someone's wife, like my mother wanted. And Tokyo was so exciting. People with tattoos and missing fingers, bright lights, excitement.'

'So you arranged to stay with your father,' George prompted, looking keenly at the glossy sweets.

'Yes. I wrote to tell him when my train would arrive, bought my ticket with a pile of coins I'd been saving and left with a bag full of clothes.'

'Brave,' George remarked, 'just getting on a train like that. May I?' He reached towards the table, and Mama took the knife and deftly lifted the sweet to his hand. 'Weren't you scared?' he asked.

'Yes, very scared. I didn't have any money and my father wasn't what you'd call a reliable person. Men aren't.'

George, who'd put the sweet into his mouth, stopped chewing. Mama smiled at him sweetly, and continued.

'I wasn't at all sure he'd turn up at the station.'

'And did he?'

Mama narrowed her eyes. The warmth and safety of her apartment made the memory of that frightening afternoon hazy and out of focus and oh so long ago.

'The station was crowded,' she said, after a pause. 'There was so much to take in after living in Kyoto. People in jeans with great big bottoms, chequered suits, leather jackets with long collars. Women had their hair in waves around their face. Charlie's Angles, you know. And there were the coffee shops and *bento* box stands and *onigiri* on sale, just like today, and rush, rush, rush. I felt like a little *aji* fish in a lake of huge, golden *koi*.'

'What happened when your father arrived?' George smeared sticky fingers on his notebook.

'I stood by the ticket gates and waited for him,' said Mama.

'My father was tall, so I kept expecting to see his head above the crowd. I waited for three hours. After that the light began to fade. The train guards kept looking, so I went to a phone booth and called Tomi, my father's friend.'

'Didn't you have your father's number?'

Mama shook her head, and her thin, black hair swayed around her pale skull. 'He didn't send me his telephone number. I asked for it, but he never sent it. The only number I had was for Tomi.'

'Who did you say Tomi was again?' George scribbled on his pad.

'A club owner. An old friend of my father's. I'd known him as a young kid. When my parents were still together and we lived in Tokyo.'

'So then what? This *Tomi* . . . he came to get you?'

'*Hai.*' Mama picked up the knife again. 'More sweet, George-san?'

George took a second helping from the proffered blade.

'Tomi came to the train station to meet me,' said Mama. 'But . . . he wasn't like I remembered. He was thinner, like a big insect, and his face was very white. When he came into the station, he had a blue can of Kirin beer in his hand, I remember that very well, and he was smoking, probably Lark cigarettes. I thought he looked like a gangster. He *was* a gangster, but I didn't know that then. I was scared, though. Intuition.'

'So what did you do? Did you run away?'

'No.' Mama smiled slowly. 'I should have done. But no. Where would I have gone?'

'Back home?' George wiped powdered sugar from his lips.

'No, I couldn't go back there.' Mama's voice rose slightly. 'My mother . . . she would have been so angry. Anyway. When I saw Tomi, I went to him and bowed very low and explained that my father hadn't come to get me and I needed a place to stay.

'He said to me, "I have a place for you, but you have to work in my club to pay your way. Okay?" What could I say? I had no money, nowhere to sleep. I thought I'd stay with Tomi until I found my father and then everything would be all right.'

'What sort of club was this?' asked George.

'A type of clip club. In Shinjuku near the soapland places – I'll tell you about them later.' Seeing George's forehead furrow, Mama added, 'A clip club, you know? Where they use a girl to bring in customers, usually foreign customers, and charge high prices for drinks. I hadn't heard of anything like that until I started at Tomi's club. It's not the Japanese way.'

George hunched over his notepad, rearranging his fingers around the pen.

'Tomi had his problems, drinking problems,' said Mama. 'He wasn't a usual Japanese man.' Noticing George's cup was nearly empty, she moved to refill it, ever the gracious hostess.

'When did you start working in his club?'

'Straightaway,' said Mama. 'We went there straight from Tokyo Central station, to what I suppose you would call the "pleasure district" in Shinjuku.

'It was very hot that evening, the height of summer. The streets were crowded, and I remember passing lots of tall, white buildings covered in ugly, black cable. The men wore suits, some of them with bright-coloured jackets, and some wore heavy, black glasses.

'Not so many ladies wore kimono back then, but sometimes you'd see one or two beautiful women, and sometimes even *geisha*, wearing our traditional dress. You always took in your breath when you saw *geisha* in Tokyo. It was like seeing a big, colourful *cho cho san*, butterfly in a dreary, grey office. So refreshing and bright. Not like me back then, with my long, black hair and blouse and pleated skirt.'

'The club – it was in the "pleasure district"?' asked George, filling line after line with blue biro ink. 'Is that a . . . How can I put this delicately . . . red-light area?'

'Yes. When we took the subway to Tomi's club, I was so nervous. I remember arriving at Shinjuku station, and feeling happy the rush-hour crowds were slowing us down. I felt so sick, I had to keep swallowing.

'The women on the streets were very elegant – Tokyo women

always have been.' Mama gave a short laugh. 'I didn't know about false eyelashes then. I thought Tokyo women were born with wonderful, long eyelashes whereas mine were stumpy and short. That's how little I knew about make-up and clothes and all that sort of thing. Quite different now, *neh*?'

Mama smoothed the faded kimono over her legs and put a hand on her hip, striking a pose. George looked at his notepad.

'So you arrived at the club.'

'Oh yes—'

'What was the club called?' George asked.

'Grandbar Tomi,' said Mama. 'It was on the second floor of a street full of nightclubs. Bar Bon Soir, Picasso, all sorts of western-style names, but it was early and the sky was still pale grey. The lights were turned off so the signs were quiet. I felt like they were whispering to me.'

'You must have been frightened,' said George.

'Yes,' said Mama, 'I'd forgotten lots of things about Tomi, having lived in Kyoto. Conveniently forgotten, I should say. He was a real drunk. I never saw him without a drink in his hand, even when I was a little kid. And he had a very bad temper. It was only when I arrived at his club I began to remember things . . . Incidents with my mother . . . and me too.'

'Like what?'

'Oh . . . I shouldn't have brought that up.' Mama waved a hand. 'Let me tell you about his club. It wasn't a particularly elegant place, but then I suppose no one cares about their surroundings when they've drunk enough whisky. Tomi sent out young girls to lure men into the club, particularly foreign men who got confused by Japanese prices, and he explained to me I'd be one of these girls.'

'And you were okay with that?'

'What could I do?' Mama shrugged. 'Tomi saw me for what I was: sixteen years old and naïve. He knew I'd do anything he asked me to, and even better, I spoke English – a useful skill in attracting the clientele he was after. He showed me around the club, and I saw the little booths where I had no doubt men and girls got up to all sorts of things. Then he showed me behind the bar to the changing-room.'

'The changing-room?' George continued to scribble.

'It was a cupboard really, not a changing-room. It smelled very badly of whisky and I think floor cleaner, and hanging on the door was my outfit.' Mama put her hand to her mouth and coughed delicately. She took a sip of tea.

'What outfit?'

'A schoolgirl uniform. The skirt was a little shorter than a usual school uniform and the blouse a little tighter. And there was a big red necktie like a scarf, quite the fashion in the seventies. Tomi even gave me a school bag with books in it. Of course, I never read any of them.' Mama gave George a cheeky grin. 'He told me to get changed and get to work.'

'And what was expected of you, exactly?' George leaned forward.

Mama yawned. 'Really, I'm getting very tired. I have to go to work soon.' She checked her watch. '*Ai*! Very soon. I have to get ready.'

'How about just a few more minutes . . .'

'No George-san. Interview is over for today.' Mama stood up.

'I'll come again? Perhaps tomorrow?'

'We'll see, we'll see. I'll show you to the door.'

8

Steph

Calamity Janes: The Biggest Hostess Club in Roppongi.

The words glowed red and yellow on black breezeblock and hung over three red-carpeted steps. At the top of the steps, two faux gold lions sat either side of a shimmering, smoky doorway, where a tanned bouncer in a tuxedo stood, his plastic skin rendering him only slightly more realistic than the lions.

It had taken Steph a long time to find Julia's club – almost half an hour of staring up at buildings. Tokyo nightspots, it seemed, were crammed seven or eight to a building, stretching up over different floors, so every three metres or so Steph would come across a handful of new clubs, bars or restaurants climbing up into the night sky.

2f Rodeo Bar, 3f Fun Time Karaoke, 4f Club Flamingo . . . The names went on. Scattered between the cramped nightclubs were American chain restaurants, brown elevators, amusement arcades, convenience stores, a shop selling puppies in boxes – but nowhere were the words Hostess club.

Eventually, as Steph had reached the outskirts of the district, where clubs and bars began to fade out and apartment blocks and trees appeared, she found it. Calamity Janes. It was wrapped around the entire corner of a main road, hogging a greedy space in the cramped entertainment district.

As soon as Steph saw Julia's workplace, her bad hand began to throb. The club looked like the seediest of strip clubs with its wolf-like bouncer and tacky Oscar-style entrance. Maybe hostessing wasn't as clean and safe as Julia made out.

Steph didn't want to go inside, but she smoothed her hair down, pulled a fallen vest strap on to her shoulder and glided up the carpeted stairs.

The bouncer turned and held up a hand.

'Yes?'

'Hi. Do you know a girl called Julia?'

'Why?'

'She's a friend of mine, she works here.'

'Who are you?'

'I told you, I'm a friend of hers. Do you mind if I go in and see her?'

'She's working,' said the bouncer. 'They won't let you see her while she's working.'

'Who won't?'

'Ricky. The manager.' He stared over Steph's shoulder at a silver BMW making a turn into the narrow side street by the club.

'How do you know that? You haven't asked yet. Where's reception – this way?'

'You can't go in.' The bouncer stared straight ahead. 'Unless you want to pay three thousand a drink plus a ten thousand yen table charge.'

'Who's going to stop me?' said Steph, marching past him into the silky darkness of a deserted lobby area, where a gleaming gold elevator was set into a wall of fake marble. Next to the elevator was a long plastic sign, which announced, amid Japanese writing and logos, Calamity Janes, 5f.

There were no windows inside the lobby, an architectural oversight in Tokyo that was becoming familiar, but the bright gold doors of the elevator dazzled as they rolled open in the semi-darkness.

'Hey,' the bouncer shouted, bounding up the red steps.

Steph jumped into the lift, pressing the fifth floor button, and the doors closed. There was a banging as the lift ascended, which Steph assumed to be the bouncer's fists punching the sealed metal. But she didn't care. She thought of the diary and Annabel's words: '*the girls at Calamity Janes always have bad stories to tell.*' Did Annabel have a bad story to tell? Did Julia? She chewed a fingernail.

Ping! The elevator doors slid open, revealing a narrow reception area that had the feel of a stage set, plywood painted matt black and gold. There was no one behind the reception desk.

'Hello?' she called out.

Next to the desk was a glass door decorated with purple chiffon curtains. The air-conditioning unit overhead fluttered the fabric to reveal glimpses of a bar beyond. Men and women sat together at tables, talking, laughing, drinking, around a V-shaped stage on which a topless blonde in a gold G string shimmied to a samba rhythm.

'Can I help you?'

Steph's gaze snapped away from the glass door. There was a man behind the reception desk, a green-skinned ghost in a white shirt. He didn't seem pleased to see her.

'Hi.' Steph gave a sultry smile, but the man's eyes remained dull. 'Is there a girl called – my friend Julia works here.'

'You're interrupting me. I'm busy right now.' The man's glare fell to the leather-bound book lying open in front of him. Inside were glossy photos of girls in exotic dancer costumes and lingerie. Steph leaned over the desk to get a better look. Some of the girls lay on beds, eyes closed, seemingly asleep. They looked peaceful, but it was a strange pose.

'Julia looks just like that girl,' Steph said, pointing to a photo of a skinny blonde sleeping on a feathery duvet. 'They could be sisters. Why are they posing with their eyes closed?'

The man slammed the book shut. 'Sorry, Julia's working. You can't see her.'

'It's important,' said Steph. Through the doorway, she could see the topless girl had begun a series of acrobatic dance moves involving a gold hula hoop. 'This is a hostess club, isn't it? Calamity Janes hostess club?'

'We're not hiring at the moment.'

'I wasn't asking about work.' Steph's smile remained bright, masking the crushing sensation she felt inside. *Not hiring* . . . Her vocal chords tightened. 'Look, I just need to speak to her for a second.'

'Julia's working.'

'Could you—' She tapped the desk and the man looked up. 'Thank you. I need to see Julia. You don't understand. It's about our friend . . . Are you Ricky?'

'What? No. You can't see Julia.'

'Well, can I have her number, then?'

'You want Ricky's number?'

'No! Julia's number. Her mobile number.'

'We don't give out girls' numbers.'

'Then you have to let me see her.'

'I'm afraid that's not possible.'

'But—'

They were interrupted by a flutter of purple. A petite, blonde woman in a creamy white trouser suit and lilac shirt strode into the reception area. She held a mobile phone to her ear and was frowning.

'No, just tell them to put it back where they found it,' she bellowed, her accent Australian and nasal. She covered the speaker, jabbed a thumb at Steph and asked the reception man in hushed tones, 'Is she looking for work?'

He nodded.

'No, I'm looking for—' said Steph.

'Has she got a visa?' The woman uncovered the receiver and barked, 'No, *not* there. Behind the files. For the love of . . .' She covered the receiver again. 'Has she got a work visa?' The woman tugged at the leg of her trouser suit, which had become caught in one of her staggeringly high heels.

The reception man took a fraction of a second to realise the last comment was directed at him. 'I don't know, I didn't . . . Do you have—'

'I heard,' said Steph. 'No, I don't have a work visa, but—'

'Then you won't be any good to us.' The woman tapped her nose and eyed Steph up and down. 'Immigration. Raids almost every weekend this month. You're new here?'

'Yes, just got here.'

'So no customers of your own. It's a shame. You're a pretty little thing – nice figure.'

'I'm looking for my friend who works here,' Steph said. 'Julia.'
The elevator chimed.

'Please,' said Steph, realising the bouncer could be up any second. 'It's important.'

'Julia!' The woman snapped the phone shut. 'English Julia? She a friend of yours?' Steph nodded. 'And I really need to speak—'

'Hold up – I'll go tell her there's a friend waiting. What did you say your name was again?'

'Steph.'

'How do you know her?'

'I've known her for years. School. College. Work. We go way back.'

'I'll be right back.'

The woman disappeared into the club.

'Is she the boss?' asked Steph

The man behind reception snorted. 'She's Ricky, the Mama-san.'

'Oh.'

Ricky reappeared, followed by a sickly looking girl who traipsed behind her like a school child being led to the headmistress's office.

'Here she is.'

Steph blinked and stared. The girl didn't look like Julia. She looked tired and spotty and there were grey-green bags under her usually sparkling brown eyes. She wore thick make-up like a circus performer, the sort of make-up that wasn't meant to be seen up close and looked like white clay, blood and marker pen.

'Julia?'

Julia was a painted picture, but there was something not quite right about the finish – bright colours painted on a dirty canvas. Or perhaps the colours had been applied with a dirty brush. There was a grey tinge to her skin beneath the thick foundation, and bumps of acne covered her chin.

She looked nothing like the Julia Steph had known back home. She was still pretty enough if you hadn't known her before, but to an old friend like Steph it was clear something wasn't right.

Steph thought of the diary, and the 'bad stories'.

'Who are you?' Julia stood perfectly still. She looked through Steph as if she wasn't there.

Next to the two painted women, Steph felt like a faded pencil sketch, dull and colourless. Her face felt bare and she could sense her hair, already dirty from the flight, swaying messily under the air-conditioning unit.

'Julia, it's me.' Steph tried to laugh; it was a joke after all. Julia, one of her oldest friends, pretending not to know who she was. Very funny. But the expression on Julia's face suggested this was no laughing matter.

'I'd better get back to work.' Julia turned and disappeared through the glass door, skinny body gliding along as if she were on roller skates.

'Wait—' Steph reached forward but her fingers found only chiffon curtain.

'There's got to be lots of girls round here called Julia,' said Ricky, sliding between Steph and the doorway and putting out her long, pink fingernails to stop Steph going any farther.

A heavy hand fell on Steph's shoulder. She turned to see the bouncer, all plastic muscle and spray tan.

'I'm sorry, Ricky. I tried to stop her.'

'She was just leaving,' said Ricky, smiling and guiding Steph towards the elevator. 'Good luck with finding work anyways.'

Steph felt the bouncer's grip tighten and watched the elevator doors close around her. Through the thick metal she heard Ricky say: 'She didn't *look* like a friend of Julia's.'

Out on the street, Steph took deep breaths and tried to get it together. The fact there was no work at Julia's club was worrying, of course. But what concerned her most right now were her friends. Especially Julia. She looked so *old*. So tired. Bad things happened to girls out here, Flin had said so. Annabel was missing. And what had happened to Julia?

Steph watched a man stumble into an open doorway and urinate. She felt a pang of despair. She was flat-broke and jobless.

If she didn't earn money in the next few days she'd be out on the street. But there were more important things to worry about right now.

She checked her watch. It was 10 p.m. Steph knew Julia finished work at 2 a.m. – she'd moaned about it enough times in her emails.

I'll find Annabel's hostess club, Steph thought. *What was it called? Sinatra's. She's probably working there right now, safe and sound. And then I'll come back here and wait for Julia to finish.*

Steph kept her head down as she negotiated the pavement, confidence and energy as flat as the squashed cigarette butts littering the pavement. Her stomach felt hollow and she knew she should eat something. But, as far as she was aware, Japan operated the usual exchange system of cash=product, meaning unless she dug something out of a bin she was unlikely to eat tonight. And she still had some dignity.

So far, Tokyo had been confusing and seedy. Where *were* all the hostess clubs anyway? Why weren't there signs?

'Hey. Girly.'

Steph felt a tap on her shoulder.

'Oh for fuck's sake, not you again.'

It was the vampire from earlier, this time without his sheaf of Club Orgasmic flyers. His shirt was open, revealing black chest hair and a silver tooth hanging on a piece of black cord.

Steph stared him down. 'I'm not desperate enough to strip yet. Ask me in an hour. I'm looking for a hostess club – Sinatra's.'

'Sinatra's?' The man was whispering, but somehow amid the noise of the crowds and the bars his voice was perfectly audible. Radio Transylvania, broadcasting 24 hours a day. 'You looking for work there?'

'I need to find my friend. She works there. Or used to.'

'I'll take you there if you tell them you're looking for a job. They give me a finder fee for bringing the right girls.' He looked pointedly at her scarred arm. 'And you never know. They might think you've got something. You're sure you don't want to strip?'

'You'll take me there right now?' said Steph.

He shrugged. 'I don't see why not.'

'Great!'

'Come with me.'

He turned and started walking through the crowds.

'Follow you?' Steph felt uneasy. *Remember why you ended up here in the first place? Because you trusted the wrong people.*

'Yes,' said the man. 'You want to find your friend, right?'

'Yes.'

'Better come with me then,' said the man.

Steph hesitated for a moment, trying to push through a myriad of spiky, worried thoughts. Then she ran after him, weaving through the crowd to catch up.

9

'Okay, look. Stop. Where are you taking me?'

Steph stood on the pavement, feet planted on foul-smelling concrete that glistened with oily water. She and the strip-club tout, who Steph had learned was called Frederico, had left the main street and entered a narrow, grey alleyway that looked like a classic Hollywood set-piece for wrong-doing.

There was no one around and the buildings were dark and empty with wooden grilles over the windows. Noxious odours – fried food and old fish mixed with *saki* and petrol fumes – rose from the yellow plastic crates stacked against the walls.

'What? Don't you trust me?' Frederico opened his pale hands, a hurt expression on his face.

'Of course I don't trust you.' Steph fought to get her breath back. 'You hand out sex club flyers and you've just led me down a dark alleyway.' She flexed her bad hand, her eyes watering as she tried and failed to make a fist.

Frederico's dark eyes took on a mock-wounded expression. 'I've told you, I'm taking you to Sinatra's.'

'Down here?'

'It's right here.' Frederico pointed to a low-lit doorway next to a red-curtained restaurant. It was sealed with thick glass and beside it was a tiny illuminated sign at chest height that read: Sinatra's Hostess Club.

'The lettering – it's the same as Annabel's business cards. This must be where she works.' Steph brightened at the thought. No doubt Annabel was safe and sound and working just a few metres away. 'Are there any more clubs round here called Sinatra's?'

'More than one Sinatra's?' Frederico scoffed. 'Is there more than one Roppongi Tower? This place is famous. No one would open another Sinatra's, it's one of a kind. Why?'

'Just checking,' said Steph, peering at the sign. It showed dated pictures of blonde girls with big grins and even bigger perms, wearing evening dresses with shoulder pads and chains of pearls or skinny gold links around their white necks.

'This is a hostess club?'

'Yes.'

'How would anyone ever find it?'

'You wouldn't. You have to be shown.'

'No, wait. Hang on. Julia's club had a great big sign . . .'

'Calamity Janes is a western-style place. This is the real thing.' Frederico pushed open the glass door and ushered Steph on to a small, fragrant landing with a bouquet of lilies in one corner and a staircase leading down. Wicker fans decorated the stairway walls, interspersed with gold-framed photographs of famous movie and music stars. Judging by the age of the actors and musicians in the photos, the pictures had been taken several decades ago.

'Who's the Japanese lady?' Steph pointed to a lady with a pixie face and huge cartoon eyes, who stood smiling next to each celebrity in the pictures.

'Mama-san,' said Frederico. 'She's famous, you know.'

Steph looked closer at the pictures. 'She knew all these people?'

'They were customers at her club,' said Frederico. 'Some of them still are.'

They reached the bottom of the staircase and stopped in front of a dark wooden door decorated with yet more wicker fans.

'This club has being going for decades,' said Frederico. 'Mama knows her business. She's got a good eye for girls. Which ones will make money. If she doesn't like you, she'll throw you out straightaway. So pray to your lucky star, or whatever you do, if you want to see your friend tonight.'

He turned around and looked pointedly at Steph's jeans, shaking his head and making a clicking sound. 'You're wearing totally the wrong clothes, completely wrong. You haven't done yourself any favours. Western arrogance, that's how she'll see it. My girlfriend spends hours getting ready when she looks for work. Hours.'

Steph put her hand on her hip. 'I didn't plan on asking for work right now. I'm looking for my friend and—'

'You shouldn't say anything to Mama about that,' Frederico added, looking at Steph's unmade-up face. 'Not at first. She'll throw you out if you start asking about her hostesses. Suspicious.' He tapped his nose. 'People come and steal girls. Play along with her, say you want work.'

'I *do* want work. But how am I supposed to find my friend if I'm not allowed to ask about the girls?'

'Just be patient, that's all I'm saying. Don't say anything unless you're asked. She has a temper. Say the wrong thing, and goodbye.' Frederico was stern. 'Maybe she'll ask where you're from, how long you're here for. She'll be able to tell if you have what it takes without you saying much. Okay? Just smile. If she gives you a job, *then* you can ask about your friend.'

Frederico pushed open the door and they walked into the club.

There was a reception desk on the right, unmanned, with an archaic brass bell welded to its wooden surface. Past that was the club itself, equally ghostly and empty, except for a three-piece keyboard combo on a tiny stage playing *Can You Feel the Love Tonight?* to an invisible audience.

Steph thought, *Tropical paradise in wicker.* There were wicker palm trees, wicker sofas, a little stage trimmed with wicker and tube lighting, and wicker snack baskets on the tables filled with two-finger KitKats, popcorn and Hershey's Kisses. Steph could imagine a young Tom Jones and Roger Moore hanging out under the huge, dusty, wicker palm leaves on the stage.

The club appeared empty, but Steph heard whispered female voices and noticed three girls tucked away in the corner near a giant cabinet containing bottles of Dom Pérignon and premium Japanese whisky.

None of them looked like Annabel, or at least the Annabel Steph remembered from school.

They wore long evening gowns in brightly coloured silk and taffeta, the sort of outfit a movie star might wear to a red carpet event. It hadn't escaped Steph's notice that Julia, despite her sickly appearance, had been wearing a slinky, sophisticated dress. Nothing like the bodices and tight jeans crammed into her own rucksack.

There was a statuesque blonde with white skin and beige eyebrows, a curvy Latina with thick caramel-coloured hair falling all the way down her back; and a very attractive willowy girl with short, glossy black hair and bright red lips.

The three girls stared at Steph. She winked at them but they didn't wave or smile.

Frederico slapped the bell with the palm of his hand and it clanged like a fire alarm.

The curtain behind the reception desk twitched. There was a scuffle. Then a slim, young Japanese man in a neat black suit appeared, nodding and issuing greetings in Japanese. His expression turned to disappointment when he saw Frederico.

'Koji. *O-genki desu ka?*' Frederico took the man's hand before he could object, and shook it rapidly. The pair began a whispered exchange in Japanese, with Frederico gesturing towards Steph, and the man, nodding politely and bowing low. Steph stood in the background, trying to appear relaxed by tapping her foot to the music. That she couldn't see Annabel in the club made her nervous. She wondered when Julia finished work.

After a while, the Japanese man nodded and disappeared through the curtain behind the reception desk, a heavy burgundy drape that delivered wafts of moth and dust. More scuffling.

Then slowly, as if by pulled by strings, the curtain moved aside and revealed a tiny Japanese woman, very pale, her face as dusty as a powder puff. She wore a striking blood-red evening gown that brought out the greeny black of her eyes.

The woman rested delicate hands with perfect red nails and glittering diamond rings on the reception desk, and tilted her dainty face towards Frederico. Steph realised this lady was the charismatic co-star of the pictures in the hallway.

'*This is Mama-san,*' whispered Frederico.

The woman looked as frail as a bird, but there was something theatrical and commanding about her. She reminded Steph of the revered old dames she'd met backstage at various theatres.

Mama had dark circles under her eyes and sagging cheeks, but her lips were bright red against white teeth and her eyebrows strongly pencilled. Her ears were decorated with dozens of emeralds and her neck adorned with a huge string of perfect, cream pearls. A musky perfume hung over her like a friendly cloud. She exuded such glamour and luxury that Steph found herself inadvertently wanting to bow.

The old lady's smile didn't leave her face as she looked Steph over from head to toe. Steph felt thoroughly scrutinised, like a piece of meat at a market.

'Hi,' said Steph, but the old lady paid no attention.

'How old?' Mama said eventually, turning to Frederico.

'Eighteen,' he replied immediately.

Mama gave a short laugh. 'No, no, no. How old?'

'Twenty-four,' said Steph, objecting to being talked about as if she wasn't there.

'Oh. Australian?'

'No, I'm from England.'

'Oh.' Mama broke into a wide, beautiful smile, transforming her face. 'English. I love England. I love the Queen. Very beautiful lady, *neh*?

Steph wasn't sure what to say.

'What's your name?' Mama leaned on the reception desk, as much to support herself as to get a better look at her prospective employee.

'Steph.'

'Oh. Short name. Like a boy. How long have you been in Japan?'

'One day.'

'You came yesterday?'

'Today. A few hours ago.'

'Today?' Mama pulled back from the reception desk and looked

at Frederico with astonishment. 'One day, *yokatta koto*? One day?'
She began speaking with Frederico in fast Japanese, and he
nodded, glancing at Steph every so often with a worried
expression.

Finally they stopped talking, and Frederico put his hand on
the small of Steph's back, moving her towards the door. The old
lady disappeared behind the curtain.

Steph batted his hand away. 'What did she say?'

'She didn't like what you're wearing. Or your hair.'

'Oh. Okay.' Manufactured brightness bubbled up automatically,
temporarily covering a dull ache in her chest. Rejection. It had
jumped into Steph's backpack and followed her all the way out
here. 'Well, it doesn't matter. It's more important I find my friend
right now. Did you ask about her?'

'Of course not.' Frederico frowned. 'I told you before. She'd
have got suspicious. People come and steal her girls. She's a very
powerful woman. You don't want to get on the wrong side of
Sinatra's Mama, believe me.'

'I couldn't see Annabel in the club,' said Steph. 'Maybe I should
look around some other places.'

'For hostess work? There are no other places. Visa problems
everywhere right now, but Mama knows *yakuza*.'

'No, for Annabel. I mean to—'

'Listen, she hasn't said no yet. She thinks you might be all
right. But she can't tell because of how you're dressed. Your hair.'

'Oh.' Some good news at least. A step closer to getting a job.
And even if Annabel didn't work here anymore, the business
cards in the diary said she *had* worked here at some point. Chances
were, someone here knew where she was now.

'So what, shall I go home and get changed?'

'No. She wants you to go into the back room and she'll try
some things with you and decide whether to give you a trial. You
probably won't get hired. But it's better than nothing.'

'Thanks for your optimism.'

'Go on, she's waiting for you. Remember, job first, questions
second.'

Frederico nodded towards the door, and Steph went behind the reception desk and pushed the curtain aside. Behind it was a tiny space, standing room for no more than four people. An office, Steph realised. There was a cluttered desk curving around two of the walls and covered in computer print-outs, record books and empty miniature drink bottles.

On the wall was a whiteboard chart with girls' names written on it in chunky marker pen and some sort of grid with numbers.

She read the names. *Chastity, Jennifer, Helena* . . . No Annabel.

'Why you looking at my girls?' Mama, who was perched on the desk, one hand pressed against her forehead, stiffened.

'Sorry.'

Mama was holding what appeared to be a dead animal. A wig. A blonde one.

'Here. Come here.' She eased herself off the desk.

Steph didn't move. 'That's not for me, is it?'

Mama's answer was simply to lift the mane of blonde hair above Steph's head and begin to pull the flesh-coloured skull cap over Steph's scalp.

'Hey! Stop! No.' Steph grasped Mama's cold hands, and the two of them struggled for a moment before Mama's hands went limp and she let the wig drop. She stepped back, looking bewildered.

'You don't want a job here?'

'I'm not wearing a wig.' Steph swallowed.

'But you'll look beautiful,' Mama said, waving the blonde curls. 'Like Barbie,' she added, as if this were ultimate proof. 'Frederico – he said you wanted work.'

'Yes. I really do.'

'Then let me see you.' Mama shook the wig at her again.

'I'm not going to put that on,' said Steph, hating herself for wanting to cry. She'd been made to wear all sorts of different wigs and outfits for the photographs . . .

'So so so,' said Mama quietly to the wig. 'Gentlemen prefer blondes. But . . .' Her frown vanished, replaced with a fabulous showbiz smile. 'How about make-up? Let me try.'

Mama reached into a drawer and pulled out a white Chanel vanity box, circa 1982, containing blocks of eye-shadow in lurid colours. The blocks of powder had old-fashioned descriptions written next to them: Mint green, Sunset pink, Lion yellow . . . but more worryingly, Mama had produced a pantomime-dame red lipstick from the case and was waving it purposefully near Steph's lips.

'I don't suit red . . .'

'You want a job here?' Mama tilted her head innocently to one side, but there was menace in her voice.

'Yes, I do but . . .'

Too late. Mama had already begun smearing the colour over her mouth.

'Please. That's enough now . . . No, that's too much.' A glance in the mirror confirmed Steph's worst fears: she looked like a plastic surgery fanatic who'd severely overdone the collagen. But Mama seemed very happy with the transformation.

'You look nice,' she announced, snapping the top back on the lipstick. 'Very pretty. I thought you would. Make-up is good. Very feminine. Men like it. Beautiful,' she announced, taking a step backwards. '*Hai, hai*, you look very good.'

Steph wiped the lipstick off on the back of her hand.

'*Ee-ai*! You'll spoil it.' Mama grabbed Steph's scarred arm. Her gaze dropped to the bumpy skin and she released her grip.

'What happened?' said Mama, a surprising softness creeping into her voice.

Steph swallowed. 'Accident.'

'Oooh.' Mama nodded as if this made everything understandable. And then, unexpectedly: 'Something to do with a man?'

Steph blinked, embarrassed that stinging tears were threatening to fall. 'He said he'd get me work,' she said, the words tumbling out.

'Men,' Mama tutted and patted Steph's arm. 'Without them we'd have no problems. And no money!' She laughed and began to cough. Then she dried her eyes with a handkerchief produced from her cleavage, picked up the wig and started stroking it.

'I have a feeling about you,' said Mama, running her fingers through the synthetic hair. 'Frederico says you went to Calamity Janes.' She used a sparkling shoe to push a pair of ancient scales out from under the desk. 'Here. Weigh.'

'They don't have any jobs at the moment,' said Steph, looking down at the scales. The red needle wobbled. 'You want me to step on these?'

'These are the rules,' said Mama, her smile charming, her eyes cold.

Steph raised an eyebrow, but stepped on to the scales, making the needle swing crazily.

'Probably they didn't like these scars,' said Mama, squinting at Steph's scarred chin and moving so she could see Steph's face more clearly under the light. 'Imperfections. But humans are more beautiful when they're not perfect. To the right man the right imperfection is very, very right. Men don't mind imperfect women.'

Mama looked down at the scales. 'But they do mind fat women. Sixty kilograms. Don't put on any more. Do you know how long I've been running this club?'

'Decades, Frederico said.'

'Yes.' Mama reached into a drawer and pulled out a measuring tape, muttering a little tune to herself *nung, nung, nung*, as she stretched it around Steph's bust, waist and hips. 'Thirty-four, twenty-four, thirty-six.' She tucked the tape back into the drawer. 'Very western.'

It really was like being sized up for the oven. Steph's

measurements were written on the back of her headshot cards back home, but to have someone whip out a tape measure . . .

Mama placed the wig on top of a cabinet and put her vanity case back into the drawer. Then she ushered Steph out and around the reception desk.

'I think I could have work for you,' she said. 'But—'

'Great!' Steph's shoulders relaxed. 'Look, I wanted to ask you this before but Frederico said I shouldn't. I have a friend who works here. Or did. Annabel. I found her cards, and I'm trying to find out where she is, and—'

'She left.' Mama's words were clipped. 'Months ago. I don't know where she went.'

'Oh. I don't suppose you have a phone number for her, do you? She hasn't replied to my emails in months. Or what about the other girls? Would they know where she might have gone?'

'She left with some of my best customers.' Mama's voice sounded distant. 'When girls do that, we don't speak about them anymore.'

'But—'

'We DON'T SPEAK OF THEM ANY MORE.'

'Okay, okay.' Steph felt something like relief. Okay, Annabel wasn't here, but she'd definitely been working as a hostess and was doing well by the sounds of things. Probably she'd just made good money and found a nicer apartment. And now Steph had got herself a job. Things were looking up.

'Anyway, you didn't let me finish.' Mama gave a dazzling smile and Steph felt uneasy.

'Taking you on doesn't make sense right now,' Mama continued. 'But I think you could be good. Come back next month, okay?'

Steph smoothed down her thick, faded red hair, dull with salt and pollution, and tried to quell the rising terror. A month? Frederico had said this was the only place hiring. Her stomach knotted as she thought of the rent due in a few days' time. She needed money. Badly.

'How about I do a trial shift?' said Steph, fighting to keep her voice steady. 'Say tomorrow night, and see how I do?'

Mama tilted her head. 'Too many girls, not enough customers right now. If you had your own customers . . . no problem. But you're too new. Sorry. Next month.'

'What if I bring you more customers?' Steph said. 'How about that?' Her voice cracked on the last word, but she managed to hold Mama's gaze. 'You must need customers. There's no one here.'

Mama shook her head, still smiling. 'No, no. Sorry.'

'If I don't bring you a new customer by the end of the week,' said Steph, knowing desperation was spilling into her voice, 'you get rid of me. Trial finished.'

Mama's tired face uncrumpled slightly, and Steph knew she had her attention.

'Not much of a deal for me.'

'I'll get you customers. I know I can do it.'

Mama didn't say anything, but she watched Steph with interest. After a moment she said: okay. Do you know what *dohan* is?'

'*Dohan*? No.'

Mama scratched at an imaginary stain on the reception desk with her fingernail. 'A *dohan* is dinner date with a customer. The girls here, they get to know customers and then the customers take them out to dinner. After dinner, the customers come here to the club with my girl and pay me for taking one of my hostesses out. This is *dohan*.'

Steph nodded. She remembered Julia telling her something about going on dates with customers. You got really good bonuses for it, apparently. The more dates you had, the more money you earned.

'So,' Mama said, 'how about this?' I'll give you a trial, but if you don't get a *dohan* by Saturday, I won't pay you.'

'That's only three days away. How I am supposed to . . . I mean I don't know anyone here.'

'Mmm, mmm, not my problem. You said you could bring me a customer. If you can find a man to take you to dinner and then come to my club afterwards, you don't have anything to worry about, *neh*? Of course, you can always win *dohan* with one of my customers. Either way, I don't mind.'

Steph looked at the empty club.

'Will you pay me for one night? Tomorrow – will you pay me for tomorrow?'

'No.' Mama's smile vanished. 'It's bad business to pay girls straightaway. But you'll get tips if you do well. Do you have a dress?'

'I have a dress,' Steph lied.

'If you come here tomorrow at seven p.m., dressed properly, make-up, cocktail dress, I'll put you on a trial. But no *dohan*, no pay.' Mama eyed Steph with sympathy. 'No girl has ever won a *dohan* in her first week.'

'I can do it.'

Mama nodded and disappeared behind the curtain, the conversation clearly over.

Steph stood for a moment listening to *Lady in Red* being played by the medley of electric keyboards. The dishes of popcorn and snacks on the tables were tempting, but she could feel the eyes of the club manager on her so didn't dare risk grabbing a handful of food before heading back up to the flashing lights and racing traffic.

As she walked the streets of Roppongi, hungry and broke, she wondered how long it would be before she could talk to Julia.

At Calamity Janes, the same bouncer was still on the door.

'I'm waiting for Julia to finish,' she informed him, head held high.

'The girls don't finish until two o'clock,' he said, folding his arms, 'and you can't wait here.'

'It's a free country,' said Steph. 'I can wait anywhere I want to.'

And with that she sat down on the pavement by the club, cold concrete amplifying her hunger and tiredness. She prepared herself for a long wait.

'. . . *tell him to test it this time . . . should be fine, but you can't always tell . . .*'

The strange words floated around Steph's warm, sleepy brain.

She sat upright with a start. Her back was freezing, and the murmur of Roppongi traffic, crowds and pumping music roared over her in a great wave of sound.

I fell asleep, she realised, rubbing the back of her neck and turning to see a man on the steps of Calamity Janes. He was talking to one of the bouncers.

'. . . and if they don't work, tell me straightaway, I'll bring more.'

The man was thirty something, with thick black hair and a large nose like a hawk's beak.

Steph rubbed sleep from her eyes and saw that the man was holding a square cardboard box bound in red masking tape.

'I'll tell him you came.' The bouncer took the box.

'Tell him *Amir* came.' Rubbing his nose, the man bounded away.

Steph checked her watch. It was just gone 1a.m. – there couldn't be long to wait now. But despite her best efforts, her eyes kept closing.

'You know, this isn't a great place to sleep.'

Steph's eyes blinked open. 'I wasn't sleeping.' Frederico loomed over her. 'Oh. Hi. It's you. I wasn't asleep.'

Frederico wagged his finger. 'You know where you are? Calamity Janes. Bad place, gangster place.'

'I'm waiting for my friend.'

'I'm telling you. Bad place. That guy that was here – Iranian mafia. Serious. You don't want to hang around out here.'

'I don't have any choice,' said Steph, yawning. 'I'm waiting for my friend to finish. Don't you have flyers to hand out or something?'

Frederico pursed his lips. 'Another friend? You won't have friends for long if you work as a hostess. All you'll care about is your business cards. How'd things go with Mama?'

'Okay. I'm doing a trial tomorrow.'

Frederico looked knowingly at her scarred chin. 'A trial? I've never heard of Mama doing that before.' He turned and disappeared into the crowd.

I'll just rest my eyes for a moment, thought Steph. *Julia's got to get out of here soon, and I'm sure she'll wake me up when she sees me.*

When Steph woke again, her spine felt like a pole of ice and the grey pavement was suspiciously dark. The Calamity Janes sign was grey and unlit. The club doors were bolted.

She got to her feet and turned a full circle, then checked her watch. 2.30 a.m.

Shit, shit, shit. The club's closed, I've missed her.

Steph rubbed sore buttocks. Julia must have walked right past her when she'd finished work. With no number for Julia, Steph knew she'd have to wait until tomorrow evening before she'd be able to talk to her.

She glided through the crowd, stepping over cracked paving slabs and a beery splash of vomit that ran into the gutter. No matter how much she wanted to see Julia, there was nothing she could do about it right now.

But there *was* something she could do about tracking down Annabel. It was something Frederico had said about business cards. There had been business cards in Annabel's diary. Tomorrow she'd phone the men on the cards, ask if they knew where Annabel was. And in the meantime she could take a look at the diary, see if there were any details about where Annabel had gone after she'd left Sinatra's. Maybe get the contact of another club or something.

Steph was sure Annabel was absolutely fine, earning loads of money as a hostess and living in some great place where she didn't have to share a room. But all the same, she wouldn't feel easy until she knew where her friend had ended up.

I I

Chastity

From: C_C_Chastity

To: CanadianDaphne

Subject: h-h-hungover

Daphs,

Nice one babes! I knew you'd get it. You will be sooo great – make sure you tell me when it's aired.

OMG, I'm so upset today. My best customer! All week he didn't phone, no *dohan*, nothing. I thought he was sick and then tonight he turned up with Helena and they sat together and left together when the club closed. I am totally SCREWED. Seriously. Without him I'm lucky to scrape number five girl, even if Juni comes in, and he never does when it's cold. I didn't even get a B request. Maybe she's amazing in bed, but OMG those girls! Like Maria and that doctor guy.

But you know how it is. It's all just competition with them. They want to win over us more than they want to make the money. It's not even as if they make much more. Maybe they get a few more outfits, some champagne kick-backs after work. All right, some of them get a boyfriend and a nice earner there. You should know. But most of them don't, the guys just sleep with them and leave them for the next girl. Helena has five customers and a boyfriend who pays for her apartment, she is just greedy, selfish eurotrash.

I'm wearing the same dresses I had on last year, I haven't had my hair done in who knows how long. And I've got to get out of here, really I have.

Roppongi's like a trap, that's what they say and it's true. You try to get out but the easy money and easy work . . . you know what it's like. I've been saying the same thing for years, *when I make this much, when I make that much,* and then, you know how it goes, you get that golden amount and you want to get more. There's something else you want to buy. But I mean it this time, really really!!!

I don't know, Daphs, listen to me. The party's over. I know. The boom years are gone, those Russians all work for half the price and do twice as much, Mama doesn't care as long as she's making money, and here I am going out every night, each night a little bit more boring, but every time hoping I'll make some big cash like I did years ago. And of course I never do. I used to watch Annabel and think, I'll work harder, I'll be as good as her . . . But it's smoke and mirrors. That golden bonus is always out of reach. There's only room for one top girl, and I'm not it. Anyway, I'm getting old.

You know the worst thing about all of this? It's not my skin or getting older or all the drugs or the hangovers. It's how I feel about men now. I see the worst of them every night, and now I just can't believe a word they say. They look like idiots to me. How am I ever going to find some nice guy when I feel that way?

What am I even talking about – boyfriend! With Tammy still at home? She scared off the last two. Anything that takes the attention off her, she can't stand it. She is such a little drama queen. The slightest thing and she's all tears. She's at it right now, going on and on. Don't think I don't know what you're doing! I know all the tricks. Now Mummy's got a hangover and she was up all night, so let me get some peace!!!!

Congrats again on your good news. All you'll hear from me is doom and gloom right now. The drugs make it worse, I'm giving them a miss this week. But hey, happier things. You've got a great opportunity and next visa run I'll come over and see you in sunny LA.

Tams is still bugging me so I better go.

Love, love,

Chastity

12

Steph

The outer door to the apartment was unlocked when Steph returned, but it was caught so firmly in the frame that she had to force it open with her shoulder. The door groaned and screeched on sore hinges as she pushed her way into the moist hallway.

It smells in here, she thought. *This place is a real dump. No wonder Annabel left. As soon as I can I'll find somewhere better.*

Tiredness had overtaken hunger and, even though her stomach rumbled continuously, she knew she'd be able to sleep through it. She'd worry about food in the morning.

Outside the bedroom door, Steph heard a noise. Like snoring. It was coming from inside the room. She turned her key carefully and peered into blackness, a blackness eased with every inch of acid-yellow light that spilled in from the hallway.

There was a girl lying on the bottom bunk, hands folded across her chest, silky yellow hair fanned out over the pillow. Steph could see the sharp points of her nose and cheekbones, her face hard and white like a stone carving. The serene effect was spoiled somewhat by the girl's mouth, which sagged open, allowing snoring noises to escape her throat.

Steph noticed there were photos stuck to the wall next to where the girl lay. One was of a brown-haired child, maybe eight years old, looking rather forlorn, and another was of a man in a lumber-jack shirt with steel-coloured hair, his lips blue with cold.

The fluorescent tube in the hallway was shining a strip of light directly on to the bottom bunk, but the rest of the room was still in relative darkness. There was no window for chinks of moonlight to creep through. Steph flicked on the light switch and the bulb fizzed and popped.

'Hey! What are you doing?' The girl threw an arm over her eyes. 'Turn the light off.'

'I need to get to my bed,' Steph said. 'Just give me a minute.'

There were bags all over the room, most of them spilling over with brightly coloured lycra clothing. The wonky shelves attached to the wall remained empty.

The girl sighed and tutted and threw herself around, pulling the duvet over her head. 'Don't take long. I need to sleep.' Her voice was accented and husky like a Bond girl's.

'I'll take as long as I like,' Steph snapped. 'You've covered the floor with all your stuff.'

She hauled luggage out of the way, not caring, after the girl's rudeness, what she trod on. As she climbed into bed, she felt under the pillow where she'd hidden the diary.

There was nothing there. She felt around some more. No. Nothing.

'Have you moved my book?' Steph said.

'What? What you talk about?'

'My book. It was under my pillow. Did you move it?'

'No.'

Anxiety bubbled around where hunger should be. But she was so tired. So, so tired.

Think about it in the morning.

Steph rested her head on the lumpy pillow filled with, what was it, rice? pulled a sticky-feeling duvet over her and fell asleep instantly.

It was hunger that woke Steph the next morning, awful, nauseating, crippling hunger that filled her intestines with air and made her mouth dry and acidic. She had a headache too. The room was pitch black, no window to signal day or night. The only sounds were gentle snoring from the bottom bunk and the rush of traffic outside.

It didn't take long for thoughts of Julia to start buzzing around. And thoughts of Annabel too. There was no way to talk to Julia until later on tonight, but she could certainly hunt down the diary. It had to be in the room somewhere and when she found it, she could phone a few numbers on the business cards. Hopefully one of Annabel's customers knew where she was now. If she was living or working nearby, they could meet up by the end of the day.

'Hey,' said Steph's new roommate, as Steph jumped down from the top bunk. 'You woke me last night. Shouting. In your sleep.'

'I do that sometimes,' said Steph, although she didn't remember having one of her usual nightmares.

'He's dead, you were saying. *He's dead.* It scared me.'

'Oh. You'll get over it. You're sure you haven't seen my book? It was right here.' Steph patted her pillow.

'I told you. No.'

Steph turned out the contents of her rucksack, jeans and vest tops spilling on to the dusty floor. A cockroach as big as a matchbox came scuttling out from under her bag strap and she leapt back in alarm as the insect suddenly sprouted wings and flew towards her, hooked legs clinging to her hair. She pulled it free, threw it to the floor and stamped on it.

'Would you keep it down?' barked the girl in the bottom bunk.

Steph ignored her, throwing sheets aside, turning over her mattress. But the diary was nowhere to be seen. And she was hungry – so hungry her vision was going in and out of focus.

The plastic racks of dust-covered food jars were still out in the hallway, but Steph would have to be a lot hungrier before she succumbed to the indignity of stealing other people's food, so she ignored the tempting packets of pasta and white bread.

I'll take a look around Roppongi, she thought. *There must be other* gaijin *houses here. Maybe Annabel's staying in one of them. A nicer one. Perhaps she even has a window.*

Looking for the diary on an empty stomach, with a bad head and a bad-tempered roommate on the bottom bunk, was silly. She'd come back when her head, and the bottom bunk, were clear.

Steph headed outside and on to the cluttered, narrow streets below. The sun was pale yellow behind patchy clouds, and dazzling to Steph's dilated pupils after so long in a room without light. *It's the afternoon*, she realised, checking her watch. *I've slept for hours and I still feel tired.*

She walked purposefully, scanning buildings for *gaijin* house signs. Tokyo by day was gentle and relaxed. The smells of boiled rice and fresh fish, the lotus flowers on the pavement, the quiet, well-tailored people buying *bento* boxes and drinks from stalls and vending machines were all very civilised.

Steph began exploring narrow backstreets, some of them cobbled, and she passed a park with little domed tents in it and scruffy shoes neatly arranged outside their entrances. Roppongi Tower, the white and orange Eiffel-Tower-esque landmark, disappeared and reappeared as she twisted and turned through the side roads.

But Steph's hunger-starved body wasn't as strong as she thought and, after climbing a particularly steep road, her vision went black and she tripped and fell. She leaned against a grey crash barrier that seemed to serve as a marker for the pavement, and blinked away orange and grey spots.

There was a glass-fronted room opposite – a fabric shop, Steph thought – its windows filled with delicately embroidered skeins of silk in sombre blues, greys and creams. Not a *gaijin* house, Steph realised, but for some reason the building took her interest.

An old lady stood in the open doorway under a wooden sign painted with black Japanese script, her sturdy body dressed in an elegant and regal green garment of silky fabric with rust-coloured maple leaves embroidered all over it, under which the dark grey of more silky fabric showed at the sleeves and collar. A kimono.

The woman's hair was steely grey and pressed into rigid curls that defied the gentle breeze sweeping along the street. Her body was equally rigid — like wood, hard and strong.

'*Ohayou . . . gozaimasu*,' Steph called out, smiling at her own poor accent, the unfamiliar Japanese as stiff as the woman in front of her. 'Do you know any *gaijin* houses round here?'

But the lady merely frowned and took a step back into the shop, cool and emotionless.

Steph shrugged. She should be getting back anyway. Her room-mate might be up by now, and she'd have a chance to search the bedroom.

Bang!

Suddenly, Steph was slumped on the pavement, legs skidding along the gritty concrete, head bruised where it had hit the crash barrier. More dark and orange spots appeared. Then blackness.

'Ouch.' Steph put her hand to her scalp and felt the beginnings of a large bruise. She wasn't sure how long she'd been unconscious when a pair of strange wooden flip-flops and bright white socks came into her eye line, and she felt herself wrenched upright by strong hands.

'I'm okay. I'm all right,' she murmured, feeling pain surge through her scarred arm. But whoever was holding her paid no attention. 'Really, I need to get going. I need to get back.'

The grey pavement moved under her and then she was indoors, in a large, light room with bamboo screen walls and shelves all around, stacked with rolls of fabric. A flat cushion was dropped on to the floor, and Steph felt herself lowered on to it. Then she was released.

She tried to stand up but found she couldn't.

The room swirled and gradually came into focus. It was bright and beautiful and smelt of flowers and silk. After a few moments, Steph noticed the woman in the green kimono was standing a foot away with her back to her, her posture stiff and unyielding.

'Thank you,' said Steph. 'I must have . . . I don't know. Thank you for helping me.'

'Alcohol? asked the woman, sounding like a school mistress.

Steph stared at the rigid back. 'Are you asking me a question?'

'There's no one else here.'

'You mean, am I drunk?' said Steph, trying to stand on weak legs. 'I really should be going.' Realising that standing was pointless for the time being, she tried to cross her legs instead but couldn't do that either. She remembered how flexible she'd been before the accident, and how easy she'd found it to sit cross-legged.

'Don't correct people. It's rude.' The lady's shoulders shook beneath the silk. 'You girls. Too much drinking.'

'I wasn't correcting you.' Steph put a hand to her forehead. 'I was clarifying. And I haven't been drinking. I haven't eaten anything today, that's all. I'm fine. I just . . . I'll get my breath back and then I really need to get going. I need to find my friend.'

Slowly and precisely the woman turned around, like cogs moving in a clock. She was tall and broad for a Japanese woman, perhaps five foot six, and had a handsome face with a strong nose and high, arched eyebrows. Steph guessed she was maybe seventy or eighty years old but she was gloriously well maintained. Her skin was soft and buttery, but she exuded icy fury as she examined Steph's face.

'You look dried out,' she said, 'like overcooked fish. I suppose you work in Roppongi. Glass, that's what you'll become. See-through.'

'I'm sure I don't look *that* bad.' *Not that it's any of your business.* 'I've just missed breakfast and – no, I don't work in Roppongi. Not yet.'

'You shouldn't miss breakfast!'

Steph glared at the cold, silky back. 'I'll just rest for a minute and then I'll leave.' *Glass.* She thought of Julia's grey skin and dead eyes.

'Again, more rudeness. You should ask me *if* it is okay to rest.'

'I don't have much choice,' said Steph, her eyes wandering towards the door. 'I feel too faint. But I'll be okay in a minute.'

The back of the lady's head moved, and Steph thought she was nodding.

'You'll sit here and I'll make you a meal. And you'll leave when I decide you're better.'

13

Mama

'So,' said Mama, as George lumbered into her apartment, large sweat patches like mould growing under his arms, 'I'm impressed you got here so quickly. You live in Mita, isn't that right? You must have hurried. Subway or taxi?'

'Subway,' said George, wondering how Mama expected him to pay for a taxi halfway across the city. There was barely enough money left to pay his internet bill that month. He sat heavily on a floor cushion, silver embroidered with tiny pink birds. The room looked the same as yesterday, but Mama seemed brighter, more energised.

'I'm glad you called,' he said, and they both knew this to be an understatement. 'Are you ready to start? The quicker we get going—'

'The quicker you get paid,' Mama finished. 'Okay. Fine. So I'll continue from where I left off.'

'Please.'

Mama yawned. 'So where was I? Ah yes. I was telling you about starting work for Tomi, wasn't I? After I'd changed into my schoolgirl outfit, Tomi sent me to a western-style hotel a few streets away from his club. I don't remember the name, Imperial something or other. He told me to find a western businessman and ask him to help me practise my English. Then I was supposed to bring the man back to the club and drink with him.

'Of course, there was a little more to it than just drinking – I'd find that out later. Let's just say other girls worked there too and they offered other services. But anyway, that first night it didn't matter because things didn't go at all to plan.'

'What happened?' George asked.

Mama stood up in one fluid movement and went to the dresser. She picked up the picture of her daughter and looked at the solemn, young face in the frame. Kaito had been seven years old when the picture was taken, but even at that age she'd been thoughtful and serious.

'I went to the hotel in my school uniform, feeling very nervous. It was a big, beautiful place I thought, with little palm trees in pots around the lobby and wicker chairs. I'd never been anywhere like it before and felt very shy. But my fear of Tomi's temper was worse than anything else, so I walked quickly past the reception desk and into the bar, which was also very fashionable, with lots of men sitting around wearing cable-knit sweaters and drinking different types of expensive whisky.'

'Very seventies.'

'Yes.' Mama smiled. 'There were western businessman there, just as Tomi had said, three of them, all sitting alone, but I was too scared to go up to any of them so I just stood and watched, hoping none of the waiting staff would ask me what I wanted. Eventually one of the men, in a checked jacket and spotted tie, smiled at me, so I went over to him and said, all in a rush: "CanyouhelpmepractisemyEnglishpleasesir?"'

George continued to scribble. Mama put the photo down.

'He was American, and quite handsome. I was so nervous, but I think that was cute to him, and also I looked vulnerable, which turned out to be what interested him. He asked me to join him and ordered me a glass of wine.'

'Had you ever drunk alcohol before?' asked George.

'No, never,' said Mama, walking carefully over the bamboo mat and coming to sit down again on her cushion. She put both hands flat on the glass table. 'I didn't want to drink it, so I made sure I tipped it on the floor when he wasn't looking. I'm sure some of the staff must have seen me, but I was more scared of taking the drink than ruining the carpet.'

'He didn't notice, this man, that you were throwing his drink away?' asked George.

'Men only notice what they want to notice,' said Mama. 'Why

else do you think every man believes a beautiful woman could be in love with him?'

George blushed. *'Touché,'* he muttered.

'After a little while, he – I think his name was David – asked if I wanted to go to dinner at the hotel restaurant,' said Mama, 'and I didn't know what to do. There was no way to ask Tomi if it was okay, and I thought maybe he'd be angry because I'd taken so long. But I didn't want to offend my new friend so I decided to go.'

'Really?' asked George. 'You went to dinner with him? A teenage girl and what – a middle-aged man?'

'He was maybe thirty,' said Mama. 'It didn't feel strange to me at the time. I was thinking of Tomi and doing a good job for him.'

'Right.'

'So, so, so. We went to dinner. And I made a big mistake.'

'Which was?'

'Let me tell you first what I thought of the restaurant. It was so fashionable, like the rest of the hotel. I was in heaven. There were yucca plants in big wooden pots, and bamboo parasols decorating the sides of the room. And I believe there was a tiger-skin rug on the floor, although that could have been another hotel.

'Silver cutlery, so much of it, maybe six pieces for each place setting, white china . . . and crystal chandeliers hanging from the ceiling. David told me they were made of diamonds, which I believed. I kept staring up at the chandeliers, wondering how many millions of yen they must have cost.

'David ordered for us, and got me an aperitif – gin and tonic. I looked at it and probably went very green, because the restaurant was bright, lots of light everywhere, and there was no way I could tip the drink on the floor.'

'So what did you do? Did you get drunk?'

'I took little sips at first – it tasted horrible! Like a soda drink with salt poured in it – and by the time the main course came I felt very giddy. By the end of the meal – I can't even remember if we had dessert – I was feeling sick, and this man, a gentleman it would seem, took me up to his hotel room so I could lie down. I was so ill, but also worried and guilty too. Tomi had trusted me and I was very frightened he'd think I'd let him down.' Mama sighed.

'It's sad. The girls who work for me, if only they worked as hard as I used to. But they're not like that. I don't know if it's western girls or just young girls today, I don't know. They wouldn't care if I paid them to do nothing. They have no sense of pride in their work.'

'So what happened when he took you back to his hotel room?'

'Of course, back then, when I came to Tokyo, there was less money,' Mama lamented. 'We had to work harder. I was grateful to have a job, any job. The girls today travel the world, they have no idea how hard their parents worked to give them their freedom. You know *yakuza* steal my girls? Every month, *yakuza* come and steal my best hostesses. I know it happens, and they go, you know? Not so long ago my best girl was taken. Annabel. No loyalty. No pride in her job.'

'So . . . at the hotel room . . .'

Mama let out a long sigh and drained her tea. 'George-san. I thought I'd be okay but . . . I'm tired. I have work tonight. It's time you were going.'

'Already? But—'

'No, no. Time to go now. We'll meet later. Later.'

'Later, when?' said George, getting to his feet, stumbling back into the cabinet as he did so. 'I'm free all afternoon. Maybe you could rest for a few hours and we'll have tea somewhere. Anywhere you like, my treat.' As he said the last words, his hand went to his trouser pocket.

'We'll see.' She led George down the bamboo-floored hallway, kimono sweeping the floor as she went, and opened the front door.

'Please, Mama.' George looked down at his shoes, scattered on the brown tiles. 'Later today?'

Mama waited a moment, then nodded. 'Okay. Anywhere I like?'

George nodded.

'Then I would like to take tea at the Park Hyatt Hotel in Shinjuku.' She smiled again, her pale lips offering little contrast against her white, creased cheeks. 'I always think they serve the best tea. Maybe if I feel better later, I can manage it.'

'Please try. There isn't much time, Mama.'

Mama smiled. 'Be patient George-san.'

'How about I call you in a few hours?'

'No, George-san, I'll call you.'

14

Steph

As Steph listened to the kimono lady preparing something behind a bamboo screen, she put her hand to her stomach and waited for her blurred vision to subside.

The thought of a meal, even from someone so strident and bossy, was certainly tempting. Perhaps she would stay. Just for a little while. And the old lady seemed to know a bit about Roppongi.

Steph couldn't decide whether she was in a fabric shop, a dressmakers, or something else entirely. Certainly there was nothing to indicate the hostess trade or the seedy side of Roppongi life.

Two sides of the room were made of bamboo screens, and there was a wooden desk in one corner with a cash register, a roll of tissue paper and a pair of scissors. Hanging on one of the bamboo screens were four beautiful kimonos.

One was ocean blue and embroidered with delicate white flowers, so soft they looked as if they'd been breathed on to the fabric. Steph felt she should sit absolutely still as her eyes followed the lines of the petals, as if her movements might disturb the pattern.

A bamboo screen was pulled back and 'Mrs Kimono', as Steph decided to call her, returned carrying a tiny four-legged tray. The tray contained a glass of iced black tea, a pair of black chopsticks decorated with silver and pink cherry blossom, a bowl of rice and a little dish that contained evil-looking brown liquid and a strange round object.

'I don't get it,' said Steph. 'No offence, I'm really grateful, but why are you being so kind? I'm nothing to you – just some stupid girl who fell down in the street.'

Kneeling with surprising grace in front of Steph, Mrs Kimono presented the tray.

'I'd help anyone in trouble. That's the Japanese way. But perhaps . . . I had a daughter once. I'd hope someone would care for her if she was hungry.'

'Once?' Steph went to take the tray.

'No!' The woman snatched it away and placed the wooden square carefully but firmly on the floor, its legs raising it a few inches above the bamboo mat.

It was then Steph saw what was floating in the dish of brown water.

An eyeball.

'A light Japanese breakfast,' Mrs Kimono announced. 'Very good for your health. I used to make this meal for my own daughter.' She looked sad.

'Thank you.' Steph stared at the eyeball, and it stared back.

The woman got to her feet and moved a few careful steps back, watching Steph with anticipation.

'Eat your meal.'

'I'm not sure I can eat this.' Steph glanced at the bamboo-mat floor. It looked clean. Still, she'd rather not throw up in this lady's shop if she could help it.

'Of course you can. Don't be spoilt.'

'I'm not spoilt.' Steph's eyes flashed a warning at the woman, who held her gaze. 'What sort of . . . animal does it come from?'

'Fish.'

Steph picked up the chopsticks. She'd had a few rudimentary practices back in the UK, but she was far from an accomplished chopstick user. And the eyeball looked like a slippery customer.

'So the girls working in Roppongi,' Steph said, her mouth turning dry as she watched the eye rotate in the dish. 'I was wondering . . . It's probably nothing, but my friend works at Calamity Janes and I saw her yesterday for the first time in ages and she looks really . . . really . . . I don't know.'

'Old?' ventured Mrs Kimono.

Steph hadn't thought of Julia looking old. But Mrs Kimono

had a point. 'Yes. And . . . Ill I suppose. And she pretended she didn't know me. It's like she's been body-snatched. And my other friend, Annabel. We were supposed to be sharing a room, but when I turned up she wasn't at the apartment. That's not like her . . . Or at least not like the girl I remember from school. She was always really reliable. I'm sure she's fine but . . . Is it safe out here?'

'Yes.' The woman nodded and made a scooping gesture with her hand. 'Very safe. The most dangerous things are the *gaijin*. Foreigners. Eat your meal.'

'Okay.' Steph felt relief at the thought of Roppongi being 'very safe', although dark thoughts still swilled at the back of her mind.

She began chasing the slimy ball around the dish with the chopsticks.

'Wait!' The woman held her hand up sharply. 'You can drink, like this.' She mimed holding the dish up to her lips, then pushed the little white saucer into Steph's hand.

'Thank you.' Steph poured the contents into her mouth as delicately as possible, chewing without breathing and feeling her toes curl as she tried to swallow without gagging. The eyeball tasted like salt and fish, not so bad, but the texture of the thing, squirts of water and goo mixed with chewy rubber, was awful. She tried to imagine herself in a west London delicatessen sampling an unusual and expensive caviar.

The woman smiled, a slight twitch that failed to reveal any teeth.

'Very good. You'll feel much better now. Drink your tea.'

'Do you think . . . it's a bit odd for a girl to leave clothes and a diary behind? Or is it the sort of thing that happens all the time out here? That's what the landlord said.'

'I don't understand you.'

'My friend Annabel. She left behind her diary and a load of clothes. That *is* a little strange, don't you think?'

Mrs Kimono shrugged. 'No. *Gaijin* come to Roppongi to make money. It doesn't surprise me that clothes would be left behind. Things from a former life. Drink.'

Steph found herself picking up the glass of black liquid, wondering why on earth she was letting this lady boss her around. 'I'm Steph, by the way. It's very nice to—'

'By the way, by the way, such a waste of words.' The woman shook her head, but her grey curls stayed firmly in place, like Styrofoam. 'You should say: "I'm Steph". Nothing more.'

'So what's your name, by the way?' Steph asked.

'By the way, my name is *Sato*, by the way. Sit up straight. You're just like my daughter – always falling forwards.'

Steph, who had always been praised for her good posture and strong back muscles, was confused. 'I am sitting straight.'

The lady looked displeased.

'No. You lean forward too much. Sit straighter.'

'Look, Sato, if you don't mind—'

'*Ai ai*! *Mrs Sato*. Shizuku Sato. Drink.'

Sato . . . Mrs Kimono, thought Steph, looking at the glass. She didn't want Mrs Kimono to think she was intimidated, so she took a delicate sip, expecting it to taste horrid. She was surprised to find it piquant, only a little bitter and actually very refreshing.

'The reason Japanese people live so long,' said Mrs Kimono, taking a cushion from one of the shelves and sitting on it. The movement was as fluid as silk unrolling. 'So.' She fixed Steph with her rather frightening eyes. 'Are you in Roppongi to work? If you're anything like the other girls, you'll be looking for a job here.'

'Yes,' said Steph, drinking more tea. 'Hostess work. I need to make a fresh start and I need money to do it. There's this course I want to take – it costs loads but once I get on it, people will see me in a different way. I can start my life all over again. They'll know I'm a serious actress. I've heard you can earn a lot out here. But to be honest, now that I'm here all I'm doing is worrying about my friends.'

Mrs Kimono frowned and her chin moved just a fraction left and right.

'It's good to care about others,' she said. 'But you can't help anybody if you're falling down in the street. It's foolish not to take care of yourself.'

Steph nodded. 'But if I'm thinking about Julia and Annabel, at least I'm not thinking about bad things . . . The fact I've got no money, no job, rent to pay . . . Things at home I'd rather not remember . . .'

'A fine way to get yourself into trouble,' said Mrs Kimono. 'In life, you must focus. Chase two hares and you won't even catch one.'

'I need to earn enough for food and rent, that's for sure,' said Steph. 'Julia's doing so well, money, money, money. I guess Calamity Janes is a good club, but—'

'*Gaijin* hostess clubs,' Mrs Kimono said. 'I'm sad to live long enough to see the *mizu shobai* so . . . maligned. It steals young girls. My daughter—' She stopped abruptly. 'Finish your tea.'

'You don't like Calamity Janes?'

'That club is worse than most. People go to *gaijin* hostess clubs and they think hostess, *geisha*, courtesan, prostitute, all the same thing.'

'But . . . hostesses are sort of a version of *geisha*.'

'NOT at *gaijin* clubs.' Mrs Kimono looked so angry, Steph thought the iced tea might start to boil under her glare. 'The things that go on at Calamity Janes . . . It has a reputation around here.' She shook her head and stared out of the window. 'I don't want to talk about *that* place in my shop. My cloth will become dirty.'

'Well, how should I know?' said Steph, but the steely look in the woman's eye didn't soften. 'I'm new here. Hostess, *geisha*, I thought it was kind of the same.'

'Just like my daughter,' said Mrs Kimono, blinking for the first time in minutes. 'She used to say the same thing. But *geisha* are arts people. Performers. They are educated. Training takes years. A hostess, she smiles and drinks. She doesn't enrich the world with her art. And at a *gaijin* place . . . it's a different matter entirely.'

'That dress,' said Steph, pointing to the blue silk garment hanging up. 'That's what a *geisha* would wear, isn't it?'

Mrs Kimono gave a curt nod. 'Handmade.' She reached out

to stroke the stitching on the hem. 'Beautiful.' Her light brown eyes looked sad. 'Everyone wants a good price these days. Even some *geisha* don't care so much about quality. They buy machine-made kimono and say it's handmade. When I used to perform, all my kimono were handmade. Many of them antiques. I never wore a machine-made kimono. I still wouldn't.'

'You were a *geisha*?' said Steph. 'Really?'

'I still am a *geisha*.'

'You must know all about men. How can you tell the difference between the good ones and the ones who want to take advantage of you?'

'What a question!'

Steph looked down at her tea. Under Mrs Kimono's penetrating glare, she felt increasingly unable to muster her usual façade of self-assurance. She wondered if Mrs Kimono could see how lost she felt inside. How desperate she was to make money out here, how much she needed a new start.

'So,' said Steph, deciding to change the subject, 'you wear that kimono when you're working as a *geisha*? Did you make it?'

'No. A craftsman makes the kimono. I help choose their fabric and design. People come here for my knowledge. What are the flowers to wear on a summer kimono, what fabrics are best for autumn, what is the best kimono for performance and which is best for the teahouse. When the kimono is ready, the client comes here to collect it.'

'Right.'

'Perhaps *geisha* and *Japanese* hostess aren't so different,' said Mrs Kimono curtly. 'Some of the abilities are the same. I didn't used to think so, but a *geisha* would, of course, make an excellent hostess. A hostess would not make a good *geisha*. Certainly not without many years of training. Becoming a *geisha* is very hard. Very, very hard.'

'How long did you train?' asked Steph.

'Many years. Nearly twice as long as most. I was an old *maiko* – nearly twenty-seven when my training finished. But being a *maiko* wasn't as hard as earning my good reputation as a *geisha*.

I worked in many low teahouses and entertainment venues before I was able to win a respectable *danna*.'

'What's a *danna*?' asked Steph.

'A patron. A customer who takes care of you.'

'I've got a trial shift tonight at a hostess place,' said Steph. 'Not Calamity Janes,' she added quickly. 'And I need to win a customer.'

'A trial? Which club? Who runs it? Western owner?'

'No. A Japanese lady. It's called Sinatra's.'

'Sinatra's.' Mrs Kimono's mouth twitched. 'She's famous, the mama there. She knows *yakuza*. Make sure you do as she tells you.'

'I met her yesterday.' Steph found she was, in spite of herself, imitating Mrs Kimono's graceful poise on the cushion. 'She was very elegant.'

'Of course she's elegant,' said Mrs Kimono. 'And so must you be, if you want to earn your money. You must know how to be around men. How to keep your dignity, even when they behave badly.' She nodded as she spoke. 'How Japanese men are, what they expect, how to serve them. Western girls don't know about Japanese men. If you work at a western place, fine. But Sinatra's is a Japanese place. At least, it was last I heard.'

'I'm sure it can't be too difficult. I've been a waitress before.'

'A *waitress*?' Mrs Kimono laughed, a rich, full sound that stopped as quickly as it started. 'If you think that's comparable, then you really do know nothing.

'This is the *mizu shobai*. The water trade. You are a night worker. You must know how to take charge. Control the men. If you don't control them, they'll control you.'

Steph unfolded her legs carefully. 'I'm not totally naïve. Anyway, I really should be getting back.'

'Of course you're naïve.'

'I'll be fine.' Steph rose to her feet. 'I'm an actress, I can play any part.'

'How can you be an actress if you haven't completed your training?'

'I have *had* training. Lots of training. I have an acting degree and I've taken God knows how many courses and my school—'

'But you said your purpose out here . . . That you were earning money for a course.'

'An MA course. It's like extra training.'

A shadow appeared at the glass door as a blue-capped postman dropped an envelope through the letterbox.

'How many years training have you had?' asked Mrs Kimono, giving the letter a quick look.

'Three . . . four . . . Three during my degree . . . Before that an entry course – that lasted a year. Then at school . . . my school specialised in drama, so I suppose you could call it nine years. Four years' full-time drama when I left school, and lots of evening classes – singing, martial arts . . .'

'It sounds like you've had plenty of training. When does the training finish and performance begin?'

'This is a . . .' Steph searched for the words, '*special* course. It's at a very good establishment. It has a good pedigree. I made mistakes back home. I was stupid. I need to make a fresh start and show people I'm not . . . I need to show them I'm a *real* actress.'

Mrs Kimono shrugged. 'They used to talk of different dance schools and music schools in Kyoto. This is the best for *shamisen*, and this is the best for dance . . . But when a *geisha* with true passion and skill performs, no one ever asks where she trained or for how long. They only know she is living her talent.'

'You're entitled to your opinion,' said Steph, 'but I know what I'm doing. When people see you in a certain light, it's hard to get the right work. I need to show everyone, I need to go to the best place . . . Well you wouldn't know about acting anyway.'

'Of course not,' said Mrs Kimono, smiling like a cat, very slowly but with no warmth reaching her eyes. 'Acting, *geisha* – they're worlds apart, aren't they?'

'I've got to go now,' said Steph, pulling open the shop door. 'I've stayed too long.'

'Well.' Mrs Kimono remained seated, looking serene. 'It sounds to me like you've had plenty of acting training. But you know nothing of men.'

'Then teach me,' said Steph, letting the door slip back. 'If I'm so ignorant, tell me what I need to know. Maybe tomorrow, after I've spoken to Julia and found my friend I can—'

'Impossible,' said Mrs Kimono. 'You're far too arrogant. You would be a poor learner.'

'Please,' said Steph. 'You're right, I don't know enough about men. That's exactly why I'm here, why I need to earn money so fast, because I was stupid and didn't know—'

'Sorry.' Mrs Kimono crossed her arms.

Steph's mouth opened and closed, but she couldn't think of anything more persuasive to say than: 'Please.'

'No. Sorry.'

Steph left then, letting the door swing closed behind her. It was only when she was halfway back to the apartment, legs a little stiff but no longer wobbly, that she realised Mrs Kimono hadn't once looked at her scars.

15

Mama

The Park Hyatt's Peak Lounge was half empty when Mama arrived, dripping with diamonds and wrapped in a silver mink stole. Most of the diamonds she wore were fake and the stole was patchy in places, but Mama felt confident that she still appeared to the staff as the glamorous lady of the night who'd dined at their establishment for many years.

A waiter came and tried to offer Mama a table, but she gave him a dazzling smile and pointed to George, who sat behind a bright green bamboo tree. George noticed her and rose quickly from his seat – so quickly he knocked over the empty coffee cup in front of him. A waiter dashed to pick it up.

'Mama!' George hurried forward and did a clumsy bow, while holding out his hand. Mama didn't take it.

'Let's take a seat and get started.' George wore a creased grey suit, the only one he owned, bought by a girlfriend years ago. The now-shiny fabric had seen good wear at many weddings, funerals and job interviews over the years.

'I'm very hungry, George-san,' said Mama, giving him a coy smile. 'Perhaps . . . a late lunch instead of afternoon tea?'

George rubbed his deeply furrowed forehead. 'The hotel restaurants will already be booked, I'm sure. I'll find somewhere nearby instead.'

'*Ni, ni ni*.' Mama silenced him with a raised hand. 'They always have a table for me here.' She nodded at a passing waiter and spoke to him in Japanese. A moment later, the pair were ushered towards one of three shiny, gold lifts, Mama stroking her stole like a favourite pet as she caught her reflection in the mirrored doors. George followed reluctantly.

'Kozue has a table for you,' the waiter murmured. 'You know the floor.'

Kozue, the Park Hyatt's celebrated Japanese restaurant, was almost full when Mama and George arrived, its dark wooden tables laden with elegant delicacies, vintage *sake* and the occasional bottle of champagne in a wooden ice bucket. The management kept special reservations for guests like Mama.

'This is one of my favourite restaurants,' she said, as a kimono-clad waitress pulled back a heavy mahogany chair for her, 'in all of Tokyo. Excellent Japanese food. And you can see Mount Fuji if the weather is clear.'

The restaurant was populated by both western and Japanese customers. Most wore slick designer suits and handled chopsticks like laser pointers, stabbing them repeatedly in the air to illustrate their high-powered conversations.

George pulled out his own seat and felt nervously for his wallet.

'I'll have the set five-course menu,' Mama told the waiter in English, 'and a good *sake* – *Tokubetsu Junmai-shu* – to start.' She turned to George. 'Have you heard of *Tokubetsu Junmai-shu*? It's a type of sake with polished rice. Very high quality.'

In other words, expensive.

'You should try it.'

'Just the noodles for me,' George told the waiter, 'and a coke.' He checked his watch.

'Let's get started.'

'Patience, patience.'

'We only have a few weeks.' George's voice reached a slightly higher pitch as he pulled out his notepad. 'We need to squeeze in all the hours we can. We're already behind schedule.'

'Your schedule, not mine.'

A waiter arrived with a bowl containing ice chips and antique *sake* cups, and George jiggled his knee impatiently as Mama took her time selecting her preferred drinking vessel. The cups were made of pottery, and many of them looked like a child's first efforts with clay. But the vessels were antiques and highly revered. Eventually, Mama chose a grey one decorated with spidery leaf veins.

'Okay, so where had we got to?' asked George, when the waiter had poured *sake* and left. 'You'd been invited to . . .' George flicked through well-scrawled notepad pages and chewed the end of his biro. '*David's* hotel room.'

A waiter discreetly placed a fizzing glass of Coca Cola next to George's notepad.

'Ah! Yes, the man in the hotel. My first customer, I suppose you could call him.' Mama took the tiniest sip of sake from the earthenware cup. 'David. Yes, I think he was called David. Let me remember.'

Mama stared out of the panoramic window which enclosed the restaurant. It was still daylight, but red and white lights were shining all over Tokyo. As she watched Roppongi Tower wink and flash in the distance, a plate of *sashimi*, served on more ice chips, was placed in front of her.

'You have to realise,' she said, picking up her chopsticks, 'I don't remember all that much about that night – especially towards the end.' She placed a shining strip of tuna between matt-red lips. 'But the hotel room . . . My memory is like a broken movie, you know? Just parts of scenes. David must have put me to bed, and I remember seeing him put my school bag on a hook behind the door and feeling confused. Perhaps he thought I'd be really upset if I lost my school books. I don't know. Anyway, he brought me water and then I was sick into a plastic bag. I was so embarrassed. Then he took his clothes off and put his penis in my mouth.'

George, who'd been taking a swig of Coca Cola, began to choke.

'I'm sorry,' he whispered. 'What did you say?'

Mama raised her voice: 'I said he put his penis into my mouth.'

A passing waiter swerved as if he'd been jabbed with a cattle prod, and several people at the adjoining tables turned to stare.

George, red-faced, bowed his head and began writing at speed.

'Okay, okay, I heard you,' he muttered.

'What could I do?' Mama's volume didn't decrease, and she added elaborate arm gestures to make her point more clearly. 'I was a young girl, I didn't know up from down. I wanted to please people, so when he explained what he wanted, I did it.

'It was okay. There are worse things. They make a big deal about that sort of thing, don't they? Sex, sex, young girls. We live through it. At least I wasn't married to him – I only had to put up with him for one night.'

George nodded, still focused on the notepad.

'I was very, very sick that night and then I fell asleep.'

Mama selected more *sashimi*, salmon this time.

'This man, where did he work? Was he somebody important?'

'How should I know? I woke up the next day in the hotel room at, maybe, six a.m. and David was fast asleep next to me, no clothes, snoring like a big bear. I had no clothes either – I don't remember taking them off. I got up and started shaking, really shaking, because I knew I had to go back to Tomi and . . . Oh, it was so embarrassing and frightening back then.' She gave a startlingly loud laugh. 'Now . . . things are different.'

'So this was—' George paused as Mama's *sashimi* was removed and an artist's palette of *sushi*, topped with two jaunty wisps of chive, was put in its place. 'Your first . . .' he lowered his voice, '*sexual* experience?'

'It was the first time I'd ever even *seen* a penis,' Mama said earnestly, not paying the slightest bit of attention to the heads turning in her direction. 'But of course there were many more to come, all different shapes and sizes. And lots of *talk* of penises. How men like to talk about their penises, you wouldn't believe it! It's their favourite topic of conversation.

'Anyway, I woke up in that hotel room and you have to remember, I was a good girl back then. I wasn't a good, good girl, not the kind of girl a mother would be proud of, but I wasn't all that bad. So you have to understand that when I took money from David's wallet, it was quite out of character.'

'You stole his money?'

'Yes.' Mama nodded vigorously. 'What could I do? I was stuck. I knew I couldn't go back to Tomi without money unless I wanted to become "black and blue", as my father used to say. I wasn't stupid. If I brought Tomi money, I knew he'd spare me a beating for taking the uniform all night and not coming back with a customer. So that's what I did.

'If I'd been in the Tokyo sex industry a few years longer, I would have taken more than money, let me tell you. Hotel soap and toiletries, credit cards, anything I could have got my hands on. They take from us so we take from them – that's how I saw things for a while. A western attitude. But as I said, I was a good girl then. I even left some yen in his wallet, I think. Yes, that's right. I didn't take all of it. And then I went back to Tomi, because of course I had nowhere else to go.'

'Was he angry?' asked George, leaning forward.

Mama smiled. 'Excuse me, George-san.' She found her bag under the table and checked inside. There were several brown jars of pills among the folds of leather. 'I have to go to the bathroom. I'll be back.'

16

Steph

The blonde girl on the bottom bunk had gone by the time Steph returned to the apartment, but the chemical odour of her perfume lingered around the stained blanket where her body had been. Steph hauled herself on to the top bunk and once again began hunting through her own bedding and under the pillow for the diary.

But it was nowhere. It had vanished.

Steph shook the rice pillow, but there was nothing inside except sharp grains – the book hadn't magically crept under its cold cover. Had it slid down the back of the bed? She checked her watch. The day was rushing along, and soon she should be starting her trial shift. She didn't want to miss it, but if Annabel's diary didn't turn up she'd feel uneasy about swanning off to work. There wasn't much time.

Steph climbed down and, sneaking a guilty glance over her shoulder, ran her hands along the cold metal of the bottom bunk. The room felt damp, she noticed, which made everything cold, and the metal frame itself was freezing. There was nothing behind the bed. But then she noticed a tiny corner of blue poking out from under her roommate's pillow.

'Hey!'

Steph turned to see her roommate in the doorway. The girl wore saggy, cut-off pink pyjamas and there were bruises on her calves.

'What are you doing with my bed?' The girl grabbed Steph's shoulder, and Steph angrily shook her off and pulled back the pillow.

There, on the damp, crumpled bedding, was the diary.

Steph snatched it and waved it at her. 'You took this from my bed.'

The girl shrugged. 'No, no.'

'What's it doing under your pillow?'

'No, I . . . I don't know how it got there. I move in my sleep sometimes. Maybe it fell and I moved it under there. I don't know. I've got a headache. Stop shouting at me.'

Steph gave her a long, cold stare, but the girl's face was impassive and Steph couldn't tell if she was lying or not.

She turned and walked into the common area, a similarly damp and cold space, but there was a window at least, albeit covered in bird droppings and exhaust-fume stains.

Steph's hands were shaking as she sat on the over-sized, battered leather couch and waited for her heart rate to slow down. She shook away the bad thoughts and let the diary flutter through her fingers, careful not to drop the wodge of business cards she knew were stuffed inside the pages.

Julia had mentioned collecting customer business cards as part of working as a hostess. 'This job is like networking,' she'd said. If Annabel was working as a hostess, the men whose business cards she had collected had to be hostess club customers. Maybe one of those men would know where Annabel was now, and Steph wouldn't have to wait to see Julia after all.

But the business cards had gone. Steph could feel that straightaway. Before she'd had time to think, she was back at the bedroom door, waving the book at her roommate.

'Where are the cards that were in here?'

The girl, who was standing on a pile of clothes, typing a text message into her pink mobile phone, ignored her, so Steph went to the bottom bunk and threw the pillow and bedding aside.

'Hey, what?' The girl looked startled as Steph ripped a grubby grey sheet from the bottom bunk and scoured the striped mattress. There were ominous brown stains between the stripes, and an empty Japanese condom packet and a rice cracker in plastic squashed against the springs. But no business cards.

'Where are they? Tell me where they are. Right now.'

'I don't know.' The girl's surly demeanour had vanished and she looked frightened. 'Look – what is it you want?'

'There were cards in here. Business cards. You know there were. And I'm not leaving this room until you give them to me.'

'I don't know what you're talking about. Maybe one of the other girls . . .'

'The girl whose book this is,' said Steph. 'I want to make sure she's okay. She left clothes behind . . . I need those cards, I want to phone her customers, see if they know where she is.'

'She left clothes behind?' The girl glared back. 'So what? Girls do that all the time. I left clothes at my last apartment. You move on. Big deal.'

Steph hesitated. The voice of reason again. Maybe she *was* making something out of nothing. Everyone was saying the same thing: girls come and go, it's safe here, people leave stuff behind.

'You must have taken them.' Steph tucked the diary under her arm and began pulling handfuls of clothes out of the nearest suitcase, which was plastic and covered in fake Gucci logos. 'And I want them back.'

'Don't touch my—'

Steph looked down and discovered she had a handful of condoms in her hand – about twenty of them. She dropped the plastic packets, embarrassed, and watched the girl stuff clothes defensively back into the suitcase. There were angry tears running down her face.

Steph wasn't sure where to look. 'We'll talk about this later,' she said, 'but this isn't over. I want those cards.'

The business cards may have vanished, but Steph still had the diary. She went back into the common area, flipped open the woven cover with its frayed, cardboard corners, and rifled through the pages. No Japanese names or telephone numbers jumped out at her, so she decided instead to read the diary page by page.

Dear God,

Not hungover – it's a miracle! Still drunk?? I don't want to go teach the kids if I am, but what can I do.

God I have a big thing to ask, they're talking about raids again. Even Sinatra's might be raided this week. The police are really cracking down, even on clubs that pay protection and . . . I don't know, it's scary stuff. Please don't let us get raided.

Work was so embarrassing last night. I asked French guy for his number. I was so drunk, but Hayley says it's good to look keen. That's what gets you *dohans*. All the best girls chase customers for *dohans*, they're always emailing and texting the guys, will you go out with me? They beg the men, please, please take me out. I didn't want to be like that, but that's how it works. You have to look desperate, that's what they like.

Got to go.

Amen,

Love Annabel

Amen. Steph remembered Annabel at school. She was always praying for something or other – good marks, not having to read out loud in English class. Her family didn't go to church, but Annabel always believed in God. It was sweet that she wrote to him.

As Steph turned the page, her watch glinted under the fluorescent light. It was getting late. She fought back sinister thoughts and replaced them with more logical ones. *No one else is worried. Everyone thinks Annabel is fine. If she was properly missing, Julia would have said something.*

She flicked through the many pages of dense handwriting and closed the diary.

There's no way I can read all this before work, she decided. *And if I don't go to Sinatra's tonight, I'll miss the chance to ask the girls there about Annabel. Anyway, Mrs Kimono's right. I'll be no good to anyone if I'm starving in a gutter somewhere. I've got to start earning money.*

In a few hours, Steph realised, she'd have a chance to talk to Julia again. She wondered which Julia would be waiting for her – the old friend from back home, or the washed-out, tired shadow who pretended she didn't know Steph.

17

Mama

'Excuse the interruption, George-san,' said Mama, as she slid back into her seat. 'Where were we?'

'You were telling me how you went back to Tomi.'

'Yes. I was still scared,' Mama continued, 'but as it happened he was very pleased with me. Probably because I gave him money. He even smiled a little I think – he did that sometimes when he was really happy – and he told me I hadn't done badly. Coming from him, that was a very big compliment.'

A dish of steaming noodle soup was placed in front of Mama. The bowl was black, with sharp corners, as if a square dish had been folded around the soup. A flat plate of noodles, king prawns and lightly fried vegetables was lowered in front of George. There were chopsticks beside his plate, but he asked the waiter for a fork.

'So you carried on working for Tomi?'

'In something of a different way,' said Mama, dipping a wafer-thin, porcelain spoon into her cloudy broth. 'He didn't send me out any more – I guess he thought I was a little too green to handle the hotel bars. I was a confident kid, but perhaps not the lone ranger he thought. Maybe he was confusing me with my mother. Anyway.'

Mama took a sip of soup. 'He decided I should work at his club instead. Not his bar – that turned out to be a pink salon – I'll tell you about those later. He would have got in big trouble if he'd put someone my age to work *inside* a pink salon. Touting was fine, but not working in the salon itself. No, he had another club. A *sunakku*. Have you heard of *sunakku* – a snack club?'

George shook his head.

'It's like a hostess club, but very low grade. Anyone can go there, any *sarariman* or student or, really, anyone. There's no entrance fee at a snack, not like a hostess club, but a snack is a *bit* like a hostess club. A poor man's version.'

'How so?'

'There are lovely young girls for the customers to flirt with and to keep them drinking, just like in a hostess bar, and of course the girls have their drinks paid for by customers. But in a snack, the customers pay for the drinks and anything they eat, nothing more, no hourly rate.

'They pay a lot, of course – more than in a regular bar – and the girls are always trying to make customers drink more. The more a customer drinks, the more the girls get paid.'

'I was wondering,' said George, scooping up a prawn and stuffing it into his mouth, 'could you explain to me a little more about the club you run now? How does it all work? I've never really been clear . . . you know . . . about what happens in hostess clubs.'

Mama nodded as George spiked two more prawns on to the same fork, rammed them into his mouth and picked up his pen.

'You mean, are the girls there prostitutes?' said Mama, and once again several diners turned around.

George's eyes grew wide. 'No, no. I know it's not the same as . . .' he lowered his voice, 'a *brothel*. But I just wanted to understand the concept a bit better. We don't have anything like it in the UK.'

'Oh yes you do,' said Mama, taking another delicate sip of *sake* and dabbing her mouth with a napkin. 'You have plenty of hostess clubs in the UK. You just don't arrange things the same way when it comes to payment.'

George stopped chewing. 'You mean strip clubs?'

'Not at all,' said Mama. 'That's a common mistake westerners make. No, no, we have strip clubs in Japan and places for men to have sex with women and all that sort of thing – the ejaculation industry we call it. A quick fix, bang bang. That's not what hostess clubs are about.'

'So what are they about?'

'Hostess clubs are a way for rich men to sit with pretty young girls and play pretend for an evening that the girls might, just might, sleep with them.'

'And do they?'

'Sometimes, yes, the girls sleep with customers. Not very often. That's part of the fun. But they're *never* paid for it, no, no, no. The customer has to win the girl, just like he would in a regular bar.

'In my bar all the girls are pretty, sexy and fun – and they all play with a customer as if perhaps, maybe, they might have sex with him one day.'

'We really don't have anything like that in the west,' said George. 'At least not to my knowledge.'

'Yes you do,' said Mama. 'What would you call your expensive nightclubs in London? I've visited many of them. They have VIP areas filled with pretty girls looking for rich boyfriends. Isn't that right?

'There are clubs, in London where men have to buy champagne or bottles of whisky or whatever to sit at a certain table, and pretty young models always want to sit at those tables with the rich men. Isn't that the same?'

'But the girls aren't paid,' said George. 'And the men . . . They don't pay for the girls to sit with them.'

'Don't they?' Mama waggled her chopsticks at him, then scooped bright, white *soba* noodles from her bowl and sucked them noisily into her mouth. 'Maybe not directly. But they pay. Anyway.' She stirred the soup with her chopsticks. 'I was telling you about working at a snack – my first proper job.'

'Yes,' said George, glancing down at his notepad again.

'So,' Mama continued. 'Tomi had another bar, a *sunakku* bar called Snack Coco in the same building as Tomi's Bar, one floor up. Much smaller, no windows and full of pretty young girls like me dressed up in short dresses and high shoes, welcoming the men and holding their hands so they couldn't touch our breasts while they drank.

'Tomi put me in an apartment with the other snack girls – the rent came straight out of my wages – and I started right away. I was still sick and headachy from drinking the night before, but with Tomi, well, I knew it wasn't smart to mess with him.

'I put on the outfit he gave me, big shoes I could hardly walk in and a tiny little skirt, and I bowed and smiled at all the customers, just like Tomi told me to.

'I must have been the youngest girl there, but the rest of the girls were young too. Maybe seventeen or eighteen. Back then, that wasn't so young, perhaps, but young enough. None of us were tough. We all had bad things happen to us while we were working – men touching us, bad language, insults, sometimes even beatings.

'One girl, a customer waited for her after work and beat her up because she wouldn't go home with him. She never came back to work again. *Hai*. Very sad.'

Mama waved at a waiter and he removed her half-finished bowl of noodle soup without saying a word.

George stopped his furious scribbling and attempted to scoop up half a plate of noodles in one fork load, holding the dish near his face so he could shovel food into his mouth as quickly as possible. A fragment of prawn shell fell on to his limp, blue tie.

'I'm making it sound terrible,' said Mama, watching the waiter refill her *sake* cup. 'Actually, it wasn't so bad. Not such a bad job for a teenager who wanted a good time and wasn't interested in marriage.

'We hated all the customers of course – *sukabai*, sleazy men, they showed us no respect – but we sang *karaoke* with them and learned about their families and I got used to drinking eventually, which made things much easier. But really, it was pretty easy work.

'The trouble came because it was "low class", I suppose. If we were in fancy hostess clubs, the clientele – well, I suppose men are men no matter how much money they have – but the girls are treated very badly in an ordinary snack. People don't think much of the girls there. The customers don't and society doesn't either.'

'Yes, I meant to ask about that,' said George. 'What do people think of girls – and *mamas* – who work in hostess clubs?'

Mama shrugged. 'Twenty years ago, a nice boy wouldn't marry a hostess. His family wouldn't approve. But nowadays, the water trade . . . people think maybe it's not so bad. Times are changing.

'I really don't know why anyone ever had a problem with snacks and hostess clubs. What's the big deal? You get nice girls working there. Many of my girls are English teachers. It's not like a pink salon, where the girls spend all night with penises in their hands.'

'I'm sorry.' George pushed his glasses up his shiny nose. 'What's a *pink salon*? You were going to tell me.'

'*Pinku saron*. Yes, let me explain. Very popular in Japan. They look like cabaret clubs, but the booths are always very dark, and you can't see what's going on in them. That's because very naughty things are going on in them. Customers pay for – there's a phrase for it. Happy endings? Happy endings. You know. When you masturbate or give oral sex to a customer. Girls do that in the booths – I did when I worked in a *pinku saron*.

'A pink salon is like, how can I say it in English? A sausage factory.' Mama raised her hand to her mouth and giggled, her large eyes going out of focus ever so slightly. 'You know. In out, in out. One man, two men, all night, many, many men. Cheap places.

'Tomi ran a few pink salons. In fact, the bar I went to that first night, when Tomi gave me the schoolgirl uniform, was a pink salon. I should have known by the smell. Pink salons always smell the same: perfume, disinfectant and semen.'

George looked at his cold plate of noodles and felt his appetite disappear.

'The snack club was a cheap place,' Mama continued, 'but sex wasn't a necessity if the girls didn't care to do it. Of course, we put up with groping customers, rude customers, but we didn't *have* to give happy endings. Sometimes we did. We could weigh up what it was worth to us.

'If a really good customer came in, sometimes we'd go back

to a hotel with him, but the other girls told me from the start: 'Make sure you take only gifts for sleeping with customers and make them promise to visit you all days of the week afterwards. Make it worth your while, but this isn't soapland – don't take money for sex."'

A plate of exquisitely arranged cod roe was placed in front of Mama, and she leaned down to inhale.

'Soap?' asked George. 'Did you say, *soapland*?'

'*Sopurando*. A soapland is a Japanese brothel. *Toruko* they used to call them when I was a very young girl. Turkish baths – but the government changed the name.

'The Turkish thought it was an insult to Turkey – can you imagine? An insult? Clearly they'd never visited our bathhouses. Any Turkish man would have been proud, I'm quite sure, to have such places named after his country. Turkish women . . .' Mama dangled a leaf of seaweed between her chopsticks '. . . perhaps not so much.

'Anyway, I was telling you about Snack Coco. Like the girls said, snack bars aren't soaplands. But sometimes they come very close.'

'Did you get to know any politicians at the snack bar? You know – important men.'

Mama shook her head. 'Of course not. What rich, powerful man would come to a *sunakku*? If you have money, you visit a hostess bar. Snack bars are for ordinary men.'

'Sorry. Carry on.'

'*Hai*, yes. Most of the Coco girls said "Don't make it a brothel, here", but those of us with ambition knew if you were to get anywhere at a snack bar you had to sleep with the customers. If you slept with them they came to see you much more often, bought you presents . . . and you got a night out in a love motel, or, if you were very lucky, one of the new western-style hotels that seemed to open every day in Tokyo at that time. You've heard about love motels, haven't you?' Mama fluttered her eyelashes provocatively.

A waiter came and removed George's plate of cold noodles and Mama's now empty dish.

'Room for an hour,' said George. 'Is that right?'

'You can rent them all night,' said Mama, shaking out a fresh napkin and resting it on her lap. 'One hour, four hours, all night, up to you. They didn't exist before the nineteen fifties, but then prostitution was made illegal and they appeared overnight.

'We always used to insist on a full-night stay, us snack girls. A night in a nice bed and a hot bath was a real bonus back then. Of course,' she gave a little laugh, 'we had to share the bath and the bed with our customer. But it wasn't always so bad. We would always say, the snoring is the worst!'

'Did you make a lot of money?' asked George.

'Some,' Mama conceded. 'It wasn't a bad wage, but when you work in the *mizu shobai* money doesn't last long. You get it, you spend it – clothes, drugs, drink, clubs . . . in your free time you want to forget everything.'

'Drugs? Really?'

'Oh yes. There were plenty of drugs around. One of Tomi's gangster friends became my boyfriend while I was working at the snack. A real gangster. He used to deal amphetamine. We had a drug romance. It didn't last long. He was killed actually.'

'Oh.' George looked up. 'Sorry.'

'No. It was a good thing. Anyway, the love motels got used to me pretty quickly. After a year or so, they started refusing me rooms. Love motels aren't supposed to be for girls coming regularly with different men.'

'But . . . didn't you say they were for prostitutes?' George flicked back a page in his notebook.

'Yes, but by the time I was using them they were more, okay not respectable, but they weren't supposed to be for working girls. Love time for cute, young, married couples, that's what they're for. Oh, you should have seen back then, all the different sorts of love motels. They have plenty today of course, plenty. Just go and look in Shibuya, but back then it was all new and exciting.

'The love motel boom. Motels like fairytale castles with four-poster beds, love motel rooms with heart-shaped swimming pools or revolving leather beds and ceiling mirrors.' Mama smiled and took a sip of *sake*. 'Fun. Or they could be. Anyway, they started refusing me a room after a while. But yes, before that I made money.'

Mama sighed and dabbed her eyes with her napkin. 'To think back . . . It's like I was a different person. So full of energy. So . . . fearless. Tomi kept me in line and I was scared of him, but really I did what I pleased, went where I pleased, dated who I pleased. And sex, sex, sex. I learned so much about men.'

The men at the next table, who were getting up to leave, all turned to take a quick look at Mama, and George's mouth twitched under the scrutiny.

'Don't worry,' Mama told George, waving a diamond-encrusted hand. 'They know me here. They know my business. Everybody does.'

George's mouth continued to twitch.

'I worked for Tomi for a few years. Yes, it must have been a few years. Lots of drinking and sex and money, but the money all went as soon as it came. I bought furs, American jeans, big sunglasses, all sorts of lovely things, but I stayed in that same apartment with the other snack girls and we were like a little family. Sisters. And then . . .' Mama paused.

'Then the *no-pan kissa* came along. The "no panty" café.'

18

Chastity

From: C_C_Chastity
To: CanadianDaphne
Subject: Same old, same old

Daph-en-neeee!

I've had such a bad day. Went on a shopping trip with a customer, this American guy, he was like something from the wild west, smoking cigars, wearing a cowboy hat, I'm not kidding. Of course he thought all hostesses were prostitutes, and that because I'd agreed to go on a date with him it meant I was fair game. He asked me to go to a hotel with him (surprise, surprise), but get this – before we'd even ordered food. You'll laugh, he took me to TGI Fridays for *dohan*. Classy, no?

He got me some really nice stuff when we were shopping, but he was SO rude. He said some shops were too young for me – too young! He's like 60 years old, I'm too young for him! OK, so HA, I got a Prada skirt out of it and a bag and a belt, but THESE CUSTOMERS!!!

We got to TGIs (TGIs!! This guy is a millionaire!!) and he decided he wanted to order for me and I let him, as you do. I'd already told him I'm vegetarian. Why did I think he'd remember? He tried to order me steak and fries, and said the steak here is really good, blah blah. And I said to him, don't you remember? I'm a vegetarian. No meat, I can't just take a holiday from it. Salads only, or whatever they have here (which I never quite figured out – what is TGIs, a burger restaurant or what?).

So he got really angry, cancelled our whole order and said, look, you'll have to get me in a better mood. Let's go to the hotel right now. When we get to Sinatra's I'll order us pizza.

You think you've seen and heard it all here, but I tell you things still come along that surprise you. Being asked to go to a hotel *before* dinner? That's a new one! Give me a break!

Customers – OK, I know they all want the same thing, but Mama's been putting me with some *really sukabai* men the last few weeks. Really bad. I mean this American guy, he's such a dirty old man, but Mama still sat me with him, even though I've been at the club for nearly two years now. I guess it just goes to show, loyalty means nothing, it all comes down to money. As soon as that Russian bitch took my customer, that was it – I got sat with whatever *sukabais* walked through the door.

No requests this week, and only one *dohan*. Mama's really pissed off with me.

It's getting pretty messy out here, more and more sleazy girls taking over the bottle-back bars. Angel (as she's calling herself now – perfect stripper name) was at Horatios last night, total mess, letting some customer sleaze all over her. Makes it so much harder for the rest of us. What's with that stupid name? It suits her though, since she has sex with all her customers now. She's even sleeping with that fat German guy now, remember him?

I'm thinking I've got to get out of this game now cause my bonuses are really sliding, and one day, honest to god, I'll crack and say, OK, come on then, take me to a hotel so I get guaranteed *dohans* all the time.

Anyway, got to get some sleep. Tammy's at her dad's house so I can finally have a lie-in tomorrow without the little madam coming in and waking me up.

Love, love, love,

Chastity

19

Mama

A waiter cleared his throat and proffered two wood-bound menus. 'Uh, excuse me, would you like coffee? More drinks?' He poured more *sake* into Mama's glass, then stood back.

'Have you heard of "no panty" café?' asked Mama, taking a menu. George took one too, but didn't open it. The waiter quickly left.

'I don't think so.'

'They came along in the late seventies, early eighties – a big novelty at first. Johnny Guitar, that was the first one. It opened in Kyoto. But by the time I was working at the snack, they'd opened all over the place – usually by railway stations. And the girls there made good money.'

'The answer is probably obvious,' said George, 'but what were these cafés, exactly?'

'Just as they sound – cafés with no panties. That's to say, the waitresses wore short skirts and no panties. The most expensive cup of coffee you ever bought – maybe, I don't know, two thousand yen a cup in today's money. Fifteen dollars. Something like that. Those cafés were a fashionable thing in the early eighties. Like a big boom. They blew up, and then very quickly went away.

'Of course, the customers were always "accidentally" dropping things on the floor for us to pick up. There were more dropped teaspoons in a *no-pan kissa* than any café in the country.

'For a while, there was no panty everything – no panty *shabu shabu*, the dipped meat restaurants, no panty *yakiniku*, grilled meat. And there were topless cafés and bottomless cafes and *no-pan kissa* with glass floors so the guests could sit underneath and look up our skirts.

'It wasn't long before the *no-pan kissa* offered extra services too, just like some of us did at the *sunakku*. There were backrooms where we'd take the customers for hand or oral ejaculation.

'We made a lot of money there, too, the girls that got into those places. A lot of money. But then very quickly, boom! Just like when they opened, boom! Men got bored, the novelty was gone and I think the government brought in some laws or something. Other coffee shops were complaining that all their customers were going to the girls with no panties. But they needn't have worried. Novelty never lasts. We were sad when the customers stopped coming.'

Mama waved over the waiter and ordered coffee and cognac.

'Your final course is already on its way,' the waiter assured her. 'Dessert.'

'Ah, the first industry I saw collapse. Sad. Very sad. Hostessing is going the same way, you know. It's collapsing. Things are different now. Men and women are different. It used to be when a man went out for the evening, the last person he wanted to bring was his wife. There was no place for her in the water trade – it was a place for men.

'Now young girls and boys go out together, spend time together. In groups. Mixed groups. Even married couples. It's not like before when a husband always went out with his work colleagues to hostess clubs or some corporate club. For me, it's depressing. Just like when the no panty cafés stopped getting customers.'

A long, thin white plate was placed in front of Mama, on which sat two gleaming, crisp chocolate globes with beads of condensation on their perfectly chilled shells. One was white, and one was a rich brown. Cognac and coffee were placed parallel to the plate.

Mama picked up the dolls' house sized silver fork resting between the two spheres and broke the darker of the two confections with a sharp crack. A rich white fondant ran out from the inside. She scooped chocolate and filling into her mouth.

'Delicious,' she announced, 'brown on the outside, white in the middle. Like me, don't you think, George-san?'

'Sorry, I . . .'

'Japanese on the outside, western in the middle, *neh*? That's what people always used to say. But now I like to think I'm the other way around. I wear western labels, have my hair in a western style, but inside I'm Japanese.' She finished the sphere in two mouthfuls and cracked the other open. Dark fondant ran on to the plate.

'So, so so. It's time to get the bill, George-san.' Mama smiled at him sweetly. 'I have a new girl starting tonight – English girl, strong face, wonderful figure, not enough make-up. She'll either be very good or very terrible. I need to get to my club, keep an eye on her.' She tapped her left eye, which was now bloodshot with tiredness.

George nodded. 'Of course, yes, of course.'

As the waiter walked towards them, Mama made a cross sign with her fingers and he turned on his heel and hurried towards the cash register.

'Next time we meet, I'll tell you all about soapland, George-san,' said Mama. 'I used to work there, you know. Yes. Don't look so surprised. After we no panty girls put our panties on again, we were desperate for work, and there were many of us coming back into the water trade – or at least the lower end of it – all at once, so very few jobs and even less money.

'We were so broke that soapland didn't seem so bad – especially when we found out how much money we could make. Well. Let's just say, the money I made there really set me on my way.'

A waiter dropped a mahogany tray with a long, paper bill on to the table and George pulled out a dog-eared, brown leather wallet and removed a series of 5000 yen notes. Each note seemed to stick to his fingers.

When the waiter had scooped the cash away with a bow, George flicked back through his notepad. It was almost half full, but his face gave away his disappointment.

'We should meet again soon,' he said. 'Tomorrow. Tomorrow morning if possible . . .'

Mama leaned her head back and laughed, revealing white teeth lightly glazed with white and dark chocolate.

'Tomorrow, George-san? Do I look like a workhorse to you? I hire other girls to work for me these days. No, no, we won't meet tomorrow.'

'Please, Mama. The deadline is coming up fast, and even with my newspaper article notes we barely have enough material to—'

'Yes, yes.' Mama waved her hands and stood to leave. 'Well, call me at the club tomorrow and I'll have one of my staff arrange another meeting. Thank you for lunch.'

20

Steph

Corset, jeans, socks, boots . . . Steph scrabbled around in the mess of crumpled denim skirts, sweatshirts and other unsuitable clothing in her rucksack, checking her watch in the hope that she'd somehow misread the time. But the silvery hands on the mother-of-pearl dial continued to race around the clock face. There was no getting away from it. She was very late.

Steph suspected Mama wouldn't tolerate lateness. She might even cancel the trial and refuse to let her in the club.

I've got to hurry.

Steph's elbow connected with the leg of her roommate, who was already preened, perfect, and taking up an irritating amount of space in the small bedroom. Standing up to get dressed, Steph battled in silence for floor space, pushing the girl's suitcases and clothes around with her feet in her hurry to get ready.

'Do you mind to look where you put your big feet?' It was the first time the girl had spoken to Steph since the morning.

'Excuse me?' Steph twisted her foot innocently into the wire of a bra, which bent under her bare heel.

'Your big feet! Watch your big feet.' The girl tutted and tried to pull her bra from under Steph's foot.

'Watch it!' Steph shouted, pushing her away. 'I'm trying to get ready.'

The girl crossed her arms across an amply padded chest.

'Okay, listen,' she said, making a T sign with her hands. 'We should . . . okay, not be friends.' She gave a snort at such a ridiculous thought. 'But . . . how about, truce? We're sharing a room. We'll drive each other crazy otherwise. I'm Natalia. What's your name?'

'Steph, and I haven't forgotten about those business cards.'

Natalia tutted. 'I told you, I didn't take your cards. I have my own business cards. Please. I work at Calamity Janes – we all have customers there.' She gave another snort and began shortening the straps on her bra so her breasts rose even higher. 'Where do you work?'

'Sinatra's,' said Steph, stepping into black jeans and hunting in her rucksack for socks.

'That place is okay,' Natalia conceded. 'If you don't care about money.'

'What does that mean?'

'It means if you want big money, you work at Janes.'

Steph thought of the empty tables at Sinatra's. She really did want to make as much money as possible as soon as possible, and she hadn't given up on the idea of winning a job at Janes. But right now the most important thing was to get to Sinatra's and, if she had the opportunity, ask the girls there about Annabel.

Steph pulled a tangle of necklaces from her rucksack, wishing she'd emailed Julia for advice about clothing before she set off for Tokyo. Going by what Natalia was wearing, the hostess look was decidedly upmarket.

Natalia was dressed in a calf-length, purple silk dress, with a string of pearls at her neck and gold rings on her fingers. She looked like the elegant wife of a high-flying executive.

The irony was that Steph had plenty of red-carpet style dresses if elegance was required (all of which, as a theatrical sort of person, she routinely wore to inappropriate occasions such as football matches and meals at Pizza Express), but she hadn't brought them to Tokyo She'd thought hostesses wore sexy, nightclub style clothes, so she'd packed three corsets, several pairs of tight jeans and acres of costume jewellery. Her evening gowns remained in the UK, stored in her best friend's loft.

'Did you ever meet the girl who was in our room before?' Steph asked, deciding, in light of Natalia's truce, to try for some information. She scraped her hair back and began frantically applying puffs of powder with an over-sized brush.

'Who?' asked Natalia, squinting at a tiny mirror in her hand.

'The girl who was here before. Annabel.'

'Annabel? No.'

'She stayed in this room. Before I came. She's a friend of mine.'

'I don't know anyone called Annabel. But the girl who was here before, I heard the stuff she left was good. Designer clothes, make-up. She must have earned a lot of money. Flin had to throw it all away . . . *Girls never tidy, never this, never that . . .* Maybe she met a boyfriend or something, I don't know. A friend of mine, Christa, she *married a customer* out here.' Natalia shook her head sadly. 'Shit happens.'

'Girls are always leaving things though, aren't they?' said Steph, the familiar uneasiness returning.

'Sure. No big deal. They were good things, that's what I was saying. She must have been a top hostess.'

'How come you moved to this apartment?'

'Why did I come *here*?' Natalia patted her hair, which was stiff with hairspray. She gazed at herself in the mirror for a moment, mesmerised. 'I worked in Ginza before. The last place I stayed – what a dump!' She dropped lipstick back into a powder-stained vanity case and arranged her long, blonde hair around her shoulders. Then she slipped into a pair of black, glittery shoes and looked Steph sternly up and down.

'That's what you're wearing?'

Steph, who was pulling shiny, patent boots over her jeans, looked up through a cloud of unbrushed hair.

'Just for tonight.'

'You need more make-up,' said Natalia, picking up a sequinned bag and heading out of the door.

'I'll be fine,' Steph said. But as soon as Natalia was out of sight, she unzipped her make-up bag and applied exaggerated eye make-up and an extra heavy coat of sheer lip gloss. By the time she'd finished, the look was verging on drag queen, but there was nothing to do but hope Mama was happy with the look. She was already very late.

★　　★　　★

'Hello? Hello?' Steph rang the reception desk bell again and again, scrunching her blistered toes together. Running in knee-high boots, tight jeans and a corset had been near impossible, so halfway down Roppongi Dori she'd given up and slowed to a brisk walk. Plenty of men had turned to stare.

By the time she'd arrived at Sinatra's, she was around half an hour late.

Mama appeared from behind the curtain, and Steph's hand froze over the bell. She'd been expecting the young, male manager and had been confident she could smile and flirt away her lateness. She doubted that Mama, already pouting with irritation, would be so easy to charm.

Please don't cancel my trial.

'I'm so sorry, Mama, I was looking for—'

'Late!' Mama's voice boomed around the reception area. It bounced off the dark vases and sank into the thick carpet. 'Late, *wakaranai*. I came back early from dinner, and you're *late* your very first night.'

'Yes, I know, I—'

'You'll be fined,' said Mama. 'Two hours' wages. And you don't even have a wage yet.' She rubbed tired eyes. 'By the time the week is over, you'll end up owing me money.'

'Fined. Okay. I can still work then.' Steph exhaled with relief. Then the full impact of Mama's words hit her. 'Hang on a minute. *Two* hours' wages?' Steph shook her head. 'You're fining me *two hours*' wages for being, what . . . half an hour late?'

'My club, my rules.'

'Well, they're very unfair rules. I think—'

'Arguing!' Mama shook her head in disbelief.

'Yes, yes, sorry.' Steph tried, unsuccessfully, to sound repentant. 'Two hours from my non-existent wages. Okay, okay. Shall I go in and get started, or . . . ?'

'Wait!' Mama held up a tiny hand as Steph made to walk into the club. 'Let me see what you're wearing.'

Steph pulled her shoulders back and made herself as tall as possible. She'd been hoping to get into the club without her outfit being examined, but perhaps Mama had forgotten about the dress request.

Mama walked around the reception desk and took a sharp intake of breath when she saw Steph's jeans.

'What's this?'

Steph looked down at her jeans.

'This won't do, Steph-chan. This won't do.' Mama waved a finger at her. 'A cocktail dress . . . Where is your cocktail dress?'

Steph blushed. 'Oh, this is just for tonight. My dress . . . my *dresses* got spoilt. I'll do better tomorrow.'

'No, you won't. Sorry, Steph-chan, you can't work like this. *Ni, ni, ni.* Won't do, won't do. I'll have to send you home.'

'No!'

Mama took a step back, surprised.

'Please, Mama. Let me work tonight and I'll have a dress by tomorrow.'

Mama shook her head, and for a moment Steph thought she'd really blown it. But then Mama sighed and took Steph firmly by the wrist.

'You can't hostess in workman's pants,' Mama announced, leading Steph around reception into a changing room, where a Hollywood-style mirror, complete with light bulb frame, lined one of the walls. Any old-school elegance offered by the mirror was ruined by the dressing table, which was made of peeling chipboard. A row of grey, school-corridor-style lockers, dented and scratched, partly blocked the entrance.

When they reached the dressing room, Mama turned on her.

'I should fire you right now,' Mama said, and Steph felt every one of her words. 'Late. Wrong clothes. You begged me for this job.'

'I know I did and I'm sorry—'

'Tonight I should say no more job for you.'

'But Mama—'

'*Hai*!' Mama held her hand up again. 'But you're lucky. We have a big party group and I need extra girls. Lucky, lucky lucky.'

Steph's chest fluttered. *Customers!*

'I'll decide what to do with you at the end of the night,' Mama continued. 'For now you can work, *when* we find you the right clothes to wear and *when* I've fixed your make-up.'

'I've already done my make-up.'

'You need more,' said Mama, pulling an electric-blue dress from one of the lockers and shaking it with care. The dress looked like something Joan Collins might have worn to a movie premiere. An abundance of sequins, sewn into elaborate sprays and fountains, glittered under the soft lighting. There were shoulder pads. Large ones. And puffing fabric at the hips.

'Oh no,' said Steph. 'Please don't make me wear that.'

'Fine.' Mama regarded the dress with a sentimental smile. 'You can go then.'

'No, I didn't mean . . . It's just too small.' Steph reached forward and lifted and arm, which was heavy with beads. 'See?'

'*Ni, ni,* fine, fine.' Mama unzipped the back. 'Try.'

Steph took the dress.

'I'll be back to do your make-up,' said Mama ominously, disappearing through the doorway.

21

Mercifully, the dress zipped up, but it pinched around the waist and under the arms, and the vamp-like points at the end of the sleeves came halfway up Steph's forearms. The skirt, which Steph was sure should be knee-length, hung awkwardly mid-thigh.

Steph put her boots back on and laughed when she looked in the mirror – the dress was so tight she was moving like a puppet.

Mama came back into the room with a case of cosmetics and swept fuchsia-pink blusher over Steph's cheekbones. She filled in her eyelids with peacock blue eye-shadow and thickened Steph's already thick eyebrows with powder. Steph gritted her teeth, thought of all the stupid costumes she'd had to wear during acting auditions and promotions jobs, and avoided looking in the mirror.

'Go wait for Hiro to seat you,' Mama told her. 'Waiting table.'

'Where's the—'

'Go, go.' Mama gave her little pushes towards the door and Steph stumbled out into the club, where a group of eight or so men sat laughing, joking and drinking at a large table by the stage. Some of them were pale and brown-haired and some were Japanese. Two western girls sat with them, pouring drinks and smiling.

Steph was about to take a seat at the large table, when the young Japanese manager appeared beside her. He wore tiny glasses and a panicked expression.

'*Steph-chan*. Girls *do not* seat themselves with customers. Waiting table.'

He clicked his fingers towards the champagne cabinet, and Steph remembered the girls hidden behind it on her first visit to the club. She could see blonde and red hair obscured by glass and champagne bottles, and when she took a step forward she found five girls sitting on a low settee, their legs crossed, faces miserable, some sipping coke from tiny glasses.

The keyboard band on stage played *Blue Velvet* as Steph walked stiffly towards the low couch and took a seat with the other girls, but she'd barely perched on the upholstery before the manager came and whispered to her:

'Steph-chan.'

'Yes?'

'Follow me.'

'Hiro wants you to sit at the customer table,' said one of the girls, her voice cool and disapproving. She had glossy black hair with a fringe, part of which was pinned up in what should have been an elegant arrangement if her hair hadn't been so short. Diamonds sparkled at her collarbone and her dress was red and full-skirted. There was thick make-up on one of her arms, which covered a dirty-looking mark Steph presumed to be a tattoo.

'Fine.' Steph stood up and followed Hiro back to the table of men, where she was offered a seat between a chubby man with whitish-blue eyes and a designer-suited Japanese gentleman with a neat beard. Both men wore loosened ties. As she sat down, the Japanese man patted her thigh.

'What's your name?' he asked, his voice playful. He smelt of cigar smoke.

Steph crossed her legs and leaned away from him. 'Stephanie.' She gave her most charming smile. 'Are you a regular here?'

The man laughed a smoker's laugh, then coughed into his hand.

'You don't even know my name. Why do you want to know if I'm a regular?'

'I just wondered, that's all,' said Steph, feeling a hand on her leg again. This time, the hand belonged to the chubby man on her other side. She leaned back the other way and turned her body completely around to face the Japanese man. 'So, what's your name?'

'Yogi Yamamoto. You call me Mr Yamamoto. What colour is your pubic hair?'

The question took Steph by surprise. 'That's a bit . . . a bit personal, isn't it?'

The man took a cigar from a golden case and shrugged. 'You wanted to know about me. Why shouldn't I get to know *you* better?'

'Whatever. Look, Mr Yamamoto, a friend of mine used to work here. Annabel. I don't suppose . . . I've sort of lost track of her and—'

The man frowned. '*Annabel?* Blonde girl?'

'I don't know,' said Steph. 'She had sort of blondey brown hair when I knew her. And a chubby face with blue eyes.'

'Where was she from?'

'England.'

'Suuurre. Annabel from England. I remember her. Barbie. She was one of my favourite girls here.'

Steph leaned forward. 'I don't suppose you have a number for her, do you? Or know where she went after here? Where's she's working? Living?'

Mr Yamamoto stared straight ahead. 'I don't know where she works now, or where she's living, but I have her number. She was one of my favourite girls. If she's your friend, why don't *you* have her number?'

'I haven't seen her for a long time. Years. And—'

Steph felt a hand tap her on the shoulder. It was Hiro.

'Drink, Steph-chan?'

'Yes, vodka,' said Steph, deciding it was going to be a long night. She lowered her voice to a whisper. '*Can I pay you at the end of the week?*'

'*For what?*' Hiro whispered back.

'*The drink.*'

'Steph-chan.' Hiro shook his head. 'You don't *pay* for your drinks. These men – they pay.'

'Oh.' Steph smoothed her eyebrows, covering her fingertips in black powder in the process. 'Fine. I'll have a vodka then.' She felt a hand pat her thigh again and smacked it away.

'We need shots!' exclaimed Mr Yamamoto. 'Tequila all round.'

'So about Annabel's number . . .'

Mr Yamamoto dismissed the comment with a wave of his hand. 'I've worked hard today. I come here to relax. Maybe when we know each other better, when we trust each other, I pass on friend's number. But not tonight. Tonight we drink.'

An hour later, Steph had consumed two double vodkas and two shots of tequila. Even though the double vodkas came in tiny, doll-sized glasses, the measures were strong and Steph was well on her way to being drunk.

When Hiro came to take her drink order for a third time, Steph pointed to her half-full glass, blinked for just a little bit too long and said,' 'I'm fine, thank you – I already have one.'

'*Steph-chan*,' said Hiro, his tone serious. '*What can I get you to drink?*'

'Really, I'm fine, I—'

'Vodka tonic,' said Hiro, as if Steph hadn't spoken. He knelt down beside her. 'Steph-chan. You always take a drink when offered.'

'Oh, I didn't—'

'And you're not refilling the customer glasses. Make sure the customers never have an empty glass. Look. Yamamoto-san's glass is nearly empty.' Hiro's jacket sleeve skidded up his long arm as he gestured to a three-quarters full glass of whisky-water on the table.

'I wouldn't say it was empty . . . Hiro, do you remember someone called Annabel? She used to work at the club. She's an old friend of mine. I was supposed to be meeting her out here.'

Hiro's jaw went tight. 'Yes. English girl. Very pretty. Very good hostess.'

'Do you know where she went?'

'Different club. She took customers. Mama wasn't happy.'

'Do you know where she is now? Where she's living or anything? Or her phone number?'

'Steph-chan, many girls work here. Many, many girls. When they leave, I don't know where they go. And we don't keep their phone numbers.'

'I don't need to be worried, do I?' Steph asked. 'I mean, girls come and go, no big deal, right?'

'Worried?'

'Because she didn't pay her rent and she left clothes and—'

'Lots of *gaijin* leave Roppongi without paying bills.'

Hiro hurried away, and Steph blinked at the array of whisky bottles and silver ice-filled buckets on the table. A dimply, wholesome-looking hostess sitting opposite winked at her and leaned forward, filling glasses with a splash of whisky from a bottle and adding water from a pineapple-cut, crystal soda syphon. She had thin blonde hair and a high, pale forehead.

'Never let their drinks get low,' she told Steph, pulling a lighter from a little handbag and lighting the cigarette of the man beside her. 'Do you have a lighter?'

Steph smiled and shook her head. 'I'll have to get one. It won't matter for tonight, will it? Can I ask you something? There was a girl who worked here . . .'

'Massa!' The girl broke into a beautiful smile as one of the men tried to stroke her hair. She took his hand and held it firmly in her lap as she sat down.

Yamamoto-san prodded Steph's leg.

'I'll give you ten thousand yen,' he said, 'if you show me your bust.'

'Are you serious?' said Steph.

'Yes.' Mr Yamamoto nodded, his eyes swimming shut, then popping open again. 'Ten thousand yen.' He reached into his suit jacket and pulled out a Louis Vuitton wallet, producing a note from a thick wodge of bills inside.

'How about I show you,' said Steph, looking longingly at the note and thinking of the many meals it could buy her, 'and instead of money, you give me Annabel's phone number?'

Mr Yamamoto frowned and shook his head. 'You haven't learned how we do things in Japan. No. When you're a better hostess, maybe.' He waved the note. 'Cash or nothing.'

'But . . .'

'Okay, nothing.' Mr Yamamoto made to put the note away.

'No, it's okay. Deal.' Steph would have done it for half the price. That sombre-looking note meant a few days grace from fainting in the street. 'Here.' She leaned forward and pulled down the high neck of the dress so the man could see her chest. When she rearranged her dress, she noticed the hostess across the table watching her, horrified.

'Beautiful,' Yamamoto-san breathed, but he held the note tightly in his hand. 'Now, what about your pubic hair.'

Steph snatched the note from his hand. 'You'll have to negotiate some new terms.' She noticed his whisky glass was empty, and wondered from which whisky bottle she should refill it. There were three on the table, all with little wax pendants hanging around their necks. The pendants were each stamped with a different Japanese symbol.

Before she could grab the nearest whisky bottle, Steph noticed some activity over the man's shoulder. The two male waiting staff, one Japanese, one a sun tanned westerner, were piling up what looked like record books on the bar – an innocent enough activity in itself, but the movements were frantic. Then Hiro sprinted across the club, holding his wrists together in some sort of secret signal that the other hostesses seemed immediately to understand.

Steph watched, perplexed, as every girl in the club got to her feet.

The hostess with the lighter whispered to Steph, 'We're being raided.'

'Raided?'

'Follow me,' said the girl.

'Reluctantly Steph stood up. 'I'll be back soon, Mr Yamamoto. We'll talk more maybe . . .'

'Hurry!' The girl grabbed Steph's arm and pulled her towards the back of the club.

22

A cluster of anxious, leggy hostesses stood by the side of the stage and, as Steph joined them, Hiro pushed his way through the group and felt around on the wall. Eventually he found a thick string, painted the same colour as the wall, and pulled it hard.

A hobbit-sized door opened in the wall.

Steph caught herself on the side of the stage as girls surged forward and through the doorway.

'Steph-chan,' Hiro whispered, holding the door open and gesturing for her to follow. 'Police raid. Go in there.' He wiped perspiration from his forehead. 'Quickly please.' There was a stack of books under his arm. 'Go.'

The dark space didn't look inviting. 'Really? Can't I stay out here?' Steph was sure that, given more time, she could persuade Mr Yamamoto to talk about Annabel.

'If you don't, the police will arrest you for illegal working. You'll be deported.'

'Right.' Fair enough. 'All the other girls are going down there too? All of them?'

'Of course. Why?'

'It's just, I can talk to them . . . I mean I can get to know them. Never mind.'

As Steph walked into the dark space, hands outstretched, a thought occurred to her. Maybe Annabel had been deported. She'd been working illegally as a hostess. If she moved to another club, perhaps she'd been caught and forced to leave the country. That would explain why she'd left so many things behind. It might also explain why she hadn't emailed for a while. She had other things on her mind.

Okay, deportation probably wasn't very nice, but it was an explanation, a *good* explanation for Annabel's disappearance.

From the light of the club, Steph could see the floor was metal and patterned with rice-shaped nodules. There was a metal rail, which she grabbed. It was cold to the touch, and led to wedge-shaped steps that spiralled downwards into darkness. Below she could hear the 'clank clank clank' of high heels getting fainter and fainter.

Steph was the last girl into the odd little secret passage and, as her foot touched the first step, Hiro pushed the door shut behind her.

Total darkness.

A little orange light appeared at the bottom of the staircase and Steph headed towards it.

The metal steps spiralled down for a good few metres before Steph reached concrete. It felt gritty under the thin soles of her boots. She could see five girls leaning against what appeared to be the double doors of a fire exit. A sixth girl stood a little apart from them – the same girl who'd been sitting with Steph earlier on – holding a lighter.

'We hardly ever get raided here,' the girl with the lighter told Steph. 'Mama must have lost her touch with the *yakuza*. Is this the first club you've worked in?'

Steph nodded. 'I'm on trial.'

She wondered which girl to ask first about Annabel. Only the lighter girl looked friendly. All the others were glaring at her like she'd stolen their wages. Steph supposed that's exactly what she'd be doing if she started winning customers.

'I'm Jennifer,' said the lighter girl, extending a plump hand. A hair-thin gold chain slid back and forth over the moles on her wrist as Steph shook it. Jennifer's accent was American and she had a broad, handsome face and fine golden hair, long and slightly limp.

'Hi. I'm Steph.'

'Stephanie. What a nice name. Don't worry, we're safe here.'

'Not for me, I was wondering about my friend, Annabel. She used to work here. I thought maybe she'd been deported.'

Jennifer looked thoughtful. 'I remember that name.' She turned to the other hostesses. 'Girls? Annabel?'

One of the hostesses stepped away from the fire exit – the dark-haired one with the tattoo, who'd spoken to Steph earlier.

'Why does she want to know?' she asked.

'*She's* got a name,' said Steph. 'And for your information, Annabel is a friend of mine. We were supposed to be meeting out here, but when I arrived she'd gone. No forwarding address, nothing. It's not like her to be unreliable – at least, it wasn't when I knew her. The sooner I find her the better I'll feel.'

'You've been reading too many newspaper stories,' said the girl. 'Annabel's fine. Girls can look after themselves out here.'

'Did you know her?'

'She left here a long time ago. You should be worrying about yourself. Mama's not going to keep you. There's no room for girls who don't know what they're doing.'

'Do you know where she went? What club she moved to? Where she's living?'

The girl shook her head. 'I don't associate with customer-stealers.'

'That's my friend you're talking about.'

'You know, I couldn't help noticing earlier, Stephanie,' said Jennifer, stepping between Steph and the glossy haired girl and putting a tactful hand on Steph's shoulder, 'it's probably not a good idea to show the customers your body – not if you want to get to know them long term.'

'Why not?'

'It sort of takes away from the mystery.'

'Oh. Right. Mr Yamamoto . . . He's got Annabel's phone number. He said if I got to know him better he might tell me it. I haven't blown it, have I?'

'Don't give her tips,' said the tattooed girl. 'If she messes up, she messes up. One less girl. We don't have enough customers for all of us as it is.' Two of the other girls nodded.

'Let's not get catty about things,' said Jennifer. 'They're not *our* customers, Chastity, they belong to the club.'

'Why hasn't she brought her own customers?' said Chastity.

'I've been here less than an hour,' said Steph. 'What – you think I can magic customers out of thin air? It's my first night. Anyway, I've got other things on my mind. What about you two?' Steph turned to the other girls. 'Do you know where Annabel is?'

Both girls shook their heads and looked away.

'If you don't have customers of your own already, I don't know why Mama hired you,' said Chastity, leaning back against the fire exit. Her face was classically beautiful, with large blue eyes, clear skin and a high forehead. 'Things are tough enough here.'

'I'm sure things will pick up,' said Jennifer, snapping shut the lighter. The darkness was absolute and everyone fell quiet as they heard men's voices above.

'Don't worry,' Jennifer whispered to Steph. 'She doesn't like the competition. Tell me about yourself – why did you come to Tokyo?'

'What's going on up there?' asked Steph.

'Oh, just a police raid. Mama will sort it. We'll be back upstairs and working before you know it.'

'When can we go back up?'

'Soon,' said Jennifer. The voices above them died down. 'But until then we have to hide. None of us have work visas. But that's the way with all Roppongi hostess clubs. It scared me at first too–'

'I'm not scared.'

'Oh. Well, I was. When we were first raided. I thought I was in such big trouble, I'd be deported. But then . . . It's funny how you get used to things.'

'But don't girls get deported?'

'Hardly ever,' said Jennifer. 'If they did, we'd all know about it. The Roppongi grapevine.'

'So no one's been deported recently?'

Jennifer shook her head.

There was a click upstairs and a strip of light appeared above them.

'Girls,' Hiro hissed from the top of the staircase. 'You can come back up now.'

By 3 a.m., the club was closing up and Steph was drunk. Really drunk. The police raid had been so artfully dealt with that none of the customers seemed at all troubled by the girls' sudden disappearance and, on their return, the party had soon got back into full swing. Drink after drink had been ferried to the table, and shots of tequila presented alongside potent spirit and soft drink mixes.

On several occasions, Steph, Jennifer and a third hostess, Helena, had been urged to slow dance with the customers to the sounds of the keyboard band, with Mama insisting quietly that dancing '*makes customers thirsty*'.

Steph had stood as gracefully as she could with Mr Yamamoto and swayed around the floor with the other hostesses and their customers, but no matter how many times she asked, Mr Yamamoto wouldn't talk about Annabel. Eventually he became angry, and Steph realised she'd better drop it. It wouldn't be long before she could talk to Julia, anyway.

When the song finished, Steph had lifted her arms to applaud and felt a disconcerting rip under her armpit. Cool air had flowed over her arm and soon blue threads and sequins were hanging loose. Mama wouldn't be happy.

When the evening drew to a close and bills were totalled, Steph fell over on her way to the toilet and the arm of the dress almost came away. It hung on the shoulder pad by a few taut threads.

A quick look in the toilet mirror showed brows no longer neat and Liz Taylor styled, but a mess of black powder. Her lipstick had all but rubbed off, save for a pale line of red pencil decorating her cupid's bow. In short, she was drunk and messy. Not the ideal look for confronting her friend and asking why she was acting like a spaced-out junkie.

As the last customers left, Hiro called her over to the bar.

'Steph-chan.'

'Hiro.'

'Mama's not happy.'

'Oh.'

'Steph-chan, you were not a good hostess tonight.'

'But . . . they had a good time.'

The men at her table had had a great night, she was sure. A few customers had to ask to have their drinks refilled because she hadn't noticed they'd run dry, and she hadn't been able to light cigarettes, but it was her first night, after all.

'Steph-chan, good hostesses pour drinks, take care of the customers . . . You did nothing but drink and make too much noise.'

'But that's what the customers want, isn't it?' Steph was too confused to be angry. 'Girls to have a good time with? Otherwise, what are we here for?'

'You're here to look after the customers, not have a good time. Mama doesn't have work for girls like you. I'm sorry, but unless you bring a *dohan* tomorrow night, the trial is finished.'

'*Tomorrow* night? But that's . . . that's impossible. Mama said Saturday. Please. It was supposed to be Saturday.'

Hiro shook his head. 'Tomorrow night, Steph-chan. If you have a *dohan* tomorrow night, Mama will keep you. But if you don't bring a dinner-date customer, then please don't come into the club.' He nodded at the trailing sleeve on Steph's dress. 'And have that dress fixed. It's one of Mama's favourites.'

Steph blinked and a wave of dizziness and depression washed over her. Having the dress fixed was the least of her problems. How was she ever going to find someone to take her to dinner and on to Sinatra's by tomorrow night? It was almost funny to think she'd come over here to earn thousands of pounds. Right now she didn't even have money for her first rent payment at the end of the week.

In a daze, Steph wandered into the changing room and nearly fell over again as she tried to pull herself free of the dress. Jennifer had left already and the other girls avoided Steph so she changed without talking to anyone, bundled the dress under her arm and headed up to the street. It was time to talk to Julia.

23

The lights of Calamity Janes were dim when Steph arrived, and the bouncer was locking the club's ornate, wooden doors.

'Hey,' Steph called, running up to the doors. 'You're not closing already?'

The bouncer didn't turn around. 'The club always closes at this time.'

Steph tasted tequila in her throat and checked her watch. She was so drunk she hadn't even thought about the time. *Oh no. I've missed her again.* 'I don't suppose you know where Julia went, do you?'

'No.'

The bouncer put the keys in his pocket and pushed past her to the street, which was still crowded despite the late hour.

Steph sat on the steps of the club and put her head in her hands.

'Bad night, *chérie*?'

Steph peered through her fingers and saw a bleary vision of a young, sandy-haired man bouncing up and down on his toes.

'You just started at Sinatra's, right?' The man was in his late twenties, but his face was heavily lined as though he spent every day of his life in the sun. His accent was Australian and he was good-looking, in a scruffy sort of way.

Steph sighed and pulled her head out of her hands, messy red hair falling around her face. 'Yes. What's it to you?'

'I saw you there tonight,' said the man, taking a seat on the step beside her. 'I'm Luke. One of the barmen. You probably didn't notice me – I was stuck in the corner mixing drinks. How are things going? Are the girls being friendly?'

'Jennifer was nice,' said Steph.

'Yeah, she's sweet.'

Steph put her head back in her hands.

'So what brings you to Tokyo?' asked Luke.

'Money,' said Steph.

'That's what they all say.'

'They're probably much better at getting it than I am,' said Steph. 'I've been here two days and if it wasn't for the tip I got tonight I'd be flat broke.'

'What are you earning money for?' asked Luke.

Steph looked up. 'There's this course I want to take. *Need* to take. A new start. I'm an actress, and people judge you on your reputation and . . . Anyway, to be honest, I'm not even thinking about all that right now. I'm looking for my friend Julia. She works here. I'm worried about her, to tell you the truth. She's acting funny.'

Smile lines appeared around Luke's eyes. 'Most people here care about themselves first, money second and everyone else last.'

'And they probably do really well, pay their rent and earn good money,' said Steph.

'Sometimes,' said Luke. 'But what's it worth, if you lose yourself at the end of it all.'

'I won't lose myself,' said Steph. 'If I'm lucky enough to earn good money out here, I'll still be me.'

'Roppongi changes people. Let's see if you're still saying that in a month.'

'I might be homeless in a month. Mama's got me on an unpaid trial.'

'Unpaid? That's a pretty lousy deal.'

'You can say that again.' Steph pushed her hair back and the gesture made her dizzy. 'And it gets worse. Mama's getting rid of me unless I get a *dohan* by tomorrow night. Anyway, look, I really don't care about any of that right now. I need to speak to Julia, but I don't have her number, her club's closed and I don't have the faintest idea where she is.' Steph put her head in her hands again. 'Nice to meet you though,' she said, her voice muffled though her fingertips.

'Your friend Julia. She works at Janes?'

Steph nodded in her hands.

'You know, the Janes girls always go to the Hollywood Bar after work – it's part of their contract.'

Steph lifted her head. 'Sorry, what was that?'

'Their contract. When Janes closes, they go sit for an hour at Hollywoods, sometimes bring customers, sometimes not. Make the bar look like it's full of pretty girls. It's just around the corner.'

Steph sat up, feeling like a string had pulled her upright.

'Really? Around the corner?'

'You want me to show you?'

'No, it's fine,' Steph smoothed down her hair and got to her feet. 'I'm fine. I'll find it.'

Hollywoods was similar to Calamity Janes from the outside, with the same golden lions gracing its red-carpet lined steps. However, the bar was altogether lighter and more open. Steph could see pool tables, a casino game and flat-screen TVs decorating the gold-tinted walls inside. A boxing match was being broadcast on the biggest TV screen and western men were crowded around, watching with blank eyes and downturned mouths.

Luke was right about the pretty girls inside. There were dozens of them, and the majority weren't just averagely good-looking, they were stunning. Granted, most of them had clearly worked hard on their appearance – flawless make-up, breast enhancements, supremely groomed and styled hair, waxed and dyed eyebrows, expensive outfits and jewellery – but the overall effect was beauty. Generic beauty, but beauty none the less.

The men, on the other hand, weren't quite so crowd-stopping. They were largely middle-aged (and in some cases verging on elderly), with dated haircuts and sagging stomachs.

At the bar sat a girl with blonde hair cut in a sharp line halfway down her back. She had a pixie face that looked Botox-frozen, and rested a frail hand on the stem of a wine glass.

It was Julia. A very odd, tired-looking Julia, but it definitely was her.

Steph went over to her. 'Hey.'

Julia turned her head, but not her body. 'Steph.' She fidgeted on her stool, and glanced over Steph's shoulder at the other girls in the bar. 'What are you doing here?'

'Thanks for yesterday,' said Steph. 'Pretending you didn't know who I was.'

Julia took a large gulp of white wine from the chilled glass in front of her.

'Look, are you okay?' said Steph. 'You're . . . I mean, you don't seem like yourself. I'm worried about you. And Annabel. She wasn't at the apartment when I arrived and—'

Julia didn't meet her eye. 'Let's talk outside.'

On the street it had started to rain, so they stood under the gold plastic overhang that sheltered the bar entrance. Julia stared straight ahead, apparently fascinated by the fluorescent tube silhouette of a naked woman on the strip club opposite. The light flashed on and off, on and off.

'Is everything okay?' Steph asked. 'You look weird, you sound weird. Is something going on out here?'

Julia's face remained expressionless. 'No. Everything's fine.'

'You don't look fine. And where's Annabel?'

'I don't know. She's her own person. I'm not her shadow.'

'When did you last see her? Seriously, Julia, she left her diary behind and her clothes. We need to make sure she's okay. It's strange.'

'It's not strange. Probably she just moved apartments. I told you, she's her own person.'

'Well, I think it's strange. I'm worried. I just want to find out where she is. Make sure she's okay.'

Two heavily made-up girls in tight, slinky dresses came out of the bar behind them, each on the arm of a different Japanese man.

'Your turn on Saturday, Julia,' one of the men whispered as he passed, and Julia stiffened. The girl on his arm, a sour-faced 20-something with a pronounced jaw, seemed to recognise Julia too and gave her a nod.

The other girl, a redhead with porcelain skin and bright pink lips, spoke to Julia in a loud Russian accent:

'Do you have a contract client tomorrow?'

Julia nodded.

'Me too,' said the girl, inclining her head towards her drunken companion, 'him.'

'You're on contract now?' said Julia, lowering her voice. A private look passed between them.

The girl glanced at Steph, then nodded.

Two green taxis pulled up and the couples climbed inside. Through an open window, Steph heard the red-headed girl tell the taxi driver in her loud Russian accent: 'Prince Regent Hotel – follow the one in front.'

The cabs drove off towards the main road.

Steph watched them go. 'Are they girls from your club?'

Julia nodded and took out a cigarette.

'Do you . . . Is that something you do?'

'What?' Julia lit her cigarette with a trembling hand.

'You know, go to hotels with customers. They *were* customers, weren't they? The men those girls were with?'

Julia took two deep inhalations of her cigarette and blew smoke towards the floor.

'Look Steph, I didn't ask you to come here, and—'

'What is *with* you? Don't you care about Annabel? And what's with the attitude?'

'Just . . . It's none of your business what goes on in my club. And don't worry about Annabel. If she didn't leave you a number, she doesn't want to meet up with you. End of.'

'But I haven't even *seen* her. Something could have happened. Have you seen her recently?'

Julia shrugged. 'Look, I'm not . . . Every girl needs to look after herself, so worry about keeping yourself safe.'

Steph stared at her friend, not wanting to believe the difference in her. Where was the fun, lively girl she'd known back home? And didn't she care at all about their old school friend?

'Excuse me for breathing, it's just I care about her that's all. And you. You don't seem yourself. Is your club—'

'You don't need to worry about me either,' said Julia. 'I'm fine. Better than fine. I'm earning so much money it's stupid and I'm having a great time out here. Party every night.'

'What about yesterday?' said Steph. 'Acting like you didn't know me. What's up with that? Your boss must think I'm mad.'

'Steph. It's . . . Look, no offence but . . . I was embarrassed. Janes is out of your league. I mean look at you – no labels, turning up in jeans with your hair a mess, what did you expect me to do? You've heard of failure by association. I'm doing well there, really well. I'm nearly the top girl.'

Steph stared at her. Julia had always been . . . Well, not snobby — she wasn't really posh enough to be snobby — but . . . cliquey. It hadn't bothered Steph back home, but maybe that's because she'd never expected the cliquey-ness to be directed at her.

Julia took a series of rapid puffs from her cigarette and watched the rain bouncing off the pavement. 'Did you find a job in the end?'

'Yes,' said Steph. 'I did, as a matter of fact.' There was no way she was telling Julia her job at Sinatra's was an unpaid trial.

'Really? Where?'

'Sinatra's.'

Julia gave a little laugh. 'Are they still taking on girls? I heard that place was dead.' Her face became expressionless again. 'Look, you don't understand how it works out here. The girls at Janes make the most money, so all the girls at all the other clubs want to work at Janes. That's just how it is. I didn't want Ricky thinking I was bringing all my friends in, trying to get them jobs when they're not Janes material. You can lose your place at Janes just like that.' Julia tapped her cigarette butt. 'One mistake and you're out.'

Steph felt something uneasy stir inside. She wanted to make money – it was true. That was the reason she was here. And if the girls at Julia's club made the most money, the truth was she *did* want to work there.

'Well, I could work at your place,' said Steph, thinking of the girls who got into the taxi cab. 'I don't see how I'm so different. I just need to get the make-up and clothes right.'

Julia shook her head. 'Don't even waste your time trying. Look at your scars. The girls at Janes are supposed to be perfect.'

'That's *really* out of order.'

'I'm just being honest.'

'Are you on drugs or something?'

Julia's frozen cheeks rippled slightly.

'And who are you to be so superior about Janes,' said Steph, 'when it's obvious the girls are sleeping with their customers?'

'So what if they are?' said Julia.

Steph put her hands on her hips. 'It's not comparing like with like, is it? If you have to sleep with your customers, it's a totally different job.'

'We don't *have* to sleep with customers,' said Julia. 'Some girls do, some girls don't. Just like at your club, probably. Anyway, like I said. There's a certain standard of girl at Janes, and you don't fit. So I was embarrassed. Sorry. Maybe we could meet up for coffee sometime.'

Steph thought of all the fun times she and Julia had shared, school, college, the various promotions jobs they'd worked on together, handing out flyers, giving away free product samples . . . No matter how bad the job, Julia always had a high opinion of herself – it was how she coped with life – but out here her arrogance seemed to overshadow all the nice parts of her.

'I can't believe how selfish you sound,' said Steph. 'And to think I was worried about you. All you care about is yourself.'

'That's life,' said Julia. 'You've got to look out for number one or you end up at the bottom of the bonus chart.'

'Do you know what, Julia?' said Steph. 'I think I'll pass on that coffee.'

24

When Steph woke up the next morning, headachy and hung over, she could hear scuttling inside the apartment walls. Cockroaches. She hoped there weren't rats. Overhead, the air-conditioning unit whirred and clicked, blasting out warm air that hurt her chest.

She lay, staring up into windowless darkness, thinking about Annabel. Julia was a worry too, but she'd made it clear she wanted Steph to keep out of her business. Well, fine. There wasn't much Steph could do about that. But she was determined to find Annabel, even if, as Julia said, she didn't want to be contacted. Then Steph could put her mind at rest and get on with the serious business of making money.

Below her, Natalia snored gently and murmured 'Dolce and Gabbana'.

Steph slid off the bunk, feeling bumpy lino beneath her bare feet, and rummaged in her rucksack for the diary. There was a hidden pocket at the back for her passport and money, and Steph slid her hand into it and pulled out the blue book. She crouched for a moment, wondering if she was crossing any moral boundary by reading her friend's personal thoughts. *No*, she decided. *I'm just making sure she's safe. I'll stop reading as soon as I find a way to contact her.*

Once Steph had retrieved her clothes from under her duvet, she decided to use some of her 10,000 yen to buy breakfast at Café Almond – the garish pink and white cake shop she'd noticed on the corner of Roppongi crossroads. Reading in the apartment hurt her eyes.

In the crisp sunshine, she breathed air that tasted of iron and heard angry traffic grinding along, but it was a relief to get out into daylight, and away from the smells of mould and burnt cheese that lingered in the apartment hallway.

Café Almond was almost full when Steph entered, and a crowd of midday lunch goers were enjoying pastries and coffees, all served with an *oshibori*, or moistened hand towel, which customers used to wipe Roppongi smog from their hands and faces. There were dozens of intriguing cakes and pastries on sale behind a long glass counter, and Steph chose a layered apple tart dusted with icing sugar and cinnamon, and a cappuccino, before taking a seat by the floor-to-ceiling glass window. The crowds outside, *sararimen* and young Japanese couples, paid no attention to the red-headed *gaijin* with a notebook on the table in front of her.

Steph opened the diary and began to read.

Dear God,

Stalked! How stupid am I? I scared myself so badly about that guy and I'm being scouted. Duh!!! He's a scout for Calamity Janes. Who'd have guessed they'd be interested in me?

Thank you God, really I am so grateful. Calamity Janes only takes on really pretty girls. But I'm not interested in that place – it's got a bad rep and I'm fine where I am.

You see, Steph reprimanded herself. *You're worrying about nothing.* But still she read on, intrigued by the reference to Calamity Janes.

So hungover today – why did I agree to drink with him? So stupid. I wasn't even being paid for it and I don't want to work for that club. I didn't want any more champagne, as if I don't get enough of that stuff. I think he was angry I wouldn't do the trial, which I feel bad about. I hate people being angry at me. He'd put all this time into watching me and following me around and I go and say no.

Hayley thinks I should have said yes, but I've never heard anything good about Janes. It's not like other hostess clubs, they let anyone in and it's all about how much the girls drink.

Lots of girls want to work at Janes because they make so much money, but it just didn't feel right to me. I see them at Hollywoods and they look like models, but they're always so tired and rude. No wonder, all those extra hours at Hollywoods after work, and Hayley says some of them work days too.

That explains why Julia looks so tired, Steph thought. Although she couldn't help wondering if there was something else going on, something more than a few late nights.

He was so pushy. Going on and on about all the money I could make. It's true, if I brought my customers to Janes (stole them from Mama) I could make loads. OK, I'll admit I was tempted. So many debts. But Janes keep your passport so if you hate it you can't leave and that scares me.

I always think of Cassie when I think of Janes too. So sweet, but *sake* first thing in the morning after two weeks at that place. Some really odd men go in there, real perverts and some of the girls have had their drinks spiked at work.

Drink spiking. Nothing out of the common in the bar scene. Still, if girls had their drinks spiked while they were working, it didn't say much for the care Janes showed its hostesses. No wonder Julia was acting so tough – it was probably a survival mechanism.

God please help me keep my customers because without them I'm nothing to Mama. She's so mean if you don't have customers. She bullied Tanya to get more *dohans* until she was so unhappy she ended up getting alcohol poisoning.

Steph's forehead began to throb at the mention of Mama and *dohans*. It was strange to think Annabel had worked at Sinatra's too, for the same Mama-san. Steph wondered if Annabel had

ever had her make-up done for her, or a blonde wig forced on
her head. Somehow she doubted it.

Panic swept over her as she thought of the impossible tasks to
be done before tonight. Magic a *dohan* out of thin air and repair
Mama's dress. Even if she possessed a needle and thread, Steph
had no idea how to sew. And *dohan* . . . Impossible. She may as
well resign now, but then what? With no rent money, no return
flight and no job, what would she do? Sleep in shop doorways
and beg for her flight money home?

Keep me safe on *dohan*. I have so many of them now and
I'm getting careless. Hazard of the job. It doesn't even freak
me out anymore getting in guys' cars.

Ken tonight in . . . wow, only two hours. My sexy chief
executive. He brings me the nicest presents, but he was SO
trying to get me drunk last time.

I think he's forgiven me now about that email, but he
could have warned me to only use his Asahi address. I hope
he smoothed things over with his wife. I'd feel so guilty if
anything happened.

That's the trouble with hostessing, you've got to be really
pushy, emailing guys, phoning them, texting them, and it
can go wrong sometimes and you feel really stupid. But
mainly it does work. Not like back home, if I chased after
guys in England like I do here they'd run a mile.

Look after my family back home. Don't let them ever
find out what I'm getting up to here.

Xxxx

Steph closed the book and took a sip of cappuccino. It didn't
agree with her alcohol-shrivelled stomach, but she took a second
sip anyway. *Now be sensible,* she thought. *Don't stress about the*
'keep me safe on *dohans*' *thing – it doesn't necessarily mean anything.*
She scanned the page again.

Ken. A chief executive. Who works for Asahi.

Steph had seen the Asahi logo on rows of beer cans in the
Family Mart convenience store down the street. If she could get

the company number and ask to speak to Ken, the chief executive, then maybe . . .

She cut a forkful of apple cake and stuffed it into her mouth, chewing quickly before she could think too much about it. There was a yellowing computer back at the apartment with a heavy, cube-shaped screen. It was covered in dust and she'd never seen anyone use it, but she guessed it was hooked up to the internet. *Asahi, Asahi.*

She took a final bite of cake and a sip of cooling cappuccino, and left.

'May I speak to Ken, please?' Having slid a phone card into the green pay phone, Steph stood as tall as she could. 'Standing tall' was a confidence-boosting technique from a course called *How to Succeed at Auditions.* Neither the course, nor the technique, had helped her succeed.

There was a pause as the Japanese receptionist deciphered Steph's words.

'Ken. Do you have a second name?'

'Your chief executive.'

'May I ask who's calling?'

'It's a personal call,' said Steph.

'One moment please.'

Vivaldi's *Four Seasons* played and then, to Steph's astonishment, a male voice clicked on to the line.

'Yes?'

'Ken. Hi.' Steph moved further inside the plastic helmet that surrounded the phone. 'I'm . . . It's . . . I work at Sinatra's. I'm Steph.'

'Sorry, I don't remember you.' There was a pause. 'Did you say Sinatra's?'

'Yes.'

'I haven't been there for a long time. How is Mama-san?'

'Oh, she's good. You know. The same as always. Um . . . Ken, I was wondering. I'm trying to track down Annabel. A friend of mine. I know the two of you were . . . friendly. I don't suppose, do you have a phone number for her or email?'

'Annabel?'

The line was silent for a moment and Steph thought Ken had hung up.

'Hello?'

'Hello. Yes, I'm still here.' Another pause. 'I remember Annabel. I saw her just last week. In a bar in Roppongi.'

'Really?' A grin spread across Steph's face. 'Just last week? That's brilliant. Thank God! Do you have a number for her?'

'No. She moved to a different club. Months ago.'

'Oh.' Steph looked down at the floor. A Tully's paper coffee cup rolled back and forth in an arc around her feet. 'Do you know which club?'

'I don't visit other clubs so I don't know. Girls change clubs, but Mama-san is the one I come to see. You said you're working at Sinatra's?'

'Yes, that's right.'

'Mmmm. *Staff*, did you say?'

'Steph.'

'Blonde hair?'

'Um . . . Depends on the light.'

'I haven't seen Mama for a long time. Maybe I'll come in tonight.'

'Oh.' Steph pushed the receiver into her ear. 'Really?' Annabel's words raced before her eyes. *You have to call guys, email them, ask them out on dohan.* 'Um, you know,' she continued, 'if you're thinking of coming in tonight, I don't suppose you fancy taking me out before, do you? As *dohan*?'

There was another long pause. Then Ken said, 'You're a friend of Annabel's?'

'Yes,' said Steph, finding she was gripping the phone unnecessarily tightly.

'Okay. Why not?'

'What time shall we meet?'

'Er . . . Let's say six p.m.? Café Almond?'

'Okay. See you then.'

Steph hung up the phone with a clack. She couldn't believe it.

After such a terrible, depressing start, now there were two lots of good news at once.

Annabel was still in Roppongi and had been seen only last week. That was the best news. She wouldn't relax until she'd seen her friend personally, but the dreadful, nagging worry that had been keeping her company since she'd found Annabel's diary had eased. And Ken had agreed to a *dohan*. Tonight. She *really* couldn't believe that.

A few minutes ago she'd been picturing herself outside McDonalds begging for change. Now there was a chance, just a chance, that she could keep her job. And if Mr Yamamoto was in the club again, she could keep working on him for Annabel's phone number.

Now there was just the small matter of the dress. And there was only one person she could think of who could help with that.

25

'So.' Mrs Kimono held open the door as Steph approached her shop. 'Something told me you'd be back. The trial didn't go so well?'

'It was okay.' Steph forced a smile. 'I have a favour to ask. A dress that needs mending. Like really quickly. I'm happy to pay for it, but I'll need time to—'

'How intriguing.'

Steph nodded and withdrew the electric-blue dress from her leather shoulder bag.

'Do you think it's fixable?'

'Yes.' Mrs Kimono pinched a few stray threads between her fingers. 'You'd better come in.' She slid the door back further.

Steph entered the familiar room, with its rolls of colourful fabric and smell of silk and flowers. Mrs Kimono was as elegantly dressed as before, this time in a white kimono covered with winding tree branches. The gnarled embroidery of wood was tipped with red leaves and a pale moon shone behind the branches.

'Have you found out what happened to the girl you spoke about?' asked Mrs Kimono. 'The one who left clothes behind?'

'Yes. I spoke to one of her customers. He saw her just last week. She's still in Roppongi.'

'I thought she'd be okay,' said Mrs Kimono with a nod. 'As okay as any girl can be in Roppongi.'

'I still want to meet up with her, though. Just to make absolutely sure she's okay. One of the club customers has her phone number. I need to get to know him better so he'll give it to me.'

Mrs Kimono went to the counter where a pair of scissors rested beside a measuring tape. 'Give me your dress.' She took the pile of sequins and beads from Steph's hands and began turning the fabric around. 'Only here?' she asked, when she found the tear at the armpit.

'Yes.' Steph nodded at the dangling threads. 'I have to tell you, I haven't been paid for my shift yet, so I won't be able to pay you right away.'

Mrs Kimono gazed at the fabric as if it, not Steph, had spoken to her.

'It's an old dress,' she said. 'Well made. Not like the clothes you see today.' She checked the label and smiled. 'Ah! I knew it. Comme des Garcons. A Japanese designer. She used to make only black and white clothing, this designer, but when the eighties came along she followed the fashion for bright colours.' Mrs Kimono sat on a little stool behind the counter and let the dress rest in front of her. 'Where did you get it?'

'Mama loaned it to me,' said Steph, feeling awkward as she stood in the middle of the shop. Mrs Kimono's rigid posture made her feel like a slouchy teenager.

'Your Mama-san. Really?' Mrs Kimono let the beads and sequins run through her fingers. 'That was very good of her, wasn't it? And yet you damaged it.'

'It wasn't on purpose.'

'Carelessness is carelessness,' said Mrs Kimono, pulling out a drawer and removing a selection of blue thread reels in different shades. She laid them on the dress. Then she looked Steph straight in the eye.

'So tell me how your trial *really* went.'

Steph's throat grew tight and she felt unexpected tears at this concern from a stranger.

'Why do you care?'

Mrs Kimono put both hands flat on the fabric. 'I told you. You're someone's daughter. I had a daughter too.'

'May I . . . Did something happen to your daughter?'

Mrs Kimono turned to the window. 'Yes. I lost her to Roppongi.'

'Did she . . .' Steph wasn't sure how to finish the sentence.

'She's still alive,' said Mrs Kimono with a smile. 'But I was too proud and now it's too late.' Mrs Kimono turned back to Steph. 'Tell me how your trial went.'

'Not great,' Steph admitted. 'I didn't do things right, I don't know why. And the men were really sleazy. It was hard to handle. I didn't know what to say half the time.'

'Ah.' Mrs Kimono nodded, and placed two of the reels back in her drawer. From the third reel, she pulled a length of cotton and snipped it free with her sharp scissors. She threaded a needle and began making microscopic stitches into the cloth. 'It's not so easy, is it? Serving men. Being a plaything. Not so simple.'

'I don't know who to trust, how to act, I've got things so wrong before. Are men ever okay?'

'Of course they are,' said Mrs Kimono, 'but if you're serving them, entertaining them, they become different creatures. They've paid for your services. What's important is to lead, to control without appearing to control. You need to be strong. To protect yourself without losing your femininity. Quite an art form.' Mrs Kimono made more stitches into the blue dress and pulled them tight so the sleeve fitted neatly back into the bodice. 'What did you expect? The *mizu shobai* life is hard.'

Steph nodded, thinking Mrs Kimono really didn't understand what she'd been through, but for some reason welcoming her commentary. The woman was cold and sharp like rock, but she seemed to talk to a part of Steph that needed company.

'Hard, like bad things happen to girls hard?'

'Tokyo is safe and so is Roppongi . . . But there are foreign bars here. Places for *gaijin* and *gaijin* have their own rules.'

'Is being a *geisha* hard?' Steph asked.

Mrs Kimono smiled, just a little, and kept sewing. 'Being a *geisha* is very, very hard. Training is hard, working is hard. My training was harder than most, and perhaps my early years were harder too.'

'Have you always worked in Tokyo?'

'No. I trained in Kyoto, like most *geisha*.'

'And then you came here for work?'

'No. When I finished my training I took work in a small town, a few hours from Kyoto.'

'Why didn't you work in Kyoto?' asked Steph.

'I was nearly thirty when I finished my training. And my teahouse closed down just as I turned my collar. Do you know what that means, to turn your collar?'

Steph shook her head.

'When *maiko* – that is, trainee *geisha* – complete their *geisha* training they undergo *erikae*, the turning of the collar. It's a very special ceremony. The *maiko* exchanges her red trainee collar for the white collar of the *geisha*. It means she's ready to practise properly as a *geisha*.'

'Oh.' Steph nodded. 'Is that when they get good at dealing with men?'

'It takes many years before a *maiko* can truly control her men,' said Mrs Kimono. 'Other things come first.'

'I don't have years. I need this guy to give me Annabel's number now.'

'*Maiko* must train very hard,' said Mrs Kimono, looking closely at the fabric and making tiny, loopy stitches. 'Life is tough. They wear heavy kimonos and hair pieces and sleep on metal neck braces to stop their hair from being spoiled. They must sit for many hours in the same position, and if they don't sit correctly, most likely their tutor will hit them with something hard until they adopt the correct posture.'

'That sounds terrible,' said Steph. 'Why would anyone go through that?'

'Why go through anything? Training is always hard.'

'Acting training wasn't hard,' said Steph. 'It was fun.'

'Then maybe you weren't doing it right,' said Mrs Kimono, pulling the thread tight and using the scissors to snip it cleanly against the cloth.

'The auditions,' said Steph. 'They're the hard part. Getting rejected all the time. And if you mess up, like I did, you can ruin your image. Be typecast. Seen in a certain way. You've got to keep proving yourself over and over again.'

'Maybe that's the real training,'

'So what happened?' asked Steph. 'When your teahouse closed?'

'No other teahouse in Kyoto would take me,' said Mrs Kimono. 'I found work in an *onsen* town. A holiday resort place. The sort of place people come to drink and have fun. Not dignified. All the girls smoking, smoking, no care for their kimonos or make-up. It wasn't the sort of work most *geisha* dream of, but I could practise my dance and music.'

'And then what?'

'I practised for many years. I learned how to control my dancing and my customers. When I came back to Kyoto, people could see the love I had for my profession. A teahouse took me in. That isn't the usual way. Usually a *maiko* trains with her teahouse and works for her teahouse. My situation was unusual. I was very proud. Too proud.'

'So how did you end up in Tokyo?'

Mrs Kimono cut away loose thread and held the dress up to the light. 'I moved here to be with my daughter. But she doesn't want to know me. Too much water under the bridge, as you say in the west.'

'Why doesn't she—'

'It's rude to ask questions.' Mrs Kimono stroked the seam of the dress. 'There,' she said. 'Perfect.' She folded the dress quickly and neatly into a square parcel and presented it to Steph.

'Thank you. Thank you so much. Now I've got a chance. I can't tell you how badly I need work right now, and without this dress . . . I promise I'll pay you for this, but at the moment—'

'It's really okay,' said Mrs Kimono. 'No charge.'

'Thank you, I—'

'So,' Mrs Kimono interrupted, 'I'm sorry to hear your work isn't going well.'

'So how can I do better? How am I ever going to win customers like the other girls do? Earn proper money?'

'You need training,' said Mrs Kimono.

'It's not even about earning money for my course any more,'

said Steph, her eyes growing warm. 'I just need to pay my rent, buy food . . . normal things. I came out here with this big stupid dream, and in two days I have less than when I started.'

'Not that training. You don't need any more of *that* training. You've trained for *many* years already.'

'No, I really do need more. You don't understand how it is with acting. It's really hard.'

'All the training in the world won't stop it being hard,' said Mrs Kimono. 'I was referring to training in the way of men. Do you think someone could act without any training at all?'

'No.'

'Then why do you think it's any different working as a hostess?'

'I don't. I mean, I hadn't thought about it. I thought I'd learn at work I suppose, but I know I've got a long way to go.'

'You're on a trial, correct?'

'Yes.'

'So they don't have time to let you train at your work, otherwise they'd have hired you full-time. If you don't train quickly, you'll be fired.'

'Thanks for your optimism,' said Steph. 'As if I didn't have enough to worry about. If you remember, I asked you for help before, and you said no.'

'I didn't say I wouldn't help.' Mrs Kimono turned and went to the shop door. 'You're somebody's daughter. I would help you if I could. But your attitude – you're not ready yet.'

'Please,' said Steph. 'Last night . . . It all went really badly, and the truth is I don't know how to do any better. The other host-esses, it was like they were speaking a different language with the men. They looked like the wives or girlfriends of whichever man they spoke to. I was just a guest at the party.'

Mrs Kimono tilted her head.

'If I don't do well tonight I'll be fired,' Steph continued. 'And then I'll have nothing. By Saturday I won't even have a place to stay. I have *dohan* tonight – what if I mess it up before I even get to the club?'

Mrs Kimono's hand fell away from the door. She crossed her

arms and gave Steph a long, appraising stare. 'I have an event planned this afternoon,' she said. 'Perhaps . . . perhaps it would be helpful for you if you joined me. You could learn something about serving others.'

'Anything—'

'So rude! You should tell me it would be a pleasure to join me, or politely decline if you already have plans.'

Steph sighed. 'Okay. Sorry. I'm really not as rude as you think I am. Back in England people think I'm quite polite.'

'Well, to me you're rude,' said Mrs Kimono. 'Are you free to join me this afternoon?'

'I don't know. I should still be looking for my friend, really.'

'You don't want help now?' Mrs Kimono gave a cold smile.

'Yes, of course. Of course I do.'

'Then you'll join me this afternoon. I'm teaching some students in the way of the tea. The Japanese tea ceremony. I think it would be good for you to join us and to learn how to serve tea. It will help you understand what's expected of you as a hostess. This customer of yours—'

'Mr Yamamoto.'

'Yamamoto-san. He sounds like a true Japanese man. If you want to invite confidences with him, you need to understand more about the way we do things in Japan.'

Steph felt pulled in two directions. A tea ceremony sounded like a complete waste of time, nothing to do with hostessing. But, with only 9000 yen in her pocket and rent due soon, she couldn't be too picky about the type of help she was offered. And, in her own way, Mrs Kimono was being kind.

'Okay,' Steph said. 'Fine. Teach me whatever it is you think I need to learn.'

26

'You hold classes here?' asked Steph, as she and Mrs Kimono walked over beige and brown carpet tiles and past giant vases of orange flowers. They were in Hotel Blossom, a five-star establishment just minutes from Mrs Kimono's shop. With its giant chains of paper lanterns suspended from the ceiling, the hotel certainly looked traditionally Japanese, but wasn't the scholarly setting Steph had been expecting.

'Yes. Once a week,' Mrs Kimono replied, leading Steph into a room filled with pots of dried flowers. At its centre was a striking rock fountain with trickles of water running around spiky crags of grey stone to a bed of gravel below. A large window looked out on to a roof terrace of exquisitely combed sand and a curving, squat tree with fiery yellow and red leaves. 'Welcome to my school. Beautiful, isn't it?'

'This is it?' said Steph. There were no plug sockets, tables or chairs in the room. In the corner was a small door, which Steph presumed was an equipment cupboard of some sort, but other than that the room seemed devoid of tea-making materials or teaching facilities. 'Where are the other students?'

'They're waiting for us already, I should imagine,' said Mrs Kimono, kneeling by the rock fountain and picking up a wooden ladle that lay there. 'Before the ceremony starts, we wash our hands.' She poured water over each hand in turn, 'and then purify our mouths.' She scooped water from the fountain into her mouth, then spat it back into the running water.

'You try.'

Steph knelt beside her and copied Mrs Kimono's movements.

'Did your daughter train to be a *geisha*?' asked Steph. 'I remember reading that it runs in families.'

'No. She wasn't interested in my world.' Mrs Kimono slipped off her lace-up shoes and nodded at Steph to remove her trainers. 'Now, we enter the ceremony room.'

To Steph's surprise, beyond the tiny door in the corner was an entire room with *tatami* matting on the floor and paper-screen walls. Three Japanese girls, no older than eighteen, knelt on the *tatami*.

They were beautifully dressed. Layers of heavily embroidered kimono hung around their tiny bodies, and their hair was set with jewels, flowers and combs, and styled with such volume that their heads wobbled under the weight. Like meticulous paintings, their faces were made up with thick, white paint, their eyes, eyebrows and lips theatrical dabs of black and red.

'The doorway is low so we must bow,' Mrs Kimono explained, as Steph followed her into the room, 'to show that we are all equal in the tea ceremony room. These are *maiko*.' The three students put their hands together and bowed.

'Hello, hello,' Steph said, bowing stiffly and smiling. She turned to Mrs Kimono. 'Are these girls going to teach me about men? Like, how I can get Mr Yamamoto to give me Annabel's number?'

'Don't walk so noisily,' Mrs Kimono reprimanded. 'And have patience.'

Steph looked down at her socks, wondering how she could walk any more quietly.

'In the tea room, we walk like this.' Mrs Kimono shuffled along the *tatami* mat. 'And we don't step on the joins of the mats.'

Steph shuffled.

'Sit down beside Keiko.' Mrs Kimono gestured with a slow, controlled wave of her hand towards a shy-looking girl in a light yellow kimono, with a cape of black silk hanging from her back. 'We'll show you how to make and pour tea.'

This is a waste of time, Steph thought. *How will making tea get Mr Yamamoto to open up to me?*

Steph sat, trying to pull her legs into the kneeling posture adopted by the other girls. It made her back ache and she knew her legs would be numb soon, but the other girls sat as if it were the most comfortable position in the world.

She looked around the room. It was larger than the fountain room, with a black, wrought iron pot sitting in its centre, surrounded by wooden and porcelain bowls.

The pot looked like a witch's cauldron, with big ring handles on its sides and steam issuing from the top, but its shape wasn't cauldron-like – rather more like a cuddly, overweight lady with a pinched-in waist. A bamboo ladle with a very long handle lay across the top of the pot, and steam billowed around it. A simple scroll of white parchment and Japanese script hung on the wall.

'Keiko will begin today,' Mrs Kimono told Steph, translating into Japanese for the rest of the group. 'Then you'll watch and imitate her movements. Watch her very closely. This is important. I want you to understand how powerful our bodies are. To control others we don't force or use aggression. We are gentle and precise. There's more to it than you realise.'

Steph nodded, privately thinking that pouring water into a cup couldn't be all that complicated. She watched as Keiko, who seemed not to feel the weight of her hair and kimono, slid forward over the *tatami* matting and took her place behind the black pot.

'Because it's October,' said Mrs Kimono, 'the ceremony is of the summer type, the brazier type. But next month will be the sunken hearth season, and the pot will be set into the floor. In a traditional ceremony, we serve sweets first, but not today. Today we only practise serving tea.'

Steph nodded and watched Keiko's delicate movements as she arranged various things in front of the black pot: a black wooden bowl, a white cloth folded into a rectangle, and a strange sort of brush with bristles made of thin strips of wood. Keiko lifted the bamboo ladle and dropped it into the pot, scooping out boiling water.

The movements were hypnotic.

Keiko used the wooden brush to whisk together water and tea powder. She produced a bowl of frothing, bright green liquid that looked like milky mouthwash. Green tea. Bowing, she turned the bowl slowly in her hands and presented it to her teacher. Mrs Kimono accepted the bowl and drank.

'We now all drink the tea,' Mrs Kimono told Steph, taking a white cloth and wiping the rim of the bowl. She passed it to another student, a tiny, smiling girl with plump cheeks and lips painted in a little red circle. She looked no more than fifteen, and there were bumps of acne under her white make-up. 'Watch Miu and copy what she does.'

Steph watched Miu take the bowl and hold it up to Mrs Kimono before taking a sip. Then Miu wiped the bowl and said a few words to Keiko, before passing the bowl to Steph.

Steph could feel everyone's eyes on her and sipped as quietly as she could. Lacking a cloth to clean the rim, Steph improvised with the sleeve of her top.

'No!' Mrs Kimono leaned forward and smacked Steph on the knuckles. 'We do *not* touch the tea bowl with impure things. You're just like my daughter – always pushing in your own direction. Never taking instruction.'

'But I don't have a cloth.'

Mrs Kimono shook her head. 'Then ask for a cloth. See how easy it is to miss what's important when you don't understand? We're performing a dance. An art form. It has to be done exactly. When we do it exactly, we command the attention of others. Here. Take this.' Mrs Kimono passed her a cloth from the silk belt of her kimono. Steph took it and wiped the bowl. Then she passed the tea to the next girl, who took it with a bow.

'You didn't thank Keiko for the tea,' said Mrs Kimono, 'or tell her how good it was.'

'I didn't know I was—'

'And you didn't hold the bowl to Miu to thank her for it. Very rude. Now, your turn to serve the tea.'

'But I don't know how.'

'You've watched, haven't you?'

'I don't really feel ready to—'

'It doesn't matter if you feel ready,' said Mrs Kimono. 'You learn by doing.'

Steph looked at the other girls, who had their heads bowed, focused on the floor. Mrs Kimono's gaze was unrelenting.

'Fine.' Steph slid along the *tatami* matting and sat behind the pot. 'I'll try.' She looked at the assortment of black bowls and pots, and laid them out around her as she'd seen Keiko do.

'No. The tea powder doesn't sit there.' Mrs Kimono slid forward and rearranged things.

'The whisk here, the bowl here. Fold your cloth and lay it on this dish.'

Steph began to fold the cloth.

'No! Not like that.' Mrs Kimono took the cloth, folded it in what looked exactly like Steph's way, and placed it on an earthenware dish by the black pot. 'Now take the ladle. No, in your *right* hand. Yes. Now ladle the water into the bowl.'

Steph poured water, spooned powder and whisked tea, but it seemed every tiny gesture and action had to adhere to some invisible template of movement, and she was corrected and reprimanded continuously.

'This is stupid,' she complained. 'I need to learn about men, not making tea.'

'How short-sighted you are. This is part of learning. To mesmerise with your body.'

'Okay, well I *feel* stupid then.'

'What – you thought you'd be perfect first time? No one is. We all have to look foolish and endure correction with patience and humility.'

'Why?' she asked, when Mrs Kimono told her to place the wooden brush into the empty bowl, and then turn it precisely three times, lifting it after each turn. 'What's the point of doing that? There's nothing in the bowl.'

'It's not about point,' Mrs Kimono said. 'It's about tranquillity. When your movements are precise, familiar, you command. People watch you. They forget about themselves and let you guide them.'

Finally, after much criticism and correction, Steph succeeded in making a bowl of frothing tea and presented it to Mrs Kimono for her approval.

'This looks like very fine tea,' Mrs Kimono said, bowing and taking the bowl. 'Good tea is made *carefully*. Time is taken. Everything is practised and well learned. Nothing is rushed. If we were to host a tea ceremony for important guests, we would plan and prepare all day, and I'd choose my best girls – the ones who can command the respect of the highest men in the country. Politicians, company directors, men who are used to being in charge. They go weak at the knees when the right girl performs a tea ceremony.

'When we present the tea, we follow the same ritual, a ritual that has been carried out for centuries. We don't ask *why*. We know our mothers and grandmothers did things this way for a good reason.' Mrs Kimono gave Steph a curt bow. 'You may go now. Training is over for today.'

Steph got to her feet, limping out on numb legs. She wondered if she'd really learned anything this afternoon except how confusing Japanese culture was and how easy it was to get things wrong.

Maybe that's what Mrs Kimono was trying to teach her – that she'd never be a good hostess and had better quit now. But quitting wasn't an option. Rent day was rushing forward like spark on a bomb fuse, and as long as she had *dohan* tonight there was still a chance she could make the payment.

It's nearly time for work, she thought as she went out on to the street, the diary burning a hole in her bag. *Now I won't have time to read*. Dusk hovered over the tower blocks. *Work first. Diary later. If I'm late again I'll be fired for sure. And then there really will be a girl in trouble.*

27

Mama

'*Coco des.*' Mama tapped on the glass and her cab stopped by a banner of red light bulbs and Japanese script. The bright sign marked out Tokyo's red-light district, Kabukicho, from the more sedate business offerings in the Shinjuku streets nearby.

Kabukicho was just waking up. Soon, the streets would be manned by tattooed *yakuza*, burly Nigerian men, and cute, world-weary Japanese girls, all trying to entice men into strip clubs, soaplands and other expensive sexual entertainments.

Kabukicho was a place that indulged the most colourful forms of prostitution, from 'subway train' venues where clients could 'harass' female passengers, to doctors' offices, school rooms and countless other stage sets for sexual play. And of course, the standard Japanese fair of soapy sex in Japanese bath houses and oral or hand relief in pink salons. All of this was taking place just metres away from some of the most conservative and upmarket hotels in the city – hotels where presidents and statesmen were regularly accommodated.

George waited by a Seven Eleven, clinging to the moral familiarity of a western brand in these streets of weird and wonderful sex for sale. He held his notepad tightly to his chest as Mama climbed out of her taxi. Mama rested against the car and waited for him to come to her.

'Mama.'

'George-san.' Mama took shallow breaths, her body sagging against glass and metal.

'Would you like to sit down?'

'No. Fine, fine.' She looked at him, surprised by his concern. Then she pushed herself away from the taxi. 'Quite a change

from the Park Hyatt, don't you think, George-san?' She slapped
the cab roof and the driver drove away. 'But the Park Hyatt isn't
so far away, you know? Maybe five minutes walk.' She sounded
as if she'd just climbed a flight of stairs.

'Business and pleasure, all mixed together,' said George,
managing a little smile and adding quickly, 'Really, Mama. Are
you sure you're okay?'

'It's exciting, isn't it?' said Mama, ignoring his question. 'Sex,
sex, everywhere. Exciting to buy, exciting to sell.'

'Not really my sort of thing.'

'Please, George-san. You're a man, aren't you?' Mama gazed
at the array of Japanese signs. There were photos of girls on
nearly all of them – cute girls, sexy girls, nearly naked girls – all
backlit to be as conspicuous as possible. 'I don't believe for a
moment all this is new to you. Western men – they come out
here for one reason, no matter what they say to the contrary.
Japanese women. But tonight isn't about women. In fact, I think
tonight will be a real eye-opener for you.'

'Where are we going?'

'A host club, George-san. I'll take your arm.'

'Hostess club?'

'No. *Host* club. A place where men are the pleasers and givers.
You've been in Tokyo for several years. Surely you've heard of
host clubs?'

'No. I never—'

'Don't worry.' Mama smiled at George's alarmed expression.
'No sex. We're here to be waited on and served, just as we would
by young ladies at my hostess club.'

Mama slid her hand under George's elbow and leaned against
him as they walked down a narrow street of restaurants, bars
and sex clubs. Mama smiled at the Japanese names and words.
'My old club is long gone, of course,' she said, pointing to a
sunakku sign. 'Tomi passed away some time ago. A heart attack.
Very common for men who work with the *yakuza*. They take
on debts, far too many debts. The stress kills them. But there
are many other *sunakku* bars – and runaway girls to work

them, I don't doubt. College students too, these days. Here we are.'

Mama stopped by a small, illuminated billboard at chest height: Club Dandy Man. Pictures of twenty-something, big-haired Japanese men in suits, doing their best Clint Eastwood impression for the camera, posed below the words.

'This is the place,' said Mama. 'Don't look so frightened, George-san, we're going to have a great night.'

'*Irashaimase!*' A chorus of young, male voices greeted Mama as she sauntered into the club, pulling George alongside her. Club Dandy Man was elegantly decorated with marble, glass tiles and white-brick archways. Cosy sofa booths were dotted around, their tables made of black faux-marble with electric blue splatters running through them. Dishes of nuts and seaweed crackers were placed along the bar, and on the walls were mounted giant glass refrigerators filled with Dom Pérignon.

'Mama-san.' A young waiter bowed before Mama, his quiff of orange hair swaying. He wore a black tuxedo with the top shirt button open and a glittery blue tie. Noting her western companion, he said in English, 'Follow me.'

'Mama,' George whispered, as they were led to a booth, 'it's . . . I've seen a few *mizu shobai* places in my time, and the bills are always rather on the high side.'

Mama laughed and fell on to the cosy sofa offered by the waiter. 'George-san,' she said, 'you have nothing to worry about. Really.'

The waiter knelt by Mama and presented her with a steaming towel.

'Look around, George-san. Isn't it funny?'

In the booth next to them, a Japanese girl was enjoying the fawning attentions of two hosts in suits, both men young, cute and clearly charming if the response of the girl was anything to go by. One host held the hand of the giggling girl to his cheek, while he gazed into her eyes and murmured softly.

'You see over there,' said Mama, pointing to a table where two hosts shouted '*Ikki, ikki*'. and women downed blood-red cocktails in balloon-shaped wine glasses. 'Just like in my club. These young men know all the tricks – how to make customers thirsty, how to make them drink more, how to make them feel loved and special. It makes me laugh. We never had clubs like this when I was a young girl. Now, college girls get into debt for this sort of thing.'

'Yes,' said George, clearing his throat. 'I should know, just roughly I mean, what the bill might be this evening. So I can get my expenses in order.'

'Don't worry about the bill tonight.' Mama leaned back into the sofa. 'My date, my money, *neh*? But yes, it's very expensive here. Maybe one thousand dollars a night for an average woman.'

George's eyes widened.

'Of course, I'm not an average woman.' Mama wiped her hands and face with the steaming towel. 'My bill is usually much more.'

'Who comes here?'

'Mainly hostesses. And sex workers. Women who earn a lot and spend a lot. I suppose you could call it the cycle of life for the *mizu shobai*. We earn money in the water trade, then give it right back again.'

The waiter took the towel from Mama and presented her with a laminated black menu which displayed, instead of a list of drinks, photographs of young men. Under each photo were listed the man's name, age, vital statistics and hobbies.

'Nobutora is always fun,' Mama told George, 'but we don't need anyone fun right now – we have work to do.' She passed the menu back to the waiter and said, 'No hosts, just Dom Pérignon.'

'You were going to tell me,' said George, as the waiter took the menu and left, 'about working in the . . . What was it called? Soap house?'

'Soapland. Ah yes. I thought you were only interested in politicians, George-san, and powerful men.' Mama's smile, all dimples and sparkle, lit up her tired face.

George blushed. 'Do . . . er . . . do those sorts of men visit soapland?'

'Not so often.' Mama took a gold-tipped black cigarette from a packet in her handbag. Immediately, a man appeared on his knees with a flaming lighter. Mama allowed him to light her cigarette and took a thoughtful puff.

'Sometimes. Certainly high men of the *yakuza* come to soapland. Sometimes, perhaps, department store bosses, that sort of level. More rarely, a chief executive, but those sorts of men tend to hire women to visit them at hotels. But. You want to know what goes on in soapland, don't you? Not just stories about the customers.'

'I suppose readers will find it interesting.'

'Do *you* find it interesting?'

'Who wouldn't?' George admitted, taking his large forearms off the table as a black ice bucket was placed in front of him. A bottle of Dom Pérignon lay inside, surrounded by ice chips infused with gold sparkles. Dandy Man coasters were slipped first in front of Mama, then George, before crystal champagne glasses were placed and the champagne opened. As the cork popped, hosts from all around the club crowded against the table, cheering and clapping.

'The champagne call,' Mama whispered to George as the hosts dispersed. 'A good idea. I'm thinking of introducing it at my club. Every time a customer orders champagne, they're treated to a round of applause and some special attention. It makes them order more.'

The champagne was poured, and Mama raised her glass to George and took a long sip.

'So,' she said, 'I'll tell you all about soapland. My journey into professional sex.'

28

Chastity

From: C_C_Chastity
To: CanadianDaphne
Subject: life and stuff

Daphs,

That's really sweet. Tammy's happy, but I've got to warn you, she's not great at walking or having her picture taken. I don't get it with her – she's such a good-looking girl, so beautiful, she could be the best model, but all she cares about is studying. When I was her age it was boys all the way, but she's not interested.

A whole plane-load of Romanian girls arrived in the 'Pong yesterday, they were all out on the streets asking about work. I told them all hostesses are prostitutes – ha! It's true – sort of!!! That's a few more young girls I don't have to deal with for a while. More and more turn up all the time, and immigration are getting wise to it. Won't be long before they raid us again.

I've booked in to have a boob job in January because God help me, everything's starting to sag, and I mean EVERYTHING. I'm thinking about dancing for a few months, just to get some money up, and obviously my boobs have to look good if I do that.

I know, I know – dancing is weird out here with all the touchy feely, but I'm tough, I can handle it, and the girls earn maybe 40,000 yen a night, sometimes more. It's more CERTAIN, you know? Not like Sinatra's, up one week, down the next. I met the Flame's manager, Johno, at Hollywoods last night. He was a cool guy, said I could do a trial for him. He gave me a few lines too, he's on the right side if you know what I mean. Better than Mama.

Another good thing about dancing is that in Roppongi the girls aren't all that special, you know? I wouldn't be the oldest girl in the place and I'd definitely be one of the prettiest. There are LOADS of 30-something girls at Flames – most of them ex-hostesses. Half of them are on ice or just look really past it, so I'd be one of the top girls in no time.

It was a good one last night, but come 3 a.m. it all went a bit strange. Daniella came in with this really REALLY drunk customer, he was all over her fake boobs and he wasn't even buying champagne, and then someone told me she's married to him. Married! She used to be the best girl at Janes, and now she's totally sold out and on the scrap heap. SAAAD.

Angel was out too, she's doing the strip show thing at Janes (so you know she's on her last legs as a hostess) and she is MAJORLY on ice. She was with Johno, and she got into a really paranoid one and started cutting this big hole in her arm with a hair pin. It was a total mess, she was crying and she got blood all over her face, it was mental.

I was like Babes, what are you doing? She said she was cutting out poison because the bar had drugged her drink, and she was just shaking and crying and wasn't making any sense. There were a load of empty baggies on the table for anyone to see, so stupid because there are SO many police around at the moment. I was just like, Look, I can't stay with you, but stick with Johno, OK? You shouldn't be on your own.

Those girls have stayed in Roppongi too long. If you do it, you've got to have breaks because it's full on, this world: drugs, drugs and more drugs.

I know what you're thinking, I can talk. But I never do coke more than three nights in a row, and ice maybe once a week, maybe less. It's the drink I need to cut down on – champagne is my oxygen!

Oh my God, forgot to tell you – you'll SOO laugh at this.

I've only gone and bleached my hair blonde! Yep! Who'd have believed it! I got it done at Syngen today, it's like platinum blonde now. It looks a bit weird with my eyebrows but I had to do something to get back in Mama's good books.

I'll love you and leave you, time to start with the make-up.

Laters Babes,

Chastity

29

Mama

Mama leaned back into the black, rubbery sofa and drank more champagne. Every time she put her glass on the table, a waiter quickly topped up her drink, then vanished into the shadows.

'Before I tell you about soapland,' she said, 'I really should tell you about my mother and father, don't you think?'

George turned notebook pages. 'We haven't covered your parents in much detail, but—'

'So, my mother,' Mama interrupted. 'A Japanese woman. She lived through hard times, like many Japanese women of her age. There is a Japanese word, *gaman*, it means to endure, and I think women of my mother's generation know that word better than most.

'She saw the war as a child and the Americans coming to Japan. Hard times. Of course, before the war, people in the countryside were very poor, often starving, but during and after the war many, many people all over Japan had no food, no money.

'My mother lived in Kyoto back then. As a young girl she was a *maiko*, a trainee *geisha*. But post-war Japan was not so easy for *maikos*. No money. She had to end her training and offer herself to men so she could care for her little sister, my aunt.

'Her mother and father weren't rich people – my grandfather was a *geiko* dresser, a man who helps *geisha*, or *geiko* as they call them in Kyoto, into their kimono, and my grandmother died young, maybe aged thirty or something like that. I never met her. I had an uncle too, but I never met him either. He was a suicide bomber during the war. I have a picture of him somewhere.

'The Americans called women like my mother "*geisha* girls" – typical Americans, they confused the term. But when she offered herself to men my mother was no *geisha*. When I was a little girl, my mother always spoke of being a *geisha* and how her life could have been different. She was sad not to have finished her training, but I never understood why. Many girls in my mother's time became *geishas* without any choice. It's a hard profession. And she'd been a "pan pan" girl. A prostitute – a comfort woman, as they used to call them. To think of being a *geisha* after that . . . The two worlds are so very different.

'She'd tell me all sorts of stories about the Americans, what they thought about the Japanese and their bad attitudes. But it didn't stop her falling in love with an American, my father, a big, burly man with blond hair. I suppose you could say it's thanks to him I did so well as a young girl in the water trade. Caucasian looks were thought to be very attractive when I was growing up. They still are, I suppose. Pale skin, rounded noses, rounded eyes. Exotic. I think I strike a good balance between the east and west, don't you?'

George scribbled away, his champagne glass fizzing, untouched. He nodded. 'He taught you English?'

'Why do you think my English is so good?' said Mama. 'Not many women from my world get an education in a foreign language. I can't really say that my father was around much to teach me, but he was there for long enough. He and my mother were together for a long time, twelve years or so, before she had enough of his cheating and lying and moved back to Kyoto.'

'Where they married?'

'No. He never married her. She would have married him, but he didn't offer. He didn't need to – they lived like man and wife. She did everything for him, brought up his daughter, earned money . . . I think he must have worked some magic spell on her, but then again, Japanese women are hard-working and loyal.

'Maybe if they'd been married, she'd still be with him now. I don't know. He wasn't a good man. He took what he could from Japan when our country was on its knees. He bought up clubs, restaurants, all sorts of things, and he made a lot of money. My mother worked hard too, of course.' Mama slumped forward, elbows on the table. 'Get the waiter, would you?'

'Of course.' George twisted around, but before he'd even managed to raise a hand, a waiter appeared at the table. Mama spoke to him in Japanese.

A moment later, a black straw was presented on a gold plate, and Mama dropped it into her champagne glass, 'Easier this way.' she said, leaning forward to drink. 'So,' she continued, after taking a long sip. 'Not all westerners are bad. Perhaps all men are bad. I didn't used to think that way but now . . . I don't know. I Know my mother wasted many years with my father, and then he took a young girlfriend and left her with no one.'

Mama closed her eyes. Her elbow slid forward, and George reached out to stop her champagne glass from toppling over. His notepad fell to the floor.

Anxious faces, both hosts and customers, turned to stare.

'Mama, I think you need to rest.'

'No, I'm fine now. Let's continue.'

George glanced down at his notepad, its pages splayed open. There were many blank lines still to fill. He looked at Mama. Her face had a saggy quality to it. Every time she blinked, it looked like she had to make a supreme effort to open her eyes again.

'Mama, enough for tonight.'

'But George-san.' Mama's words were crisper than he'd expected, considering her jaw looked so limp. 'Soapland. I need to tell you about soapland and—'

'No. I'll take you home.'

'But I'm working at the club tonight.' said Mama.

George looked around for a waiter, and, as he'd seen Mama do in the Park Hyatt restaurant, made a cross with his fingers for the bill.

'I don't think that's a good idea.' said George. 'I think it best I take you home.'

30

Steph

There were plenty of western girls waiting outside Café Almond when Steph arrived, all looking expectantly into the crowds. Steph had drawn on eyebrows so dark they looked like tattoos and added bright pink cheeks and lips. Coupled with Mama's electric-blue dress, she looked like a 40-something divorcée. All that was missing was a waft of Chanel No. 5 and a designer handbag full of mints and tissues.

She'd left Annabel's diary back at the apartment, hidden in her rucksack. The afternoon with Mrs Kimono meant time was short and once again she'd had to rush to get ready for the evening.

At the crossroads, Steph waited. One by one, the other girls were approached by older men in suits and whisked away in taxis or chauffeur-driven BMWs.

Seven o'clock came and went.

Across the street, a shaven-headed American shouted at a *massagie* girl and everyone turned to stare. The girl wrapped her sleeping-bag style coat around her and bowed her head. When the American walked away, her eyes were red. '*Massagie*,' she said to men who passed, but her voice was downbeat.

A navy blue BMW cruised along the street, and Steph noticed a Japanese man with rigid posture looking at her through the passenger window. He seemed to be examining her face in some detail, but when she looked directly at him he turned away and said something to the driver. The car sped on.

Steph waited. And waited. When two hours had passed, she felt sweat creeping under the tight armpits of the dress. She had a bad feeling that Ken had been the man in the car, the one who'd stared at her face so intently. Not everyone liked scars. If Ken had decided he didn't like what he saw she was in trouble.

A skinny white girl came and lounged against the Café Almond glass next to her. She looked all of eighteen, but took hard drags of her cigarette like someone with a 40-a-day habit.

'Hey,' said Steph. 'Is this the only Café Almond in Roppongi?'

'Are you meeting someone?'

'Supposed to be.'

'Then yeah.' The girl had an angelic face, acres of long, sandy-brown hair piled high on her head and the cracked voice of a heroin addict. 'There's one down the street, but no one meets there. This is the one we all meet at. Amir!' The girl waved at a craggy-faced, Arab looking man wearing blue jeans and an Armani sweatshirt.

Steph watched as he stopped and kissed the girl on both cheeks. He looked familiar. She turned her head just a fraction so she could get a better look, and then remembered where she'd seen him before – he was the delivery guy outside Calamity Janes on her first night. The one Frederico said was a gangster.

The girl rubbed her thumb and fingers together, and Amir nodded, then dropped something into her Chanel handbag. He was short and muscular, with a quiff of thick, black hair and looked young for a man in Roppongi.

'You want to pay me later?' Amir asked.

'Pay you tomorrow,' she said.

'No worries. Hey, if you're short you know . . . Like I said before . . .'

'Thanks for the offer, babes,' said the girl. 'but I'm not that hard up. Not yet. See you later.'

'Sure.' Amir turned to Steph. 'What are you waiting for, baby?'

'*Dohan*,' said Steph. 'I think I've been stood up.'

'I'm surprised,' he said, looking her up and down. 'You're new here?'

'I have a friend out here,' said Steph, 'so I'm not totally, you know . . .' She blinked hard to stop the tears from coming. It was all so humiliating. Being stood up where everyone could see. The man tilted his head.

'You're sad, baby?'

'No, it's just . . . I . . . It was important I had *dohan* tonight, that's all.'

'You want to use my phone? Call the guy?' Amir pulled out a pink NTT Docomo mobile and flipped open the lid with his thumb.

'It's too late to call now. I only have his work number.'

'Okay. You need someone to take you to your club?'

'No, I need a *dohan*.'

'So how about I take you as *dohan*?'

Steph blinked at him. 'As a *dohan*?'

'Sure. What time do you have to be there?'

'Listen, the club's really expensive. It's a hostess club.'

'That's okay. When do you need to be there?'

'About now.'

'Okay. Let's go.'

'Really?' Steph wished there was someone to ask if it was okay to go with this guy. If he was a gangster, so what? He seemed friendly enough, and anyway, what choice did she have? A *dohan* was a *dohan*.

Hiro was polishing the reception bell when Steph arrived, and he looked alarmed to see Amir standing next to her. 'Steph-chan.' He wiped his forehead with the back of his hand. 'This is . . . You've brought *dohan*?' He looked over Amir's loose jeans, tattooed forearms and dirty white trainers.

'Where's Mama?' Steph asked.

'Mama's not very well. She's off sick tonight.'

'Oh.' There were no customers, and the keyboard band played *The Great Pretender* to empty seats.

'Please go to the waiting table, Steph-chan,' Hiro said, rubbing the bell even harder with the cloth. 'Mr . . . Your friend is a new customer. We have to talk . . . fill out paperwork.'

Amir leaned an elbow on the reception desk. 'No problem.' He winked at Steph and pulled a chewed biro from his top pocket.

As Steph approached the waiting table, all the girls craned their necks to get a better look at the man in reception.

'You got *dohan*?' said Jennifer, as she sat down. 'That must be some kind of record. On your second night.'

Steph smiled and stuffed her leather shoulder bag under the sofa.

'Nice suit he's wearing,' said Chastity, whose hair had been dyed an unflattering, yellowy blonde. It clashed with her grey-black eyebrows and made her hair look wiry and dull. 'Good luck getting him to pay the bill.'

'Who's your *dohan* tonight?' asked Steph.

Chastity folded her arms.

'You've done really well,' said Jennifer. 'I don't think anyone's ever got a *dohan* in their first week.'

'Annabel did,' said Chastity.

'Okay, Annabel probably did,' Jennifer conceded. 'But she was a legend. I mean, you can't really compare—'

'I wish someone could tell me where Annabel's living now,' said Steph. 'Or working. We were really good friends at school. It's weird to hear people talking about her and not knowing where she is.'

'You're still worried about her?' asked Jennifer.

'Not as much as before. I spoke to one of her customers. He saw her just last week.'

'That's good news,' said Jennifer. 'I mean, it's not really dangerous out here, but you never know.'

'I can't wait to see her again,' said Steph. 'She was really swatty at school. A good girl. I can't imagine her as a hostess. She's good at it, you said?'

'Oh yeah,' said Jennifer. 'I got here after she left so we never met, but I heard she was good. Like *really* good. The best customers.'

'Do you think she's still working in Roppongi?' Steph asked.

'Maybe,' said Jennifer. 'Talk to Luke, the bar guy. He goes out in Roppongi all the time. If she's still around, he'll probably know her.'

'Luke? I think I met him already.'

'The Australian guy,' said Jennifer, pointing to two men in tuxedos watering down whisky behind the bar.

Steph looked over her shoulder and saw Hiro and Amir deep in conversation, a pile of forms on the reception desk between them. Amir was rolling down his sleeves, covering his tattoos.

Steph smiled. 'Thanks.'

'Don't let Hiro see you.'

31

'Luke?' Steph addressed the two tuxedoed backs bobbing up and down behind the bar. Luke's head popped up. Although his shirt was white, there were grey marks around the collar and cuffs, and Steph could tell he wasn't a person who wore a suit out of choice.

'Hello again,' he said. 'The girl who cares about other people. How can I help?'

'Hi.' Steph found herself smiling back. 'I forgot to ask you the other night. Did you ever meet a girl called Annabel? She used to work here.'

'English Annabel?'

'Yes,' said Steph. 'We went to school together.'

'Yeah, I've heard of her,' said Luke. 'Really sweet girl by all accounts. Always top of the bonus chart. Mama loved her, but then she left. Just like that. I think she must have done something bad – taken customers from the club, maybe – one of the customers asked about her and Mama got really angry.' He screwed the lid back on a bottle of mineral water with slim, muscular fingers. 'How are the girls treating you?' Luke leaned on the bar, making a perfect square with his upper arms, shoulders and forearms.

'Okay,' said Steph. 'So . . . Do you know what happened to her? Where she went?'

Luke shrugged. 'I'm not the person to ask. I never met her.'

'Jennifer thought maybe you'd heard about her outside the club or something.'

'No,' said Luke, removing a funnel from a whisky bottle. 'Never anyone called Annabel. What do you think of Mama?' He raised an eyebrow. 'Bit of a dragon, hey? Wait . . . Hiro's coming. Is that your *dohan?*'

Steph turned to see Amir being led to a table by Hiro. 'Yes.'

'I've seen *him* around Roppongi. Not a great guy. Make sure he pays his bill. You'd better go back to the waiting table – I don't want you getting in trouble.' He gave her a final smile, then ducked back below the bar.

'Thanks so much for doing this,' said Steph, as she took a seat opposite Amir. Hiro had seated them in a dark corner on one of the worst tables in the club, small and cramped, with cushioned stools instead of sofas.

'No problem.' Amir ordered a bottle of wine and leaned forward on his stool, legs spread wide. 'So tell me all about yourself.'

'Shouldn't I be asking you about *yourself?*' asked Steph.

'I'm sure you're much more interesting.' Amir gave her a perfect smile, straight white teeth gleaming against tanned skin. There was a slightly devilish set to his face when the light caught him in a certain way. The muscles above his eyebrows protruded and his sharp cheekbones cast shadows.

'Really, I'm not.'

Hiro appeared with a bottle of red wine and two glasses.

Steph took the bottle and a glass, pouring wine and making sure to tip the glass carefully so it didn't splash. Thinking of the tea ceremony, she used a napkin to wipe away dust from the bottle, then took a coaster and set the glass in the centre of it. Amir's face relaxed as he watched her.

'Why not tell me why you came to Tokyo?' said Amir. 'That's always an interesting story.'

'Same reason as every other girl. To earn money.'

'Any particular reason?'

'I made some mistakes back home. I need to make a new start. You know, I really should be asking about you.' Steph was aware of Hiro lingering somewhere nearby. *You just made noise and got drunk, you didn't serve the customers.* 'What brought *you* to Tokyo? I take it you're not from here originally.'

'I'm from Iran,' said Amir. 'I came here to earn money too. I

have a son back home, I wanted to make lots of money for him
– enough so he'd never have to worry. I thought it would be
better out here, but . . .'

'It isn't?' Steph finished.

'No, it is better. Sometimes. I can't go back anyway, even if I
wanted to.' He stood up. 'Bathroom.'

When he came back, there was white powder on one of his
nostrils.

'What do you do out here?' Steph asked.

'What do Iranian men usually do in Tokyo?' said Amir, leaning
back and putting his hands behind his head. 'Make money from
nose powder.' He sniffed and tilted his head back. 'I can help
you out if you need something.'

'Thanks for the offer,' said Steph. 'But I don't even have rent
money.'

'Get a good customer and he'll pay,' said Amir. 'I sell to most
of the working girls round here, Greengrass, Janes, and the strip
clubs. They all get their stuff from me and most of the time,
when the girls want pick-me-ups their customers pay.'

'You go out a lot in Roppongi?'

'Every night.'

'Did you ever meet a girl called Annabel?'

'Annabel? Sure. She used to work here.' Amir squeezed his
nostrils together.

'Really?' Steph leaned forward. 'You don't happen to know
where she is now?'

'I haven't seen her for a long time – she was with some bad
people last time we met. *Yakuza.* Gangsters.'

'Bad people?' Steph felt chilled again. 'But she's still in Roppongi?'

'That would be my guess, if it's the same girl. She was pretty
much into the Roppongi life-style – drink, drugs, customers.'

Steph thought about the sweet, clean-living girl who scribbled
hearts all over her school folders and gave her friends handmade
cards on their birthdays.

'That doesn't sound like my Annabel. You must be thinking
of someone else.'

'Check at Janes. Last time I saw her was at Hollywoods, so maybe she's working at Janes now.'

'You think she might be working at Janes? My friend Julia works there . . . I think she would have said something.' *But then again Julia's so keen to keep me away from her club, maybe she decided not to let on that Annabel's working there.*

'Australian Julia?'

'She's English.'

'I thought she was Australian. You sure I can't help you out with anything? Did you try ice yet? I get the pure stuff. Ask anyone.'

'I'm fine.'

'I can give you credit. I do that with a lot of girls. Or you can pay in other ways, you know? A lot of guys pay good money for time with pretty girls. Nice guys. Clean. I can make connections for you.'

'Thanks but no thanks.'

'Suit yourself.' Amir checked his Rolex. 'Then I guess I'd better be going.' His wine glass was still half full. 'See you around. Steph, isn't it?'

'See you around.'

32

It turned out to be a long night. A few party groups came into the club at midnight and Steph knocked back drink after drink until finally, at 1a.m., Mr Yamamoto arrived. Hiro chose Steph to sit with him and, although the other girls didn't look pleased, Steph couldn't help beaming with delight.

Once she was at the table, Steph poured drinks slowly and carefully just like she'd learned at the tea ceremony, taking care over every gesture. She made sure the glass was always centred on the coaster and the whisky bottle faced the same way, ignoring the cold stares from the waiting table.

Yamamoto-san seemed to enjoy the care and precision with which Steph attended to him, and told her he'd ask for her the next time he came in. But try as she might, she couldn't get him to reveal Annabel's phone number. 'Next time, next time. Maybe, maybe,' was all he said on the subject.

In the changing room at the end of the night, Chastity and Christiana made their feelings about Steph even clearer. '*She doesn't even have her own clothes . . . There's no way she's good enough to hostess here . . . Why did Mama even hire her? What's with all those scars, who likes those?*'

As Steph changed, they jostled her and crowded around the lockers so she couldn't get her bag. She pushed and shoved as good as she got, but it hurt to feel so isolated and disliked, even though her name was now on the bonus chart and she felt assured of a full-time job as soon as Mama came back.

Steph was set free at 3 a.m. and walked uphill towards Roppongi crossroads with the stagger of someone who was slightly drunk and had been in high heels all evening. As Steph passed a *sushi* restaurant, its window decorated with cartoon pictures of raw fish and rice, she spotted a familiar face behind the glass.

Julia.

She hesitated, guessing she'd be met with another frosty response, but knocked on the glass anyway.

Julia turned round. She had chopsticks in her hand, and was perched on a stool next to a fat, forty-something western man with no eyebrows. She looked fragile and skinny.

Even though no invitation was forthcoming, Steph pushed open the glass door to the restaurant, the odour of warm, slightly stale fish greeting her as she stepped inside. There were huge hunks of raw fish, some of them with dried-out edges, lying under a glass counter.

A sturdy Japanese man stood behind the fish, slicing *sashimi* with a giant cleaver. Julia sat at the bar beside her companion; they were the only customers in the restaurant.

'Steph? I'm busy right now,' said Julia, staring at a little dish of soy sauce and *wasabi*. The man had his hand on her thigh.

'It won't take a minute. I just wanted to ask . . . Does Annabel work at your club?'

Julia's eyes were red and tired. 'I don't know. Janes is a big place. You could work there for months and not meet all the hostesses – there are like fifty or something. Not that it's any of your business *who* works there. If you're looking for a way in, just forget it. I told you, you're not . . .' She glanced at her male companion. 'Look. Forget about working at Janes, Okay?'

'I'm not trying to work at Janes,' Steph said. 'Guess what? I just want to meet up with my old friend, that's all.'

The man with the cleaver stopped chopping.

'I'm not going to talk about girls who work at Janes,' said Julia. 'It's confidential, anyway. We're not supposed to . . . Well, anyway. If you don't mind, we're having dinner.' Julia turned her back to Steph and prodded a little dish of rice with her chopsticks.

'Fine. I'll just go to Hollywoods and see if Annabel's there,' said Steph, crossing her arms. 'Or better still, I'll just hang outside your club at chucking out time.'

Julia laughed. 'Shows how much you know. Not all the girls *have* to go to Hollywoods *every* night. Some don't ever go. You could go to Hollywoods every night and not meet half the girls working at Janes. And we don't all finish at the same time either. Different girls, different contracts.'

'Don't you care about the three of us meeting up?' said Steph in a desperate bid to evoke some sort of emotion from Julia. 'Friends reunited, after all these years?'

'Goodbye.'

'You know what Julia? There's something really wrong with you.'

'Steph . . .' Julia put a hand on Steph's shoulder. For a moment she looked like the old Julia. Just for a moment. 'I'm a different person out here,' she said. 'When I get home, I'll be me again. But for now . . . I think it's best we go our separate ways.'

'Thanks for nothing.' Steph's usual grace abandoned her after fifteen vodka tonics, and she tripped over the step as she left the restaurant.

Steph forced open the sticky door to her bedroom, drunk and tired enough to fall into bed fully clothed. She got the diary out of her rucksack. Natalia wasn't in, so she flicked on the light and threw the book on the bed.

I will find you Annabel, she thought. *And together we'll work out what on earth is wrong with Julia.*

She leafed through the pages until she found where she'd got up to. Turning on to her stomach, she began to read.

'Dear God,

I feel so worthless, useless, empty. No *dohans* this week, absolutely none, zero. Mama is so angry, she won't even look at me any more . . .'

She must be talking about the Mama at Sinatra's, Steph thought.
It was comforting to know that her old friend had problems with
Mama too. She continued to read.

. . . it's such a knock, so scary, going from top to
bottom. I could never believe it when I was at the top of
the chart, I always knew it was only a matter of time
before I'd fall right back down to the bottom again, and
here I am, no *dohan*, two requests, worse than when I
first started out.

Maybe moving to Janes would be a good idea, but the
manager gives me the creeps. Do I really want to work for
someone who's into that sort of thing? He didn't even hide
it. All those pictures were out for anyone to see. I know sex
is different out here, but it's still creepy. Naked girls are one
thing, but when they're tied up or lying with their eyes
closed it looks really weird.

And how could I ever do a trial for them anyway,
when Sinatra's will never let me have a night off? Big
fine if I miss a night, and Mama's fired girls for less.
Take care of me God, help me work out the right thing
to do.

Amen. Love Annabel.

Dear God,

Japanese painkillers really work. Headache gone, finally,
but still feel sick. Last night was mad, I've never drunk so
much in my whole life and those girls do it every night. Feel
sick just thinking about it right now. And in an hour I've got
to do it all over again.

Please, please help me do well, make my customers
change clubs. I can't keep drinking like this. Without champagne customers, it's four cocktails an hour until I'm dead
from the alcohol.

Cassie didn't have any customers, and the management
wouldn't sit her on any tables so she just sat around earning
nothing for weeks, watching all the other girls. That's why

she ended up such a major alcoholic – the only money she
got was from drink kick-backs.

I don't like working at Janes, I really, really don't . . .'

Wait. Steph reread the last section. *So she* did *move to Calamity
Janes . . . That's what it sounds like.*
Steph read on.

The manager here is so sleazy. He keeps putting his arm
round my waist, standing really close, yucky, yucky. He said
because I didn't have an entertainment visa I'd have to work
hard to make customers *extra happy.*

Now I think, Mama wasn't so bad. Except that she fired
me. How did she know I went to Janes? I hate thinking
about that night, no more work for you, no more work. It
gave me the shock of my life. My eyes are still red from
crying and it's two days later, I was in pieces but she didn't
care. Out, out, no more work for you.

I'd go back there in a second if I could. I hate it here,
it's so sleazy. After work, some of the girls get in cabs and
go to hotels with their customers, extra contracts they
call it.

God help me. I really mean it!
Love Annabel.

Steph laid her head on the diary. It sounded like Janes was a
really sleazy place, but more interestingly, it was clear Annabel
had worked there at some point. *Shame this diary doesn't have
any dates* . . . Was Annabel at Janes the same time as Julia? Was
she still there now? Steph didn't believe for a moment that if
Annabel still worked at Janes, Julia didn't know about it.

On a whim, she flicked to the back of the diary to see if the
last entry was more illuminating then the ones she'd read so far.
Perhaps it would offer a clue as to where Annabel had worked
last, or a new address. But the last page wasn't filled with
Annabel's usual, dense handwriting. Instead there was a neat
list. It read:

WW + 1
VT + GL
R&C + USA

On the page before, the last diary entry was a scrawled mess, much harder to read than earlier entries. Steph scanned it quickly, but it was too hard to decipher and she couldn't see any words that looked like the name of a hostess club or an address.

She closed the book.

If somehow I got a job at Calamity Janes, thought Steph, *then I could find out for myself if Annabel still works there. Or at least ask the girls there where she's living now.* Then another, less virtuous thought occurred to her. *And I'd be working at one of the best clubs in Roppongi. I could make some serious money . . .*

She was about to read more when the bedroom door banged open and a waft of perfume and alcohol flowed into the room.

Steph closed the book and did it under her sheet.

'I need sleep,' said Natalia, turning out the light.

33

I look like a vampire, Steph thought, examining herself in the mirror. Her eyes were sunken, her cheeks greeny-white and her mouth tasted of sour milk and vodka.

It was nearly 7p.m. She'd woken up approximately two hours before, and was now in the hostess toilet at Sinatra's touching up her make-up before work. It had been dark when she'd woken up, the Roppongi disco on the street below already in full swing. She'd been furious at herself for sleeping in, and shoved Annabel's diary in her bag on the way out of the door, planning to read a few pages at work.

The girls had made sure there wasn't an inch of space in the changing room for her when she'd arrived, so she'd hurried to the toilet, a tiny, plastic cell no bigger than a washroom on an aeroplane, to finish getting ready.

The customer toilet was a lavish, marble affair with a gold-plated toilet-roll holder and scented tapers in a polished glass jar, but the toilet for hostesses was cupboard-sized and dirty, with a mould-encrusted shower over the toilet and a sink that caused bruised knees at every turn.

There was thumping on the plastic door. 'Hurry up.'

Steph emerged to find Chastity, skinny arms crossed and a pot of stage foundation in her hand. She hadn't yet covered up the tattoo on her arm, and Steph could see a tacky picture of a little elf and *Tammy* written underneath in greeny-black letters.

'You're wearing *that* dress again?' Chastity said. 'I think you'd better change the record – you're making the club look cheap.' She pushed past Steph into the toilet.

'Mind your own business.' Steph headed to the waiting table, but Hiro blocked her path.

'Steph-chan, you can't wear that dress again.'

'Did Chastity say something to you?'

Hiro shook his head. 'No, Mama likes a different dress every night. She wasn't in yesterday, and you're new so . . . you know. I gave you a break. She's in now. She won't let you work in that dress.'

'Please, Hiro.'

'Borrow something from one of the other girls. You'd better hurry. You'll be marked late if you're not on the waiting table in three minutes.'

In the changing room, three girls were getting dressed – a sandy blonde, an ice blonde and a platinum blonde. Steph had learned their names last night: Billy, Christiana and Helena. Billy was from Israel, Christiana from the Czech Republic, and Helena from Russia.

'Where's Jennifer?' Steph asked.

Christiana and Billy ignored her, but the girl with ice-blonde hair, Helena, said, *'dohan,'* and continued applying her lipstick. She was tall and powerfully built, with a strong jaw and superior expression.

'Look, does anyone have a dress I could borrow?' Steph asked.

No one said anything. Then Helena clicked the cap back on her lipstick and said: 'You can rent a dress from me. Five thousand yen.'

'You're joking.'

Helena shrugged and swung her thick hair from one shoulder to another. 'Up to you. Mama won't let you work in the same dress night after night. So lose a night's pay, why don't you.'

'Why can't you lend me something? It's just a dress.'

'Why should I give you something for free?'

'Steph-chan.' Hiro called from the doorway. 'You have one minute. Do you have a dress? No dress, no work.'

'Okay, okay, fine.' Steph withdrew 5000 yen from her bag. 'Look, how about five thousand for a week's worth of dresses?'

'I'll loan you three. For three nights.'

'Okay.'

Helena nodded and presented her with a long, black lycra dress with a split up the leg and a gold sequin dragon prowling around the skirt. It was cheap and gaudy, but Steph pulled it on as quickly as she could and hurried to the waiting table, Annabel's diary tucked under her arm. The club was empty, so she seated herself right in the corner, out of Hiro's eye line, and began to read.

Dear God,

I'm so ashamed. I promised I never, ever would, but last night I did and now I feel so bad I just want to die. God, if my parents ever found out I would just kill myself, they would be so ashamed of me. I can't blame anyone, it was me, me, all the way, my choice and now I can't take it back.

Please forgive me. I feel so tired today and sick, and the worst of it is that I'm supposed to teach English, but I can't do it now, not the way I'm feeling. My head hurt so much earlier I thought I needed hospital, but those painkillers again, they are a life saver.

I never thought Janes would be so hard. Sleazy, yes, but it's *hard*. Start at 7pm, work until 3am, then do another hour at Hollywoods, and the whole time it's drink, drink drink, four drinks an hour or we get fired. It's so high pressured, we have to look immaculate, I mean absolutely perfect. If Ricky doesn't like our hairstyle, or she thinks we haven't taken enough time over it, she sends us to the hairdressers across the street and we have to pay for a blow dry. And they do weight checks and stroke your legs to check you've shaved under your stockings and nothing short of perfect will do.

It's hard enough getting ready with a hangover every day, but when you have to look perfect it is PRESSURE and seriously stressful. They have a weight chart on the wall, and it makes me feel so fat to look at it because I'm the heaviest girl in the club by about a stone – everyone here is tiny.

New girls get sat on *all* the tables and I'm so tired of it, drinking from 7p.m. And I have to be laughing and joking the whole time, even though the men here are so slimy and roaming hands all over the place. No fake drinks here (I miss Sinatra's orange vodka!) – it's all wine or champagne so you can't pretend.

There's so much cocaine here and I hate drugs, but last night I was so tired, really, really exhausted, and . . . I was supposed to get a break, but then this massive party group came in.

I was so tired I just went to the toilet and started crying. And I was thinking, what am I going to do? They'll sack me if I don't come out, but I can't do it.

Geraldine came in the toilets to do her stuff, and she said you look tired, you should have some wake-up powder, and I just thought I really need it. I don't know what it was, too much drink, I don't know. I wasn't even scared until my nose really hurt and I saw blood on the banknote. But then I just had this awake feeling like, yes I can do it.

I was talking to everyone, being the *best* hostess ever, then it was all edgy scary, like everyone was looking at me. I felt really down and sad and just totally empty.

Geraldine said I should take some more, and I thought I'd really better not, I don't want to get addicted, but all the girls here do it and Geraldine can take it or leave it.

Work went so quickly, we went out to Hollywoods and stayed out drinking and talking. 9am I got back! I did more and more all night. I won't lie, I had a good time. But I won't do it again. I'm going to take another painkiller.

34

'Steph-chan!'

Steph snapped the diary closed.

'No reading at the waiting table.' Hiro clapped his hands at her. 'Mama wants to speak to you in the office.'

'Okay.' Steph put the diary under the sofa. She'd been feeling a little uneasy about reading on anyway. Finding out where Annabel was working was one thing, but nosing into her secrets and personal feelings was something else.

In the office, Mama was sitting in a swivel chair, a pair of diamond-studded glasses on her nose. She looked old and tired, and was breathing oddly.

'Steph. Big problem.' Mama put her hand on a ledger book filled with numbers. She let out a sigh and her shoulders sagged forward. 'Your customer.'

'My *dohan*,' said Steph, a sickly feeling creeping around her intestines. 'What about him?'

'He's no good.' Mama tapped a Parker pen slowly on the pages. 'Didn't pay his bill. Bad credit card.'

'Right . . .' said Steph.

Mama shook her head. 'Steph-chan, you're in some trouble. When a customer doesn't pay his bill, the hostess must pay his debt.'

'What? You're not serious.'

Mama took off her glasses and dabbed at a runny eye with a tissue. 'If I'd been here, I never would have given him credit,' she said. 'I know a good customer from a bad one. But Hiro . . . He's still learning. Unfortunate. But it's still your mistake. Bring bad customers and they're your responsibility. You owe the club sixty-three thousand yen.'

Steph's mouth opened and closed. She wanted to scream. She wanted to cry. She wanted to find Amir and break his legs. Why did this keep happening to her? It was just like back home – a man coming along, pretending he was her knight in shining armour, and then totally messing her around. If Mama hadn't been watching she would have burst into tears. *Stupid, stupid, stupid. Why can't I work out by now who to trust and who's taking me for a ride?*

More than anything Steph wanted to be out of this room, out of Japan, somewhere where things were simple and easy. But that place didn't exist. Things at home hadn't been simple and easy, and she'd brought exactly the same problems out here with her.

Mama patted Steph's forearm. 'You were lucky. It could have been much more.'

'I . . . Mama, I can't pay that.'

'Hiro says you weren't so bad last night. An improvement. Which isn't saying very much. But if you continue to improve, I'll let you carry on working here until you've paid your debt. If not, the trial will finish and you'll have to find some other way to pay.'

'Even if you do let me work here, how am I going to pay my rent? Buy food?' Steph thought of the 5000 yen she'd just given Helena. Apart from that she only had a few silver coins.

'Not my problem, Steph-chan.' Mama turned to the ledger book again. 'You'll find a way. You can go now.'

Steph stood gawping for a moment before she turned and left the office. Somehow, her legs carried her across the club. *60,000-something yen.* She wouldn't pay it. She couldn't.

Feeling eyes on her, she turned to see Luke watching from behind the bar. He smiled and gave a little wave. Steph put her head down and kept walking.

Jennifer was at the waiting table when she got back.

'I think Luke likes you,' she said, as Steph sat down. 'He's been staring at you all night. No wonder Chastity . . . Well, she can't be too pleased.'

'Why not?' said Steph, rubbing her forehead.

'Chastity really liked him, but he dumped her because she's
. . . Oh you know Chastity, it's always money, money, money.'

'Where are the other girls?' said Steph. The words sounded
faraway, as if someone else were speaking.

'*Dohan*. Tables. Everything okay?' Jennifer ducked her head
down so she could see Steph's face. 'Stephanie?'

'I'm fine, I'm fine.'

'You don't look fine. What did Mama want?' asked Jennifer.

Steph stared at the bar, where Luke and the other waiter were
throwing spirits and sodas into tiny glasses.

'I heard your customer, Amir . . . His card wasn't good?'

'Who told you?'

'Chastity. You know how she is with Mama. They're like that.
She's seen her without her wig.'

Across the club, Steph watched Luke fling ice into the air and
catch it in empty glasses. 'I owe the club his bill.'

'I'm really sorry,' said Jennifer. She smelt of flowery perfume
and her large, mottled thighs radiated heat. 'What are you going
to do? Stay here and work it off?'

Steph shrugged. 'Even if I do work it off here, how am I going
to live for the next week? My rent's due in two days.'

'You're not going to skip out on it, are you?' said Jennifer.
'Please don't do that. Mama knows *yakuza* and . . . If you do
that, don't stay in Roppongi.'

Steph put her head in her hands. 'I'll have to try and find him.
Force him to pay up. But that could take days . . . weeks . . . I
have no idea how to track him down. I don't even know his last
name.'

'Okay, listen,' said Jennifer. 'Promise to keep this to yourself.
Okay? Did your friend out here tell you about bottle-backing?'

'No.'

'Okay. Well, bottle-backing is like . . . You need to earn some
money right?'

'Yes.'

'Right, well, it's sort of like a sales kick-back system. For every
bottle of champagne you get a customer to order, you get some

money. Usually three thousand yen, sometimes more if it's a really expensive bottle and—'

'I do know about that,' Steph interrupted. 'Hiro said something about it on my first night. If I bring a customer in I get a percentage of his table or something.'

'No, not *here*,' said Jennifer, lowering her voice. 'Outside. In the Roppongi bars. Hoggies, Square Mile. They pay you straight-away. In cash. But listen, it's strictly against the rules. If Mama catches you, you'll get fired.'

'Why's it any of her business?' said Steph. 'What we do after work is up to us.'

'Not if we bring customers from the club out with us,' said Jennifer, looking over her shoulder. 'For the kick-back, it has to be champagne or like really fancy wine. Usually that's hard to get, but they're all rich here. Champagne is like their breakfast cereal. So you bring a club customer to a bar with you after work, he orders champagne at a kick-back bar and bingo – we make money.'

'Can we go tonight after work?' said Steph, seeing a glimmer of light at the end of the tunnel.

'Sure,' said Jennifer. 'We'll have to leave the club at different times, or Mama will get suspicious. We'll finish early tonight – no one ever stays late on a Saturday. Let's meet at Square Mile? Do you know how to get there?'

'I'll find it,' said Steph. 'By the way, I left a blue book here. Under the sofa. Did you see it?'

'A blue book?' Jennifer got up. She wore a floaty dress, which looked soft, pretty and very feminine. 'No, can't see one.'

'It was here.' Steph felt around the settee.

'Was it your customer book?' Jennifer gasped. 'You didn't leave it lying around, did you.' One of the other girls might have . . . Wait, you've only just started. What was it, a notepad or something?'

'Something like that. It's okay. Maybe it's for the best. I've got more important things to worry about right now.'

35

'I've got some bad news.' Jennifer pulled up a barstool. She and Steph were in Square Mile, a notorious hostess and stripper bar where sex tourists, American soldiers from the nearby army base, and Japanese men with a fetish for western women, hung out and drank, often until 10 a.m. 'My customer can't make it tonight.'

Steph nodded. It figured. Bad news was following her around.

'So how are we going to make money?'

Steph downed her glass of wine and slid it forward on the bar, where it was immediately topped up by King, the six-foot-five Nigerian barman who owned Square Mile. The bar served free white or red wine to hostesses, equally stale and warm and hidden in five-litre bottles just under the bar, a far cry from the range of chilled champagne and premium wines displayed for the customers.

Of course, the run-of-the-mill clientele enjoyed more reasonably priced drinks: Ebisu beer (brewed just a few subway stations away) for the Japanese, Budweiser for Americans who wanted everything to be just like home, and tiny glasses of vodka coke for the handful of lady drinkers who weren't associated with the sex industry and didn't qualify for free alcoholic vinegar.

The regular customers hardly ever bought champagne, but that didn't stop the hostesses and strippers, positioned on stools along the bar in short skirts and low tops, continually asking them for it.

'Let's try with some of the bar customers,' said Steph.

'The regulars?' Jennifer pulled out a sickly pink lip-gloss and spread it around her lips. 'That's tough. Uh oh . . . Here go the strippers.'

The strip clubs in Roppongi played the same sexy songs over and over, and whenever these familiar tracks were played in Square Mile, or indeed any after-work venue where strippers hung out, the girls would leap up on to the bar and give everyone a free show – clothed of course, but with lots of hair swinging, buttock circling and legs opening and closing.

'Hardly anyone has money in here. King. King!' Jennifer gave her best sweet-little-girl smile.

'Help you?'

'Any good customers? You know. Champagne good?'

'Maybe the guy at the end of the bar.' King pointed to a ginger man in a brown coat. It was warm inside, and the coat gave clear 'stay away' signals. No one sat within a few metres of him, even though the bar was packed. 'He works in movies. They're shooting some action movie over here, he's staying at the Prince Regent. Might be worth a shot.'

'Let's go talk to him,' said Steph, pushing her way through the crowds. She crashed into a hard chest. 'Hey, sorry,' she said, noticing she'd spilled wine down the anonymous torso.

'Someone's in a hurry.'

It was Luke, now with white wine down his red T-shirt, smiling benevolently as if Steph had just offered him a beer.

'Looks like you've emptied your drink,' said Luke. 'Do you want another? A proper one?'

'No, I'm fine.' Steph looked over Luke's shoulder at the brown-coat man, aware that one of the strippers dancing on the bar was sidling towards him. 'I'll get another free glass in a minute.'

'You're sure?'

'Yes, really. I'm okay.'

'Hey, I think I might have remembered something about your friend,' said Luke, as Steph tried to push past him. 'Annabel, was it?'

'Oh. It's okay.' Steph continued to work her way past him. 'Someone saw her last week, I'm not really worried. Talk to me another time, okay? I've got other things on my mind right now.'

'Okay. Well, at least let me get you a drink before the end of the night.'

'Thanks.'

Jennifer appeared beside them. 'Too late,' she whispered to Steph, pointing to the brown-coat man. A young girl, maybe eighteen or nineteen, was kneeling in front of him on the bar, running a knuckle down his cheek. 'But look at the booth over there. They're wearing *suits*. Might be worth a shot.'

They pushed back through the crowds, Steph smiling at Luke's chivalry as he tried to move people aside for them. When they reached the booth, the three men inside it, all western-looking and wearing suits and square-framed glasses, were clearly delighted to see them.

'Girls,' said one. His accent was American. 'How you doing?'

'Oh, you know,' said Jennifer, with a coy smile, 'just looking for somewhere to sit.'

The man smiled back. 'Ted,' he said, shaking Steph's and Jennifer's hands. 'This is Manny and Jo.' He gestured to the other two men. 'Take a seat. Do you girls want something to drink?'

Jennifer giggled and threw her hair around. 'We thought you'd never ask. It's *so* expensive here.'

Ted stood up. 'What'll it be?'

Steph started to say 'Champagne' but Jennifer cut in.

'Vodka cokes,' she said.

'What do you girls do?' asked Ted, when he returned with the drinks.

'English teachers,' said Jennifer. 'We barely make our rent each month, it costs so much out here. But we still like going out and having a good time.'

Ted raised his glass in agreement.

A few drinks later, Steph and Jennifer retreated to the bathroom, where Jennifer let Steph know her master plan.

'When we go back out,' she said, 'we tell them it's your birthday. Then we ask for champagne. Got it?'

'Got it.'

'We'll never see them again, so don't worry about lying.' Jennifer sidestepped a pool of dirty water on the floor. 'You heard them. They're business tourists. And they're lying to us, just as much as we're lying to them. Did you see the wedding bands? They're not buying us drinks out of the goodness of their hearts.'

Jennifer pushed open a toilet door, revealing a bleached-blonde, sickly-looking girl with a huge chest giving a man oral sex in the cubicle.

'Could you fuck off,' said the girl, turning around.

Jennifer closed the door. 'That's Angel,' she whispered to Steph. 'She does the floor show at Calamity Janes. Total mess. She's always in and out of toilet cubicles with guys. Chastity says she does it for cocaine. Not even money. So sad. I hope I never end up like that.'

Twenty minutes later, a champagne bottle stood on the table and Steph and Jennifer were knocking back glasses of it as quickly as they could. Jennifer showed Steph all the hostess tricks of spilling champagne from the bottle as they poured, saying 'cheers' a lot to encourage the men to drink, and knocking full glasses to the floor. It worked. Within an hour, they had a second bottle.

Hours passed and more bottles arrived. A fight broke out in the crowd as one of the customers tried to stuff ice down a girl's chest. She slapped him, he slapped her, and the bouncers threw them both out.

'I've got to go home,' said Jennifer, when the fourth champagne bottle was nearly empty. 'Seriously, I'm so drunk.' She grabbed her bag, which fell open on the dirty, champagne-puddled floor, spilling make-up, coins and scraps of paper around her feet. After rescuing approximately half the contents, she clutched her bag to her chest and leaned on Steph's shoulder. 'Are you coming?'

Steph, holding Ted's hand while he refilled her champagne glass, shook her head. 'I'm staying here,' she whispered. 'I think maybe they might get another bottle.'

'Steph, I really think . . .' Jennifer put her hand to her head. 'Wow. Everything's spinning. Look, I can't leave you here.'

'I'm fine. Really.'

'No, Steph, I think . . .' She grabbed the side of the booth. 'Okay, I've really, *really* got to go. I'll ask Luke to look out for you.' Jennifer swayed into the crowd and vanished.

And then Steph's world went weird. Really weird. Like it had fragmented into little pieces. She was in the toilets, but they'd changed shape, like in a dream, and the door led to somewhere different. And then she was crouching behind the bar, hiding. Someone said her name, and she saw the man in the brown coat waving a pair of handcuffs at her. Then Luke was there, his shoulder warm and solid, carrying her past the pink and white canopy of Café Almond.

36

'Drink some water.'

Steph tried to open her eyes. They felt stuck together and her eyelashes pulled against her cheeks. Finally her eyes fluttered open. A bottle with Japanese writing on it was being waved in front of her.

'Luke?'

'Yes, it's me. Water for you.'

She took the bottle, broke the seal and drank. It satisfied her mouth, but not her stomach, which immediately cramped painfully around the cold liquid.

'You must be feeling rough,' said Luke, crouching down beside her. 'You were pretty far gone last night.'

'Where am I?' Steph sat up, and felt the battered, plastic-leather of a cheap couch sticking to her legs. Her evening dress rode up around her thighs. She smelt exhaust fumes and heard traffic. The window behind her rattled, and a nicotine-stained computer sat in the corner. 'I'm at my apartment. How did I get back here?'

'No, you're at *my* apartment,' said Luke, taking the water bottle from Steph's shaking hands. 'You passed out in the bar. A guy was trying to get you into a taxi. While you were unconscious.'

'No, this is *my* apartment,' said Steph, blinking and taking the water again. 'It is.' She stood up, but her legs shook so she sat back down again. 'I can see my room. Where's my key. Where's my *bag*?' She felt around on the floor.

'Don't worry, I have it,' said Luke. 'It's in my room down the hall. I promise, you're at my place, not yours.'

'No, I'm certain,' said Steph, noticing the familiar pattern of grease on the computer in the corner and turning to see the motorway overhang at the window. It was dark outside, but the view was familiar. 'We must be staying at the same place. I thought it was all girls . . .'

'Weird,' said Luke, kneeling down beside her. 'What's your room number?'

'Ten.'

'You know, you were pretty stupid last night.'

'No . . . Why was I? I made some money. I'm fine.'

'You nearly weren't fine,' said Luke. 'Watch who you drink with in future. How's your head?'

'Fuzzy,' Steph admitted. 'What time is it?'

'Gone six. Nearly time for work.'

'Shit. You're joking.' Steph leapt up, holding on to the sofa for support.

'I'll walk you.'

'Thanks for getting me home,' said Steph, as Luke stopped at a pizza van and ordered a slice of pepperoni for a pre-work dinner-on-the-run.

'Do you want pizza?' asked Luke, pulling out a couple of thousand yen notes.

'No, I'm fine.' Steph's stomach felt hollow, but she was too embarrassed to take food when she wasn't sure she could pay Luke back.

'So you wanted to know about Annabel, right?' said Luke. 'There was something I wanted to tell you.'

'Do you remember her from the apartment?' asked Steph. 'She stayed in my room, before I came.'

'I didn't know *you* lived there until today,' said Luke, 'and we work together. There are like thirty people staying there. Everyone comes and goes. You're sure you don't want a piece?'

'Yes.'

Luke took his slice on greaseproof paper and they walked down towards Roppongi Tower, its orange and white metal struts criss-crossing the night sky.

The tower watched over the district and saw everybody: the

nice young ladies who flew over to be models and left as escorts with drink problems: the men who squandered millions of yen on the attentions of beautiful, uninterested women: the female travellers who, hypnotised by piles of yen in Tokyo's western-sleaze central, ended up staying in Roppongi for years, their dreams of seeing the world put on hold one more month, one more month.

'When I tried to talk to you about Annabel last night,' Luke said, 'you didn't seem all that interested.'

'I wasn't,' said Steph. 'To be honest, last night I realised I need to take care of me and earning money. Annabel . . . Everyone says she's fine, someone saw her a week ago and no one's worried about her. I still want to meet up with her but . . . There are other priorities right now.'

'Well I remembered she went to work at Calamity Janes. One of the barmen had a crush on her.'

'I already knew she worked at Janes,' said Steph. 'I was thinking about getting a job there too so I could try and get in touch with her. But actually now, if I was trying to get a job at Janes, it'd be to pay off my debts.'

'He was heartbroken when she left,' said Luke. 'He wanted to marry her. I remember him going to Janes, trying to see her. He really loved her. She must have been a real sweetheart. He goes for nice girls.'

'She was when I knew her,' said Steph, feeling a pang of homesickness. After Julia's cold dismissals, the idea of Annabel was reassuring, like a warm cup of English tea. 'A really nice girl. Do anything for anyone.'

Luke held the floppy pizza with both hands and lowered it into his mouth. After he'd finished chewing he said, 'She stole a customer from Mama, though. I saw him in Square Mile last night. That's what reminded me. Mama was so angry. It's bad when girls do that. Mama trusts the girls and they take her customers. She's in debt herself, you know. And she's sick. She doesn't deserve that.'

They started walking again. Steph wished Luke would walk

more quickly. He had a bounding pace that seemed to move him more from side to side than forward. Her head hurt.

Inside the club, Steph changed into another of Helena's hand-me-downs and applied layer after layer of make-up. The dressing room was empty, so she reasoned she must be slightly early.

'Steph-chan.' It was Hiro, calling from the doorway.

'Yes?' Steph's head was pounding, and she prayed there weren't customers waiting already. She went to the changing-room door, lips pencilled with liner but no lipstick, and only one eye made up.

'Steph-chan. You left your customer book here.' Hiro produced Annabel's diary. 'Don't leave it out again. You have to keep your customers private. Very important. Go to the waiting table.'

'Okay.' Steph yawned and took the book. After she'd finished her make-up, she sat alone at the waiting table, the diary absent-mindedly tucked under her arm. She flicked through the pages, picking up where she'd left off. *Maybe I shouldn't be reading this*, she thought, ordering water from the bar. *I don't think Annabel would be happy about me knowing some of this stuff.* Her thumb held her place in the diary.

Steph pushed herself into the furthest corner of the waiting table, checked Hiro was still occupied elsewhere, and began to read:

I'm so low and just ashamed of myself. And fast enough, here comes work again, like Groundhog Day, every night the same. At least if I'm working all the time I can't go out spending money, and maybe, maybe I'll finally be able to get my credit cards paid off.

Annabel. Xxx

Dear God,

I'm completely buzzing, I want to talk and talk but there's no one to talk to. Did *so* much coke this week and ice too, but I swear this is the very, very last time I touch that stuff. That's it now, no more drugs. Please make sure my parents never find out. I feel so stupid, I spent my bonus money, and I feel so sick and weird today. Stupid, stupid, stupid.

Being sacked hasn't sunk in yet. It's for the best, I know. I can't hack teaching English. I hope they didn't see me throw up. I hope that wasn't the reason.

When I take coke or ice I can just drink and drink, it's like nothing affects me, but then the next day I really feel it. But I'm always better by the evening. Probably cause I know I can have another drink again soon. Bad I know, but it's not just me, all the girls do it.

I used to be such a good girl, I used to be sensible. God, I don't even know what ice *is*. I blame Geraldine, giving me coke all week, she said I needed to ease out of my come-down, and I was feeling so, so low at work I could barely even look at the customers, let alone smile or have fun, so I did need just a little bit.

That stuff costs so much, I knew I should get my own bag and share some back. Maybe have a line at Hollywoods, give the rest to Geraldine and go home.

But when we were in Hollywoods I got this, I don't know, sort of itching or . . . I just really, really wanted to do lots more coke, just stuff my nose with it and say what the hell and just go for it, just for one last night.

I asked Geraldine and she found this guy, Amir . . .'

Amir. Steph gripped the diary so hard that a pain shot through her hand. If she ever saw him again, she'd kill him.

. . . but he didn't have any, only ice, which made Geraldine happy. I wanted coke, but she told me ice is the same but with less comedown (true – I don't feel low today, just weird).

I asked to buy a few lines for me and Geraldine and I'd buy coke when he had it, but they both laughed and Amir said I could only buy a gram, which cost practically all my bonus money. But I bought it and just thought, what the hell, let's do this instead and this can be my last fling.

I won't lie, it was so fun. Can't believe we met Boy Ambition! And they do coke too! Of course I ended up buying more after sharing so much. I was just on one, no control, and it makes you feel *great* this ice stuff, really great. Even better than coke. I felt like the queen of everything.

Most of the Janes girls are on drugs – that's how they're so party, party all the time. I always wondered how they're so on it, even when they look tired, but now I know.

The manager *loves* me now, he puts me on all the best tables and my customers keep coming in here so I'm making a *lot* of money. But it's a bit like, the more you work out here, the more you need coke and stuff to keep you going. It's going to be hard to stop doing it, especially since the other girls all take it and I don't like the idea of them having the edge over me because they're such bitches anyway, most of them.

All the Russian girls sleep with their customers, and they're so competitive and they really hate me because I'm doing well, but I don't like them either because they make things really sleazy. They sleep with customers, so men at Janes think there's a chance with all of us.

I seriously have so much energy.

Jacqui said those girls get paid half what we do, so if that's true I suppose I should live and let live. But who knows in this crazy place? Roppongi myths, so many of them.

Like there's a rumour that a customer spikes girls' drinks, and the management know all about it but doesn't warn us. Jacqui said Honey's drink was spiked and she woke up in a customer's apartment with no knickers on and the customer was like 'oh, you were so drunk' but she never passes out and she was sore. And the management still lets him in, even though Honey told them about it, but now it's all hush, hush. Even she won't talk about it. But again, fact or fiction? Maybe it never even happened. You never know out here.

Wages this month – 1,000,000 yen, £5000 in English money. If I save it that will be my debt paid off just like that. I'm doing so well here. I've been really good, I paid my rent straight away and went to the supermarket (no restaurants this month) and bought all my food for the next week and I've hidden the money away and I WILL NOT spend it.

Amen, Annabel. Xxx

37

Steph looked up from the diary.

Drink spiking, girls working as prostitutes . . . It was all so unsettling. But what really caught Steph's eye was £5000. Annabel had earned £5000 in one month.

Steph had been so absorbed in the book, she hadn't noticed some of the other girls had arrived and were arranged around the waiting table, legs crossed, chests out, vacant eyes staring at the keyboard band as it plinky-plonked through its set. Jennifer wasn't there, probably on *dohan*, but Helena, whom Steph felt she'd formed something of a bond with since the dress deal, sat beside her.

'How much do the girls here usually earn in a month?' Steph asked.

Helena shrugged. 'At this club? Depends on her bonuses.'

'Do you think a girl could ever earn, maybe seven thousand dollars in a month?'

Helena gave a little laugh. 'Sure. If she had a magic wand and filled the club with customers. You want that sort of money, work at Calamity Janes.'

'Really?'

'Yes. I have a friend who works at that place. She makes *mucho* yen, but she's always working, working, and the whole time pressure from the manager. I like it here better – more easy.'

'Do they . . . Is there some special look you have to have to work there?' asked Steph, trying to forget Annabel's comments about the sleazy manager, girls sleeping with customers and drinks being spiked. If she could earn £5000 a month, her worries would be over.

'They're beautiful girls,' said Helena, 'but we're beautiful girls too. No, it's not about looks. Okay, sometimes it's about looks, but when they hire the really beautiful girls at that place, sometimes those girls don't stay long. It's all about customers. If you have a customer, they'll take you. That's it.'

'Just one customer? They told me I needed an entertainment visa.'

'If you have no customers, that's true. Janes always want girls with something extra to offer. A visa – it's like big boobs, you know? Something extra.'

'You have customers,' said Steph. 'Why don't you work at Janes, earn double, more than double, what you earn here?'

'And have double the headache and double the hangover?'

'But leave twice as quickly.'

'What's the rush?'

'Steph-chan.' Hiro swooped towards Steph, his arms in a praying gesture. 'Request for you.'

'A request?' Steph leapt to her feet. 'Really?'

'Yes. Yamamoto-san.'

As Steph left the waiting table, a foot stuck out to trip her up. Chastity's. She neatly stepped over it, giving the patent leather shoe a little kick as she calculated how much money she could earn working at Calamity Janes for six months. Enough to pay off Mama and save her course fees.

Just one customer. That's all she needed. She'd already put in a lot of hard work with Mr Yamamoto in an attempt to get Annabel's number. Maybe with a little more effort, and a little help from Mrs Kimono, she could win him as a customer.

Mrs Kimono was locking up her shop as Steph came rushing up the hill, breathless, her lips pale with cold. She'd run all the way from her apartment in the hope of catching Mrs Kimono and running with a hangover was really no fun at all.

'Mrs . . . I'm glad I caught you. I didn't know if you worked on Sundays or . . . I wasn't sure.'

'You look blue,' Mrs Kimono remarked. 'Frozen.' The sweeping wind stirred brown leaves in little dusty circles on the street, but Mrs Kimono herself, dressed as usual in layers and layers of silk, seemed unaware of the weather. 'I wasn't sure if you'd come to me again. What's gone wrong this time?'

Steph pulled down the sleeves of her sweatshirt and clicked her teeth together to stop them from chattering.

'Nothing. Nothing's gone *wrong*.'

'Really?' Mrs Kimono raised a long, neat eyebrow and deposited the shop keys in a little tie bag she carried on her wrist. She had another bag, a large leather one, hanging from her shoulder. It looked very full. 'Then why have you come to see me?'

'This hotessing thing is still so hard, I don't get it, and . . . To be honest, I did *loads* better after you showed me all that tea ceremony stuff. Mr Yamamoto—'

'Yamamoto-*san*.'

'He requested me yesterday. A request! Can you believe it? So I'm getting there. Now I need him to start taking me out to dinner. Will you help me again?'

'I thought you wanted this man to give you your friend's telephone number.'

'I did, but . . .'

'You've forgotten about her.'

'Not exactly. But I know she's okay now. Someone saw her last week, and Julia isn't worried about her. I'm in a lot of debt. I really need to focus on earning money. How do I get Yamamoto-*san* to start taking me out before work?'

'You're in too much of a hurry,' said Mrs Kimono, taking tiny steps along the street, the silk of her skirts keeping each movement clipped and exact. 'Patience. Too western, like my daughter. He's a Japanese man and patience is the Japanese way. These things take time.'

'I don't have time,' said Steph, following her along the tiled street. 'I owe a lot of money, and until I pay it back I'm in trouble. And I need rent, clothes, all sorts of things.'

'Yes.' Mrs Kimono nodded at Steph's thin University of Exeter sweatshirt and ungloved hands, red with cold. 'I can see. But you must be making money somehow. I haven't seen you for weeks. You must have paid rent in that time – landlords in Roppongi don't wait that long.'

'I've found another way of earning money,' Steph admitted. 'Me and another girl, we go to the bars after work and get bottle-back money. Kick-backs. It's kept me going – I paid my rent so far and bought a few dresses – but it's really hard work, and you have to drink so much and if I just get one customer I can pay off the debt in no time. Then I can start earning for my course and get everything back on track.'

'I see.' Mrs Kimono carried on walking, and Steph had to slow her pace not to overtake her. 'So what do you want?'

'I want you to tell me more, give me more insight into what the men like out here. If Yamamoto-san starts taking me on dates, he sort of becomes "my" customer. And I get good bonuses.'

'I see. Like *geisha* have *danna*, I suppose.'

'What's a *danna* again?'

'You don't listen, do you? Again, like my daughter. A *danna* is a *geisha*'s patron. So you need a patron. Someone to fund you. To take care of you.'

'Sort of,' said Steph. 'I was thinking . . . Maybe if I get another customer, it gives me the option . . . I can go to this other club and bring my customer with me.'

'Steal the customer, you mean?' said Mrs Kimono.

'I suppose when you put it that way . . .'

'Not very honest,' Mrs Kimono remarked. 'What about your Mama-san? He's her customer, isn't that right? She won't be happy with you. She gave you a job and you want to steal her customers.'

'I know, I know.' They reached the corner, and Steph saw the circle sign for the subway station in the distance. 'You're right. It's not a good thing to do. Probably I'll just try and get him as a customer so I can do better where I am. But I'm looking at paying off months of debt before I start saving anything. And I don't even know if I'll make my rent. This kick-back thing, it doesn't always work and it's exhausting.'

'What new place are you thinking of?'

'Calamity Janes.'

Mrs Kimono's lips pressed into a thin line. 'Calamity Janes? *Manuke!* Where is your . . . instinct?'

'Are you feeling okay?' It was the first time Steph had heard Mrs Kimono pause to consider her words, or lapse into Japanese.

'You are a very, very foolish girl.'

'Why? What's so bad about Calamity Janes?'

'If you can't feel something is rotten at that place . . .' Mrs Kimono shook her head. 'Money is worthless if you've given your soul away.'

'It's not just for money,' said Steph. 'I think Annabel might work there. She definitely did at some point.'

'If your reason for stealing a customer and working at *that* club is to find an old friend, then I suppose I must admire you,' said Mrs Kimono. 'But you're playing with fire. I already lost one daughter.'

'I don't get what's so bad about—'

'I won't speak of that place anymore. You're old enough. Find your own way.'

They walked past a Tully's coffee shop and a Japanese pot restaurant with fake steam blowing from a pretend charcoal grill at its doorway.

'I know you say I ask too many questions,' said Steph. 'But . . . will you tell me about your daughter? We're friends now. Aren't we?'

Mrs Kimono's bottom lip quivered ever so slightly. 'I'm happy to be your friend. All I will say about my daughter is that she made bad choices. Choices that shamed me as a mother. My *danna* asked me to cut communication with her. So I did. It was only later in life I realised the bad choice I myself had made. A mother's love shouldn't come with rules.'

'Sorry,' said Steph. 'I hope you make friends again.'

'Don't forget about *your* friend in your search for the next yen.' They had reached the subway station and Mrs Kimono turned into the entrance. She looked strange against such a modern backdrop, vaguely ghostlike against the dazzling concrete and glass offices and hotels soaring into the greying, dusk sky.

'No, that's exactly what I do need to do,' said Steph. 'I need to forget everyone except myself. I've been looking for Annabel, asking around, and all that's happened is I've landed a great big debt. I'm in more trouble now than when I arrived. The next yen – that's what I need to be focused on.'

'Then you'll be in good company in Roppongi,' said Mrs Kimono.

'Is it so awful I want to make money out here?' Steph waited at the top of the subway steps, feeling she needed an invitation to accompany Mrs Kimono. 'I need it, I really do. My life back home is a mess. I need to get things on track. And I've had some really bad luck so far. My customer turned out to be no good. I'm in debt.'

'Follow me.' Mrs Kimono waved her hand, descending the subway steps, one hand stroking the metal rail, her Kimono fanning around her.

'Where?' Steph took a step downwards.

'I'm going to the temple. You can come.'

'And you'll teach me more about being Japanese? Like you did at the tea ceremony?'

'Yes.' Mrs Kimono nodded, her stiff grey hair remaining perfectly in place.

38

'This is *Kaminarimon* – the Thunder Gate,' said Mrs Kimono, taking staccato steps towards an enormous red pagoda stretching up into the sky.

The ancient wood structure took up a staggering amount of space in the rundown, riverside district of Asakusa, and made the shabby office blocks nearby look even more sad and tired. The pagoda was as big as a church, but more intricate and beautiful, with tiers of carved wood boldly painted in red, white and gold. The layers were supported by shiny, red pillars, between which hung a red lantern as big as three men.

'It's a beautiful temple,' said Steph. 'Where do you pray, or worship or whatever you call it?'

'Don't you listen?' Mrs Kimono snapped. 'This is the gate, not the temple. There are two gates before we reach the temple itself. *Senso-ji*.' She said the word as if she were breathless.

'It's my favourite temple. The oldest in Tokyo.'

'It's amazing,' said Steph. 'Right in the middle of all this . . . this . . . you know.'

Mrs Kimono nodded. 'Do you know anything about Japanese religion? Culture?'

'A little,' Steph lied.

'This temple is a Buddhist temple for Guan Yin, the goddess of mercy. People come here for all sorts of reasons – to give thanks, to ask for help, or simply to feel at one with others. We pass through the Thunder Gate, and along *Nakamise Dori*.'

They walked under the lantern on to a street lined with souvenir sellers and food stands. 'We've built and rebuilt this street so many times,' said Mrs Kimono, 'it's seen world wars and earth-quakes. But still it survives.'

A Japanese man and a western girl stood by a rice-cake stall watching a young boy flip saucer-sized rice cakes on a charcoal fire, then dip then in briny liquid before leaving them to cool. The man was maybe fifty and dressed in a suit, while his female companion wore jeans and looked about twenty. They seemed to be having fun, the man smiling adoringly as the girl attempted to say some words in Japanese.

'What is it that Japanese men want from hostesses?' Steph asked. 'I do the same as the other girls, but I've never been asked on *dohan*. It's been weeks now.' She noticed an ice cream shop with a display of twenty or so plastic ice cream cones in the window and shivered. Some of the ice creams were the most bizarre colours – green, purple and cherry red – and the English translations of their flavours were equally unusual: green tea, soy bean and sweet potato.

'I've never experienced a hostess club,' said Mrs Kimono, 'but I imagine the men who go there go to feel like *men*. They want to feel every woman at the club desires and respects them. And they also want to relax, be taken care of.'

'Is that what *geisha* do?' asked Steph. 'make men feel desired and taken care of?'

Mrs Kimono was silent for a moment, and Steph could hear the rustle of silk as she walked, *chiff, chiff, chiff*. Eventually, she spoke. 'Yes, perhaps we do make men feel like we desire them. And we certainly take care of them and help them to relax.'

'How?'

'All sorts of ways. The tea ceremony, you already saw. And we play music, perform dances. Very often we play drinking games to help the men have fun and, 'loosen their ties,' as they say. We're also their friends. We know about their business and maybe even offer advice if we're asked – although of course we always make it *look* like the man has come up with the answer he needs. We're never too clever. We take the hard work out of their social lives. Our customers work so hard all day, we do everything for them when they visit us. Even the conversation is taken care of.'

'Everyone works so hard here,' said Steph. 'I see Japanese people asleep everywhere – on subway trains, in restaurants. Sometimes the customers at work fall asleep on us.'

'Most Japanese men work maybe sixty hours a week,' said Mrs Kimono, ushering Steph under another beautiful pagoda at the end of the street. 'The Treasure House Gate,' she annouced, 'and now we're in the main complex.'

Beyond the gate, there were more red pillars and low roofs surrounding a central, concrete square – chilly under the setting sun. Natives and tourists milled around, and several older Japanese people stood by what looked like a little well at the centre of the complex, which issued thick, fragrant clouds of silvery incense smoke from its centre.

Mrs Kimono walked towards the smoke and took her place in the crowd surrounding it. 'After work, men don't want any pressure of problems,' she said. 'They want someone to take the hard work from their shoulders. Make all the *effort*.' She wafted the smoke towards her with soft gestures, breathing the fumes deeply into her lungs and closing her eyes.

Around the fuming incense, others were also encouraging the smoke towards them – some waved it towards arms or legs, others directed it towards their heads. They were all older people, white-haired, and some were bent or weary. There was chanting coming from somewhere, washing over the temple in waves.

'So,' said Mrs Kimono after a moment, slowly opening her eyes. She looked tranquil and unusually benign. 'You'd like to learn something you can use at work. Something that will make you popular with you customer. Come with me.'

Mrs Kimono led Steph under one of the green rooftops and produced a cushion from her bag. She put the cushion on the cold, concrete floor and knelt on it.

'Kneel with me.'

'On the floor?'

'Yes.'

Reluctantly, Steph knelt on the cold floor, noticing disapproving looks from other temple visitors, including two elderly women in kimonos.

Next, Mrs Kimono removed a black wooden cup from her bag and placed it between the two of them.

'Can you hear the chanting?'

'Yes.'

'Good. Pay attention to it. The rhythm of it. I'm going to teach you a *geisha* drinking game. *Konpira fune fune* – the slapping cup game. I've been commissioned to entertain a group of very important politicians tonight, old friends of mine, and they love to play this game. It looks easy but it isn't. Watch.'

Mrs Kimono began slapping the cup in rhythm to the chanting, placing her hand behind her after each slap. Occasionally she'd pick up the cup, put it behind her, then place it back between them, but always in time to the rhythm of the chants. When the chanting was slow and mournful, she went slow. When it became quicker and more chatty, her pace picked up.

'Now we try together,' she said, and she and Steph slapped the cup in turn. 'If one of us takes away the cup, the other must touch the floor with a closed hand,' she explained. 'If we make a mistake, we drink *sake*. I don't have any *sake*, so you'll have to pretend.'

It sounded simple, but Steph found herself forgetting to close her hand, or dropping the rhythm.

'Good fun, isn't it?' said Mrs Kimono. 'Simple, good fun. That's what Japanese men like. We arrange fun and games for them, so they don't have to think. But always with gentleness and femininity. You must always let the man win.'

'That's it?' Steph was sceptical. 'A game like that will make me more popular at work?'

'Try it with your customer,' Mrs Kimono urged. 'He'll love that you've learned something of Japanese culture, but most of all he'll love someone else taking care of things for him. Taking away the responsibility. Letting him relax and be in someone else's care.' She coughed suddenly and violently, turning away from Steph and bringing her hand to her chest. 'I have a meeting now. Perhaps you'd like to come and see me again. I'd like to hear your progress. It's been a while since I've had a *maiko* of my own.'

39

Mama

'Don't be shy, George-san. Come in.' Mama was in her dressing gown when she came to her apartment door, and George hesitated on the threshold, this time remembering to remove his shoes before entering.

'I hope you don't mind, but I have to get ready for work.' Mama took laboured steps down her hallway and turned into a side room – her bedroom. 'We've come a long way together, haven't we? Good friends now.'

George followed, but waited at the bedroom door, his cheeks red. 'I'll wait for you . . . er . . . Where would you like me to wait?'

'No, no, come in.' Mama had her back to him and was rifling through clothes in a beautiful wardrobe of polished wood. The doors were inset with porcelain panels and painted with silhouettes of tree branches.

It looked out of place in Mama's simple apartment, a relic from an earlier, more affluent time, but it suited the splendour of garments hanging within. Stiff bodices in red and blue velvet, sweeping evening gowns with puffed sleeves, and innumerable slinky black dresses were squashed side by side among furs, cashmere shawls and tailored wool coats. Beneath them a heap of shoes, mainly stilettos and most of them red, were piled up, almost to knee height.

'We're doing well, aren't we, George-san? You must have nearly everything you need.'

'Perhaps but . . .' George took a tentative step into the bedroom. 'I feel there's something . . . The book needs more somehow. More of who you really are. I have a sense you're hiding something from me. A secret. The reader needs to see inside you. Into your soul. I need to know everything.'

The table by the window was littered with medicines: white plastic pots labelled in Japanese and blister packets of pills held together with solemn, black rubber bands.

'Take a seat.' Mama motioned to the simple futon on the *tatami* floor, and George sank clumsily to his knees. She muttered as she flicked through dresses: 'No, too uncomfortable. No, needs a repair. I feel like *red* today, red, red, red . . .' Her movements were slow and cautious, as if fearing pain at every stretch. 'We'll do the interview here, while I get ready. You'll be anxious to get started, I imagine.'

'Will you help me, Mama?' said George. 'We need to speak very frankly today. Not just about your career, but . . . There's something else, isn't there? Something you're keeping from me?'

'You think so?'

'I'm a journalist. I know when people are holding things back.'

'I'm a little better today,' said Mama, as if she hadn't heard him. 'I just needed bed rest, nothing more. They've given me new medication now, it helps a lot. Reduces the swelling. Much more powerful. It means I can carry on working. I thought last week maybe that was it. Retirement.' She took a long, red dress from the wardrobe and hung it over the door. 'Now. I was telling you about my mother and father, wasn't I?'

'Yes, but—'

'You have enough about them?'

'Yes. I was thinking—'

'Okay. So I'll tell you about working in soapland.'

To George's obvious embarrassment, Mama removed her dressing gown and let it fall to the floor, revealing peach-coloured underwear, blue veins latticing her rail-thin legs and transparent skin around her ribcage. Every time she inhaled, the skin on her chest looked as though it might tear with the pressure. She stepped into the dress.

'Yes, I suppose we can start with that,' said George, looking at the floor.

'After the *no-pan kissa*, there were many girls looking for work and where else would we go, those of us who weren't looking for marriage, but back to the water trade?' Mama worked the dress up her tiny frame. 'I'd never been paid for sex at that time, not directly, but after several years of using my body I saw no reason why not. Going back to the snack club seemed like a lot of hard work for not much money.

'You have to make relationships, you see – something I was good at, but not for the rates the snack bars were offering. I'd heard of hostess clubs, but I'd heard better stories about the money on offer in soapland – five thousand dollars a month. This was in the eighties when that sort of money could buy you a new car, near enough.

'I wasn't scared of the sex industry. I'd seen enough things working for Tomi and also in the *no-pan kissa*, and most of us in those cafés ended up offering something like sex anyway by the end, so the idea wasn't entirely new or unpalatable.'

'Where did you go – back to Tomi?'

'No, not to him. But I did go back to Kabukicho. Girls told me I could find work there, and right away I got a job in a place near the fancy Shinjuku hotels. I remember it very well, the name of the place was written in neon-tube lighting over the door and there was a picture in the entrance – cute, young girls giggling, sitting on a bed of stuffed toy animals.

'When I told the manager, who was a quiet, family man, as a matter of fact, and treated the girls very well, that I'd worked in a *no-pan kissa* he gave me a job right away and I was shown to my own room. Will you help me, George-san?' Mama was struggling with the zip of her dress. 'The perils of living alone,' she said. 'Usually I ask my cleaner to help, but I gave her the afternoon off.'

George zipped her up, then settled his weight back on to the futon.

'What was I saying? Ah yes. I had my own room to service customers and we girls could decorate it however we liked. Stuffed toys, sexy photos, whatever we wanted. There was a private bath in there, of course, and a shower, all part of the soapland experience. We had to buy our own condoms, toiletries, that sort of thing. Shampoo. Oils. You know. Really, we were our own boss.

'A very tough girl, her name was Peach in English, showed me around and told me how everything worked. She had tattoos, which I'd never seen on a girl before, and a very hard attitude. I think she'd been abused quite a bit along the way, and she was very tough with customers and told me I didn't have to take any nonsense from anyone.

'A lot of the girls, she told me, got a hard time, sometimes physical abuse from customers, and took it. You know how Japanese girls are — sweet and shy and obliging. But if someone was rude, she said I should tell them to get lost.

'Peach had bright pink hair, and some of the other girls had orange or blue hair. They had some great outfits too, very sexy, cheap looking really, but they looked great on young girls, something like a Japanese punk. We have a name for that look, we call it *yanki*. It's worn by people from the wrong side of the tracks. In comparison, I was quite plain but I had a western look which set me apart.

'Anyway, Peach talked me through what the girls offered. It was basically a set menu for a set price, about an hour from start to finish, like every other soapland. The man comes in, you undress him and give him oral sex. Then you soap him down and wash him, and sit him on a special chair with a hole in the bottom. You lie under the chair and lick his anus and around his testicles. Then there is a bath, and you massage him with your soapy, naked body before moving to the bedroom for full sex. It's quite a service. Lying under a man performing oral sex with soap falling in your eyes, it's not easy. People were always jealous of the money we girls made, but it was hard work.'

Mama reached up to a shelf in her wardrobe and took down a round box, removing the lid with care. Inside it was a mass of black hair. She took out the wig and shook it around, then placed it over her scalp.

'I was quite excited, especially when Peach told me how much we earned per customer. It's always the way with sex work – you get so excited about the money, you're able to forget about everything else. But let me tell you, the first day in particular was hard. So was the second. And the third. Very difficult. Emotionally, you see, it drains you.

'You do more than just give sex, and that's hard enough. No, you have to give emotion and make a man feel special, maybe eight different men in the same day. It's hard work. And then, of course, you meet the strange characters too, and you're never certain you can be safe with somebody.

'The manager was very good, but he couldn't be in every room at once, and those were the days before security cameras. So, from time to time, I did worry about things happening when my door was closed. Sometimes they did. Those things, we tried to forget, as if they never happened. Don't talk about it, don't remember. Otherwise you wouldn't be able to carry on.

'I had a rather strange customer for some time, I think maybe he was mentally ill, quite a few clients were, or physically disabled, and he followed me wherever I worked. When I left the first soap place, he followed me to the next, even though I didn't give him my details. And the one after that. It was frightening.'

40

From: C_C_Chastity
To: CanadianDaphne
Subject: hungover again

Daphneeee!

I do read your emails, I promise! Sorry babes, I've just got a lot on my mind, you know how it is out here. Yes, I think it's awesome you passed the audition. That Grey guy, what an idiot. Sounds like there's too many good-looking women out there, just like here. The men end up thinking they're gods.

In Roppongi girls like us are just average and it does warp you. Look at girls like Angel and Katrina. They both used to be top girls, customers falling over them, but they do it with anyone for a bag of coke and a B request these days, they don't think they're worth anything more. And me, I can't say I've escaped it. I'm always looking for the next dress or haircut or surgery or whatever. Anything to make me stand out.

A few nights back Hiro sat this new English girl (loads of weird scars, doesn't know the first thing about hostessing, why did Mama hire her? Why?) with Yamamoto. I was so, so angry. Yamamoto ALWAYS requests me, but I think this new girl must have pulled some strings with Hiro or something, she's sleeping with someone, mark my words. Yamamoto always orders champagne too, so that was my good bonus out of the window. I'm lower on the bonus chart than ever.

I feel so stuck right now. If things keep going the way they're going, how am I going to pay rent in this crazy city?

Sometimes I just feel like running home, but going back there . . . it's easy to forget how mad my family are. Your family is supposed to make you happy, but mine makes me sad. And working back home is just ten times harder – London is the worst place, at least out here we're respected. Sort of.

I was so depressed last night I was seriously thinking about taking a stripping job. At least that way you're in control of your wages and you can hustle for business. And when you strip, it's not like you have to get into these creepy relationships with customers, you know what I mean? That always ends with them asking you to a hotel room, and you just hang on for as long as you can and spend the whole time fending them off.

It's like Fiona was saying, with stripping you just get in, do your thing, take the money and go home. OK, yes, it's all touchy feely out here, which does sort of suck, but I was thinking I could handle it as long as I know there's money coming at the end. That's the thing with hostessing, you can put in a load of work and then your customer takes off with another girl, and bam! You're right at the bottom of the bonus chart.

But then I woke up this morning and had a 'what was I thinking!' moment. It's bad enough for Tammy that her mum's a hostess, let alone a stripper. And all the strippers out here end up in a bad way.

My hair is coming out in chunks! No kidding! Peroxide has done something really bad to it. Tammy had a fit when she saw it. Honestly, she's like a mum sometimes. I swear, she's more of a mum than I am. I'm always the one wanting to go out and have fun and she stays in and does her homework.

The promotion thing with Mama, I'm pretty sure now it's not going to happen. It really hit home last night when Hiro sat that new girl with my customer – why could they hire me as a second Mama-san when they can get someone younger?

You know what, a few years ago I had money saved and still had time to take courses and all of that stuff and was still

young enough to start new things. But when you're thirty
with a kid, starting at the bottom doesn't feel good. If I went
back to London, I'd be training as an office junior or just
stripping with a load of eighteen-year-olds who are better
looking than me and have better skin and no tattoos. At least
out here, they think we look young, even when we're not. I
couldn't go back to some dingy flat in Shepherd's Bush, I just
couldn't do it, even as a stepping stone.

I can't believe you remembered that million yen thing. It
was such a long time ago. I'm a long way from that now – a
million yen wouldn't even keep me in skin cream. I've had it
and spent it twenty times over.

Now, if I quit work, I'd need billions to keep me and
Tammy living the way we're used to. And even that wouldn't
buy us our own place. Do you know how long mortgages last
out here? 100 years. No kidding. Mums and dads pass on the
debt to their kids.

I'm having a bad day today, hun. I just feel like I've got
nothing, no training, no skills, I wasted all my time being a
stupid model and a hostess, thinking I was all important and
the next big thing. I should have got in, got out.

Love you babes,
Chastity XXXXX

41

Mama

'Frightening?' asked George, shuffling on the futon. 'Was it dangerous, working in soapland?'

'A little,' said Mama. 'In soapland, no matter how good the manager is, you're really on your own. It's lonely. Your only company all day are your clients, and you're in a room with a little window and not much light or air. I never wanted to chat to clients. I thought it was a waste of time.'

Mama opened a large drawer on the vanity unit in the corner. The drawer was full to the brim with necklaces, brooches, bracelets and a host of other jewellery, all tumbled together like a pirate's treasure chest. She examined chains of diamonds and pearls, eventually deciding on a giant ruby hanging from a black velvet string. She fastened it around her neck.

'I worked there for many years,' said Mama, 'and I did plenty of drugs, drank too much, ate bad food and spent time with bad people. I didn't realise when I took the job, but when you work at soapland you cross over.

'The snack bar was borderline acceptable. But working at soapland isn't something nice girls do – or certainly they don't admit to doing it. I actually met a few nice girls there, girls saving for weddings or earning money to care for elderly parents. But there's a stigma. No one would marry a soapland girl, and the girls saving for weddings were doing it in secret, terrified their fiancés would find out.

'I spent money like you wouldn't believe when I worked soapland. It made me feel better to spend, like I was part of real, normal society. But as soon as I earned it, I spent it on clothes, drink, friends, boyfriends . . . In my hand one minute, gone the next.'

'What made you leave?' asked George.

'I don't know, probably the weird guy was a big part of it. The customer who kept following me. I heard stories about him, but the police wouldn't do anything and wherever I moved he always found me. I realised that as long as I was working in soapland, I was vulnerable.

'Japan is a very safe place, but that's because many groups in our society don't report crimes. The *yakuza* and sex workers keep their troubles to themselves.

'And of course, there was the stigma. I'd had enough of being frowned upon, looked down on. At first I was earning so much money that I didn't care about the looks I got. But after a while it got to me. All my friends knew what I did, but when I met strangers I'd lie about my job. I could never keep a boyfriend – the lie wouldn't hold for long enough.

'So I decided to save money and get out. Lots of girls *say* they're saving money, every soapland worker has a story about her big dream when she's earned this many yen, or that many yen. But usually the goal changes, the dream shifts, and they stay stuck, always talking, talking about the day they'll move on. But when I decide to do something, I do it. I'm strong, you know?'

George nodded.

'So. Just like that, I cut out everything – my bad friends and all my bad habits. And I worked and saved, worked and saved. The other girls were a little cold, jealous of my determination, but I didn't care. What I did care about was *how* I was going to get out of soapland. This is why it's easy to get stuck, you see. Once you're known for working soapland, other places don't want you.

'Tokyo is a big place, but the water trade is small. People knew me. I wasn't the sort of girl more respectable places, like hostess clubs, wanted. But that was okay, because I didn't want to work for someone else anymore. I wanted to earn enough to run my own place. My own hostess club, I decided.

'There was *real* money in hostessing back then. Clubs with western hostesses in particular, they were quite the thing in the eighties. Hostess club owners were making obscene amounts. As a young girl I'd seen my father run businesses in Tokyo, and I was smart enough to realise I wanted other people working for me.'

Mama put her hand to her head and closed her eyes. Her jaw twitched, then relaxed. She opened her eyes again. 'It was hard saving the money at first. At soapland, I was with the wrong crowd. Most of the girls there drank or took glue or drugs, and no one was supportive or encouraging. I realised I needed a different scene, so I found a new place, a masturbation-only place. Much less work.'

'A different type of soapland?' asked George.

'No, a different type of place altogether. I don't know if there's an English word for it, but it's a place men come just to be masturbated, without even seeing a girl. Less emotion, less stress for me, and the girls there were nicer. Many were students.'

'I'm not sure I understand,' said George. 'How could you . . . you know, without being seen by the customer?'

'Oh, it was no problem,' said Mama. 'The customers came in and put their penises through holes in the wall.'

'Okay.'

'From the customer's point of view, the place looked a lot like changing rooms with curtains, the sort of changing rooms you find in a department store. The man would go into a booth, close the curtain behind him and put his penis through the hole in the wall. We'd sit on the other side of the wall and masturbate them, bish bish, just like that, and then we'd wipe them with a wet cloth and we were done.

'The holes had pictures of famous women above them so the customers had something to fantasise about, and of course for all the customers knew there could have been men servicing them behind the walls, but we were busy enough.

'After my experience at soapland, I was very good. So good, I got complaints, would you believe, for being too quick.' Mama chuckled. 'My secret was to make noises. And I had a special technique with my hands. I could service maybe twenty, thirty men a day, twice as many as the other girls, so I kept my income as high as when I was working soapland.'

Mama bent down by the wardrobe, her knees clicking as she rummaged in the piles of shoes at the bottom. 'I wonder if . . . No, not *those* shoes, not today. My lucky shoes . . . Oh, I can't find the other one. Ah! Here's a pair.' She stood up slowly and put the shoes on her vanity unit. 'It was while I worked at the penis-hole place that something wonderful happened. Something wonderful and terrible at the same time.'

'What?'

'I fell in love.' Mama smiled at the memory. 'For the first time. I'd had boyfriends of course, but this was different. He was an American. Repeating my mother's mistakes, you could say, and he was somewhat like my father. But I fell for him like falling off a mountain.'

'Was he a customer?'

'No, no.' Mama's mouth puckered. 'I'd never fall for a customer. No, I met him in the street on my way to work one evening. He was very dashing and handsome, and he had the bluest eyes I'd ever seen. He looked like a film star, you know? Bright white teeth and a strong jaw. He asked me for directions, and straightaway I knew I'd just die if I didn't see him again.

'He was staying at one of the Shinjuku hotels, but he told me he was lost. I had a feeling he wanted to find out a little more about the delights of our red-light area. So I offered to give him a tour, and in turn he offered to buy me dinner.

'I'd never missed a day of work in my life, but for this man I didn't give work a second thought and we went out together that night. What's the time, George-san?'

'Six thirty.'

'Ah! So late. I really have to get to the club. There are men trying to steal my hostesses again, spreading bad rumours about me, my club.' She yawned. 'It's important I'm there all the time right now. Without me, things would fall apart. I don't know. The water trade – it's a hard world. Sometimes I think I was better off at the bottom of the pile seeing twenty penises a day. No responsibility.

'The girls are always quitting, you know. My hostesses. They're not career girls, not like I was. Most of them are travellers. Not good news for the business.'

'Would you like me to call you a cab?' asked George.

'No need. A friend of mine lends me his driver. I've made good friends in this business, important friends. But it's hard, so hard. I'm in so much debt, George-san. Just like my father. But I'll keep working.'

George looked at his notes. 'We're nearly there, Mama. So close. But there's still something . . .' He shook his head. 'What is it you're not telling me? This is all fascinating, but it's too easy. What don't you want to share? What feels too hard?'

Mama smiled. 'Everything is hard right now.'

'Maybe you should rest tonight.'

'No, no. No time, no time. No one to look after me, I have to look after myself. George-san, next time, let's meet at my club, okay?'

'Sure.' George watched her stiff movements, saw the tiredness in her eyes. 'Whatever time you can give me.'

42

Steph

It was 2 a.m., and Hiro was behind the reception desk, stuffing bank notes and silver coins into slim, white envelopes. Steph and the other hostesses stood a few feet away, watching him, shifting their weight from one high-heeled shoe to the other.

Some of the girls twiddled their hair, others gnawed the skin around their fingernails. The collective nervousness was catching, and Steph found herself breathing a little too quickly and chewing her lip.

Hostesses at Sinatra's were paid every other week, and pay hour could be nerve-wracking since a low wage packet signified low bonuses and could mean immediate dismissal.

But as Steph watched Hiro count out notes, she felt a cautious optimism. She'd been doing well at the club. Yamamoto-san had been requesting her on a regular basis, and he always bought champagne which meant his table bill would be very high. Maybe, just maybe, she'd earned enough to pay off her debt and leave a few yen spare for food and other necessities.

'Chastity.' Hiro slid an envelope over the desk. Chastity snatched it and studied the figure written on the white paper. She held the envelope close so no one else could read, but she clearly wasn't pleased.

'Helena.'

Helena smiled when she saw her figure, and tucked the envelope into her shoulder bag.

'Steph.'

Steph could tell, without even picking it up, that the white envelope was empty. The bubble of hope burst. She took the envelope anyway, her name written in *kanji* and *Zero yen* pencilled underneath.

Chastity nudged Christiana and smiled.

'How long until I actually get paid, Hiro?' asked Steph, ignoring the smug look on Chastity's face.

'At least three months, Steph-chan.'

'Three?'

You have fines to work off now, as well as your customer debt.'

'What fines?'

'Five lateness fines, dress fines, hair fines, chewing gum fines . . .'

'What? A chewing gum fine? You *are* joking?'

'You were chewing gum in the club. So we fine you an hour's wages.'

'Four lateness fines – I've only been late twice.'

Hiro pulled out a time sheet. 'Last Monday, and the Thursday before that, you were at the waiting table two minutes past and three minutes past.'

'That's not late.'

'Yes.' Hiro gave a curt nod. 'Late.'

'And for that I get fined, how much?'

'Two hours' wages.'

'This is a joke.'

'No joke,' said Hiro. 'You should have chosen your customer better. Then wages wouldn't be a problem for you. I told Mama, a girl who brings in customers like that doesn't understand the club. She deserves her debt.'

'If *you'd* vetted him better, I wouldn't have a problem either,' Steph countered. 'Mama said she'd never have let him in.'

'I knew he'd be a problem,' said Hiro, with a little nod. 'But *your* problem, not mine. You needed to learn. A bad customer means hostess debt.'

'You mean you knew his card would be bad?' Steph said, her voice rising. 'And you let me bring him in anyway?'

'I had . . . an idea.'

'I can't believe this.' Steph screwed up her empty pay packet and threw it on the desk. 'You got me in debt on purpose. To

teach me some stupid lesson. Months of debt just for not knowing
. . . How could you do this to me? Don't you have feelings?'
She'd said very similar words before, under different circum-
stances, and it hurt just as much to say them a second time. 'I
should have known,' she said. 'You couldn't care less, no one
could. Fine. Well, from now on I'll be just like everyone else round
here. I won't care about anyone but myself.'

Steph was at Roppongi crossroads within minutes, having
marched out of the club before anyone saw the tears come. She
was crying now, pushing back and forth against the crowd with
no idea where she was going, lost again.

Three months.

It was like a prison sentence. She'd been surviving so far on
bottle-back money, but it was hard work, both physically and
mentally, and she wasn't sure her liver could survive the amount
of champagne she'd have to drink to pay her rent for three
months.

Ahead, the sign for Calamity Janes shone under the churning,
black sky.

I'll go in there and ask for a job, Steph decided, roughly wiping
away tears and leaving mascara streaks on her cheeks. *I'll make
them take me. I won't take no for an answer.*

She marched up the club steps with such authority that the
bouncer ignored her, and when she reached the unmanned
reception desk on the fifth floor she banged her fist on the thin
wood.

'Hey! Anyone? Is anyone here?'

A blonde head poked through the glass door by reception.

'Can I help you, love?' It was Ricky, the mama-san, this time
dressed in a grey trouser suit, almost identical to the white one
that had hung loosely around her petite frame the last time Steph
had seen her.

'Yes, I met you before,' said Steph, hoping her eyes didn't look
too red. Her gums felt bruised and tender from crying. 'You . . .
I'm looking for work.'

Ricky leaned against the glass door, clearly gearing up for a 'not right now' speech.

'I got a job at another club,' said Steph, 'but everyone knows this place is the best. And I've got a customer.'

Ricky pulled herself upright. 'Really? That was fast work. What's his name?'

'Yamamoto-san.' *At least, soon he'll be my customer. I hope.*

Ricky's long fingernails tapped the glass door. 'As in Yamamoto Pharmaceuticals?'

Steph nodded.

'And he takes you out, does he? On *dohan*?'

'Loads of times.'

'And he'll come with you? If you switch clubs?'

'He told me he would.'

'Well, great!' Ricky took a plastic folder of contracts from behind the reception desk. 'He'll come to Janes? You can bring him here?'

Steph nodded again.

'Take one of these.' Ricky waved a contract at her – Japanese script with English translations written underneath. 'Fill it in, come to the club with your customer and we'll start you working. Here, let me sign it for you. What's your surname?'

'Coen.' Steph watched Ricky scribble her name in the blank space on the back page, then sign *Ricky Demarco* in the spot marked *Manager*. She dated the contract and passed it to Steph.

Steph glanced at the pages of writing, noticing **We take your passport to ensure a minimum three-months working commitment**, written in bold letters.

'But listen, Ricky. Yamamoto-san is busy this week. What if I start tomorrow and bring him next week some time?'

Ricky gave her a cynical smile. 'I don't think so, love. How do I know he'll make the switch? How do you know, for that matter, unless you actually bring him in?'

Steph flinched. 'He will. I'm sure he will.'

'I work on certainties. Customer first, then we'll sign you up.'

Through the glass door, the club lights dimmed.

'Closing time,' said Ricky.

Girls and customers began to flow out into reception, the girls dressed in tight jeans, scarves and coats, their 'civvy' clothes for an hour's shift at Hollywoods.

Steph noticed the customers were mostly western and hardly any of them wore suits. Rather than the classy group of Japanese business men who visited Sinatra's, the Janes clientele had the air of a stag group, disorderly and noisy, showing little respect for the establishment or the girls with whom they linked arms or held hands.

She watched the throng of hostesses, scanning their faces for the fresh-faced, long-haired girl she'd known at school. There was no way to get a good look at every girl, but no one looked remotely like Annabel.

Julia was one of the last hostesses through the glass door, holding hands with a tall, black man in a baseball T-shirt. She wore tight-fitting, pale blue jeans, high-heeled boots and a low-cut top, which seemed to be the standard Calamity Janes after-work outfit, and looked ill and washed-out under her mask of make-up. When she saw Steph, she gave a little jump of shock.

'Steph! Ricky, I'm so sorry, I told her not to—'

Ricky put up a hand. 'No, it's all right, Jules. Sounds like she's doing well for herself. I might be taking her.'

Julia looked mortified. She shook her head. 'But . . . there's no room. There isn't space for any more girls here.'

'Always room for girls with customers.'

'But she's . . . Look at her scars, Ricky. She's not right for us.'

Steph couldn't believe what she was hearing. 'Julia, what's wrong with you?'

'Now, now, you two.' Ricky knocked on the desk. 'None of that. Julia, she's a good-looking girl, scars or no scars, and if she's got a customer, well – what more do I need to know?'

Julia's jaw went tight. 'She won't be any good. She doesn't even care about making money. She's looking for our friend and she's got it into her head that she works here.'

'I know she definitely *did*,' said Steph, her cheeks flushing. 'And it was probably while you were here too.'

'See?' Julia implored. 'That's all she's really interested in. I bet she doesn't even *have* her own customer.' She marched out of the club tugging her man behind her, and Ricky watched her retreating back with interest.

'Like I said.' Ricky didn't look at Steph as she spoke. 'Come back with a customer and we'll talk. But FYI, we don't talk about girls who work here. Confidentiality.' She tapped her nose, thought for a moment, and then said,' 'Lots of our girls go on to be famous – supermodels, big movie stars. They don't want people knowing they used to work at Janes.'

Ricky nodded and smiled as the last stragglers left and the lights were turned out. 'Anyways. You'll see in the contract. We like to keep things private. If you work for us, you'll be expected to do likewise. Come back with your customer and I'll see what we can do with you.'

43

The rain fell in great sheets against the glass window of Freshness Burger as Steph poked her salad with a pair of chopsticks. It was the sort of weather, she thought, that tugged down the corners of your mouth until you couldn't help but look miserable. She stared at Annabel's diary, which sat on the table beside her 'freshness' salad, *teriyaki* tofu burger and green-tea latte.

Steph had persuaded herself that Annabel was fine. In fact, Steph wasn't even sure why she'd been so worried about Annabel. It seemed foolish, in The light of her own debt and problems, to have wasted time worrying about her friend when she should have focused on winning customers.

But something else had occurred to her. Another reason for reading the diary. *Annabel was a top girl. Everyone at Sinatra's said so. And she wrote before about how to get* dohan *... That you need to be pushy, to email and telephone. For all the good that did me. But maybe I can learn more from her. What was it that made her such a good hostess?*

Despite what Steph had told Ricky, she knew she was a long way off offers of *dohan*. But she was determined to start earning real money at Calamity Janes, and maybe, just maybe, the remaining pages of Annabel's diary held information and advice that would help her.

Steph didn't feel particularly virtuous about reading her friend's private diary for personal gain, but out here it was every girl for herself. Annabel would understand.

She began to read.

Dear God,

Sincerely I want to die. I want the ground to swallow me up. I am so so embarrassed, I can't even look at myself. I just wish there was some sort of magic pill I could use to forget last night so it never happened. But there's nothing I can do except hide away here, talk to you and hope these painkillers start working soon because my head is pounding.

Why Lord, why did I do it? OK, he's younger than most of the customers and he's sort of cute, sort of, but he's still a customer and . . . and . . . oh, it's just too too embarrassing. Not just that I slept with him . . .'

Steph took a sip of her latte and stared at the words. Annabel? Sleeping with customers? When Steph had known Annabel, she'd never even kissed anyone, and she got embarrassed during sex education classes. She hoped that sex wasn't the secret of successful hostessing. But Annabel had never mentioned sleeping with customers before.

Steph carried on reading.

. . . but why did he have to leave money, like I'm some prostitute. God, I'm so ashamed. I feel so dirty. I'll never get over this, never. Please make sure no one at home finds out. Please, please please please please.

I will never, ever get drunk again. If I wasn't drinking, I wouldn't have gone back to the hotel with the guy, and . . . I completely quit as of now. But I can't go into work tonight, God. Ricky's been ringing me and ringing me, please make her leave me alone. I can't stand to speak to anyone, I just want to be alone with my painkillers.

If the other girls at Janes find out what happened (what if they do, God? Please, please make sure they don't. Please.)

My mobile's ringing again. Make her go away. Make her go away.

Annabel xxxx

Steph closed the book and took a bite of tofu burger. As hungover as she was, food at this time of the day was kill or cure. Luckily, the burger seemed to cure.

I don't get it. Truly I don't get it. What made Annabel such a good hostess?

Annabel seemed to be getting herself in more and more of a mess. How did she get customers? Did she sleep with them? No, it didn't sound like it. From what she'd written, this guy was very much a drunken one-off.

It wasn't all about looks. Annabel was good looking, but out here everyone said some of the best looking girls made the worst hostesses. Maybe it was about ambition, but Annabel didn't seem to *have* any hostessing ambition, besides paying off her debts. Why did customers like her so much?

Concluding that the diary wasn't revealing anything useful, Steph finished her food. Swallowing her green tea along with her pride, she decided to pay another visit to Mrs Kimono.

'How did you find me?' Mrs Kimono sat behind a simple market stall just outside Kamakura station, an array of delicate silk birds covering the wooden table in front of her. The silk had been stiffened and the birds created by folding the silk, *origami*-style, to create angular creatures with long necks and square wings. It was the most glorious array of patterns and colours – a bird for every taste.

Steph couldn't be sure, but she thought Mrs Kimono gave the tiniest hint of a smile as she approached. Her kimono was black and embroidered with a winter scene: bare tree branches with snow-tipped ends and a blizzard running up and down her skirt.

'Your friend in the bakery told me where you were.'

'Bakery?'

'You know – the apple pie shop next to yours. She said you were at the seaside today and drew me a subway map.' Steph picked up one of the cranes and turned it in her hands. 'These are really lovely.'

'Aren't they beautiful?' Mrs Kimono had been kneeling behind the stall, but now she rose to her feet, like a flower opening. 'Too good for Tokyo, but good enough for Kamakura. It reminds me of Kyoto down here. I love to be by the water.' She inhaled salty fresh air. 'I don't suppose you've been here before.' It wasn't a question.

'What are they?' asked Steph, replacing the bird and knocking over two others in the process. She hurriedly picked them up.

'*Origami* cranes,' said Mrs Kimono. 'Made from silk. I treat it specially to make it hard. Usually we make cranes from paper. We say in Japan, if you fold a thousand *origami* cranes, any wish will be granted. Any wish – long life, good health, recovery from illness.' She dropped her eyes.

'Why don't you sell these in your shop?' asked Steph.

'I don't *sell* them. Sometimes I have a wish I'd like granted. So I fold cranes and people take them and make a donation for the giant Buddha nearby.'

'What are they for, exactly?'

'They make wonderful gifts. The Japanese often give them as wedding presents – a thousand years of happiness for any married couple. Young girls use them as matchmaking charms too. Tradition says that when a girl turns thirteen, she can fold a thousand paper cranes and give them to the boy she'd like to marry.'

'And does it work?'

'Sometimes. So, you've come here for more advice? I take it you haven't yet won your *danna*?'

'How did you know?'

'I can tell by your face.'

'I played your drinking game with Yamamoto-san and he loved it. I take my time pouring the drinks too, doing everything properly, carefully. I know what you mean about controlling things. I feel much more like I'm running the show, like he has to ask my permission before he can try anything sleazy. He's been good as gold, actually. But he still doesn't take me on *dohan*. I'm missing something. I don't know what.'

'My friend can run this stall,' said Mrs Kimono, waving at a woman a few feet away behind a table of tiny, painted wooden cats. The woman wore a tired kimono, nothing like the grand, brightly coloured affair worn by Mrs Kimono. She nodded as Mrs Kimono spoke a few, soft words to her in Japanese. 'Let's go for a walk into the hills,' said Mrs Kimono. 'You've been drinking too much. You look like a sour prune in *shotu*. The fresh air will clear the alcohol from your skin.'

44

'Can I ask you a question?' Steph and Mrs Kimono walked up well-worn, wooden steps surrounded by green trees. The air was fresh and cool, and the path was pleasantly shaded from the winter sun.

'You may.' Mrs Kimono was wheezing slightly, but her pace was still fast, almost too fast for Steph.

'Do *geisha* ever sleep with their customers? I think some hostesses do. Is that the way to get a *danna*?' Steph was fully prepared for a tart telling-off for such an impertinent question, but to her surprise Mrs Kimono nodded.

'Years ago, when I trained to be a *geisha*, it was expected. When a young *maiko* completed her training, she would not undergo the turning of the collar, *erikae*, as girls do today, but a *mizuage* ceremony. *Mizuage* – it means being taken from the water. The *maiko* had her hair cut and lost her virginity to her *danna*. Then she entered a relationship with him, usually for the rest of her life. History makes it sound romantic.'

'Did you have a *danna*?'

They walked on, past a tiny tea restaurant tucked into the trees. Frothy bowls of foaming green tea were being served, alongside jellied cubes of Japanese confectionery.

'Yes.' Mrs Kimono lifted her robe slightly as the ground became flatter and rockier. 'A very famous, very important man. A politician. He was my *danna* for many years, and I learned to love him. He bought me antique kimonos, wigs, combs, all the things a *geisha* needs to carry out her trade. It costs a lot of money to keep a *geisha*. But . . . things weren't to last.'

'What happened?'

There was silence, and Steph feared she'd over-stepped the mark. Mrs Kimono was being extremely agreeable today, which was confusing. In many ways, a telling-off would be a relief.

'In the end, he had to give me up.' Mrs Kimono's wheezing eased as they walked along the flatter ground. 'His wife insisted. A great scandal. And a lot of shame and heartache for me. For a long time, I was ashamed to walk the streets in Kyoto. And I missed him. He'd been my patron for many years. But then, only a year after we were parted, he died. It was very sudden.'

'I'm sorry,' said Steph.

'I was heartbroken all over again,' said Mrs Kimono. 'I wasn't even allowed to attend his funeral. *Geisha* usually aren't. His wife, of course, was allowed to mourn his death.'

'But . . . He gave you up,' said Steph.

'Love doesn't turn off like a tap.'

Steph thought for a moment. 'You're right. It doesn't. Can I tell you something?'

'Certainly.'

'There was this guy, before I came here. Really bad news. We had arguments all the time and he had a temper. We'd fight, but usually I wasn't scared. I thought I could trust him, I really, really did.

'He promised me all sorts of things — that he'd get me work, acting jobs. He took pictures of me. Naked pictures. He had some story that there was this film coming up and they had to see me like that. Then he sold them. I thought he cared about me. But he didn't, he was just using me. And do you know what? I still love him. Is that stupid?'

'No. It's not stupid.'

'But now I feel . . . like I don't know how to read men. What their agenda is. I thought I knew, but I got it so wrong. Maybe deep down I don't want a customer – I'm too scared.'

'You're still learning, that's all,' said Mrs Kimono. 'I think you're probably not such a bad judge of character. You just need to know how to control the men in your club. Draw them into here.' She clasped her hand into a fist and held it to her chest. 'But you have to be strong to do that.'

They reached a place from where they could see the ocean far below, foaming and crashing around grey spikes of rock that jutted out of the water.

'*Geisha* are like those rocks,' said Mrs Kimono. 'We stay strong. Serene. Even though life around us can be harsh and uncertain. No matter what is happening in our lives. We absorb the emotions of others.'

Steph shook her head. 'I just don't understand . . . Annabel . . .'

'Your friend.'

'Yes. She was a top hostess. But I'm reading her diary and she doesn't sound strong. She doesn't sound like you at all. I don't think she slept with customers – not regularly, anyway. Why was she so popular?'

'You're reading this girl's diary?'

Steph blushed. 'I didn't start out reading it for bad reasons. But now I have to get better at this hostessing thing, one way or another. You have to understand – I'm in lots of debt.'

They walked past a Japanese couple taking pictures of each other by a huge, beautiful tree, its roots lying above the ground like tentacles.

'And you think her diary will help you?'

'I don't know. Everyone says she was a good hostess. I wanted to find out her secret. Can you blame me? I don't have a single customer, and I have months of debt to pay off and I just want a good job at a good club.'

'No, I don't blame you.' Mrs Kimono looked out at the sun, floating just above the ocean. 'But that sort of thinking, it's not the way. There's a demon in Roppongi. It gets under people's skin, makes them people they're not. Like my daughter. I hope you haven't been touched by it. At one time you wanted to find your friend. Have you already forgotten?'

★   ★   ★

Mrs Kimono took Steph along the pier, past stands offering dried squid on sticks, rice cakes and gambling games with cork guns.

'This is what I'll teach you today,' she said, as they stopped at a pretty, wooden shop selling wrapped hazelnut sweets and embossed *origami* papers. 'Folding cranes.' She bought a packet of paper and led Steph to the pier edge, where they sat with their feet dangling over the water. 'Watch me.' With a few deft folds, Mrs Kimono turned a piece of gold and black paper into a tiny crane.

Steph took a piece of paper and started to fold.

'Not like that! Keep it tidy.'

'What's this got to do with anything?'

'It's about prayer. Humility.'

'And . . . ?'

'A good *geisha* is humble. I imagine a good hostess is the same. She's strong, but at the same time she understands life flows around her and there are many things she has to accept and cannot change. She prays for something better when life is uncertain.'

Dear God, Dear God, Dear God . . .

'Annabel wrote to God in her diary,' said Steph. 'She prayed. She was humble. But what has folding cranes got to do with praying?'

'I told you. Fold a thousand cranes and your wishes will come true. But more than that. As you fold, it brings you peace. With peace comes humility.'

'I'm never going to fold a thousand.'

'The longest journey starts with a single step.'

Steph kept folding, trying to keep her edges as neat as possible. As she turned the paper in her hands, a man and a woman walking along the road by the pier caught her eye. The girl was Natalia, her pale skin luminous under the setting sun. She wore jeans and a puffy coat with a fur collar, and held hands with a Japanese man who came up to her shoulder.

As Steph watched them, Natalia and her companion turned into a hotel. Steph looked down at her bird and kept folding.

'You've made a very ugly bird,' said Mrs Kimono. 'There are some bad folds here, and this isn't neat. You need to practise. By the time you fold a thousand, you'll be better.'

'Maybe I've got better things to do.'

'Really? Like what?'

Steph took another sheet of paper. 'Like making money.'

45

'What are these things?' Natalia plucked a paper bird from a line of twenty that sat on the bedroom shelf. 'Good luck charms or something?'

'Something like that,' said Steph. She sat on the top bunk, applying her make-up. The paper cranes were all over the bedroom now, running along the metal bar that ran between her bunk and the wall, floating like ducks on the folded piles of clothes in her rucksack and balanced on the chipped light switch.

'I haven't seen you for days,' Steph commented. 'Not since . . . I saw you in Kamakura.'

'How are they made?' Natalia began to unfold the bird.

'Don't unfold it.'

'Okay, okay.' Natalia tucked the paper back in place. 'Why so many of them? Are you on ice or something?' She wiggled her fingers. 'Trying to keep your hands busy?'

Steph shook her head.

'I'm so tired.' Natalia rubbed her eyes. 'Another day, another *dohan*.'

'No wonder,' said Steph. 'Evening *dohan*, daytime *dohan* – you must be exhausted.'

'Daytime *dohan*?' Natalia looked confused.

'In Kamakura,' said Steph conversationally. 'I saw you with a customer. At least, he looked like a customer.'

Natalia put the bird back on the shelf. 'Janes . . . It's different from other clubs. Some of us have daytime shifts. More money. I suppose it is a little like *dohan* . . .' She carried on dusting powder over her already powdery cheeks, then cocked her head at Steph.

'Do you have *dohan*? You never do your make-up this early.'

'Yes,' said Steph. 'I do.' She smiled. Her first real *dohan*. She didn't know how or why exactly, but Mrs Kimono's advice had paid off. One thousand cranes later and she'd got her wish: yesterday Yamamoto-san had asked her to dinner.

'I thought you'd have been sacked by now.' Natalia pouted and drew lip liner around her lips. 'You have so few clothes.'

Steph ignored her, calm in the face of such obvious provocation. A car horn beeped from the street, and she slid off the bed.

'That's my customer,' Steph said, strapping on second-hand high-heels she'd bought from an ex-hostess advertising in *Tokyo Notice Board*. 'Have a good *dohan*.'

'I *always* have a good *dohan*,' said Natalia.

Outside, a black Mercedes sat on the curb, swallowing up half the pavement. Tinted black windows revealed the silhouettes of a driver in the front seat and a passenger in the back.

Steph knocked on the window and the car door opened. Yamamoto-san was inside, his body slumped against thick, leather upholstery. He was fiddling with his mobile phone. Despite being over fifty, he was a spritely, youthful character and Steph often felt more like his babysitter than his lady companion.

'Yamamoto-san, good to see you.' Steph smiled and bowed.

Yamamoto didn't look up, but smiled at his phone. 'Ready?' he asked.

Steph thought, *I should let someone know where I'm going.*

She saw Luke on the balcony smoking a roll-up. He smiled and Steph knew he'd been watching.

'Luke. Hey, Luke.' Steph waved. She poked her head into the car. 'Where are we going, Yamamoto-san?'

Yamamoto fidgeted. 'Restaurant.'

'Which one?'

'Ninja. In Akasaka.'

'Okay.' Steph called up. 'Luke, I'm going to Ninja in Akasaka. See you at the club, okay?' Luke stuck two thumbs up.

Steph was glad it was Luke who knew where she was going. Her safety net. She trusted him – something she couldn't say about many of the people she'd met in Roppongi. She hoped she was right to put her faith in Luke. Trust was still something she struggled with.

Although Yamamoto-san had a bad habit of pulling up Steph's top like a naughty schoolboy, overall he was unobjectionable and their dinner together was almost enjoyable. In fact, Steph felt rather foolish to have worried about getting into his car. After all, he was a very rich and upstanding member of Japanese society. The stories about girls going missing were unpleasant but, in reality, the odds were against anything bad happening. Tokyo was one of the safest cities in the world.

They'd enjoyed a meal of meat dipped in salty, boiling water and green-tea ice-cream for dessert, and now Yamamoto-san was calling for the bill.

Steph sat as tall as she could manage, cleared her throat and breathed deeply for the big question.

'Yamamoto-san?'

Mr Yamamoto sighed. 'You're going to ask me again for Annabel's number, right? I told you. All in good time.'

'No.' Steph shook her head. 'I wasn't even thinking about that. I . . . How long have you been a customer at Sinatra's?'

'Years.'

'Really?' Steph pressed her knee against the table leg. 'Do you . . . Have you ever been to any other clubs?'

'Of course not! Only your club, my dear.'

'No, I wouldn't mind,' said Steph. 'In fact . . . Look, I was thinking, would you like to take me to a different club after dinner?'

'A different club?' Yamamoto shook his head. 'In Roppongi? A hostess club?'

'Well . . . yes. I was thinking, Calamity Janes.'

'Oh.' Yamamoto-san thought for a moment. 'You're sure. Calamity *Janes*? It's a very . . . western place. How well do you know it?'

'Really well,' Steph lied. 'My friend works there.'

'You know how everything works there? Not altogether the same as Sinatra's.'

'Yes, yes. Fine.'

'Okay, I don't mind.' Yamamoto-san wagged a finger. 'But Mama won't be happy with you. I've been her customer for a long time.'

'It'll be fine,' Steph insisted. 'Mama's doing really well right now.'

'Not what I heard.'

'No, she is. She won't miss us.'

'Just for tonight?'

'It depends,' said Steph, twiddling her napkin in her lap. 'I'm thinking . . . Probably I'll move there if things go well. I don't know yet.'

'Oh.'

The waitress presented Yamamoto with an embossed, leather bill holder and he dropped a big pile of notes inside. He took Steph's hand. 'We're getting closer, aren't we? Becoming good friends. So for you, I'll change.'

'Thanks,' said Steph, her heart still pounding and her hand sticky inside Yamamoto's dry one.

'So . . . We're going there now?' asked Yamamoto.

'Yes,' said Steph. 'Does your driver know how to get there?'

Yamamoto laughed. 'Everyone knows how to get to Calamity Janes.'

46

Mama

Mama sat on the rickety chair in the tiny office at Sinatra's, drinking a *genki* drink from a brown bottle. George sat opposite her on a tatty, cushioned stool that was now too stained and threadbare to be used in the club. There were barely thirty centimetres between them and George's knees were bunched up against his stomach, his notepad close to his chest.

'Money,' Mama announced, slapping her hand on a leather accounts book. 'That's what this business is all about. You can never have too much of it.'

The low murmur of male voices could be heard from the club.

'That's why I got into this business and believe me, George-san, there's still money to be made, no matter what people say.' There was a row of brown *genki* bottles lined up on Mama's desk, and she added her now empty bottle to it.

'You look better,' said George. 'I trust hospital . . . not too gruelling?'

'I'm bored with talking about hospitals and illness, George-san. Let's talk about other things.'

'Okay.' George's shoulders bumped into the wall as he pressed his pen to the notepad. 'Well, how's business?'

'So, so,' said Mama. 'The police raided last month. I've just received the fine. Counterfeit whisky. *Yakuza* tell me they'll be after illegal workers soon. We'll see.' Mama sighed and put her head in her hands. 'It's very hard. I've had to take out a bank loan to pay the girls their wages. But I'll keep working. I have to. Otherwise, Kaito will have nothing.' Tears appeared quite suddenly.

George's pen faltered on the page. 'Mama . . . I know this is hard. But when you talk about your daughter . . . I feel we're getting to the real you. The heart and soul. You haven't spoken much about Kaito. Is this what you're holding back?'

Mama's neat bottom teeth showed for a moment. '*Hai*,' she said, with emotion. 'Yes. You think I have a secret? I do. I've been a terrible mother, George-san. That's my secret. I was too busy working, working.' More tears. George reached forward and took Mama's hand.

'You were working for her. Just like you're working for her now.'

'She didn't need any of the things I was working for. She needed my time. And I didn't give it to her. Now she doesn't want my time. All I can give her is money.'

George gave Mama's hand a squeeze. 'Go on.'

'No, it's too much. Let's talk about better things. How about when I fell in love?' Mama nodded. 'I can't say falling in love was happy. It was probably one of the hardest times of my life. But I'll tell you the story.'

George looked disappointed and took his hand away.

'After that first dinner, Conrad took me out almost every night. We went dancing and to cabarets and wonderful restaurants. He showed me a Tokyo I'd never seen before. We made quite a pair at first, me in my cheap *yanki* clothes, him in his expensive suits. He introduced me to the high life. Expensive clothes, Japanese fashion designers. It wasn't long before I had my own furs and diamonds. I was smitten.'

'By him or the lifestyle?'

Mama smiled. 'Both. It was all so new, so exciting. I felt I'd found my place at last, on the arm of my suited gentleman. It felt so right. He told me he'd move to Tokyo so we could be together, and of course I believed him. I was young. Foolish. It's true, love makes you blind.

'Within a month I became pregnant, and I expected he'd find us a nice apartment in the city. We'd have a happy family life together. I had no idea he was married. That he had a wife back in America.'

George nodded sympathetically. 'How did you find out?'

'Mama-san.' Hiro poked his head around the office door.

'*Hai*?'

Mama and Hiro began a rapid exchange in Japanese, and Mama nodded and took another *genki* drink from her desk drawer. Her eyes faded.

'A problem with one of our girls,' said Mama, when Hiro left. 'Steph-chan. She was on *dohan* but hasn't turned up. *Yakuza* tell us she's gone to another club. Stolen one of our best customers. She owes me money, too. I'll have to send *yakuza* to deal with the problem, and they cost . . . oh, more than money in the long term.'

'Stolen?'

Mama nodded. 'Customers get attached to girls, not clubs. It's my fault. I got it wrong. I thought she was trustworthy.' She shook her head. 'I don't know . . . If things keep on going this way . . . I don't know. What was I telling you?'

'How you found out Conrad was married.'

'Yes. I found letters from his wife in his hotel room. A big pile. Blue paper with the American flag at the top. She'd sent one probably every day he'd been away, there were so many. He hadn't even bothered to hide them. They were in the drawer of his bedside cabinet with his cigarettes. Maybe he thought I couldn't read English. Or maybe he wanted me to find them. I don't know.

'I was three months pregnant by then. We'd planned to go out to an American-style restaurant that night, but Conrad invited me to his hotel to spend time together before we went out and, as was becoming a regular occurrence, he changed his mind about going out. He used me for sex. I realised that in the lonely years that followed.

'As soon as I found the letters, I shouted and screamed and cried, but Conrad showed no emotion. He was like a different person. Not the warm-hearted man I'd known. He told me he thought I knew he was married. I was too proud to tell him about the baby, so I left.

'I was totally alone. No money, no one to take care of me and soon, I knew, I wouldn't be able to work. But I'm not a weak person. I don't wait for life to do what it wants with me. So I decided to go ahead and open my own hostess club in Roppongi. That way, other girls could work for me while I cared for the baby. I thought I could do it before the baby was born, but I needed money. My savings weren't enough, and I didn't want to take *yakuza* loans.'

'So how did you—'

'My first hostess club,' Mama gestured to the bamboo-patterned paper on the walls, 'wasn't like this. It was in a different location. In Akasaka, a cheaper part of town back then. It wasn't fancy. There was no office or reception area, no stage or keyboard band. Just a room with a bar. That was it. I found furniture from old cabaret clubs. I couldn't afford to buy champagne so we didn't sell it.

'But even renting a place like that cost hundreds of thousands of yen, plus of course "thank you" money to the landlord and various other expenses. The girls were the biggest outlay. After so many years in the sex industry, I had a good idea about what men wanted, the sorts of girls they liked to spend time with. But hiring the right girls is never cheap. And I simply didn't have the money to get everything started.'

'So how did you get it?'

Hiro appeared at the door, and motioned to his watch.

'George-san.' Mama got to her feet, holding on to her desk for support. 'The club needs me tonight.'

'But we've hardly . . .' George flipped back through his notepad. 'We're getting there, but I need more from you. Time's running out.'

'Not tonight, George-san.'

'But you're in hospital this week. When will we—'

'So come with me. To the hospital. Hiro will give you my appointment times. We'll talk there. Good-night, George-san.'

47

Steph

Steph smiled broadly as she approached Calamity Janes reception area, but her taut jaw gave away her true feelings: fear, verging on panic.

Please, please let this work out.

When she saw Ricky behind the desk, Steph clung to Yamamoto-san, her human version of a Calamity Janes gold membership card. To her relief, Ricky greeted her like an old friend, and gave no sign that Steph had turned up uninvited.

'Steph. How are you, babes?'

'Good, thanks. We've just been out to dinner.'

Ricky winked, none too subtly, and put a hand on Yamamoto's chest. 'Good to see you. Yamamoto-san, right? Come on in, the floor show's just starting.'

She led them both through the glass door and into the main room of the club. It was vast, with an L-shaped bar running around two of the walls. In the middle of the room was a catwalk-style stage, painted to look like marble and decorated with gold pillars, semi-circled by a dance floor and row after row of high gold tables and stools.

Already, many of the tables were full of customers and girls, and Steph counted at least fifteen champagne bottles floating in ice buckets. Quite the contrast with Sinatra's.

'Steph, you go get yourself ready in the dressing-room, babes.' Ricky winked again. 'You know where it is,' she added, shoving her towards a matt-black door by the bar.

I am ready, Steph wanted to say, but then she glanced at the other girls — long, exfoliated and moisturised legs swinging from high stools, hair immaculately pinned up or swinging, shiny and perfectly straight, around designer-dress straps. It was like being inside a glossy magazine. Steph touched her own hair, clean but slightly wavy, and realised she should probably at least try to straighten it. And maybe touch up her make-up, make sure it wasn't smudged.

'I'll be back in a minute, Yamamoto-san.'

Through the black door, the dressing-room was even pokier than the one at Sinatra's and crumpled clothes and bags took up much of the floor space.

There was another girl in the room staring into a cracked fragment of mirror, which was balanced on two nails against the wall. An archaic, green punch-clock hung next to the mirror, and beside that were dozens of punch cards squashed into a rusty, wall-mounted holder.

The other girl, a scrawny, bleached blonde with a deep cleavage, didn't seem to notice Steph's arrival, and began spraying perfume all over her hair and bare shoulders. She looked familiar, but Steph couldn't quite place her.

'Hi,' said Steph. There were hair straighteners on the floor next to an empty McDonalds bag. 'Anyone using these?'

Silence. More perfume.

Steph knelt down and plugged in the hair straighteners.

The girl took a tiny, transparent packet of white powder from her bra, along with a 500-yen note. She rolled up the note, stuck it into the powder and sniffed. Within seconds, the whole bag, maybe two teaspoons of powder, had disappeared up her nose. She patted her nostrils.

'I need a little coke for the show,' she told her reflection in the mirror. 'I'm useless without it.'

'A *little* coke?' said Steph, noting the girl's clothes. She wore a mask of chiffon scarves that revealed her bare flesh as she moved. It was an unusual outfit for a hostess.

'Are you a dancer or something?' asked Steph, remembering the topless girl on stage the night she'd come to see Julia.

'Dancer and hostess,' said the girl, somewhat defensively. She put gum in her mouth and chewed at a rapid pace. 'Are you new?'

'Just started.'

Without bothering to look at Steph, the girl plucked a card from the wall holder and punched it into the machine.

'So *that's* why you don't know who I am. You'll learn. I'm one of the best hostesses in this place.' The name on the girl's card was Angel.

Suddenly Steph remembered where she'd seen Angel before. 'You were . . . I saw you in Square Mile.' *In the bathroom. Giving some guy a blow job.*

'I go there sometimes.' Angel flipped her hair from shoulder to shoulder and studied her nails.

'Do I need to punch in?' asked Steph, noticing a hand-scrawled bonus chart tacked to the wall. Julia's name was written on it near the top. She was doing well, the fourth best hostess last week. Angel, despite her boast, was right at the bottom. Steph panned up and down the names on the chart, but couldn't see an Annabel.

I guess she doesn't work here any more, Steph thought, oddly deflated despite her resolve to forget about Annabel and concentrate on work. *Perhaps she moved to another club or flew back home.*

There were letters and numbers scribbled next to some of the girls' names.

'What does SB mean?' asked Steph, pointing to the scribble next to Julia's name, among others. 'And twenty-four?' The latter was written next to three names: Natalia, Kirsha and Anastasia. Steph wondered if it was the same Natalia she shared a room with. It must be – there wasn't another Natalia on the list.

'They should clear this thing,' said Angel, ignoring the question and shoving her card back into the over-crowded holder. 'Half of these are old cards.' She plucked out one that said Geraldine, screwed it up and dropped it on the floor. 'Girls who don't even work here any more.'

As Angel hurried out into the club, Steph stared at the punch cards. There were many more cards in the holders than there were names written on the bonus chart, and . . . *Geraldine* . . . Annabel had written about a girl called Geraldine.

A thought occurred to Steph. Maybe Annabel's card was still in the holder. If it was, it would show whether Annabel had clocked in that night, or had stopped working at Janes some time ago. She tried to push away the thought. *Leave it. She's fine. Don't get distracted or you'll end up messing up at this place too.* But she found herself folding back the tops of cards, reading all the names written on them.

Yasmin, Chole, Honey . . . Julia. Steph felt a tug as she read Julia's name, and the card tore slightly as she folded it back to see the one underneath. *Carrie, Jessica . . .* She kept flicking. Only a few more now . . .

The door flew open and Steph jumped away from the cards.

'What do you think you're doing?'

It was Ricky.

'I . . . just, I thought I needed a punch card,' said Steph, feeling blood in her cheeks.

'Michael should have sorted these,' said Ricky, stepping forward and touching Julia's torn card with irritation. 'There are dead girls in here.'

Steph flinched.

'Girls who've left,' Ricky clarified. 'It needs clearing out. I'll sort your times tonight. Don't worry about punching in. You read the contract, right? Do you have it with you?'

Steph pulled the slightly crumpled contract from her bag. 'I haven't signed it yet,' she admitted. 'I thought I might as well wait until I got here.'

'You've read it though, right?' It occurred to Steph that, without her shoes, Ricky was probably only five foot one or two.

'Yes,' Steph said. *Well, glanced at it.*

'And you've got your passport with you?'

'My passport.' Steph thought of the red booklet at the bottom of her shoulder bag. She carried it everywhere since she didn't trust Natalia not to steal it from the bedroom.

'I have to take it, or you can't work,' said Ricky.

Steph lifted her passport from her bag and reluctantly held it out. 'I can take it back though?' she asked. 'If I need it?'

Ricky shook her head. 'Not for three months. We keep them to make sure girls don't . . . It takes a while to build relationships with customers. It's hard work here. We want to make sure you give it a chance, give *us* a chance, before you think of quitting.' Ricky smirked. 'Of course, if you're not any good you'll get your passport back in a few days.'

Steph's grip tightened on the passport, but Ricky snatched it and tucked it inside her jacket.

'We'll take good care of it, don't worry.' Ricky ran her hand along Steph's legs. 'No stockings. You need clear stockings – it's in your contract. I'll let you get away with it tonight, but this is your last warning. A few more things. No more than three minutes in the bathroom, and you have to drink four drinks an hour here, no ifs, no buts. Whatever the waiter brings, you drink okay?'

Steph nodded dumbly.

'Ready to start work?'

48

Steph soon discovered Calamity Janes was very different from Sinatra's.

Those four drinks an hour arrived at tables like clockwork, tick, tock, tick, tock, every fifteen minutes. Second, toilet time was monitored. More than three minutes on a bathroom break and Ricky came hammering on the door. Third, every half-hour girls were moved to a new table so, according to Ricky, they could 'meet as many men as possible'.

Steph spent barely ten minutes with Yamamoto-san before Ricky called her to another table. She was reluctant to leave her customer, especially when she saw her replacement – a willowy, brown-haired girl with a Colgate smile who greeted Yamamoto like an old boyfriend. But table-hopping was by order of the management. As Ricky said, rules were rules.

Steph was moved on to another table, and then another, offering introductions again and again. There wasn't enough time to learn the customers' names, let alone get to know the other hostesses placed and replaced around the various tables, so she nodded and smiled and listened.

By the fourth table, Steph's voice had become decidedly robotic.

'Hi, I'm Steph, I'm from England. What's your name?'

'John.' The man wore a baseball cap and had a South African accent.

Ricky appeared at the table with another hostess on her arm. Julia.

'Another girl for you Mr Taylor.'

'Hello,' said Julia, shaking the customer's hand as she sat down.

Steph and Julia nodded at each other.

'Ricky said you should take a bathroom break,' Julia told Steph, her eye twitching just a fraction.

'You're joking.' Steph turned around. 'She can't tell me when to go to the toilet. Where is she?'

'You have to do as you're told here, Steph,' said Julia, her voice hard. 'Just go, okay? Your mascara's running, you should sort it out.'

'It's too much,' Steph complained. But she got up anyway, deciding not to rock the boat on her first night.

Sinatra's and Calamity Janes have something in common, thought Steph when she reached the toilet. *This bathroom is a dump.* The floor was gritty and damp, with grey toilet roll trodden into it, and the hot tap leaked, making the room tropically muggy.

Steph went to check her make-up in the mirror, but there was so much condensation it was like looking at herself through water. She cleaned a space and noticed thin, wavery letters written in the steam:

Rum and coke flag
Vodka tonic G1
Wine 1

What was it – some sort of drinks order? Maybe a hostess had forgotten to bring a notepad, and was taking down customer drinks so she could make conversation at a later date.

When Steph returned to the table, Julia was holding hands with Mr Taylor and admiring his business card.

'Did you sort out your make-up?' Julia asked.

'What? Oh, yes. Why? Does it still look smudged?'

'No,' said Julia, without looking at her. 'It's fine now.'

The rest of the night passed in a blur. Steph got so drunk it became a patchy tapestry of memories held together with sellotape and staples. She'd knocked over drinks, smudged her make-up and fallen off her stool several times, but in Janes, where all the girls consumed alcohol as though it was a marathon race, she was in good company.

When the club lights flashed on and off and *Leaving on a Jet*

Plane began to play (the club's signature 'haven't you got homes to go to?' song), Steph followed the other girls, all walking with as much dignity as they could manage on rubbery, drunk legs, to the dressing room. It was mayhem as girls fought their way in and out of the cramped space, some even crawling between other girls' legs to pull their bags from dusty corners, and having fingers stamped on in the process.

Steph would usually have been equally keen, but she thought of Mrs Kimono and decided to be calm and dignified, and to wait outside until the free-for-all died down.

Ricky approached her as she stood by the changing-room door.

'There's a guy waiting for you downstairs,' said Ricky, adding ominously, 'Japanese. Black suit.'

'What?' Steph blinked in confusion. 'Yamamoto-san? He left hours ago. But we arranged to meet—'

'Not your customer,' said Ricky. 'Another guy. Tattoos.'

Steph shook her head and a thousand Rickys danced around in front of her. 'I don't know who he is.'

'Well, he knows who you are.' Ricky headed towards the office. 'You better hurry up and meet him. He's making my lobby look unfriendly.'

Girls were now flowing out, in jeans and jackets, so Steph went into the empty dressing-room and found her bag. She was so drunk, not to mention distracted by the idea of a visitor, she nearly forgot about the punch cards, but just as she was leaving she noticed them on the wall.

I may as well check the last few.

The order of the cards was completely different now and, she noticed, with a sense of despair, that they'd been thinned out. Around half had now been removed – presumably those belonging to 'dead' girls.

Steph slapped the wall in frustration. Annabel must have left the club, or there would still be a punch card for her. But where had she gone?

Why are you getting so angry? Forget about Annabel. She's fine. Focus on making money. But as pins and needles spread across

Steph's palm, she knew she couldn't forget. She may end up broke, but she just couldn't help herself – she wanted to find her old friend. Here they both were, in Tokyo together, and they hadn't even met yet. She had to work something out somehow.

A girl came into the waiting room and picked up a punch card labelled Caroline. She had blue-black hair and a square, handsome face, and looked at Steph with glazed eyes.

'Did you ever meet a girl called Annabel?' asked Steph.

'No. Who is she?'

'She used to work here.' Steph scanned the bonus chart again, using her finger to steady her eyeline. No sign of Annabel's name. She hadn't really expected there to be.

'We're not supposed to talk about the girls who work here. Or used to work here.'

Caroline snatched her bag and left.

Throwing off her high heels, Steph pulled on jeans and trainers and followed her. The club was almost empty now and, since she didn't have a customer waiting, she headed straight to the elevator and down to the lobby.

A Japanese man with thinning, gelled hair and dark glasses was waiting there.

'Stephanie.' He took her arm.

'Who are you?'

'I'm here for Mama-san. You owe Mama some money.' He gripped her arm tighter and walked her to the carpeted steps, nodding cordially at the bouncers on the way out to the street.

'I know.' Steph staggered, nearly falling down the steps. 'I'm going to . . . Hey, careful. I was always going to pay her back.'

'Good.' The man turned to her. His face was totally still, like a stone tablet, and his lips barely moved as he spoke. 'But I have to give you the terms.'

'I'll pay her as soon as I can,' said Steph, feeling . . . not scared, but uncomfortable, despite the crowds of people on the street. 'I was always going to. That's why I moved clubs – so I could pay her back quicker.'

'The terms are two days.'

Steph felt her stomach lurch. 'I can't do that.'

'If you don't, the debt will double. And a few days after that, it will double again.'

'She'll have to give me more time.'

The man let go of her arm. 'Two days are the terms. I hope you understand, uh, how serious this situation is. You have until Wednesday to pay.'

'I can't,' said Steph, but the man had already disappeared into the crowd.

Steph had a lot to think about as she walked home. Money, mainly. But also the fact that Annabel didn't seem ever to have existed at Calamity Janes. The customers she'd spoken to hadn't remembered her. That was very strange. And there had been no glimmer of recognition in Caroline's eyes when Steph had said Annabel's name.

The same went for Natalia, and yet she'd been hostessing at Janes for some time. It was like Annabel had been erased out of history. She'd become a ghost.

As Steph turned into the back street behind Café Almond she heard a sound – like a cracking or spitting. She blinked up at the dirty buildings, momentarily forgetting, in her drunk state, which iron staircase led to her apartment. They all looked the same.

There was a pressure on her throat, then a shooting pain in her arm.

'Ow. Ouch! Who—'

A large, cold body pressed against her back.

She was pushed forward towards an alleyway stacked with crates of empty bottles.

'Get off me!'

Steph's bad arm twisted back on itself against scarred, useless muscles. It burned as if someone was holding a lighter to her skin, and she couldn't squeeze her hand to make a fist. Every survival instinct was deadened, forgotten. She couldn't decide whether to step left or right, which way to move her arms.

Surprise gave way to fear as hands tugged at Steph's clothing and she fell to the floor.

She started to shout, still struggling.

'Get off me.'

The hands paid no attention.

There was shouting from across the street, and Steph forced her shoulders left and right.

'Get off, get off!'

More shouting and a knee came towards her face.

Suddenly, the knee withdrew. Pressure lifted from her arms. She felt gritty water from the pavement splash on her cheek, heard running, and saw a big, muscular man careering down the street chased by two Japanese men.

After a few seconds, her saviours abandoned the chase and returned, breathless, to Steph, who was picking herself up from the pavement.

'Are you okay?' One of them looked about eighteen, with spiky black hair shooting up from a baby face, and was clearly more shocked than Steph that she'd been grabbed in the street.

'I'm fine,' said Steph. She turned and threw up on the street.

Upstairs in the apartment, Steph boiled water for green tea and sat shaking on the common room sofa. She tried a few centre punches, but her bad arm was stiff – much stiffer than it had ever been – and wouldn't stay straight.

She felt bruised, frightened and vulnerable. Bad things did happen out here. Tonight was proof. Was it something to do with the guy who'd come to the club earlier? The one Mama had sent?

Her hands began to shake.

Somehow, I've got to pay back that money. In two days . . .

49

At precisely 8 p.m., spotlights illuminated Calamity Janes' faux-marble stage and Angel began her performance. She wore long, black layers that swung around her white skin and, as the music began, she removed her clothing one layer at a time. There was a forced smile on her tired, sad face.

The club was packed, and little by little customers turned their chairs to face the stage. Hostesses, who'd seen Angel dance a hundred times before, used the distraction to pour their drinks on to the floor.

Steph hadn't slept well the night before and felt too sick to drink. But the little glasses of vodka tonic were mounting up on the table, one delivered every fifteen minutes. Pay packets were 100% dependent on what the girls drank, and their minimum wage was delivered to them in little glasses throughout the night.

The club didn't care how hostesses disposed of the drinks, as long as the customers believed them to be drunk and enjoyed by their party companions.

Steph looked at the wall of fizzing alcohol. She'd been unlucky tonight. Ricky had seated her on a spot-lit table over hard flooring, which meant dumping drinks wasn't an option.

Angel is a mess, she thought, between the flow of worried thought that had become the soundtrack to her mind since yesterday's attack. It was true. Angel did look a mess. Rough, peeling skin, the frantic eyes of a long-term cocaine user, and a mouth that looked incapable of smiling. There were scars on her wrists, too. Every rib could be seen as she shed layers until she was topless and gave the tired dance she delivered night after night at two-hourly intervals.

'Stephy.'

Steph felt a bony finger on her shoulder. It was Ricky.

'Michael says he'll talk to you now.'

Steph jumped up. When she'd arrived an hour earlier, she'd asked Ricky about the possibility of being paid a month in advance. A month's wages, she was quite sure, would cover Mama's debt, but she was equally sure there was no way the club *would* pay her upfront. After all, at Janes everything worked on drinks bonuses, not hourly rates. But she couldn't think of any other way to get Mama's money in two days. Ricky had shrugged and said, 'I doubt it, but I'm not the person to ask. You need to talk to Michael.'

Michael was the club manager – another Australian. He was a real sleazebag. Aside from the fact that he looked like an ageing pervert, with his jet-black, oiled hair and tinted prescription glasses, he'd come into the girls' changing room unannounced and stare openly at the girls as they rapidly dressed under his gaze. Steph also noticed him sliding his beefy palm, uninvited, on to one of the girl's rear ends as she punched her shift card.

'What do you think my chances are?' asked Steph, feeling slightly sick as yet another round of drinks was unloaded on to the table. There were three full drinks waiting in front of her. By the time she got back from speaking to Michael, there'd be four.

'Depends on what you've got to offer him.'

Steph hurried past the stage where Angel, naked except for a crystal-covered thong, was swaying her hips back and forth completely out of time to the music. Steph felt a wave of pity – Angel was already drunker than most of the customers, and who could blame her? She was a tired, joyless old woman using the last of her looks to make money. If Steph was her, she'd be drunk too.

Steph knocked on the office door.

'Come in.'

The office was expensively decorated, with a huge, dark desk taking up most of the floor space. Michael sat in a leather executive chair behind the desk, swinging back and forth. He wore a suit, but his thick orange neck would have been more at home in a T-shirt.

'Well, well. Steph-an-nie. Our newest little lady.'

Behind the desk were shelves stacked with box files.

Steph took a seat without being asked and noticed three stacks of colourful booklets on the shelf behind Michael's elbow. They were passports, bound together with rubber bands. She could see one very much like hers, a scuffed, burgundy booklet sitting on top of the smallest pile. So much for the club taking good care of it.

'You wanted to speak to me?' said Michael, lighting a cigar.

'Yes. Um. This is difficult.'

'You want some money.'

'I'm in a bit of a situation,' Steph admitted. 'It's . . . nothing I can't handle. But. I just wondered if there was any way . . . I need some wages in advance.'

'I notice your customer isn't here tonight.' Michael leaned forward. 'Janes is all about customers. If you don't have customers, you're nothing here.'

'Okay.' Steph nodded. 'But about—'

'The best girls spend time with customers outside the club.' Michael tapped his cigar on to a gold ashtray. 'Girls who aren't so good – they don't make the extra effort. Maybe they'll keep their customer for a little while, but it never lasts. The customer gets bored. Stops coming in so often. Are you going to be one of my best girls?'

Steph swallowed. 'Yes,' she found herself saying. 'I'll work really hard for you.'

'Good.' Michael slapped the table. 'Keep the customers happy, that's what we're all about. Be a "yes" girl. What the customer wants, he gets. He wants to take you to lunch, you say yes. He needs you to pick a present for his wife, you say yes. He asks you to a hotel room, you say yes. Got it?'

'If I spend time with customers outside work,' said Steph, choosing to ignore the hotel room reference, 'will you give me my wages in advance?'

'No.' Michael sucked on his cigar and blew smoke. 'You don't get any extra favours for doing the same job all the other girls do. I'm just telling you how to keep customers sweet.'

Steph nodded. 'And my wages?'

'Sure,' said Michael. 'A month in advance. Pick them up from reception at the end of the night.'

'Really?' Steph wondered what the catch was. She didn't have to wait long to find out.

'We're not like other hostess clubs.' Michael rolled his cigar between his fingers. 'Girls work extra hard here. Have the girls told you?'

'I . . . Well, not exactly.'

'We pay well, but the girls really have to earn their money,' Michael said. 'By whatever means necessary. You have to do *everything* within your power to keep your customer coming back. Is that clear? If I give you your wages in advance, I want it *crystal* clear.'

'Right.'

'If I hear that for some reason it's *not* crystal clear, that you've lost your customer, you won't have a job here any more. And I'll want those wages back with interest.' Michael laughed. 'That guy who came to see you yesterday?'

'How did you—'

'Ricky told me. He's well known around here. Some hot water you're in. But he's nothing to the people we know. So don't even *think* about skipping out on *our* debt. We'll find you wherever you go.'

Steph got up and left, not quite remembering how she made it to the door.

You've got your money, she thought. *As long as you keep Yamamoto-san interested, everything will be fine.*

Outside, Ricky was waiting for her.

'You look a mess,' Ricky said, picking up a strand of Steph's red hair and letting it drop through her peachy fingernails. Steph's dyed hair had faded in the weeks she'd been in Tokyo. 'You need to get it coloured. Maybe blonde.'

'But I—'

'First and last warning. Come like this tomorrow, and I'll send you to our hairdressers upstairs. They charge ten thousand yen a cut, so Lord knows what they'll charge for a dye. And I want to see some jewels on you tomorrow. Diamonds. Something like that.'

Steph nodded, digging her nails into her palms. Back at her table, four drinks waited for her. She knocked them back, gagging on the last one and stared, red-eyed, across the club.

Julia stared back. She was the other side of the dance floor on a table with just one customer, her ankles crossed, slim fingers around a champagne glass and little finger raised. She wore a forlorn expression, but as soon as Steph locked eyes with her she turned back to her customer and grinned a candy-floss grin, sickly and synthetic. The customer's hand was under her skirt and moving higher up her thigh.

Another vodka tonic appeared. Steph took a sip and when she looked across the club again she saw something alarming.

Julia was . . . swaying.

Vodka caught in Steph's throat as she watched Julia's head and shoulders roll around, like a puppet with slack strings.

There was a crash as Julia's champagne glass fell to the floor and Julia slumped forward on to the table, her blonde hair covering her face.

Steph was running now, past girls and customers, skidding on the champagne-damp floor.

'Julia! Hey, Julia!'

My Girl boomed over the speaker system, and hostesses tip-tapped around the dance floor with their customers. Steph felt bodies closing around her. She couldn't see anything but leggy dancers and their short, balding companions spinning and turning.

Nobody moved out of the way, so she shoved her way through until she reached the other side of the dance floor and Julia's table.

But Julia wasn't there. Nor was her customer. There was

nobody but a waiter wiping spilt champagne from the gold table top.

'Where's Julia?'

The waiter looked as though she was mad.

'Julia.' She grabbed his arm. 'Julia! She was here . . . She was . . . She passed out on the table or something.'

The waiter shrugged, and Steph wanted to shake him. *You must know! She was here a second ago.* She scanned the club for Julia's silky blonde hair, her skinny, pale shoulders, the black dress she was wearing . . .

The glass door leading to the reception area gave a tell-tale *clank*, and Steph ran across the club and pulled it open. She knew it was against the rules for hostesses to leave tables of their own accord, and she certainly wasn't supposed to go wandering into the reception area during working hours, but she didn't care.

It was cool in reception. Cool and empty. An over-sized, fake-marble vase of plastic flowers sat in the corner, gathering dust.

Steph stood for a moment, hand tingling, vision blurry with drink. The reception desk was unmanned. But the elevator . . . The red and black LED display indicated it was rising to floor six. It stopped.

Steph ran to the lift and pressed the call button.

After a moment, the elevator began to descend.

Six . . . five . . . ping! The doors rolled open.

Just as Steph stepped inside, she saw the shadow of Michael approaching the glass door from inside the club. She jabbed the number six inside the elevator and the doors rolled closed. Had he seen her? She wasn't sure.

50

The lift jerked upwards.

But when it reached the sixth floor the doors didn't open. Steph jabbed the 'six' button again, but the elevator just hovered, going neither up nor down, its doors closed. It took a moment for Steph to notice a slot with a red light around it, glowing against the gold wall. What was it – some sort of swipe card lock?

She dug her fingers between the elevator doors and managed to prise them open a centimetre or so. Through the gap was a dark hallway lit with strange blue lights, but no matter how much she pulled, the doors wouldn't open.

Frustrated, she let them slide closed, and then, quite unexpectedly, the elevator began to descend. Steph jabbed the 'six' button again, but the lift paid no attention.

The doors rolled open on the fifth floor.

Michael stood outside.

'Young lady, what are you doing?'

'I'm looking for Julia.'

'Who?'

'Julia?'

'Nope, doesn't sound like a customer name,' said Michael. 'Sorry, you're confusing me. I don't know why you'd be out here unless you were seeing off a customer. Get out of the lift.'

Steph got out.

'One of the girls here . . . my friend Julia,' Steph said. 'I think she just passed out, but . . . She went out here maybe. I wanted to check she was okay. She just vanished into thin air . . .'

'Reception isn't a place for hostesses,' said Michael, putting his hand around Steph's waist. 'Nor is the elevator.'

'But Julia—'

'Julia's fine.' He steered her through the club and into the dressing room.

'See?' Michael plucked Julia's punch card from the row on the wall. 'She punched out a few minutes ago. You must have just missed her. She was booked in for an early finish this evening – arranged it with Ricky earlier.'

Steph nodded at the punch card, realising, as the numbers jumped around, just how drunk she was. So she'd been seeing things.

'Okay,' she said.

'Good,' said Michael. 'Now get back to work.'

'What's the time?' asked Steph.

'Two-thirty,' said the girl beside her, a pretty eighteen-year-old hostess who reapplied her bright red lipstick every ten minutes.

Steph was sitting with three Calamity Janes hostesses in a booth at Hollywoods, counting down the minutes until she could finally finish work. There were thirty still to go.

'Do we have to come here *every* night after work?'

'Some of us,' the red-lipstick girl said. 'Read your contract.'

'Shouldn't Julia be here?' Steph asked, still worried, despite seeing Julia's punch card earlier. The pile of blonde hair on the table . . . It had looked so real.

'Depends on her contract,' said the girl. 'If she's on a special contract, she doesn't have to come here.'

'Maybe that explains it. Hey.' Steph leaned forward. 'That's . . . I think that's . . . I don't believe it.'

'Who?' asked the girl beside her, following Steph's eyeline. Amir had just walked into the bar, and was handing a cardboard box bound with red tape to the barman.

'Someone who owes me money,' said Steph.

'*He* owes you money? Steph . . . He's with the mafia, he helps Michael with, like, the *bad* side of the busines. Seriously. If he owes you money, just forget it.'

But Steph was already marching towards Amir.

'Keep it under the bar for Michael,' Amir was saying as Steph approached him.

'Hey.' Steph tapped him on the shoulder.

Amir turned to her, his eyes red and agitated.

'Remember me? You took me on *dohan*, remember? At Sinatra's. Your card failed and they stuck me with your bill. You owe me money.'

'Sure. I remember you. I couldn't help you out before, right?' He turned his back to the bar and rested both elbows on the shiny wood. 'But now you've got a problem. Maybe I can help you after all.'

'What?'

'I'm a good friend to girls who need money.'

'That's great,' said Steph, folding her arms. 'But all I need is for you to pay off the debt you owe my club.'

'Hey.' He shrugged. 'If you were stupid enough to bring a *dohan* to your club who didn't pay, that's your problem. But if you need money to pay your club back, I can help you. I told you. I know plenty of guys interested in girls like you.'

'And I told you. Forget it. You owe me that money.'

'You don't want my help?' Amir's eye began to twitch. 'Then you want a war. You don't want a war with me. Don't make problems.'

As Steph watched the veins in Amir's neck pulsate she realised he wasn't going to back down. He clearly saw no reason to pay back her club and wouldn't take kindly to her continually reminding him what he owed. All he was interested in was using her for his own financial gain. No, she didn't want a war with him. She'd had enough of wars.

'I don't need your help,' she said through gritted teeth. 'I'll find the money somehow.'

Amir turned to leave. 'You've got my number, right?'

As Steph watched him disappear through the door, Luke came into the bar.

'Hey, Luke!' She waved at the red-shirted figure. 'LUKE!'

Luke had a book under his arm, and he walked his bouncy walk towards her.

'Long time no see, I thought you were sick.' His wavy hair was slightly frizzy from the cold air outside, but despite the winter weather he wore no coat.

'No, not sick exactly.' Steph looked at the hostesses beside her and felt ashamed. Did he know she'd moved clubs, taken one of Mama's best customers? But what else could she have done? Hiro had set her up.

'Sure, okay.' Luke looked confused. He came to join her by the Budweiser and Becks pumps and offered her a stool.

'So where have you been? You're going to have so many fines by the time you get back. You get fined even if you call in sick. Didn't they tell you that?'

'Oh, I just . . . I fancied some time off,' said Steph, twiddling her hair.

So he didn't know. Steph wondered what he'd think of her when he found out. It was just business, wasn't it? Girls took customers to new clubs all the time. And she had a better reason than most. But something told her Luke might see it differently, and she hated the idea of him thinking badly of her.

'Yamamoto-san hasn't been in since you left,' said Luke. 'He's usually in every night, every other night.'

'Let's not talk about work,' Steph said. 'Let's talk about . . . oh, I don't know. Other things. What's the book?' There was a picture of a *geisha* on the front with heavy red make-up around her eyes.

'Guidebook,' said Luke. 'Time I saw more of Japan.'

'That's something I'd never even thought about doing.'

'There's a lot to see. We all eat, sleep, work in Roppongi and think we're living in Japan. But Roppongi's not Japan. Tell you what, how about I take you out tonight? Show you a few proper Japanese places?'

Steph couldn't help but smile. The thought of going out with someone her own age, and whom she didn't have to serve, was liberating. And seeing new things outside the polluted zone of sex clubs, over-priced bars and western restaurants in Roppongi sounded wonderful.

'I . . . Wow, that sounds great.' Steph checked her watch. 'But . . . Maybe in half an hour or so.'

'Why half an hour? Are you meeting a customer or something?'

'No, it's not that.'

'Come on. This place is boring. There are hundreds of bars like this all over the place. Let's get out of here.' He offered her his hand.

Steph looked at the rows of Janes hostesses in booths, all of them clearly bored, miserable and sleepy. There was no Michael or Ricky to keep an eye on things, so perhaps management didn't bother checking on girls here. Maybe they trusted the girls to manage themselves.

'Okay, let's go,' said Steph, taking his hand and laughing as he tugged her out of the bar. She looked over her shoulder, wondering if the other girls would notice her leaving, but they all looked dead-eyed and uninterested. *It's only half an hour*, Steph thought. *Management will never find out.*

'So did you find your friend?' asked Luke, as they walked inside an eight-storey mega-building with the words *Big Echo* written on the outside.

'Where are we?' asked Steph, blinking at the neon-pink decor and young Japanese couples queuing at what looked like a post office counter.

'*Karaoke*,' said Luke.

'Oh.' Steph smiled. She loved performing in public. 'Do you like singing?'

'No, but that's not the point. I wanted to take you somewhere properly Japanese.'

Steph had to admit *Big Echo* was different from anything she'd experienced so far in Roppongi. For a start, everyone inside was Japanese. And they looked wholesome. No drunk businessmen with teenage girls on their arms.

The tube lighting highlighted the scars on Steph's arm, turning them bright white like lightning bolts. She saw Luke notice them.

'I suppose you want to know where I got these.'

'Not really,' said Luke. 'I'm more interested in what's going on with you. Did you ever find that girl you were looking for?'

He went to the cashier. '*Ni, arigato*,' he said, and took a printed slip from the woman behind the desk.

'Annabel you mean.' Steph followed him to an elevator. 'No, it's weird. It's like no one remembers her.'

'Weird things happen out here,' said Luke, checking the receipt and selecting the fourth floor.

'I suppose.'

'You don't think so? You've only been here a few weeks and already your drink's been spiked.'

Steph stared at him. 'My drink hasn't been spiked.'

'You don't think, maybe, someone dropped something in your drink that night at Square Mile?'

Steph thought about it. 'No.' She remembered the three Americans. They'd been touchy-feely, but spiking her drink? They wouldn't do that. Would they?

'It happens a lot out here – you have to be careful.'

'I was just drunk.'

'I'm serious,' said Luke, leading Steph down a corridor with door after identical door lining the walls on both sides. 'Drink spiking happens all the time. That girl, Natalia, who shares your room? She had her drink spiked *inside* Calamity Janes. That's a hostess—'

'I know Calamity Janes,' said Steph. 'Really? She had her drink spiked? Poor girl.'

'Here we are,' said Luke, trying a door handle.

'Where's the bar?' asked Steph, as Luke opened the door. Inside was a tiny room with a two-person sofa, a plastic table, jumbo *karaoke* book and remote control. On the wall was a flat-screen TV with the words *Big Echo* bouncing around on it.

'No bar.'

'So how do we . . . I thought there'd be other people. So we just sing . . . Just the two of us?'

'They bring us drinks when we ask for them.' Luke pushed a laminated menu towards Steph as she took a seat on the sofa.

'Jennifer's missing you, by the way. You're going to be in for it with Mama if you're not back tomorrow.'

'Yes, I—' Steph looked over the menu. 'Can I have tea or something? I've had enough alcohol. Say hi to Jennifer for me.'

'Say hi to her yourself,' said Luke, picking up a phone on the wall and ordering their drinks. 'You'll be in tomorrow, right?'

'Well, here's the thing,' said Steph. 'I don't know about that.'

Luke picked up the *karaoke* book and flipped through the pages. 'Not that you're missing much. Mama-san's in a bad mood, worrying about customers, hostesses . . . She's in so much debt. She's sick, did you know that? I know she can be an old battle-axe but she needs us. We need to help her, help the club pull through.'

To Steph's relief there was a knock at the door and a waitress unloaded their drinks on to the table: a Kirin beer and an oolong tea with ice cubes in it so square they looked as if they'd been measured with a ruler.

'Did you want to know about my scars or not?' said Steph, grabbing her drink and taking a large gulp.

'Only if you want to tell me.'

Steph hesitated. Luke's expression was kind. Okay, she'd got it wrong before, trusted the wrong people. But she couldn't carry that around for ever. Like Mrs Kimono said, it was about being strong.

'I do,' she decided.

Luke put down the *karaoke* book.

'This guy . . . He was sort of my boyfriend. He was supposed to be helping me with my career. He promised me so many things. Films, soaps, pop stuff. But he was really . . . It was all lies. I was like his pet. He wanted to control everything I did.

'He took all these naked pictures of me, and filmed me in these sexy outfits, and like an idiot I went along with it. I thought I could trust him, that he had my best interests at heart. But he didn't. He sold the pictures and the film, and . . . It was all so embarrassing.

'After that, every audition I went to, every time I tried out for Shakespeare or something, no one was taking me seriously. That's why I'm saving for an MA course – so people know I'm like a respectable actress.'

'How did you find out about the pictures?' asked Luke.

'A friend of mine saw them in a magazine. He used my real name and everything. I went mad when I found out. We had a fight in the car. And he . . .' Steph took a deep breath. 'He turned the wheel. On purpose. He was a bit, you know, mental, I think. I was like his property, he could do what he liked with me.

'The car hit someone coming the other way. Head on. I was a miracle case – my seatbelt was broken and I went through the windscreen but I was okay.' She put her head in her hands. 'He was wearing a seatbelt but he died. I shouldn't have fought with him. I never thought he would . . . And now he's gone, and my life back home . . . It was ruined.'

Luke put his arms around her.

'You sing first,' said Steph, her voice muffled. 'I don't know how things work in here.'

It was 5 a.m. when Steph and Luke got back to the apartment.

'I'll see you tomorrow at work, okay?' Luke said, when they reached Steph's bedroom door.

Steph looked at her feet. 'I'd better . . . you know, go in.'

'Okay.' Luke took both her hands in his. 'You're the best girl I've met out here, you know? Don't change. Girls change out here.' He leaned forward and kissed her. 'Have a good sleep.'

'Okay.' Steph squeezed his hands, then went into the bedroom. Natalia wasn't in – she rarely was at 5 a.m. – and Steph suspected she was with a customer, enjoying the soft bedding and en-suite bathroom of a Roppongi hotel.

As she climbed into bed, she thought about Luke and how caring he was. *Mama's sick . . . She needs us . . .*

I've done a selfish thing, Steph thought, shivering as she pulled the damp duvet over her. *But I can make it right again. As soon as I've worked for a month and paid off my debt, I'll take Yamamoto-san back to Sinatra's.*

51

Mama

The hospital receptionist led George into a yellow room with yellow tables and yellow chairs. He held a bunch of yellow flowers in his hand, and wondered if he should have chosen a different colour.

'Mrs Tanaka is still with the doctor,' the receptionist told him, indicating a closed door. 'She'll be out soon. Please read this.' She handed him a folded leaflet with slightly wonky English lettering on it.

'Your visit will relax patients and encourage them for regaining health,' it read. 'Please be attentive to patients' condition and offer refreshing talks.' Did interviewing count as a refreshing talk?

The door opened.

'George-san.' Mama came out. She was dressed in a faded floral trouser suit with a gold chain handbag on her padded shoulder. The bag was large, but clearly not large enough as various papers spilled out as Mama walked.

George picked them up, catching medical insurance forms and a 'consent form for hospitalisation' as they fell to the floor. He tried to cram them into the bag, alongside a pair of slippers, medicine, chopsticks in a clear case and lipsticks, eye-shadows and powders rolling around loose at the bottom.

'They're preparing the results right now,' said Mama, taking a seat on a hard chair. 'We only have a short time to wait. Shall we get started?'

George handed her the yellow flowers, which she appeared delighted by. 'George-san! You shouldn't have.' Her delight soon faded, however, and she dropped the flowers on the chair next to her. 'Tell me where we were up to.'

'I was really hoping for something more personal today. Perhaps about Kaito—'

'Let's not go through all that again.'

'Mama. Please don't take offence. But . . . you're keeping something hidden. For the book to work, you have to tell me everything.'

Mama ran her hand through her thin black hair. An ugly red scar was visible as her hair parted, running all the way over her scalp. She winced when she touched it. 'So. Conrad, Conrad, Conrad. That's what I was telling you about.'

'Yes,' George interrupted. 'You were telling me about your club. How you found the money. How it all started.'

Mama nodded. 'You're right, of course. Yes, I had nowhere near enough money to get started. But I was determined to have my club. So. I decided to try blackmail.'

'Really?' George pulled his notepad out of his jacket and clicked his pen. 'Who did you blackmail?'

'Kaito's father.' Dimples appeared in Mama's cheeks. 'I found his home address on all those letters she'd sent him. She was very prim and proper, his wife, a regular, boring American house-wife. She always wrote her address at the top of the letters. Can you imagine? Even on letters to her husband.

'I wrote to her saying I was a good friend of Conrad's and I'd like her telephone number because I had some news about her husband. I told her I'd pay the call fees.

'She must have had an idea, from my letter, what sort of news I meant. But I was clever about it. I didn't say straight out, "Dear Jane, I'm having sexual relations with your husband and I'm pregnant with his child". I was patient. I waited for her to call Conrad, which I knew she'd do as soon as she received my letter, and then of course I knew Conrad would come running to me, begging me not to reveal his secret. And he did.

'It was summertime. He took me to a noisy bar in Roppongi and I gave him my terms. I wasn't pregnant enough to be uncomfortable, but I was hot and sick and seeing him again was hard. But I knew unless I got my money, I'd be stuck. So I asked for the highest figure I could think of, and he wrote me a cheque then and there on one condition – that I never contact him or his wife again.

'I agreed and he knew he could trust me to keep my word. My interest in him evaporated as soon as I found out he'd lied to me. The illusion, the love bubble, had burst, and I had no desire to keep him on the scene. Far too uncomfortable. As a matter of fact, I don't think he would have been good for Kaito anyway, but . . . You want secrets, George-san? You want me not to hold back? I wasn't thinking of my daughter. I wasn't at all in the habit of thinking of someone else. The sex industry had made me selfish. Selfish and greedy.

'So. I had my money and I began looking for venues, advertising for girls. I was lucky because I spoke good English so my English adverts worked well. Lots of young models from America, Australia – even England – came to see me. Some of them I've seen since in the movies or on TV. Good-looking, ambitious, just what I needed. I wanted western girls – I knew that was the big trend, and with my language skills and western looks I couldn't have imagined running any other sort of place.

'Back then it was easier to find good girls. Now universities steal all the really young ones, and I only get them when they're twenty-two, twenty-three. But I had some real wonders, let me tell you. Big Hollywood film stars, supermodels. And the way they were with men, so charismatic some of them, the actresses usually – oh, they had men eating out of their hands.

'Most of the girls now, they have no idea how to treat a man. I have to teach them. But those girls taught me how to ask men for what you wanted.

'The western thing was the smartest business move I ever made. Other hostess clubs did well in the eighties, but international clubs . . . Well, I pretty much had a licence to print money.

'By the time Kaito was born, I'd employed a manager and four hostesses. Not many girls, but enough.

'One of those girls, one of the first hostesses I hired, went on to be a very famous model. Internationally famous. On billboards for big perfume houses and all sorts of things. Of course, many of my girls have become famous.' Mama smiled and put a finger to her lips.

'I came to the club with Kaito every night. It was hard work, but the girls loved my daughter and they'd look after her in the office while I spoke to customers. Those first few years, I made enough money, not lots, but enough. Until Kaito was five. Then . . . Everything exploded!' Mama threw her hands out. 'Customer, customer, customer . . . It was like I'd unlocked a magic door and the money came pouring in. The club was too small, we couldn't keep up, so we moved to bigger premises, the premises we have now, and hired more girls.

'It was a wonderful journey. I bought a red Ferrari, a nice apartment. I drank champagne every night, before, during and after work. Kaito had a nanny, of course, and I shipped her off to boarding school as soon as I could.' Tears appeared.

'You want to know the truth? I didn't want her around, spoiling my fun, because I really *did* think I was having fun, George-san. I really did. I didn't spend time with her – my own daughter. Some days I just wished she'd disappear . . . That's the truth. I was so selfish. There is no excuse. Things were hard, but lots of women have lived through harder.'

Mama plucked a petal from the yellow flowers and held it up to the light.

'I thought happiness meant freedom from responsibilities. Being able to do exactly as I pleased. I didn't think about Kaito at all. She was nothing more than my entertainment. When I was bored, I gave her back to her nanny. I told customers she was more precious to me than the diamonds they gave me, but the truth is I loved my diamonds more than I loved her.'

'Every parent is different.'

Mama shook her head. 'No. I was a terrible mother. You're right. I shouldn't hold back. It's time to be honest.'

A doctor came into the waiting area, a bulky brown envelope in his hand. He paused when he saw Mama and George talking, but Mama smiled and reached for the envelope.

'This is what they wanted me to wait for, George-san,' said Mama. 'Test results. Very important, according to the doctor.'

'What was the test?' asked George.

'A scan to show if the treatment worked. If my tumour has gone.' She sounded oddly cheerful, given the subject matter. 'We'll meet at my apartment next time, okay?'

George opened his mouth to reply, but Mama was already heading out of the door.

52

Steph

'Julia.' Steph had been in the changing rooms since 6.30 p.m., watching hostesses clock in and out, waiting for Julia to arrive.

Julia didn't acknowledge Steph as she sauntered through the door.

'I'm glad to see you,' Steph said. 'I wanted to check. I thought . . . Where did you go last night?'

'Your hair looks better,' said Julia, sliding her punch card free from the holder.

'Thanks.' Steph touched her newly dyed blonde hair. She'd picked up a packet of hair dye from a Japanese supermarket and asked Luke to translate the instructions. After she'd transformed herself into a blonde, she'd told Luke she needed to phone a customer and dropped by Sinatra's, where she'd paid off her fine in full.

Janes really did pay well – she even had yen for rent. But of course, she'd just traded one prison for another. It would be many weeks, months really, before she would make enough money to be free from Roppongi.

'Are you all right?' Steph went on. 'I thought . . . It looked like you passed out last night.'

Julia missed the slot as she tried to punch her card. Her hand was trembling.

'No. Passed out? Don't be stupid.'

'That's just what it looked like,' said Steph. 'But, well, you're obviously okay. So. Fine. Sorry for caring. I wanted to ask you something.'

'For goodness' sake.' Julia managed to feed her card into the slot. 'You're not going to ask me about Annabel again, are you? Stop being paranoid. Leave her be.'

'No, not that,' said Steph. She hadn't really thought about Annabel since the attack on the street. Once again, money had become the priority. 'I wanted to ask, are you on a special contract or something? You weren't at Hollywoods last night.'

'What?' Julia regarded her coldly.

'The girls were saying last night . . . about contracts. Is it true you can get on a contract that means you don't have to go to Hollywoods every night? Is that why you weren't there?'

'You really don't know anything, do you?' said Julia. 'If *that's* the contract you want to get on, you can get on it no trouble. Just ask Michael.'

'I didn't say I wanted to change my contract. I was asking if that's why you weren't at Hollywoods last night.'

'Every girl's contract is private. I don't have to talk about it.'

'Girlees!' Michael appeared at the door. 'Hurry, hurry. Time for work.'

Clouds of blusher hung in the air as girls pulled on their shoes and hurried past Michael, but as Steph tried to leave he put his hand on her shoulder.

'Not you, young lady. We need a little chat.'

The office smelled of stale beer, cigar smoke and aftershave. Steph noticed a pornography magazine on the desk as Michael ushered her into a seat. He sat himself in his leather chair, which fanned out above him like raven wings, and tossed the magazine into a drawer. Then he slapped his hands on the desk.

'We had a nice talk before, didn't we?'

'I—'

'I gave you wages in advance. We came to a little agreement.'

Steph nodded.

'So. I was surprised to hear you finished your shift early last night.'

'Early? No, I was here until closing time.' Steph felt uneasiness creep up her intestines.

'But you left Hollywoods early.'

'Not really early . . . I stayed until—'

'Two-thirty, I heard. And you left with a young man. Not even a customer.' Michael wagged his finger at her. 'Very, very bad. You haven't read your contract. Our hostesses aren't allowed boyfriends who aren't customers.'

Steph didn't know where to look. 'Sorry, I didn't think half an hour mattered—'

'It does matter,' Michael shouted. 'It matters very much. You're contracted to work those hours. Listen to me. WE OWN YOU. For the next three months you belong to us. The trouble you had after work last week. You don't want that sort of thing happening again, do you?'

Steph shook her head.

'Because I'm telling you, step out of line again and you'll be in so much trouble. I don't care if you're dying, you come to work, you come on time and you stay until your shift finishes. If I hear you're so much as a minute late, there'll be trouble. Understood?'

'Yes,' Steph said, placing her hands flat on the desk to stop them shaking. 'No need to shout.'

'Now, if you want a different contract, that can be arranged. I notice your customer isn't with you tonight.'

'He's—'

Michael put up his hand. 'Save it. I don't want to hear excuses. Just listen. We have a . . . What would you call it?' He looked up to the ceiling and caressed his chubby lips with a finger. 'An offer we make girls when they're not bringing in customers regularly enough.'

He waved his hands around. 'I wouldn't say you're in the danger zone just yet, but I can see the signs. And I like to be fair. Give everyone the best chance of making money. So. You've come to us with a customer. Great. Terrific. We hope you get many more customers here.

'But let's say you don't. And you lose the one you have. Let's say he goes cold on you, finds someone else before you've worked your first month. Usually, we'd fire a girl. Say she hasn't lived up to the terms of her contract. With you that could be especially tricky.' He patted his forefingers together. 'Don't you think? Considering you've *borrowed* your first month's wages before you've even earned them?'

Steph nodded, blood throbbing in the bags under her eyes. Pressure, pressure, every day more and more.

'But we're not *monsters* here,' said Michael. 'We always give girls a chance to earn money.'

'Thanks so much,' Steph said, 'I'm a really hard worker, and—'

'You didn't let me finish.' The words hung in the air. 'At any stage, if you feel you're not doing well, if you'd like to boost your earnings . . . we can offer you a special contract.'

'Is this the contract where girls don't have to go to Hollywoods?' asked Steph.

'Exactly.' Michael flexed his fingers. 'Instead you're on call. Twenty-four hours. For the customers.'

'Like freelance?' said Steph.

'No, not freelance. You still belong to us. But customers can call you any time, day or night, and you attend to them. Provide them with whatever they need. We give you a special mobile phone and you keep it with you at all times. Customers call you, ask you to come to where they are, they book the hotel rooms, all that is taken care of. The pay is quite extraordinary – an extra four hundred thousand yen a month, plus you can bring your special customers into the club, get drinks bonuses. Girls have made an absolute fortune.'

'You mean be on call to sleep with customers,' said Steph.

'What girls do with customers is up to them,' said Michael. 'We don't get involved with that side of things.'

Steph thought of Natalia, going into a seaside hotel with her customer in the afternoon. And Julia, leaving the club early and not going to Hollywoods. Was Julia on a special contract? It made sense. If Julia was sleeping with customers, of course she wouldn't want Steph working at Janes.

I'm a different person out here. When I get home, I'll be me again.
Julia, with her 'sophisticated young lady' persona, wouldn't

want Steph telling people back home what she was up to. Not that Steph would tell. But Julia wasn't the most trusting of people.

'Thanks for the offer,' said Steph. 'The other girls can do what they like. I don't judge them for it. But I'm fine.'

'For now,' said Michael. 'Well, the offer's there if you need it. Sorry, *when* you need it. Off you go then.'

Steph got up.

'Come to me when you change your mind,' said Michael.

53

'Very good, Yamamoto-san.' Steph clapped her hands as Yamamoto bellowed 'She was a DAAAAAY TIPPER . . .' into a gold microphone. He was breathless as he followed the English words on the TV screen, but managed a smile.

Steph watched from a white leather couch, holding a glass of champagne. On Yamamoto-san's insistence, they were in the VIP room at Hollywoods – a private space for celebrities and very rich men. Yamamoto had refused to sit in Hollywoods' main bar, and Steph was more than happy to accompany him to the VIP area, where she got double drinks bonuses as she whiled away her 3 a.m. shift.

She topped up both champagne glasses, being careful to spill as much as possible on the spotless glass table in the process. Then she poured a good quantity of the fizzing liquid into the ice bucket. Another few units of liver damage saved. She would have poured the champagne on to the floor, but the bouncer had whispered a severe warning about the disposing of alcohol, particularly red wine, on the VIP room's white carpet.

'You're wonderful, Yamamoto-san! Much better than me,' Steph called out. It was funny, but since folding the paper cranes she found it much easier to be around Mr Yamamoto. And he seemed to like her more. In fact, all the customers seemed to like her now. She'd only been at Calamity Janes a few nights, but already she was popular.

Maybe, thought Steph, *I'll stay here six months instead of three. Earn more than my course fees. A few extra thousand so I can buy some nice clothes and things. It seems a waste, now I've got this great job, not to make the most of it.*

There were raised voices near the door and Steph sat up. A man in a red T-shirt was talking to the suited doorman.

It was Luke.

Steph wanted to slide down the back of the leather couch and become invisible. But there was nowhere to hide. She and her stolen customer were in plain view.

'One minute. Then I'll go,' Luke was saying.

The doorman nodded.

No, don't let him in . . .

Steph gave a half-hearted smile as Luke came over to her.

'Hi. Fancy seeing you—'

Lines of disappointment appeared all over Luke's face. 'Mama told me. You've taken one of her best customers. I thought you were different. I thought you cared about people . . . You just seemed more . . . I didn't think you were the type to screw someone over for more money.'

'I can't see you,' Steph whispered. 'I'm not supposed to . . . Anyway, he's *my* customer, he chose to come to Calamity Janes with me. Look, it's just business, isn't it?'

'Business, sure.' Luke stuffed his hands into his jeans pockets. 'Just to make a few extra thousand yourself. After Mama gave you a job.'

'You'd do the same if you were me,' said Steph, aware that Yamamoto's song was finishing. Did he know about Amir not paying his bill? About the debt Mama had saddled her with, and Hiro setting her up? Steph felt a surge of anger. Who was he to judge her?

'Okay, so what if I'm at Janes to earn money?' said Steph. 'I need money to get on with my life. Is that so bad?'

'Then it'll be the next yen, the next yen. You cared about finding your friend not so long ago. I don't see you looking for her now. I told you you'd change.'

Steph watched him leave. There was a glass panel in the door, and through it she saw a girl approach Luke.

Chastity.

Jennifer had suggested bottle-backing here, Steph remembered, so probably it was a popular venue for all hostesses, not just shackled 3 A.M. girls from Janes.

Chastity threw her arms around Luke's neck. Her nose was inches from his, and she stroked his hair with one hand. Luke looked uncomfortable, but his hands were around Chastity's waist. She felt a sting in her chest.

I'll show him, she thought. *I do care about finding Annabel. I just got sidetracked, that's all. It won't be the next yen, then the next.*

Yamamoto came back to sit beside her. 'Want to go shopping?'

'Shopping? It's four o'clock.'

'Don Quijote. It's open all night.'

Don Quijote was a seven-floor duty-free department store on Gaien Higashi-Dori. Its logo was a cute, winking penguin in a Santa hat and it sold anything and everything. Wigs, costumes, digital cameras . . .

'No thanks.' She checked her watch. It was gone 4 a.m. – time to clock off. 'There's something I've just remembered. I . . . Thanks for everything, I've really got to get going.'

Where are you?

Steph threw aside sheets and rummaged in her pillow case. She turned out her rucksack, throwing aside clothes and make-up, but the diary was nowhere to be found.

She went into the common area, its artificial light clinical and harsh in the early hours of the morning, and felt down the back of the settee. To her relief the diary was there, tucked into a fold of sweaty, plastic leather. She remembered now, leaving it on the sofa a while ago. How could she have been so careless?

Flicking through the pages, she greeted the familiar writing like an old friend. The diary was messier and harder to read as the entries went on.

Luke was talking nonsense. She still cared about finding Annabel.

The next diary entry didn't start with 'Dear God' like the earlier ones had. Steph flicked forward a few pages and noticed

Annabel had dropped it from the entries until the end of the diary. *It's probably easy to lose your faith out here*, thought Steph. *I'm amazed she stayed talking to God for as long as she did.*

> 'My customers are slipping, down to three now, got to
> pick up the pace. But this Takka guy might be really good, if
> he works out I'll have four . . .'

Steph heard the front door crash, and Natalia stalked past the common room, heading to their bedroom.

'Hey!' Steph shouted. 'Hey, Natalia.'

Natalia's sour-looking, pointy face appeared at the doorway. Steph could smell the mixture of alcohol and perfume from several metres away.

'You're working at Janes now?' Natalia accused. 'I saw you tonight.'

'Yeah, I just started. You know that girl who was in our room?'

'I told you I didn't know her.'

'She worked at Janes. Did you know that?'

'No. I never met her.'

'I guess the club has lots of girls working there. Michael offered me a contract tonight. You know – like the one you're on.'

'A twenty-four-hour contract? On call? Do it. It's good money. Hard work, but good money.'

'I didn't know it was called that,' said Steph, and she thought of the bonus chart on the dressing room wall at Janes with *24h* written next to Natalia's name. So what did SB mean? Those were the letters written next to Julia's name.

'Do you mind?' asked Steph. 'Doesn't it bother you, you know . . . that they're old men? Being with them like that?'

Natalia put a finger to her lips. 'We keep it quiet, you know? Everybody knows, but nobody talks about it. We say special contract, Okay? But we don't say more.'

'But does it?'

'No, it doesn't bother me,' said Natalia. 'I like it better. I spend maybe twenty minutes with a guy, I don't have to talk to him, I don't have to make nice or play pretend. Not even when I bring him into the club.'

Natalia disappeared into the bedroom.

Steph watched her go. She thought for a moment about how draining it was being on your best behaviour around customers, always laughing at their jokes, pretending they were wonderful. She could see how not having to do that would be a relief, and she certainly had no moral objection to Natalia, or Julia for that matter, sleeping with men for money. She just wouldn't want to do it herself.

54

Annabel's handwriting was increasingly illegible, but Steph held the diary close to her face and read slowly.

'That was such a weird one, just meeting him in the apartment. But that's what this place is like. Crazy. And I'm good. I'm really good. I'm one of the best hostesses. Who else gets customers when they're not even at work?

And he seems like an OK customer, maybe a bit funny but aren't they all?

I've got to stop taking ice, it's making me soooo paranoid. When Takka asked me out I thought, This is too good to be true, instead of I'm a pretty great hostess.

Coke is OK. It clears your head, helps you handle the drink better, but ice is just so bad. It feels great, but it's just too, too hardcore. Plus it's so expensive. I haven't kept my bonus money in weeks.

But then, I'm not so worried about wages any more. Easy come, easy go, that's how everyone lives out here and that's the best way. I'm earning so much it's just silly, so I'll worry about my debt some time later. I can pay it back in three months if I want to. I'll just get really tough and sort it out.

There are so many things I want to buy, clothes, shoes, bags and jewellery. Girls in cheap dresses are the real losers at Janes, the ones at the bottom of the chart. You can tell the best girls by their clothes and I'm a best girl.

Best clothes are free clothes, but I love spending my own money. It feels so good. Nothing beats pay day and all those notes you take home.

I hope it works out with Takka. His wife was English so it does sort of make sense, maybe I look like her or sound like her. It would be really good if I remind him of his wife (how bad does this sound?).

Michael's going on and on at me to go on special contract. If things work out with Takka I think he'll stop. The other girls here are such vultures, they've got their claws into my Sinatra's customers, so I've got fewer now than when I started and Michael won't shut up about it. But if Takka comes in with me every single week (I really, really hope he does) Michael will leave me alone.

Annabel xxx

Steph closed the diary. Her eyes hurt. There was plenty to prove Annabel *had* worked at Janes, despite no one seeming to remember her. It was weird that neither the customers nor the other hostesses knew who she was. *She's fine, she's fine*, said the sensible voice again. *You'll bump into her at some point. Get on with earning money.*

Head heavy and intelligence dulled by alcohol, Steph closed the diary and went to bed.

Drunken evenings became drunken weeks, and before Steph knew it a whole month had passed at Calamity Janes and Christmas was approaching. The club was decorated with Santa hats and boots bought in bulk from China, and puffs of cotton wool from the 100-yen store were stuck over doorways and hanging from the ceiling on long strands of fishing wire.

Steph's routine had become a simple one – work until 2 a.m., get bottle-back bonuses until roughly 5 a.m., sleep until 5 p.m., eat fast food, put on make-up, go to work.

When wages came, far from the empty pay packet Steph had been expecting, she received a pleasant cash sum, her percentage from Yamamoto-san's bottles of champagne and food orders. It was good news. She was free from debt and now everything she earned belonged to her. And she was working at one of the best clubs in Roppongi.

When, one Sunday morning, Steph decided to visit Mrs Kimono and, as promised, keep the old lady up to date on her progress, it had been many weeks since they'd last met.

At first, Steph didn't realise the vehicle outside Mrs Kimono's shop was an ambulance. But as she came closer, she saw that the big white camper van had an oxygen mask and orange blankets inside.

A crowd had gathered around the window of rolled silks, and a stretcher emerged from its midst. A grey-haired woman was strapped to the stretcher with an oxygen mask on her face and white silk around her shoulders.

It was Mrs Kimono.

'Hey,' Steph shouted, running to the stretcher. 'Excuse me, she's a friend of mine. Mrs Sato, are you okay?'

It was a stupid question, but for once Mrs Kimono didn't tell her so. Instead, she pulled the oxygen mask away, slapping at a paramedic who tried to put it back in place, and said:

'I didn't expect to see you again.' Her voice was gravelly. 'I thought you were hard at work, earning money.'

'What happened. Did you fall?'

'No. Why did you come?'

Steph held out the bean curd cake she'd been holding under her arm. It was wrapped in white paper, and Mrs Kimono reached out and touched the wrapping.

'I brought you cake,' said Steph. 'To say thank you for your advice.'

'That was some time ago. I thought you'd forgotten all about me.'

The stretcher reached the ambulance.

Steph shook her head. 'I meant to do it ages ago, but somehow . . .'

'You were distracted,' Mrs Kimono finished.

'But I never forgot you,' said Steph. 'I promised I'd tell you how I was getting on, so here I am. I know it's been a while.'

'I suppose we all get distracted,' said Mrs Kimono. 'It doesn't mean your heart is bad. As long as you get back on the right path.'

'I am on the right path.'

'Are you?'

'I think so.'

'Will you get something for me?' Mrs Kimono asked, as she was lifted into the ambulance.

'Of course. What?'

'There's a letter inside.' Mrs Kimono coughed, and momentarily took another gasp of oxygen from the mask. There was blood inside the clear plastic. 'On the mat. I fell before I could pick it up.'

Steph went to the shop, found the white envelope by the door, then ran back to the ambulance just as the doors were closing.

'Wait! Please.' She waved the letter at the paramedic. 'Let me give this to her.'

The paramedic nodded and Steph jumped inside the cramped interior, taking a seat on a green cushion opposite Mrs Kimono's stretcher. The old woman was struggling for breath under the oxygen mask, but when she saw the letter she reached out for it and pulled the plastic from her face.

'The wrong name,' she said, opening the envelope. Inside were two items. One was a map, made up of pastel-coloured squares. There was a star-shaped compass at the top of the page. Mrs Kimono folded it carefully and placed it back into the envelope. Then she held the other paper close to her face and read. When she'd finished, she put it to her chest and dabbed her eyes.

'What's wrong?' asked Steph.

'Nothing is wrong.' She took a deep, rattling breath. 'I've been waiting for this news a long time.'

'You look so . . . *thin*,' said Steph. Mrs Kimono's usually handsome face was drawn, and bony shoulders poked up under the orange blankets. Her weight loss was startling.

Mrs Kimono shivered as the paramedic jumped into the ambulance and banged the door closed. 'Yes,' she conceded, coughing into her hand. 'But you don't look healthy either. Working too hard?'

'Maybe. The more I work, the quicker I can make money.'

Mrs Kimono reached out again and touched the wrapped cake in Steph's hand.

'I know this store. Very traditional. This is a good cake to bring a *geisha*. Who told you?'

'No one. I looked it up on the internet.'

'Very good. I want to give you something in return. There's a Japanese company, not far from here. They hire English-speaking girls to act in commercials. Let me give you their address.'

'No, it's fine,' said Steph. 'Really. I'm not ready for that yet.'

'It's not fine. It's important you carry on with your acting, get work.' Mrs Kimono withdrew a biro from somewhere under the blanket. The grandeur and beauty of her white silk kimono looked odd against hospital-issued bedding. Tearing a corner from the envelope, she wrote a name, address and phone number in stiff, spiky letters. 'Here.' She handed the paper to Steph.

The ambulance began to move, and Mrs Kimono's watery eyes locked on Steph.

'I may not be here much longer.'

'Don't say that. You'll be fine.'

'This letter – they've given me permission. Aoyama cemetery. I've found my burial plot. I'm not afraid of dying. This is my family plot, no more Mrs Sato.'

'No more Mrs Sato?' said Steph.

'Sato is my *danna's* name. We didn't marry but I gave myself that name. Many years ago. To feel close to him. He isn't my daughter's father.

'Now I want to be close to my real family again. In life my daughter and I weren't together, but we can be together in death.' She closed her eyes for a long moment.

'Your daughter . . . She passed away? I didn't know. I'm so sorry. When did it happen?'

'She didn't die.' Mrs Kimono relaxed back on to the bed. 'She's still here. But when her time comes, we'll be together.'

The ambulance pulled up in front of the hospital, and the paramedic began unclipping the stretcher. 'You can't stay, I'm afraid,' he told Steph in careful English. 'She'll be moved to intensive care. Maybe you can see her later today.'

'Yes, no reason for you to stay here,' said Mrs Kimono. 'But listen to me.'

'I'll wait in the hospital until they let me see you.'

'Did you move to a different hostess club?'

'Yes,' said Steph. 'I did. I moved to Calamity Janes.'

Mrs Kimono closed her eyes. 'I thought so. I could tell by the cracks on your mouth and your bad skin. I wish you'd listened to your feelings. Calamity Janes has a bad reputation. Be very careful.'

'What reputation?'

'The western girls who work at that place. Glass *geishas* I call them. Fragile. Breakable. Empty. Roppongi is a place to stay if you don't want to grow up. But it's not a place to live. You can't be a *maiko* for ever.'

They wheeled Mrs Kimono into the hospital, and Steph heard the squeak of the stretcher on the rubbery floor. She took a seat on a wooden bench in the lobby.

Outside, it began to snow.

55

Mama

When Mama opened her apartment door, there was nobody there.

'*Konnichi wa?*' she enquired.

'Hello, Mama.'

The voice came from around her knees. George was bending down by her shoe rack, slotting his brown lace-ups beside rows of cotton slippers.

'So. George-san. Last interview today. Do you think you'll get all the material you need? Has there been enough time?'

George straightened. 'I'm hoping.' He crossed his fingers. 'We'll see how today goes.'

'But it's important, isn't it?'

'Yes,' said George. 'I suppose so. But in the scheme of things . . .'

'The deadline must be getting close,' said Mama, waving him into the apartment.

'Yes.' George followed her down the hallway and into her sitting room. 'And there's still something . . . I've got a lot of information, but I feel there's still something you're not saying. We have to work hard today. Anyway, you look . . . well. Very well.' Although Mama wore a dressing gown and slippers and her hair was patchy and thin, her face was radiant. Energised.

The floor cushion was as uncomfortable as it had been during George's first visit, but he sat with more acceptance now. He didn't fidget as Mama pottered in the kitchen.

'No tea today, I can't be bothered with it,' Mama declared, bringing in two plastic yoghurt-pot-style cartons of supermarket-made milky coffee which she'd warmed in the microwave. She set them on the coffee table with two KitKats. 'Here. Help yourself.'

George took a chocolate bar and watched as Mama lowered herself on to a cushion. Her left leg didn't seem to be working properly, and she had to pull it into a cross-legged position.

'We have work to do,' she announced, taking a carton of coffee.

'Yes.' George took out his notepad and pen. He looked at his writing materials, then at Mama. 'May I just say what a truly humbling experience it's been working with you. Truly. And if at any point you need to stop, to rest . . .'

'Yes, yes,' said Mama cheerfully. 'I'm fine. Really.'

'How were the test results? You look well. Good news?'

'We don't have long. Okay? So let's get started.'

'Okay.'

'I was very sad last time we talked, wasn't I? Remembering Kaito's childhood. What things were like while she was growing up. I did exactly what every parent shouldn't – I gave her a childhood similar to the one I had. Ignored. Second best to men. I should have known better.'

Despite the melancholy topic, Mama's tone was still cheerful and George's shoulders sagged as she chattered away. During the last interview, when she'd talked about Kaito she'd been vulnerable. The real woman behind the Mama-san façade. But now she was hard and impenetrable again. Fun and light-hearted, yes. Interesting and honest, of course. But most certainly tough and unyielding.

'I hated and resented my own mother for letting me down, for putting herself and her men first, and yet I did the same thing.' Mama sighed. 'So stupid. Do you have children?'

'A son,' said George. 'Christopher. I don't see him as much as I'd like to.'

'Oh. Divorce?'

George nodded.

'And you don't see your son so much, because . . . ?'

'He lives in England. And his mother likes things her way.'

'So does every woman,' said Mama. 'That's how we are. Your

job is to make sure things *go* our way. Then we all get along just fine.'

George laughed, but Mama was serious.

'His mother – you let her down in some way?'

'You could say that.'

'I *will* say that. And she left you?' Mama didn't wait for an answer. 'That's always how it goes. A man doesn't live up to a woman's expectations and he has to go. Who's wrong – the one with the expectations, or the one who doesn't meet them? I don't know. Anyway. You should try harder to see your son.'

'It's not so straightforward,' George insisted. 'His mother—'

'His mother this, his mother that. I don't believe a mother would stop a man seeing his child without good reason. If you're such a good parent, why move away? Some men have a hard time taking responsibility.' Mama gave him a bewitching smile. 'I'm being hard on you, George-san. Don't be offended.'

'No.' George stared at the page. 'You're right. She doesn't . . . I mean, it's hard but . . .'

'You should try harder,' said Mama, taking a sip of coffee.

'Did you try hard?' asked George. 'With Kaito?'

Mama looked down. 'You really won't let this go, will you, George-san?'

'The book needs your soul laid bare. I need you to tell me everything.'

'*Hai.* Probably true. But what about me? What about what I need?'

'Maybe it'll be good for you to get things off your chest.'

Mama nodded. 'I suppose, if there was ever a time, this is it. Well.' Her voice sounded young suddenly, and unsure. 'Don't think too badly of me, will you, George-san? But I'll tell you. Things were very hard for Kaito when she was young. I was running the club, the glamorous woman of the night. Diamonds, pearls, champagne, perfume. I tumbled in and out of Kaito's life when I felt like it and she loved me. Oh, she adored me back then. She wanted to be just like me. She was too good a daughter for me. I didn't deserve her.

'I'd bring different men home all the time, boyfriends, married men, billionaires. Men who took the two of us on exotic holidays. I used to say to her, 'Nobody can say your life isn't exciting, Kaito. And you have things none of your friends have. Your own colour television, a personal computer, lots of clothes . . .' But of course, she didn't want any of those things. She just wanted a normal mother who didn't sleep all day and the children at school didn't gossip about. She wanted my love.

'I knew she was suffering, George-san. I knew her pain. It's so hard to talk about. I kept it a secret from myself for so long, you know? I pretended I didn't know how much she suffered. I hid her pain a long way down where nobody could find it.

'She was bullied terribly at school because of me. That's the Japanese way, I'm afraid. The nail that stands up must be hammered flat. Her mother worked in the *mizu shobai*, so she was picked on. She told me about it, but I didn't pay attention. She was an inconvenience to me, particularly when she complained about my men.'

Tears trickled down Mama's face.

'This is the worst part, George-san. I hope you're ready for it. Some of my men didn't treat her well. My own daughter. I knew, but I pretended not to know.'

George's pen was racing along the page.

'Yes, keep writing, George-san. You're right. People should know everything. What I'm really like and what I really did. Not a sugar postcard. I was a real westerner back then, just like my father.

'Many of my boyfriends were gangsters. They were cruel to Kaito and I did nothing. One would ridicule her acne and her skinny body, another . . . He beat her. And I would laugh about it. That was how I dealt with it. Pretend it was no big deal, just a joke. I didn't want to make problems with my men, back then. I look strong to you, don't I? But when it comes to men, relationships, not customers, I'm not strong. I never thought I deserved much, so I let him hurt my daughter . . . Let him spoil the way she thought about herself . . .'

Mama took a deep breath and George leaned forward and patted her hand.

'You're being very honest,' he said.

'I don't want to be a westerner any more, George-san,' Mama said. 'But I have to keep working like a westerner. The club – I have to make it work.' She smiled, and her face softened. 'Back when my club started, things were easy. You wouldn't believe that, would you? I was pregnant, and after that of course I had a young child to look after, but it was easy. The money came in like rain falling from the sky. I should have known. Life shouldn't be that way. It wasn't balanced.'

'And it's not like that today?' asked George.

'No.' Mama's eyelid began to twitch. She stopped it with her fingers. 'Back then, within five years my club became the best-known hostess bar in Roppongi. And I was making money, money, money. Every big business knew my club was the place to take clients for after-work meetings, and I had many famous customers. Film stars, music stars . . . Oh, so many.

'You know, the American film stars who came were all badly behaved. They were married men, most of them – some married to great beauties of the time, famous women. Models. Actresses. But they all asked for sex with hostesses, all of them except one. James Bond.'

George inhaled. 'James—'

'Yes, yes.' Mama held up her hand. 'Him. Very famous. He didn't ask. But the others did. And they talked about themselves. Oh goodness me, did they talk about themselves.'

'Who were they?' asked George.

'I've written all their names, I'll get them for you.' Mama went to a wooden dresser, leaning heavily on her left leg. 'Here.' She removed pages of lined paper and gave them to George. 'I wrote notes too. See?'

George took the papers, his eyes widening as he saw the names. 'You had . . . and . . . They were all customers?'

Mama nodded and sat down again.

'And he asked for . . . This one wanted a girl to . . . I can't read what it says here.'

Mama leaned to look at the paper. 'Watch *Deep Throat*. The movie. He wanted one of my girls to watch that movie with him and then perform oral sex while he phoned his wife at home.'

'I thought your girls weren't prostitutes,' said George.

'Anyone can be for the right price. How about this one?' Mama pointed. 'You wanted politicians, George-san. You don't get much more famous than that.'

George stared at the paper. 'I wish you'd shown me this sooner.'

'I wrote it in hospital. See how he behaved? For someone from the White House, he wasn't such a gentleman.'

'*Had bad body odour,*' George read, '*and fell asleep in the club after vomiting on one of the girls, whom he later demanded come back to his hotel with him.*'

'Of course, as a good Mama-san I never told customers' secrets,' said Mama. 'But times have changed. The musicians were the worst. Pop stars. They thought they were God. Something happened in the eighties, in England . . . Band Aid it was called. Do you know it?'

'Band Aid? The charity thing?' said George.

'I think so. Lots of bands, all together. Anyway, a few of those bands came here and they thought they were Jesus, you know? Telling us we should give to charity and save the starving people in Africa.' Mama laughed. 'But of course, they were spending thousands on girls and champagne!'

George nodded again and again as he scanned the pages. 'This is . . . It's just great, Mama. Just what we need. And . . . These are the girls who worked at your club?'

'The famous ones, yes,' said Mama. 'You see this one? Blondy she used to call herself when she worked here. One of my favourites. I see her in all the big movies now. She had fairy dust in her smile – the men were mad for her. She did drugs, though.' Mama shook her head. 'And this one . . . An American model, very famous, *neh*? I thought she was cleaner than clean, but the waiter saw her having sex with a customer's son in my club bathroom.' Mama put a hand to her mouth and giggled. 'Oh, she was beautiful, but I thought she was too tall and skinny. The magazines liked her, though. And now she does work-out videos, all sorts of things.'

'This is all superb,' said George, smiling at the girls' names. 'And with all the other material, I have everything I need.'

'I'm glad.' Mama beamed at him. 'Those days are long gone now. The gift diamonds, the big expense accounts. Now companies have budgets. Everything is watched carefully. And Japan isn't as exotic as it used to be. There are lots of American places. Western stars go to western clubs and restaurants and pretend they're still in America. Of course, I didn't know who these customers were when they came to the club.' She smacked the list. 'They were just clients to me, and usually quite badly behaved ones. I only slept with a few. The really handsome ones.

'I'm not proud of being a bad mother, but I am proud of my club. Through everything, police raids, *yakuza* threats, I always take care of my club and my girls. My hostesses. They're my daughters too. I'm always with them. When Kaito was growing up, I saw my girls more than I saw her, and maybe I even treated them better. My hostesses are always paid, no matter how desperate things are for me. And they always will be.'

George nodded. 'That's admirable.'

'Maybe. Maybe I'm just a young fool who turned into an old fool,' said Mama. 'Girls leave me all the time, you know. They take customers. They don't care about me, or my club. They're not Japanese, these girls. They don't have loyalty or honour in that way. But you know what, George-san?'

'What?'

'I don't care. I'll still look after my girls. I won't do what I see these western clubs doing – working girls too hard, not paying them right, bringing in sex, sex, sex under the table, letting in bad clients, making the girls unsafe. I won't do it, no matter how many girls take my customers. Never. Even though sometimes the girls hate me, George-san.'

'I'm sure they don't h—'

'They do. I can be mean. But I'm their Mama-san, I have their best interests at heart. I always make sure they're paid. I take care of them in my own way. So, you have everything you need for the book now?'

George nodded. 'Mama . . . More than enough. And you've been so ill. I really thought it was going to be touch and go . . .'

'You thought I'd let you down?' Mama raised an eyebrow.

'No I . . . Not let down. But you've been so ill. Mama, how were your results?'

'No news is good news, isn't that what they say?'

'No news? The results . . . They didn't tell you anything?'

'I haven't opened them.'

'Why not?'

'Why should I? So some doctor can tell me whether I'm living or dying? That's my choice. I'm grateful for every twist and turn, kink and corner of life. I'll die when I'm ready.'

'But . . .' George shook his head. 'What if the results . . . What if you need more treatment?'

'I've had enough treatment.' Mama folded her hands in her lap and sat up straight. 'I'm not having any more. Listen, George-san. If you tell yourself you're dying, you'll die. Poison. You see? Poison for the mind. And I won't take it. I believe I'm well. I have to be well, because I have to pay my hostesses and make money for my daughter.'

George stuck out his hand. 'Mama, it's been a privilege. Let me know if there's anything I can do.'

'Just make the book a success.'

56

Steph

'Is Mrs Sato ready for visitors yet?' Steph asked the hospital receptionist, a nervous-looking woman sitting behind a desk that ran the entire length of the entrance hall.

'Oh. Sorry. She's still too sick for visitors.'

'Are you sure?' Steph leaned over the desk. 'The ambulance people told me I could see her later today.'

'Let me call the doctor.' The receptionist picked up her phone and said some words in Japanese, but after a few seconds she hung up, shaking her head.

'The doctor's not available right now. Not until six p.m. Would you like to wait?'

Steph nodded. 'Please.'

The receptionist gestured to the hard benches, dotted between well-tended pot plants decorating the hospital lobby.

Steph took the same bench she'd been occupying for the last four hours. The aches from an afternoon sitting on hard wood instantly rolled back into her joints.

She checked her watch. 5 p.m. Another hour to wait.

Steph yawned and looked inside her bag for chewing gum – anything to distract her from the tedium of clock-watching – and saw Annabel's diary amongst the empty food wrappers and loose make-up. She remembered Mrs Kimono's last words to her.

The western girls that work at that place. Glass geishas I call them.

A shiver caught her. *I'll finish reading this, she thought. I've been here months and I still haven't tracked Annabel down.*

Lost another customer. And yet again it's to a contract girl, surprise, surprise. Michael keeps saying Why don't you go on contract? Look at all the customers you make, and I'm scared if things don't pick up . . . I don't know. I suppose I could always find a different club, but I'm used to the money here, it would be such a step down.

A group of nurses walked past, their white coats buttoned all the way to their necks, and disappeared down a hospital corridor. Steph thought about the contracts at the club.

Girls, it seemed, could sleep with customers to make extra money, and the club sanctioned it – even arranged it. In fact, it seemed if you weren't doing so well, management put you under a lot of pressure to go on a special contract and offer customers sexual services.

Maybe that was the secret to good hostessing, although it didn't seem like Annabel was sleeping with customers. Steph hoped she wasn't. It would be such a turnaround from the sweet girl she'd known at school.

Being at the club is really freaking me out at the moment. This sleeping beauties thing – the Japanese are weird, weird weird sometimes. Who gets off on a girl being passed out? I'm always watching my drink now, it's made me so paranoid.

An arc of white light washed over Steph's eyeballs, and her face began to throb in time to her heart. *Sleeping beauties . . . always watching my drinks . . .* There was something about the phrase 'sleeping beauties' that made her hair stand on end. She thought of the photos she'd seen behind Calamity Janes' reception desk on her first night in Japan. Beautiful girls asleep in their underwear.

'Excuse me.' She waved at a man in a hospital coat. 'Is there an internet café near here?'

'Sleeping beauties' was an immediate hit on Google, but the websites it brought up were far from Walt Disney. Steph sifted through pages of pornography, showing photo after photo of unconscious women in various stages of undress.

'Sleeping beauties,' she read, 'are unconscious, drugged or sleeping girls used for sexual gratification. Named after the cult Japanese book, *House of the Sleeping Beauties*, by Yasunari Kawabata, 'sleeping beauty' pornography films feature unconscious women having sexual acts performed on them.'

Steph checked her watch.

6.30 p.m. I'll be late for work.

The hospital probably wouldn't let her see Mrs Kimono today anyway. She'd come back tomorrow. But the thought of going to the club made her limbs feel full of sand.

Luke said Natalia's drink had been spiked, and now Annabel was talking about 'sleeping beauties' and watching her drink . . . But there was probably nothing to worry about. 'Roppongi myths', as Annabel herself had written. And to miss work, when there were so many bonuses to be had . . . Well, it just wasn't an option.

As she hurried into the warm cave of the subway and on to the spotless train platform, Steph opened the diary again. She was hoping Annabel would elaborate on 'sleeping beauties' and scanned down the page, but the phrase wasn't used again.

It's been such a bad week. I hate Sundays. I'm so lonely at the weekends, all the customers go back to their wives and none of the girls want to do anything but sleep off the drugs. Not that I ever go out with the girls anyway – it's not like that here. None of us are friends.

The sad thing is, the customers are the nearest thing I have to friends and when I'm drunk or on ice or something, we get on so well. When I'm sober, they're boring as anything.

The subway train pulled up to the platform, exactly on time as always. Steph climbed aboard and continued to read.

As usual, I'm on a massive comedown, but I can never sleep through it so I'm just sitting around, trying to distract myself. I've got a bag with half a line of ice in it, so maybe

I'll take it and go to the cinema or something. Anything to cheer myself up. SOOO bored.

The train pulled into Roppongi station, and Steph realised she'd need to hurry. As she rushed out of the station, past fast food restaurants and amusement arcades, she wondered about Julia.

Had Julia's drink been spiked the other night? And if it had, why was she back at work the next day as if nothing had happened?

57

Chastity

From: C_C_Chastity
To: CanadianDaphne
Subject: re: re: life and stuff

Guess what babes?

Luke's leaving. I'm over it. He was fun, but let's face it, he was never going to buy me an apartment or a big enough diamond ring. I was only ever really with him for a mess around.

Everyone moves on in the end. I swear, I'll be here when Mama-san finally pops her clogs. She's not well these days, she forgets where she is half the time, it's like having an old mental patient walking around the place. Last night she fell asleep on Nishi, she was snoring and everything. So funny. Someone should tell her she's getting old.

I feel bad for Mama, but she's being a real witch right now. She just lost another good customer, actually one of my request guys, Yamamoto-san, so she's tearing into all of us. *Make customer, bring customer, I can't trust you girls. You steal my customers.* You know what she's like.

It was her own fault she lost him. She hired this new girl with scars all over her, and after a few weeks this girl got really friendly with Yamamoto-san, probably started sleeping with him, and talked him into going to a different club – Calamity Janes we heard. In which case, she's got her punishment, hasn't she?

I'm just sick of it all, to be honest, all that customer stuff. Dancing is looking better and better. I took dirty doctor guy (remember him?) to Flames last night and you know what? It's not sleazy AT ALL. Champagne on every table. The girls seem OK, one of them says she'll show me how to dance on the pole.

Of course, dirty doctor guy thought I was warming him up for a night of action, so I had to peel his hands off every five minutes, but I made good drink-backs and Johno kept asking me to come back again.

When we were watching the dancers, dirty doctor asked me to strip for 100,000 yen and I would have done (Johno's been on at me to do a trial for so long now, I've got my head around taking my top off) but then something kicked off. One of the customers bit one of the girls and everyone had to leave. There were police vans on the street when we got out, they're REALLY cracking down on this area, stopping girls in the street to ask for visas, it's scary. I need to marry someone FAST! Ha ha ha.

Dirty doctor said we should get a hotel room (surprise surprise), and I was so drunk I thought, why not? Most of the girls here end up doing it with customers eventually, and I'm tired of working, working, working and never knowing what bonuses I'm going to make.

OK don't judge me for this but I did it. It was pretty icky the next day, waking up to find this old, fat lump next to me, but the rest I hardly even remember so it can't have been that bad. We got in the bath so he was clean before, and as long as the champagne and coke was coming I was fine.

He's visited me every night this week, and he bought me a diamond necklace the next day (a really small one, but he left the receipt in the box so I can take it back and get the money – 40,000 yen) and he hasn't even asked if we can do it again. Mama's been so happy with me, I'm like her top girl again. I think she felt pretty badly stung by that other girl. She's realising she can rely on the old guard like me and Christiana.

So I know you're probably thinking ew ew ew right now, and you're right but I've got to tell you, it's good to have the pressure off this week. Tammy will never find out and if it gets her school fees paid, it can't be such a bad thing.

Chastity

58

Steph

Steph shivered as snow fell on her shoulders and hair. She wore jeans and two hooded tops, but no coat, despite the downy flakes rapidly covering the pavement outside Calamity Janes.

'Can we go into the club yet?' Steph asked Ricky, who wore a cashmere coat and leather gloves. A cigarette smoked in her fingers. The rest of the Calamity Janes hostesses huddled around her, about fifty of them in total, smoking and complaining.

'Fuck knows,' said Ricky.

Almost as soon as she'd arrived at work, a potential police raid had been announced. The girls were hurried out in a panic, Ricky shouting, herding them into the lift one group at a time, *hurry, hurry, hurry*.

Down the street, police loaded hostesses from Club Greengrass into the back of a police van. They wore skimpy evening dresses. Most of them were crying.

'Greengrass never gets raided,' said Ricky, throwing her cigarette butt into the gutter. 'Never. *Yakuza* are losing their touch.' Her mobile phone vibrated and she flicked it open. 'Hello? Ya. Okay Mikes, I'll tell them.' Ricky turned to the girls and shouted, 'Back inside! Keep your casual clothes on, you're just having a drink at the club, right? Just girls having a drink and a night out.'

Angel pushed forward. 'None of us have visas,' she said. 'We're just going to sit inside and wait for them? I can't get busted. I've got debts to pay. If I can't work—' Her voice rose to hysterical volume.

'Angel, calm it down,' Ricky barked. 'You're all in casual clothes, Mike's taken your contracts to a safe place. He's talking to friends right now. They say the police have nothing on us.

There's nothing they can do. They can't stop girls drinking with men in a club.'

'What about our passports? They're in the office. Anyone could see them.'

'It's not a crime to keep girls' passports,' said Ricky. 'Passports don't prove anything.'

Everyone went into the lobby and Steph piled into the lift with Angel and three other hostesses. Since the lift could only fit five at a time, the girls left behind folded their arms, tutted and generally expressed their irritation at having to wait in the open lobby, where an icy breeze whipped their pale cheeks pink.

No one spoke as the lift rose, each girl staring down at her own high heels. Steph remembered Annabel's diary comment. It was true – the girls here weren't friendly.

The club was empty when the lift arrived on the fifth floor.

'Wow,' said Steph. 'It's like a ghost club.' The bare stage looked out at tables of half-drunk drinks and melting ice buckets. 'Where did the customers go?'

'Hollywoods,' one of the girls said. 'That's where Michael always sends them. They'll be back up when Ricky gives the all-clear.'

'I can't stand this,' Angel shouted at the bar. She smoothed her eyebrows over and over again. 'I can't stand it. We're going to get caught. We'll be deported. I've got debts to pay.'

'Stop stressing,' said one of the other girls. 'You're making *me* stressed. We're just having a drink in a club, like Ricky said.'

'I can't stand it. I can't stand it!' Angel turned around on the spot. 'They have papers on me. They're setting us up.' She went to the office.

'Wait.' Steph called. 'Don't go in there. If Ricky catches you . . . Don't be stupid.'

But Angel was already inside, tearing papers from the shelves.

'Don't.' Steph followed her. 'You can't be in here. They'll sack you for sure. Come on—'

Angel turned and looked straight past Steph, her watery eyes staring out into the club.

'Look, you'd better get out of here,' said Steph.

Ricky's voice floated through the wall.

'. . . *getting worse and worse, I don't know how we . . .*'

Angel looked bewildered, then horrified. She bolted from the office, hand over her mouth.

'. . . *and they're just on at us the whole time right now, like a pack of Rottweilers . . .*'

There were papers all over the floor.

Steph looked at the mess and realised Ricky would know someone had been in here. After Michael catching her in the lobby and finding out she'd knocked off from Hollywoods early, she couldn't risk even the suspicion that it could be her.

Hurriedly, she picked up the papers and stuffed them back on to the shelves.

'. . . *who came up already? No, Michael's gone . . .*'

There was a square box on the floor, bound with red tape. *The box Amir keeps delivering*, thought Steph. *What's in it? Drugs? Porn?* It looked too small for magazines or videos, and if it was full of cocaine there'd be enough to last Michael for a whole year. The box was thoroughly sealed, wrapped many times with reams of shiny tape. Although she was curious, Steph ignored it and carried on picking up papers.

The passports were sitting on the shelf, just like before, and as Steph stacked papers next to them she noticed the British passport she'd assumed to be hers was no longer on top of the pile. She felt uneasy. The passports were so exposed, so easy to steal . . . What if someone had taken hers?

She picked up a pile, pulled off the rubber band and began leafing through, looking for the familiar British lion and unicorn crest, gold on burgundy.

The passports were mostly red, since the majority of Janes' hostesses were from Russia and the Czech Republic, but there were a few navy Australian or black American booklets in the mix. When Steph found a UK passport, her breathing quickened. She was fairly certain it wasn't hers, the scuffs weren't right, but she flicked it open to see the name and the photo anyway. A white-faced girl glared back at her.

Julia.

Steph could hear the tramp of feet as more girls came out of the lift. She put Julia's passport back in the pile and kept looking.

American, Russian, Russian, Czech, Russian . . . UK.

Steph flicked open the passport.

A gentle-looking girl with thick, browny-blonde hair smiled at her. She looked healthy and wholesome, like a farmer's daughter.

The name under the photo was Annabel Jones.

Steph's hand began to shake as she stared at the photo and read the name over and over again.

Annabel.

There was a clank as the glass door banged outside, and Steph snapped the passport closed, shoving the pile back on the shelf. She ran outside and took the nearest stool, trying to slow her breathing as she watched Ricky saunter between the tables.

'Did you . . .' Ricky looked at Steph. 'Where did you come from?'

Steph shrugged. 'I've been right here.'

Ricky shook her head. 'I'm getting as paranoid as Angel.'

59

The evening was a carousel of customers as Ricky moved Steph from table to table, allowing her barely twenty minutes at each one. There were so many newcomers to meet, so many names to remember, that by 1 a.m. Steph was dizzy and exhausted.

But still, Ricky wasn't content to leave her be.

'Stephy. New customer for you.'

'Okay.' Steph was so tired she could barely keep her eyes open. All she could think about was the passport, lying just metres away in Michael's office.

'It's just one guy. You and Julia. No fighting now.'

'Julia?'

'Over here.' Ricky led her to a table, where Julia sat in a long, red dress, gazing into the eyes of a customer with extremely heavy eyebrows.

Julia didn't look up as Steph sat down.

The customer had a brown coat folded over his arm, and Steph recognised him as the man she'd seen in Square Mile the night she'd been out with Jennifer. She turned on her actress's smile and gently clasped the man's hand.

'What's your name?' she asked.

'Si*mon.*' He pronounced it like she was stupid for asking.

'And what are you doing in Tokyo, Simon? Do you live here? Visiting?'

'Always the same questions over and over,' said Simon.

Steph smiled serenely. 'I'll talk about me then. Julia and I used to go to school together. Isn't that interesting? With a friend of ours.'

'A long time ago,' Julia interjected.

'And guess what? Our friend's passport is in the office at this club. Isn't that strange?' Steph looked Julia straight in the eye, and Julia shifted her gaze.

'Don't make a big deal out of nothing, Steph.'

'Big deal out of nothing?' Steph leaned over the table. 'It's *weird*. The club has Annabel's passport, but she doesn't work here. Where *is* she?'

'Just drop it,' Julia hissed. 'Seriously, forget about Annabel. Or you're going to find out things you'd rather not know.' Julia glanced at the customer, who was watching them both with interest.

A waiter arrived and unloaded two drinks on to the table – glasses of white wine, one with ice cubes floating in it.

'You've got the wrong table,' Julia told the waiter, making an urgent T-sign with her hand. He ignored her, threw down coasters and placed the drinks.

Ricky appeared behind Simon's shoulder. 'Excuse me, Mr Finch? I have er . . . About your requirements, can we talk in reception?'

Simon followed Ricky across the club.

Steph picked up her drink, but Julia snatched it out of her hand before she could take a sip.

'Don't drink that.' She poured it on the floor.

'Why not?'

'He got the wrong table.'

'What are you talking about? They bring us drinks, we drink them. How can they have got the wrong table?'

'Just . . . Trust me, okay? You don't want that drink.'

Steph stared at the empty glass. It looked perfectly innocent – just a normal wine glass with ice cubes melting in the bottom.

'Was there something in the drink?' she said.

Julia gave her an urgent look and put a finger to her lips.

'What does that mean? Yes or no?'

'I'll order you another one.' She waved at the waiter.

'How did you know?'

'Simon's coming back,' said Julia, sitting straighter so she could see across the club. 'Just forget it, okay?'

'Do they spike girls here?' asked Steph. 'Annabel . . . I read something about sleeping beauties. Drugging girls for sex.'

'I really don't . . . Some of the customers . . . I don't know.' Julia lowered her voice. 'You just have to be careful, that's all. Plenty of hostesses here have woken up in strange beds. You have to watch out.'

'How are my ladies?' Simon sat between Steph and Julia and put his arm around their shoulders. 'Time for another drink?'

'I've already ordered us another,' said Julia.

As Steph walked home that night, the smiling picture in the passport haunted her. Annabel looked out at her from bars and clubs and even down from the night sky, where a few stars managed to twinkle through the polluted gloom.

If Annabel wasn't working at the club any more, *why* was her passport there?

She needed to speak to Luke. He was the only person around here who made sense. Inside the apartment, she banged on his door. The stiff wood was wrenched open, and Luke stood in the doorway, his slim frame made bulky by the huge rucksack on his shoulders.

'Luke, I'm so glad to see you.'

'I can't stop.'

'It's important, Luke. Please talk to me.'

Luke checked his watch. 'Look, I've really got to run. I've got a train booked.' There was a green envelope in his hand.

'At this time?'

'At this time.' He headed to the front door.

'Fine,' Steph called out. 'Have a good trip.'

It looked like Luke was going away. The thought wasn't comfortable. She wanted to ask him where he was going, why he needed luggage. She wanted to tell him she'd only taken Mama's customer because Mama had put her in so much debt and Hiro had set her up. And she wanted to ask him to help her find Annabel. But she wasn't sure he'd be willing to listen.

The front door banged and the noise rattled through the walls. Steph's throat felt sore.

Annabel's passport is at Calamity Janes, she thought. *But Annabel isn't. Should I go to the police about that?* She remembered the tough-looking, crew-cut policeman and his warnings about visa checks and deportation. And she thought of the 'people' Michael had said the club knew. Bad people.

I'll finish her diary first. If it doesn't tell me where she is now, then I'll go to the police. There's probably a perfectly good reason why the club still has her passport. Maybe she skipped out before her contract ended, took a job nearby and never bothered picking her passport up again. There's no point getting paranoid until you've read more.

She reached into her bag. But the diary wasn't there.

60

Chastity

From: C_C_Chastity
To: CanadianDaphne
Subject: roppongi weirdness

Daphs,

I swear to God, I'm going mad. No jokes. This is just the
weirdest thing that's ever happened to me. Since I've been
doing the dirty with dirty doctor guy he's been sweet as, but,
this is so mad, I'm getting JEALOUS. No word of a lie. Me!
Jealous of this old guy with moles all over him. But it's true.
When the other hostesses sit at the table with us, I hate it. I'm
like, look at me, talk to me! Mental!

Dirty doctor has been requesting me three, four times a
week (and shopping trips, *dohan*, you name it – new jewellery,
we went to Disneyland a few days ago . . .) and Mama's
started talking about 'Oh Chastity-chan, you'll be Mama-san
number two soon' again, so it's all good.

I really, really don't know why I didn't do this years ago –
all those girls, those top hostesses, they knew the easy way to
do things. We were killing ourselves, chasing round customers
for bonuses and all it takes is a few 'love moments' maybe
once or twice a week, and you've got a great customer for life.
Sleazy, all right a bit. But we're talking maybe an hour a week,
that's it. That's it! For all this peace of mind it's well worth it.
Not for you, you're going places, but for me, what else have I
got?

Dirty doctor is paying for my boob job! I'm booked in for
two months' time, a really good clinic too.

What was it like living with that old movie guy who paid your bills? Cause dirty doctor has offered to move me and Tammy into his apartment and I'm thinking . . . maybe. Tammy would have her own room and he says I would too, but I'm not stupid. I know what he wants, and I know I'd have to play the headache game as many times as I could get away with. He's away on business a lot though, and he has this yacht he could take us to on weekends and his apartment is so nice.

I used to see hostesses living with old guys and think, What are you playing at? But now I get it. Those girls know what they're doing. Old guys look after you, and all that worry, money, money, money, it's just gone. Such a relief. They take care of everything and you can just relax and go with the flow.

Chastity

61

Steph

'Miss Stephanie?'

Steph felt hardness against her head and hip. She opened her eyes and saw white light all around. And plant pots. She'd fallen asleep on the hospital bench.

'Yes.' She sat upright, shielding her eyes from the bright lights. 'Sorry. I didn't sleep well last night.' Rubbing her hip, she remembered the restless night she'd had on her rickety bunk bed.

There had been plenty to think about, but the absent diary had been foremost on her mind. Her bag had been in Janes' dressing room while she'd been working, which meant someone could have taken the diary from it. Or it could have fallen out, either in the changing room or on the way home.

Steph had retraced her steps to the club as soon as she'd discovered the diary was missing, but there'd been nothing on the iron stairs or the pavement except for old chewing gum, spilled drinks and fast-food wrappers. Calamity Janes had been closed up, dark, its heavy doors sealed. She wouldn't be able to check the dressing room until 6.30 p.m. tonight when the club reopened.

There was nothing she could do until then, except talk to Mrs Kimono. Ask what she knew about Calamity Janes. Whenever Mrs Kimono had talked about Janes, her face had puckered, as if she had a bad taste in her mouth, but Steph had dismissed this as dislike for western culture. Now she wondered if there really was something more going on at Calamity Janes – something Mrs Kimono knew about.

'You're the doctor?' Steph asked.

The man had grey hair and a gentle voice. 'Yes.' He stared at Steph's scarred chin. 'Have . . . Did you visit before?' he asked.

'I was here yesterday.'

The doctor took a step back. 'Ah! Sinatra's? I've seen you at Sinatra's.'

Steph tried to picture the doctor without his white coat. Then she remembered a similar-looking man, his face slack with drink, wearing a grey suit and sitting with Chastity by the side of the stage at Sinatra's.

'You're a friend of Chastity's,' she said.

'*Hai*, yes.' The doctor nodded. 'Chastity. My fiancée.'

'Your fiancée?' Steph looked at him, bewildered, and then realised perhaps the doctor hadn't quite got the English word right. Presumably he meant 'favourite girl' or something.

'What a small world.' Steph moved from one foot to the other. 'So . . . Mrs Sato. How is she?'

'Come with me.'

The doctor took Steph down to the basement level.

'This way please.'

He led her into a strange-smelling room. Mrs Kimono lay at its centre on a hospital bed. She was wrapped in a pink kimono and her hands were folded across her chest. She was perfectly still. There were white-petalled flowers everywhere and incense burned on the bedside table. Two nurses knelt by the bed, their heads bowed.

It took a moment for Steph to understand.

'I only saw her yesterday,' she whispered, approaching the still figure.

Mrs Kimono's forehead was wrinkled into a frown. It suited her. Even in death she wasn't quite satisfied. Steph smiled through her tears.

'She left something for you,' said the doctor, and one of the nurses went to a cupboard and removed a folded, white kimono with a note on top.

'She was wearing this yesterday,' said Steph, taking the note. The writing was shaky and angular.

'For my *maiko*,' it read. 'This is the first kimono I wore as a *geisha*. I was presented it by my *danna* when I finished my *maiko* training. It is an antique, from my old *ochaya*, or teahouse.'

* * *

Steph stared at the note, bewildered. 'She wants me to have this kimono,' she told the doctor. 'I'm happy to, but . . . Shouldn't it be something for her family?'

'She doesn't have any family,' said the doctor.

'She has a daughter.'

The doctor shook his head. 'The daughter won't be . . . She doesn't want . . . She would like the state to take care of everything. She doesn't want to be involved.'

'So there won't be a funeral?'

The doctor looked uncomfortable. 'She'll be cremated within a few days. You can go to the crematorium. Pay your respects.'

'She had a burial plot,' said Steph, looking away from the stiff figure on the bed. She held the kimono to her chest. It smelt of damp and soap. 'Here.' Steph went to the cupboard where the kimono had been stored and found the letter Mrs Kimono read yesterday. 'It's in here.' She passed it to the doctor. 'She wanted to be buried.'

'In Japan, people are cremated before they're buried,' said the doctor. 'But in any case, we were aware of her wishes. She can't be buried in that plot.'

'Why not? It's what she wanted.'

'The family won't allow it,' said the doctor.

'The daughter?'

The doctor didn't reply.

Steph looked at Mrs Kimono again, pleased she couldn't hear. 'Will there even be a ceremony?' asked Steph.

The doctor shook his head. 'There's no one to arrange it. She has some friends in Kyoto, but they're too old to travel. As I said, you're welcome to accompany the body to the crematorium.'

'She seemed so well yesterday.' Steph clutched the kimono. 'Yes, I'd like to go to the crematorium. When will you be moving her?'

'As soon as we can,' said the doctor. 'There are no facilities here to keep her longer. There's little space for the living in Tokyo, let alone the dead.'

62

When the heavy doors of Calamity Janes swung open at 6.30 p.m., Steph was already waiting.

'Good to see you're taking things seriously,' Ricky commented, as Steph hurried past the reception desk and into the dressing room. 'I heard Michael had a word with you.'

'I think I left something behind yesterday,' Steph replied.

She pulled aside crumpled clothing and strings of laddered stockings.

And there it was. Under a scuffed pair of strappy high heels. The diary. It must have fallen out of her bag.

Steph snatched it up and flicked through the pages, then hugged the blue book to her chest.

Thank you.

She kicked aside takeaway wrappers, revealing a frayed square of brown carpet, and took a seat to read.

Work is AWFUL. I hate it so much. Someone told Michael I slept with basketball guy, and now he won't leave me alone. I've been on the waiting table all week, even though the club is packed, he's doing it to get at me because I won't go on contract. It's like punishment, he did the same thing to Geraldine. That's why she ended up being a floor-six girl all the time. I swear she'd have been fine otherwise. She did a lot of ice, but it was the sleeping beauty stuff that really sent her over the edge.

A floor-six girl. Sleeping beauty stuff. Steph read and reread the phrases. She thought of the lift not opening on the sixth floor, the strange key slot and the glowing blue lights in the hallway.

Maybe it was just a closed-up office floor, off-limits during the evening. But . . . *sleeping beauty stuff*. The lift had gone to floor six after she thought she'd seen Julia pass out.

I'm just desperate to get back on tables, get working, get earning money. I've earned NOTHING this week. No drinks, no pay. Takka hasn't come in for me like he promised, he's found another girl, a Polish one at another club who does the hotel-room circuit. I knew he was too good to be true. Only two *dohans* before he asked me to sleep with him, that's a record. He must think I'm desperate. Or so ugly I can't get customers any other way.

I need some ice tonight to level me out, make me confident, help me handle Michael. I deserve it after this week, especially now Geraldine's gone. I spent all last month's wages on clothes, I quit my teaching job and now I've got nothing. Sad, sad, sad, but it has to get better.

Annabel

The next entry was more worrying.

I feel so so sick and dirty and I can't handle this, help, help help, please help me someone. I can't stay here but I've got nowhere to go. I can't fly home broke, a failure, I've got no money, just a room full of designer clothes.

My insides feel disgusting, like I want to go into them and clean them with a brush, and no matter what I do I just can't get those pictures out of my mind. Julia lying there. Passed out after they'd spiked her. She was just a piece of meat to them. I was so scared when they caught me. I wasn't supposed to see anything.

Oh my God. Julia's drink was spiked. And Annabel saw something happen to her. Steph's hands shook as she tried to read on. *So where's Annabel?*

It should have been me as well. It would have been if I hadn't been sick. I must have thrown up whatever they spiked me with. I just can't stand to think of it. Those men, doing whatever they wanted. Maybe, it's like Geraldine says, I would have woken up none the wiser and not worried about it. It's probably worse that I woke up and saw. But Geraldine had a breakdown . . .

I've been watching my drinks for weeks now, but it's so hard when you're drinking the whole time and the drugs make you sloppy. But if I hadn't taken bad ice with those tequila shots I never would have thrown up and I would have slept right through everything. It makes me feel so dirty.

I wish I hadn't seen what I saw. And I was SOO frightened.

Girls were drifting into the dressing room, throwing clothes to the floor, grabbing punch cards.

Steph felt a tap on the back of the diary.

'What's this?' Caroline leaned over her. 'Customer notes before work?'

'Just a book.'

'You're in everyone's way.'

'Give me a minute.'

'We're trying to change.'

'A MINUTE, okay?' Steph shouted, her eyes racing across the page.

Flower money. That's what they called it. We'll give you flower money to keep quiet. I phoned Takka over and over again today, he's my only friend out here now Geraldine's gone. I can't tell him what happened, but I can let him look after me like he said he would.

Annabel.

Steph felt someone kick her knee.

'Hey! Watch it.' She snapped the diary closed and saw girls cramming their punch cards into the clock. The display read 7.00 p.m.

Jumping to her feet, Steph grabbed her own card from the holder. She was the last to punch in, just before the clock rolled over to 7.01 p.m., and as the girls rushed out to the club, Steph felt the diary against her fingers. There were only a few pages left to read.

'Steph!' Ricky appeared at the door. 'Hurry up and get sat down. I've got a special customer for you, very rich.'

'Coming,' said Steph.

'That's a big customer book,' Ricky noted, as Steph followed her across the club. 'You want to get yourself a smaller one. And didn't I tell you to wear some bling? Last warning.'

Steph found an overweight, ginger-haired man waiting for her on a table by the stage. He had a red face and told her he was from Germany. She sat down, but the moment Ricky was out of sight she got to her feet again.

'Excuse me,' she said. 'Bathroom break.' She hurried across the club, feeling the woven cover of the book rub against her scarred arm.

Inside the toilet she flicked quickly to the last few pages.

63

I slept with Takka last night. He's so old and everything was wrinkly and it was so embarrassing. I cried and cried right in front of him. Then I went to my own room and it was OK. Takka says I can move in with him, and truly I hate this apartment so much. Being here reminds me of what happened and I can't get my head straight here, too many other hostesses around and it's dirty.

I had a dream last night I went to the police, but I didn't know what to say to them. It was just a dream. Here I am, still working at Janes. I need to be here. I need the money for coke right now, not for ever, but right now I need it, it's the only thing that gets me through. I haven't said a word to anyone, and I won't. The police would deport me anyway, and that would just finish me off.

Takka looks after me. I don't like some of the things he wants me to do, but he lets me do lines, not like some of the customers here. And he buys me nice clothes and he says he'll pay my rent.

He keeps on asking and asking me to move in with him. And he would never spike any girl's drink, he's told me he's not into that whole 'sleeping beauties' thing. He's talked to the club to make sure my drinks are left alone. I'm safe with him.

I thought it was just the Russian girls who got spiked, but now I know different. Every new girl will get spiked sooner or later. That's how it works. They get more money for us if we're new. We're like a prize, it doesn't matter where we come from.

⋆　⋆　⋆

Steph perched on the toilet seat and stared at the handwriting, which was increasingly irregular, scruffy and full of spelling mistakes, so different from Annabel's first neatly written entries. But she could hear Annabel's voice as clearly as ever.

Every new girl will get spiked.

Steph thought of the drinks waiting for her outside, probably two or three by now. And the drink Julia had poured away last night. She thought about what Annabel had written she'd seen – Julia passed out after having her drink spiked, and having things done to her while she was unconscious.

But was Annabel seeing things as they really were? Or was she drugged up, paranoid and believing her own hallucinations? It was sad hearing her gentle, good-natured friend get lost in the Roppongi fog.

> I never thought they'd do it to me. But they did, and now I know you can't trust anyone out here, only yourself. Some guy was lined up to do things to me while I was passed out, just like they did with Julia.
>
> How long are they going to let me stay here now I know their secret?

There was a banging on the door.

'I'll be right out,' shouted Steph.

'Out *now*,' came the reply. It was Ricky. 'You've been in there *way* more than three minutes.'

Steph closed the pages and flushed the toilet, then stuffed the diary under her arm.

'Okay, okay,' she said as she came out, 'My, erm . . . Just checking my make-up.'

She could feel Ricky's eyes on her as she returned to the table, and clutched the book tight against her ribs. A tequila waited for her at the table, alongside a glass of vodka tonic. The drinks looked like little barrels of poison.

'Take a shot,' the customer demanded. As he talked, flecks of spit danced under the spotlights. 'Shot, shot, shot!'

Steph picked up her tequila and kept her lips tightly closed as she threw the contents at her face. Alcohol ran over her mouth and down her scarred chin. It dripped on to her bare cleavage, and she wiped it away, taking care not to let her tongue touch her lips.

The German man frowned. 'You didn't drink much. I'll order you another.'

'No, really. I'm fine.'

'Your manager won't be happy with you. You're supposed to make my drinks bill high, isn't that right?'

Steph looked around the club for Julia, desperately wanting to talk to her, to ask how she'd known to throw Steph's drink away yesterday.

There were blondes everywhere.

A few tables away, a peroxide-blonde Angel sat with an obscenely old man, seventy if he was a day. They were side by side, not talking. Angel ground her teeth and gazed out at the club with dead eyes while the man sat with his arm snaked around her waist. She looked like a shell of a person, joyless and paranoid, and too out of it to care who touched her and where.

But Julia was nowhere to be seen.

Steph looked at the vodka tonic in front of her. As usual, it was decorated with a mean sliver of lemon, thin enough to be transparent. Fruit was expensive out here.

I've drunk vodka tonics ever since I got here, Steph reasoned. But she still didn't trust the drink.

The German man was staring at her.

'I have to go to the bathroom,' she said.

'Again?' asked the customer. He was sweating, Steph noticed, and had barely touched his own drink.

'Yes,' said Steph. 'Cystitis.'

The man was quiet.

'Back in a minute.'

64

There were only a few pages left, all of them so messily written
that Steph had to concentrate hard to make sense of the words:

Fuck everything, who cares any more? I don't care, I don't
care, I don't care. It's all about the money, who has it, who
doesn't. No one will give it to you, you have to go out and
take it. I'm someone who has it. Money, money, me, me me.

All this old stuff, this old life, it's gone now, I'm leaving it
all behind. Takka's going to buy me everything new and I'm
going to make a new start with him, new clothes, new home,
new everything. I'll never wear any of these clothes again,
write in this book again. This is a fresh start.

She left all her things behind, Steph thought, *because she moved
in with a customer. So she* could *still be here. In Roppongi. But if
she doesn't work at Janes anymore, why is her passport still at the
club?*

Takka's closing it all up, paying my old credit card debts
and he's going to take care of everything from now on.

The singing, I'm not good enough, I never was. There's
too much competition, too many other good girls. It's time
to live in the real world. You don't get anywhere without
using your body, and I've got a good body, I'll make the
most of it while I can, take Takka for what I can get while I
can still get it. I mean, let's face it, if I was forty he wouldn't
have looked twice at me.

I just don't care anymore – I did a line of coke when
I got up, who cares, who cares? What's the big deal? If it

feels good do it. Sunshine line, that's what Geraldine called it. Whatever gets you through the day and keeps the money coming in. And I can afford it, I earn enough.

I'm 24. That's old out here. I'm lucky to have found someone like Takka. Really, really lucky. No one at home would understand, but it's different out here. It's normal for young girls to date older men.

Age isn't really anything to do with it, it's all down to money. The prettier you are, the richer your customers and the better presents they buy you. I don't know if I can go home anyway, knowing what I know, doing what I do. I'm a different person out here.

Just like Julia . . .

That was the end of the diary, except for the list at the back:

WW + 1

VT + GL

R&C + USA

As Steph closed the book, she noticed the greasy writing again in the steam of the mirror. It was more faded than before, but still visible on the gloomy glass.

Rum and coke flag

Vodka tonic G1

Wine 1

She turned back to the diary. Then she looked at the mirror again. Three lines on the mirror, three lines in the diary.

Rum and coke.

R&C.

Steph glanced back at the diary.

VT. Vodka tonic.

So that would mean . . . WW. *Wine.* White wine?

Maybe it was just a coincidence. The initials Annabel had scribbled could be anything, clothing designers, shops, customers . . .

Steph checked her watch. She'd been in the bathroom for five minutes, and anticipated a thump on the door at any moment. She closed the book and went out into the club.

The German man watched her legs as she sat down, his fat stomach squeezed over the table.

'Sorry to rush off like that,' said Steph.

The man smiled. 'Fine, fine. You're new here. How are you finding it?'

'It's . . . okay,' said Steph. 'Good. I'm not so new, I've been here a few months now. I've never seen you before though – have you been coming here long?'

'A long time. Years. I always come to Janes when I visit Tokyo.'

'Right.' Steph picked up her vodka tonic and took a stiff gulp, tiny slivers of partially melted ice stinging her back teeth. 'Girls stay here a long time too, don't they?'

'Some do.'

'Probably not so healthy to stay too long.'

'Maybe,' said the German.

'Girls change out here,' said Steph. 'Their ideas change. Their ambitions . . .'

The man took a gulp of beer. There was sweat on his forehead again, but he didn't wipe it away. He was staring at Steph, and as he did so his eyes multiplied like a spider and spread all over his face. Steph blinked and his eyes went back to normal. But she felt strange. Her heart raced for a second, then slowed down to a steady thump, thump, thump.

The German man took her hand under the table, and Steph could smell detergent from his shirt. For a moment, it looked like his body was melting into his stool. Then everything snapped back to normal, and Steph found herself staring at the empty vodka tonic glass.

The last page of Annabel's diary swam around before her eyes.

WW + 1
VT + G.

Annabel thought drinks were being spiked at Janes. What

if she'd written a code to remind herself which drinks to avoid? And someone else had written something similar on the mirror . . .

Steph felt a flutter in her ribcage. *WW* and *Wine* . . .

White wine and ice. The drink Julia had thrown away.

Vodka tonic G1

So what did G1 mean?

G1, GL . . .

Lemon. Something lemon.

Steph stared at the sliver of under-ripe fruit in her glass.

Green lemon.

The German man stared at the glass too. He knew.

'Got to . . . toilet,' Steph said, leaping from her chair and careering across the club.

She reached the bathroom and slammed the door, locking it with shaky, loose-jointed fingers before jamming those same fingers down her throat and retching over the sink.

Strings of saliva dangled as she threw up clear liquid.

She ran the tap and wiped her mouth with toilet roll.

After that, everything went black.

65

Steph came to in bluish darkness. Her head felt as though someone had smashed it with a hammer.

Shadows moved by her feet and she lifted her neck but found she couldn't move her hands or feet. In panic, she struggled and found her limbs restrained, useless. Something burned at her wrists and ankles like rubbing alcohol. On the wall was a square, dark blue light – some sort of TV or projector screen.

'Wait,' said a voice. 'She moved.'

A grey silhouette came near to Steph's face, and instinct told her to lie perfectly still. She felt warmth on her cheek.

'No, she's out,' came another voice, a female. 'We set up in the other room.'

Every muscle in Steph's body tensed, but she stayed still, fighting to keep her breath even.

Breathe in, breathe out.

Whoever these people were, they couldn't know she was listening.

There was a click as a door opened, letting more blue light into the room. Steph could see the outline of a bed around her and feel soft sheeting under her body.

The door closed and locked with a snap. The room went dark again.

Steph let her body relax, trying to calm down, trying to think. Every muscle felt taut and frightened, but the burning sensation around her wrists and ankles was what worried her the most.

She moved her wrists, which were resting on her stomach, and after establishing they were bound together, squirmed back and forth in alarm, only just managing not to scream.

Breathe in, breathe out, breathe in . . .

Her ankles were bound too, but not together. They were tied – presumably to the corners of the bed.

The door handle rattled. There was a click as the lock rolled open.

Breathe in, breathe out . . .

A shadow came into the room. The door was relocked, and the shadow approached the bed.

Steph thought . . . No, she was *sure*, if she caught the shadow at the right angle with her tied hands . . .

What happened next was unexpected.

Steph felt gentle movements around her wrists, and a slipping, burning sensation as ropes slid away. Then her hands were hot, pulsing with blood. Free.

The figure was at her feet now, feeling around her ankles.

Steph grabbed the bulk of human being with both hands and secured her arm around its neck. The movement wasn't fluid or controlled, like it would have been before the accident, but she got a firm hold and pulled.

A startled voice said, 'Wait!'

It was a female voice, and Steph was aware that the body, despite its apparent size in the shadows, was slender and light.

'Shush,' said the voice. 'I've locked the door. No one can get in.'

Steph gave a little gasp.

The voice, the perfume, the build . . . They were all so familiar.

'Julia?' said Steph.

'Just be quiet,' the voice replied. 'You've got to leave before they come back.'

Steph released her grip, just a fraction.

On the wall, the blue screen began to flicker.

'We have to leave.' The voice was more urgent now. 'I heard them setting up the cameras. We've got ten minutes, maybe less. They'll start filming soon. The lights will come on. They'll be watching from the other room.'

'I know it's you Julia,' whispered Steph, releasing the pale figure. Her arms felt heavy, but blood was beginning to flow.

'Yes, it's me.'

The mattress under Steph yielded as Julia sat beside her.

'You should have read the mirror,' Julia said. 'I wrote it all out for you. On the mirror. So you'd know what not to drink.'

'Julia, what's going on?'

'I didn't want you to get spiked,' said Julia. 'It's just because you're a new girl. They won't spike you again.'

'Who's they? Who spiked my drink?'

'The management.' There was a long pause. 'Don't worry, it won't happen again. At least, not unless you agree to it.'

'Agree to it?'

'You can choose to be spiked. To earn more money.'

'What?' Steph shook her head. 'Why would anyone do that?'

'It's one of the club's special contracts,' said Julia. 'Some of the girls go on call, twenty-four hours, sleeping with customers. Hard work but lots of money. That's one type. The other is the sleeping beauty contract. No work at all.'

'A contract?'

'A few of the men out here have a thing for girls when they're passed out. Unconscious. Helpless. It's sort of a fetish. Not just Japanese men – men from all over the place. So some of the girls get drugged at work. Voluntarily. It's sexy for the customers – they play pretend the girl doesn't know what's going on. They go upstairs together and what they get up to is their business. The club makes a video for them. A souvenir. Everything's consensual. No one is paid directly – the club just puts bonuses on a girl's pay packet.'

'But who would . . .'

'It's a good deal,' Julia insisted. 'Girls don't have to do anything, they don't have to worry about pleasing customers or going to hotels. Just one drink. Bang. They pass out and wake up in the morning with a nice big bonus.'

Steph could see shadow on Julia's grey face, and the greenish circles under her eyes. She thought about Julia's blonde hair splayed over the table that night, and the fact she had vanished and the next day pretended nothing had happened. And on the bonus chart . . . *SB* written after her name, just like *24* was written after Natalia's name. Sleeping beauty.

I'm a different person out here . . .

'You're on a sleeping beauty contract,' said Steph. 'Aren't you? They spike your drink at work.'

'It's all right,' Julia said. 'Like taking an anaesthetic. You wake up none the wiser. Everyone's happy. Before I asked to go on contract . . . The pressure was so bad. All I thought about was customer, customer. And the men always leave you if you don't sleep with them. It's better this way.'

'Except that girls who aren't on contract, girls like me and Annabel, get given the wrong drink,' said Steph.

Julia's shoulders hunched over. 'They're not that careless. They would have given you a fantastic bonus for it, and like I said, you would have wroken up none the wiser.'

'What are you talking about?'

'It's an extra service they offer customers – new girls, the real deal, genuine innocents. The pay is good. Really good. Enough to persuade you to go on a sleeping beauty contract, probably. Lots of girls do after their first time.'

'Like you did?' Steph filled in the silence.

'They'll do the same for you, you know,' said Julia. 'Even though you woke up. Come back tomorrow and they'll make you a good offer. You won't even have to go on a contract, they'll just give you money to keep quiet.'

'What's the catch?'

'You've got to stay loyal to the club. Work until your contract ends. And you can't ruin the secret for other new girls – it doesn't hurt them. They wake up in their own apartments and half the time they don't even work out what happened.

'It's only when they give them the flower money talk a few weeks later and offer them the sleeping beauty contract they work out they were spiked. It happens all over Roppongi anyway. At least the way we do it things are safe. The girls are kept an eye on.'

'Why has no one gone to the police?' Steph said. 'Surely one of the girls would have gone to the police by now – one of the new girls?'

'If we tell, it would be us getting into trouble. Not the management.'

'Why?'

'We're illegals. We're lucky to be working.' There was a rustling sound as Julia stood up. 'You don't need to worry, they never spike girls a second time. They give you the drink codes so you know which ones not to touch.

'Once you're in the know, you count as a veteran. Customers won't pay any more for you, so they offer you the standard sleeping beauty contract.'

'There's no way—'

'I wouldn't blame you for turning it down,' Julia said quickly. 'Waking up must really freak you out. Don't worry – you'll get your bonus, provided you stay until your contract ends.'

There was a whirring sound. Julia moved toward the door.

'I've got to go. Wait a bit before you follow me. They can't know I helped you.'

'Why *are* you helping me?' asked Steph.

'You were sick. I was outside the bathroom. Another girl . . . She was sick, threw up her drink. And she woke up too. It's worse to wake up. Better to sleep through. Otherwise you might see things . . . Hear things you don't want to. I didn't want that to happen to you.'

Steph's head was pounding, but the words from Annabel's diary spoke clearly through the fog of pain:

I just can't get those pictures out of my mind. Julia, lying there. She was just a piece of meat to them . . . I wasn't supposed to see anything . . . It should have been me as well. It would have been if I hadn't been sick . . .

'Annabel's drink was spiked,' said Steph. 'But she was sick and she woke up, like me. She saw you . . .'

There was a silence.

'What happened to Annabel? Did they hurt her?'

'I told you, forget about Annabel—'

'Julia—'

'It wasn't a nice thing for her to see. It freaked her out a bit, but they took care of everything. And I had passed out, I didn't know what was going on. No one told me anything until the morning.'

'So where is she?'

There was a silence.

'Julia. *Where's Annabel?*'

'Listen. There's no time. You're on floor six of the club. Wait a few minutes for me to leave, then take the elevator downstaris. I've unlocked the door. You should go home now, to your apartment. I can't stay. I've got to punch out or they'll get suspicious.'

'I'm still in the club?' said Steph.

There were movements and a sound like a brush running over silk. Then the door opened and closed and Julia was gone.

Steph sat on the dark bed, fear threatening to overwhelm her. Had a few minutes passed yet? Time was impossible to calculate.

On the wall, the screen flickered again and lights came on, acid bright.

It was then Steph realised twenty glass eyes were staring down at her.

Cameras. Like shark's eyes. Everywhere. Wall-mounted in the corners of the room and free-standing on tripods around the bed.

The screen, which had been an eerie dark blue, now changed to white and Steph saw herself projected on the wall, sitting up on a double bed with red marks on her wrists and ankles. She touched the rope burn on her ankle and watched the Steph on TV do the same thing.

Then she ran.

And she was tearing down a long corridor with blue lights flickering under doorways, running towards a gold elevator and jabbing the call button.

Come on, come on . . .

Footsteps shuffled behind doors and a door handle rattled.

The passports . . . I've got to get mine and Annabel's from the office and get out of here. I'll take them to the police. Tonight.

The elevator doors opened.

66

Chastity

From: C_C_Chastity
To: CanadianDaphne
Subject: new apartment

Daphs,

OK, don't kill me but guess what? I'm getting married!!!
I'm not joking! To dirty doctor. Shit happens!!!

Who'd have guessed it? ME shacking up with a customer.
Tammy doesn't know what to make of him yet, they've got
to get used to each other, but he doesn't mind having a little
kid around and anyway, she's at school all week so it's not as
if she's in his way much and she's been in her bedroom
basically since we moved into his place.

He's got such a nice apartment, honestly Daphs you'd be
so jealous, right near Roppongi Hills, right near the club and
all those shopping places in Azabu Juban. I love it, so cool.

Dirty doctor, OK, he bothers me more than I thought he
would. Every night so far it's been the creeping hand game.
Makes me feel a bit sick sometimes, he sweats in the
weirdest places and he has moles EVERYWHERE, but he's
so funny and, you know, apart from the bedroom stuff it's
been fun.

And maybe, OK get this – we might even have a big, white
wedding. I'm serious. I was talking to him about immigration
raids and all that stuff, and he said Well you know how to fix
it? We should make it a big wedding to make sure you get
your working visa.

Seriously Daphs, he is RICH. I'd only have to be married

two, three years, divorce and then I get half of everything. He wants a pre-nup, but I'll talk him round.

It'll be such a relief to have a proper visa. Everything's got tighter and tighter, every time I do a visa run so many questions. I was getting scared to leave the country. They raided my bag last time, all that coke, it must have stuck to my clothes cause they searched me all over.

Tammy was crying, and I was thinking, fuck fuck fuck, they're going to deport me, all sorts of horror stories were going round my head. That was a stress I could have seriously done without. But no more of that when I'm a married lady.

The new apartment and everything, it's all good, but . . . do you ever wake up sometimes and think what's the point of it all? I thought once I'd got somewhere nice to live and no money worries, life would be excellent. But it feels . . . I don't know. A bit empty? Like I'm missing something. Don't get me wrong, I'm not knocking it. Maybe I'm bipolar, up one minute down the next. That's why I take so many drugs!!

Chastity :(

67

Steph

The club was dimly lit, the blue of the fire exit sign giving the empty tables and stools a radioactive glow. Steph checked her watch and realised the hostesses and customers must have only just left. The club was deserted, except for whoever was upstairs.

To Steph's relief the office wasn't locked. She wondered if anything in Japan was ever locked – it seemed to be a country of perpetually open doors. She snapped on the office lights, her eyes watering in the brightness, then froze as she heard a noise. A scrabbling sound. It was coming through the plastered cardboard wall separating the office from the girls' changing room.

Maybe one of the girls is still here.

The scrabbling stopped and Steph heard the irregular, muffled footsteps of someone unsteady on their feet. It sounded like they were heading towards the club's main room.

I've got to get the passports and get out of here.

She straightened up and grabbed the stack of booklets on the shelf. But as she did so, she noticed the square cardboard box she'd seen before – the one bound in red tape and delivered by Amir. It was under the bottom shelf by her feet with a stack of Calamity Janes ashtrays on top of it. Razor-neat lines ran through the red masking tape.

The box had been cut open.

More footsteps. And now they were definitely coming nearer.

Steph fell to her knees, pushed the ashtrays to one side, and the box leaves sprang outwards to reveal rows of white boxes. They were labelled in Japanese, but below the criss-cross symbols the words 'Rohypnol, flunitrazepam, 1mg' were written over and

over again, under a blue hexagonal logo for Chugai pharmaceuticals and the words Controlled substance.

There was a scrawled note resting on the boxes, written on a
piece of torn newspaper.

Michael. Won't turn drink blue. Any problems call me. Amir.

Rohypnol. The date rape drug. Amir was supplying it to Janes
in large quantities.

If this isn't proof for the police, I don't know what is.

Steph grabbed the box and stuffed it under her arm.

A shadow fell over her.

'What are you doing here?'

Steph's shoulders leapt almost to her ears. She turned to see
the loose, haggard face of Angel, white and washed-out, in the
office doorway.

'Nothing,' Steph said, getting to her feet, squaring her shoulders. 'Just go home.' She put the box on the desk and began
leafing through the passports.

Czech, Russian, Russian, USA ... UK. She checked the back
page. Inside, her own photo, smiling and healthy, mocked the
pale, frightened face looking back at it. She stuffed the passport
in her bra.

'I can't go home.' Angel gazed at the shelves. 'They've got
papers on me.' Her frantic eyes dropped to the passports in
Steph's hands. 'Why do you have those?'

'I'm getting out of here,' said Steph, flicking through more passports. *Russian, Swedish, Czech ... Another UK passport.* She flicked
it open. Annabel's face stared back at her. 'They spiked my drink.
They're spiking people's drinks here. And my friends is missing—'

'Did you wake up?'

Steph glanced over Angel's shoulder. 'Look, I need to get out
of here . . . I don't have time to—'

'They give you a great bonus if you wake up,' said Angel. She
began grinding her teeth. 'Four million yen.' She stumbled forward
and pulled papers from the bottom shelves. 'I won't let them
deport me.'

Steph's hands went numb. She couldn't feel the passports any more. Julia hadn't mentioned just *how* much the bonus might be. Four million yen. That was around £20,000.

The passport in Steph's bra was cold against her skin.

I could just put my passport back and go to the apartment. Come back tomorrow, work until my contract ends and collect my bonus. I could do in two months what I'd planned to do in a year, and fly back to England early. Start my life all over again.

Then Steph thought of Julia, so cold, so ill looking. And she remembered Mrs Kimono's remark before she died:

'You don't look well . . . Working too hard?'

And Annabel.

She looked down at Annabel's passport photo. Annabel had changed since school. Her cheekbones had sharpened and her hair had grown thicker, but she still had that scholarly, prefect look that Steph remembered.

There was a tearing sound as Angel ripped papers, her bony back wriggling under a tight lycra dress.

Steph stared at the passport photo. Then she looked at Angel.

Working too hard . . . I'm a different person out here . . . Four million yen . . .

Steph watched Angel throw torn paper to the floor.

No. It can't be. Please God, it can't be. Suddenly Steph knew what had happened to her friend.

'Annabel.' Steph held out the passport.

There was silence. For a moment, Angel was absolutely still. Then she turned around, sucking at hollow cheeks.

'This is you, isn't it?' Steph stepped forward. 'You're Annabel.'

Now Steph could see the similarities between her old friend and the girl in front of her. The spongy nose, icy blue eyes and a top lip slightly larger on the left side than the right. Bleach the hair to a straw-like consistency, rub the skin with sandpaper, add ten years and you had the same girl.

Angel stared at her. 'I don't use that name any more.'

'But you are, aren't you?' said Steph. 'You're Annabel.'

Angel blinked and for the first time looked Steph square in the face. 'Steph?'

Steph nodded. 'It's me. Long time no see.'

'How long have you been working here?'

'A few months,' said Steph.

'I asked Julia not to . . . I didn't want you to see me like this.' Annabel turned back to the shelves. 'She said she'd make sure you wouldn't find out. She told me she'd stop you getting a job here. I just need a few more months to sort myself out.'

'You won't sort yourself out in Roppongi,' said Steph. 'You should leave. Come with me. I've got your passport.'

Steph held it out to her.

Annabel's head began to bob, her eyes flicking open and closed, open and closed. 'I can't leave yet.'

'Why not?'

'I need more time here. The money's so good here. Just a few more months.'

'It's never just a few more months.' Steph thought of Mrs Kimono's peaceful, cold body. 'Not out here. Come with me.'

'No . . . You do what you want.' Annabel carried on sorting through papers. 'I can't leave. Not yet.'

'You're so different,' said Steph.

'Girls change out here,' said Annabel. 'They grow up.'

'Is that what you call it?'

Annabel didn't reply.

'Please come with me.'

'Stop asking me that,' Annabel snapped. 'Just . . . get on with your own life and I'll get on with mine.'

Steph hesitated for a moment. Annabel didn't want to be found. Not right now. So there was nothing Steph could do.

She took one last look at the girl she'd known. Then she picked up the red box, turned, and walked stiffly to the elevator.

Out on the street, a pinky-purple sky shimmered around Roppongi Tower. Sunrise. Steph turned her back on the cold, dead lights of Calamity Janes and headed downhill.

68

'Hello? Miss?'

The orange light of the sun burned Steph's eyelids. Her limbs were stiff, folded around concrete steps and the red box, and she shivered in her evening dress, feeling cold right through to her bones.

'You can't sleep here.' It was a young policeman. Behind him, a woman in uniform was unlocking the police station doors.

'I came to see you,' said Steph. 'I'd like to make a statement.'

'Come inside.'

The interview room was hospital-warm, and after a hot tea and plate of rice and fish from the station canteen, Steph stopped shivering and was able to give her particulars to the young policeman.

'You understand,' he said, 'that now we have a record of you, if you're . . . uh . . . *working* here we may investigate your accommodation and means of income and . . .'

'I'm not working here,' said Steph. *Not any more.*

'Oh.' The policeman nodded.

'But I'd like to make a report on a hostess club.' She pushed forward the red box. 'See the note inside? To the manager of Calamity Janes. It's Rohypnol. It was in the office at the club. They use it on the girls there.'

'*Oh.*' The policeman looked concerned as he lifted out white boxes. 'Yes. Illegal. Thank you for, uh, bringing this to me. We will take this very seriously.'

'There's something else too.'

Steph handed him the Calamity Janes contract, still unsigned, which had been lying at the bottom of her bag for some weeks.

It was crumpled and grubby with fluff. Ricky had signed and dated it in swirly handwriting, and written Steph's name above. 'Calamity Janes. They gave me this contract. Three months of work. It's illegal, isn't it?'

'Yes. Unless you have an entertainment visa.'

'If you want to deport me, then go ahead.'

'You haven't signed this contract,' the policeman noted.

'No.'

'And you say you're not working?'

'No.'

'Then I don't see how . . . uh . . . It doesn't seem to me against the law to be given a contract by this club.'

Steph considered correcting him and admitting she'd been working at Janes. But she thought better of it. Why burden him with the paperwork and herself with a deportation fine? There was a difference between honesty and stupidity.

'But you'll investigate the club?'

'Yes. Certainly.'

'What'll happen to the girls working there?' asked Steph.

'I don't know,' said the policeman, sliding his feet in and out of his rubber slippers. 'The club may be fined. Maybe closed. But nothing is certain. Police matters take a long time in Japan.'

'Okay,' said Steph.

'You're travelling in Japan?' asked the policeman.

'Maybe,' said Steph. 'I think I might do. Just for a little while. I need to see an old friend before I leave, too. But really it's time for me to go back home.'

'Oh.' The policeman nodded. 'Back home to England. What do you do there? Work? Study?'

'Work,' said Steph. 'I don't need to study any more.'

From the outside, the crematorium looked like a giant factory. There were gleaming silver pipes running all around it, carrying thick black smoke along and up into the sky.

It was only inside, where groups of mourners sat on plastic chairs, drinking *miso* soup and hot coffee from plastic cups, sobbing and holding one another, that the building's purpose became clearer. The crematorium operated twenty-four hours a day loading dead bodies on to shiny metal trays and feeding them into industrial ovens.

Dead bodies were disposed of quickly in Tokyo.

A man in a black baseball cap led Steph into a grey-walled room with a metal table. On the table sat a vase of plastic flowers, a china urn and a silver tray. On the tray lay the charred bones and powdery ashes of Mrs Kimono.

'Please.' The man removed his cap and handed Steph a pair of long chopsticks. 'Take the bones from the ash. Choose the best bones for the urn.'

The china urn beside the ashes was about the size of a biscuit tin and painted with blue flowers.

Steph took the chopsticks.

'Tradition,' said the man, nodding as Steph brought the chopsticks towards the tray. The bones were coated in light grey streaks, but were surprisingly white, given that they'd just been incinerated. 'The bones only, not the ash.'

'The doctor told me,' said Steph, arranging the chopsticks in her hand, 'one of Mrs Sato's family could come here . . . Her daughter wouldn't come.'

'Wouldn't come, wouldn't come.'

She picked up a small piece of bone, ragged like a snapped twig. 'In here?'

'*Dozo.* Please.'

She dropped the bone into the urn. A tear ran down her cheek. 'And he told me Mrs Sato can't be buried where she wanted to be buried.'

'No.' The baseball cap man shook his head. 'No . . . *permission.* Sorry.'

'She wanted to be with her daughter,' said Steph, picking out more bones. The ash swirled around the chopsticks.

'Needs *permission.* Without permission, no burial. Her daughter wouldn't allow it.'

'Mrs Sato was from Kyoto,' said Steph. 'A *geisha.* Could I post the ashes to her old teahouse?'

'Post? No. You can't post. Illegal.'

'Maybe I could speak to her daughter.'

The man laughed. 'But would she speak to you? Daughter is famous. Very famous. You can read about her in the newspaper. To talk to her you need *appointment* and to you I don't think she'd give.'

'Famous? Who is she?'

'Owner of Sinatra's hostess club,' said the man with a nod. 'She's written a book. Already a waiting list to buy and not even, uh . . . *printed.*' He blushed. 'My wife is on waiting list.'

'You're joking.' Steph let the chopsticks rest on the urn. 'Her daughter . . . is *Mama-san* from Sinatra's? Mrs Sato's daughter?'

'*Hai.* Yes. Her daughter.'

Steph felt like laughing. Mrs Kimono must have been laughing herself whenever Steph mentioned Sinatra's. It must have hurt her and pleased her at the same time. Steph's hand throbbed when she realised Mrs Sato knew she'd moved to Janes with one of Mama-san's customers.

'You're wrong,' she said. 'I don't need an appointment. I'll go and see her tonight. There's something I should tell her anyway.'

The man held his cap and was silent for a moment.

Steph carried on picking bones until there was nothing but grey ash left, as fine as grains of sand. When she'd finished, the man handed her the urn.

'I'll take them with me,' she said, 'when I go to see Mama.'

'Do what your heart tells you.'

Outside the crematorium, snow began to fall. Soon the city was white, and the pavements a hazardous cover of toffee-hard, grey ice.

Steph held the urn close to her chest, then reached in her pocket and took out the torn envelope Mrs Kimono had written on a few days before. The handwriting, despite its spikes and points, looked warm and alive. It was strange to think its owner would never write again.

She wanted me to look for acting work, thought Steph. *And I will. But first I should visit Mama-san.*

*   *   *

A giant bouquet of red roses decorated Sinatra's reception area, and Steph played with the petals as she waited for Hiro to tell Mama she was waiting.

The minutes stretched out like elastic. Waiting was painful. Then the curtain twitched.

'What are you doing here?' Mama wore a red velvet dress with a plunging neckline, ruby earrings that weighed down her earlobes and a web of emeralds on gold strands around her neck. It was the sort of ensemble an actress might wear on Oscar night and Mama wore it as though she were collecting her award. The Sinatra's reception desk was her podium.

Mama nodded at Steph's rucksack. 'We're not a youth hotel. You can't stay the night.' Then her eyes fell to the urn. 'A souvenir for your family? You've made a poor choice. In Japan, we hold the dead in those vases.'

Steph clutched the urn tighter. 'Look, I've got something to tell you.'

'Oh?' Mama cocked her head to one side.

'I came to say I'm sorry.'

Mama shrugged. 'You paid back your money. We have no business with each other any more.'

'I know, but I wanted to thank you for giving me a chance,' said Steph. 'And I wanted to say . . . Yamamoto-san . . . I'm not working at Janes any more. I've asked him to come back here.'

Mama's face remained serious, but Steph thought she saw the hint of a smile.

'He's been coming here a long time. We'll make him very welcome.'

'Sorry for taking him,' said Steph.

'Business, business.' Mama waved her hand.

'I know it is,' said Steph. 'But I shouldn't have done it. It's just . . . Okay, I wanted to earn more money. Pay off your debt quicker and –'

'And work in the big league,' Mama nodded. 'I know. The best club.'

'Anyway,' said Steph. 'There's something else too.' She put the urn on the reception desk. 'I knew your mother. Mrs Sato.'

Mama-san stared at the urn.

'We were friends,' said Steph. 'I was at the crematorium, and I thought you might want her ashes.'

'Friends, *neh?*' Mama's gaze didn't leave the blue and white porcelain. 'My mother and I weren't friends. She abandoned me for her *danna*. She was *geisha*, you know. Finished her training very late in life – she had to fight for it. When she found her *danna* suddenly her own daughter was too much of an embarrassment.'

'She wanted to be buried at your family plot,' said Steph.

'I told the hospital,' said Mama. 'No permission. Not from me. She abandoned me, so I abandon her.'

'But it's what she wanted.'

Mama shrugged. 'People want lots of things. I want loyal host-esses but I don't always get them.'

'Please, Mama—'

'No!' The word made a whooping sound that made Steph jump. 'Take it.' She pushed the urn forwards.

'But what should I do with it?' asked Steph. 'It's for her family. You're her family.'

'*Wacarini, wacarini.* Don't know, don't care. Yours now.' She looked away from the urn and patted one of her eyes. Then she whispered to the floor, 'Take her to *Kyoto*. She was happy there.'

'I will,' said Steph, picking up the urn. 'I'll take her there.'

'Fine, fine.' Mama coughed into her hand and didn't meet Steph's eye. 'You're not working any more?'

'Not here,' said Steph. 'But I will do back home. Time to face things. Rejection, embarrassment . . .'

'That's life.'

'I hear you've written a book,' said Steph with a little smile. 'I'm looking forward to reading it.'

Mama beamed at her. 'So are lots of people. Waiting list this long.' She stretched her arms out. 'Most pre-orders ever. They're fighting over me – TV shows, newspapers . . . I can afford to take on more girls. You still want a job? I have room for you.'

Steph smiled. She'd come to Roppongi begging for work, and now two clubs wanted her and she wasn't interested.

'I can't stay here, Mama,' said Steph. 'It's not real, you know? Just hiding.'

'You see it how you want to see it.'

'I need to get on with my life. Auditions, trying out for things . . . Failing things. Living, you know.'

'I understand,' said Mama. 'Girls stay here too long. You don't want to end up like me, old, with no one to take care of you. Go. Maybe I'll see you in the movies some day.' She disappeared into the office, leaving Steph alone in reception.

'Steph-chan.' Hiro slid out from behind the curtain. 'I have something for you.' He offered her a folded piece of paper. 'Luke asked me to give you this.'

'How did he know I'd come here?'

'I don't know.' Hiro pushed his glasses up his nose. 'Lucky guess maybe.'

'Thanks,' said Steph, opening the paper. 'But it's just a phone number. I don't recognise the code.'

Hiro leaned over the desk to read it. 'It's not Tokyo.'

Steph tucked the note in her pocket.

69

Kyoto train station – an architectural wonder of steel and glass. It wasn't what Steph had expected. She thought Kyoto was supposed to be an ancient city. Where were the temples?

She wandered from the train, newly-dyed red hair blowing around her shoulders. Following a yellow line set into the tiled floor, she passed displays of sponge cakes with festive holly on top and hand-wrapped *onigiri*.

She held the china urn of bones and Mrs Kimono's white silk kimono, its scratchy black embroidery creeping over the arms and back of the garment. There was plenty of space in her ruck-sack for both items since she'd given all her hostess dresses to Natalia. But she hadn't thought it right to keep the beautiful kimono crumpled among her socks and knickers on the long journey, nor risk the urn being chipped or cracked as she tugged her rucksack on and off train storage shelves.

When Steph handed over the dresses, Natalia had stared at the floor, then lifted her bed sheet and reached into a little frayed cut at the side of the mattress. From it, she'd removed a handful of business cards and passed them to Steph, biting her bottom lip as she did so.

'*I took them from your book,*' Natalia had said. '*Sorry.*'

But for Steph there was nothing to forgive.

Steph made her way through the lunchtime crowds, weaving left and right between suited men, families and young couples.

Suddenly the crowd parted.

A *geisha* walked towards the train platforms, her wooden shoes clacking on the tiles. She held her long silk skirts just above the floor, but still they trailed along the ground at the back, *swish, swish,*

swish. Perhaps she was thirty, perhaps she was fifty – with her face hidden under thick, white make-up it was impossible to tell.

When the *geisha* saw Steph, or rather, saw what Steph was carrying, she stopped. The combs in her heavily lacquered wig jangled. She smiled.

'May I?' The *geisha* gestured, with a soft wave of her hand, to the kimono Steph held.

Steph nodded, and the *geisha* stroked the fabric, turning parts over in her hands, reading the embroidery like a storybook.

'I know this teahouse,' she said with a smile. 'Shijo-dori Street. And I know this *geiko*. Shizuku Tanaka.' She glanced at the urn. 'My condolences.'

'Thank you,' said Steph.

'Did you know this lady?' the *geisha* asked.

'Yes,' said Steph, 'she was my good friend. It's thanks to her I'm not hiding from life any more. I'm living for real now. I hope she knows I listened.'

The *geisha* bent down by Steph's feet in a swift, athletic gesture.

'Yours I believe,' she said, scooping up a scrap of paper from the floor. 'It fell from your bag.' She passed Steph the paper. It was the note Luke had left at Sinatra's. 'The number for your guesthouse?'

Steph juggled the urn from hand to elbow and took the scrap of paper.

'I don't know what that number's for. It could be anywhere.'

'It's a Kyoto number,' said the geisha. 'See the code? Seventy-five.' She nodded and swished away, *swish, swish, swish*.

'Thank you,' Steph called after her. She walked on, past a billboard advert showing three smiling Japanese girls. Part of the sign was written in English.

'Smile is best make-up,' it said.

Steph looked around her. She saw only Japanese people, some wearing suits and negotiating a clipped pace through the station, others carrying small children or chatting with friends. Against her scarred arm, the urn grew warmer.

Steph looked down at the phone number and smiled.

Dear Reader

If you enjoyed this book, please share your thoughts on Amazon.co.uk

How to write an Amazon review

1. Visit Amazon.co.uk and log into your account (or create a new one).
2. Search for *Glass Geishas* in 'Books'.
3. Scroll down to customer reviews, and click the 'Create your own review' button on the right-hand side. Easy!

If you've been affected by any of the issues in this book, please contact www.missingabroad.org

Acknowledgements

Lovely reader, my first thanks go to you. I'm delighted you decided to spend so many hours in my company.

Whom to thank next? My name is on the front cover, but the truth is a whole team of people created this book. Thanks go to:

My soulmate Demi, for endless support and being the best dad to our little girl.

My brilliant sis for incredible insight and a genius creative mind.

Piers Blofeld, agent extraordinaire, whose changes made the book so much better.

Susan Fletcher, for being the perfect, clever, confident editor (and also making the book so much better).

The publishing team at Hodder.

Lesley Downer, author of *Geisha*.

Lisa Louis, author of *Butterflies in the Night*.

Shoko Tendo, author of *Yakuza Moon*.

Amanda Preston for her time and excellent suggestions.

Sheila Thompson for doing a great job of checking the manuscript and having an eagle eye for things that don't add up.

Kevin Harris for his fantastic creative mind and poet's soul.

My Dad for believing anything is possible and my Mum for all the stories.

Swati Gamble for all her hard work and being kind enough to explain things to me that I should already know.

And my little girl Lexi – just because I like seeing her name.